The Hope

John Wilton

For Philip,
A good 'Ischian' friend.
John.

ISBN: 978-1-291-80461-4

Copyright © 2014

All rights reserved, including the right to reproduce this book, or portions thereof in any form. No part of this text may be reproduced, transmitted, downloaded, decompiled, reverse engineered, or stored, in any form or introduced into any information storage and retrieval system, in any form or by any means, whether electronic or mechanical without the express written permission of the author.

Although partly based on true events, this is a work of fiction. Names and characters are the product of the author's imagination and any resemblance to actual persons, living or dead, is entirely coincidental.

Cover photograph of Wenceslas Square, Prague, November 1989 by Brian Harris. Copyright of The Independent.

PublishNation, London
www.publishnation.co.uk

CONTENTS

Part One: 1994 and a second chance?   1

     1   The signs and the hope   2

Part Two: Tom's hope and 1989 beginnings   15

     2   Recollections of earlier hope   16
     3   A thought provoking pummelling   26
     4   At Liberec   51
     5   To Brno   67

Part Three: 1994 - The Czech Republic five years on and the hope of the Czech people   81

     6   At Brno   82
     7   The seventy-two year old man and the seventeen year old girl – can't wait to be old!   94
     8   The Brno early evening and the time of day he both loved and hated   103
     9   The 'Titanic' of romantic disasters   111
    10   A Brno Friday afternoon and reflection   122
    11   To Slavkov, with Napoleon, Josephine, magical mirrors and thoughts of Tom's Waterloo   145
    12   Janácek and a different type of tune – the music of youth   160

13	To Ostrava – the shortages and the excesses	177
14	A Marlboro manoeuvre	184
15	The panelak and two different lives in the new post-revolution Czech Republic	199
16	Stalin's granny	218

Part Four: 1989 and 1994; decision time for Czechs, Slovaks and an Englishman — 222

17	"One of you is going to die."	223
18	17th November 1989	231
19	18th November 1989 and the beginning of Tom's 'revolution'	249
20	The 'Revolutionary Days' and change – for everyone	261
21	Tom Carpenter - 'voice' of the reform communists	276
22	December 1989 and the cold reality	289
23	The end of the line?	299
24	The hope	321

Part One: 1994 and a second chance?

1
The signs and the hope

For four-and-a-half years he'd told himself this was never going to happen. He'd hoped it would of course; planned it in his mind. But he never really believed the chance would come again. Now there she was, sitting opposite him in a Prague restaurant in the late Spring of 1994 reeling off her recollections of the exciting 'November days' of 1989 that they had experienced together. Speaking faster and faster about the crazy days of the 'Velvet Revolution' they'd shared in Prague.

"What about your bruises Tom? Your scars of the revolution?" she teased him.

A smile spread across his face at her reminder of the events they were in the middle of on the evening of 17th November 1989, a night when his life and the history of her country, Czechoslovakia, began to change forever. It was that steely cold Prague evening that Jana was recalling and Tom's own particular personal introduction to the full force of the communist State police.

Back then the two of them had been on the huge student demonstration, halted by massed ranks of the State police in Národni Street. They had stood motionless, demonstrators and police, for over an hour. Tom had an increasingly dry taste in his mouth from the tension of the silence broken only by the intermittent singing of the demonstrators. Then, without warning, waves of police waded into the demonstrators from the front and from the nearby side streets, thrashing all in front of them with their long batons. Partly through the force of the numbers of police attacking the front of the march ahead of them, and partly through their own instincts, they were pushed under some nearby passageway arches on the side of the street.

Suddenly Tom heard a loud aggressive Czech voice shout something behind him, followed swiftly by a barely audible low hiss as a long white baton cut through the cold night air and hit him hard.

A thud landed across his shoulder blades, immediately accompanied by hot searing pain across his back and down his arms. He lurched and stumbled forward, fortuitously out from under the arches and straight through the seemingly hundreds of charging State police racing past him. Another one of them caught him a sharp blow with his thick white baton across the back of his legs as he charged past the stunned falling Englishman.

Despite only the briefest of glances, Tom could see that the face wielding that baton landing the second blow was one full of anger, but also full of fear. It was a very young face, maybe nineteen years old at the most, with eyes open wide and very large pupils betraying the fear. The young voice shouting and ranting in Czech displayed the anger. There was a fine line between the two blurred instantaneous emotions of anger and fear, and they produced an extremely volatile mixture when added to the wielding and thrashing through the air of a long thick stick making contact with Tom's body. Later, when reason had replaced pain in his senses, he was convinced that it wasn't that the baton-wielding young guy was necessarily angry with him specifically; it was just that he was angry at having to be there at all, and to be in such a fearful and seemingly dangerous situation. Despite possessing and wielding the long thick stick he obviously felt no longer in control of the situation and was totally unsure of just what might happen next. It was a mirror image of the situation the Czechoslovak communist leadership increasingly found themselves in – wielding a long coercive 'stick' over the Czech and Slovak people, but no longer able to control the situation or what might happen next in the country.

What did happen next for Tom, of course, was that the stick made rapid and extremely painful contact with his legs, immediately followed by his yelping cry as the pain now raced through that part of his body. His cry of pain was accompanied by yet more, and faster, screaming abuse from the young police guy as he raced on and into the main body of the brutal violent madness under the arches in the passageway in Národni. As Tom hit the cobbled street from the second blow he felt physically sick, from the pain and from the fear of what might still be coming his way in terms of a beating. The police though were too busy charging past him to get at the main body of marchers still trapped under the arches. In the hazy corner of his brain he heard Jana screaming at him. "Tom! Tom! Get up! Get up! Quickly, get up now!"

Now he knew precisely where all the church bells of Prague that the communists had banned for years were – ringing loudly in his head. He tried to shake his stunned head and get his brain to tell his body to move, muttered "I'm okay," although he clearly wasn't and Jana put her hand under his arm and hauled him up.

"Come on, quick," she implored him.

"I'm bloody trying," was all he could reply as he gasped for air. They could still hear the screams and shouting from the continuing mayhem behind them as they stumbled off down the side street of Mikulandská and into the relative safety of the dark and cold Prague night.

Jana pushed him into a doorway in a street about half-a-mile from Národni and propped him up for a minute to get his breath and try to recover a little. In a very low and serious tone she whispered in his still ringing ears, "Well, Tom, now you know. Now you have seen what it's like. What the problem is. Why we want to change it all and how much they are determined not to let us. Now you have seen the reality of it. It's a good, but painful lesson don't you think? I'm sorry that you had to experience that very practical lesson. I'm sorry I asked you to come. I didn't want you to get hurt. I really didn't think that would happen."

"Yes, well I've certainly seen and experienced the painful reality, but you don't have to apologise for bringing me. It was my choice, I wanted to come," was all he could think to say through deep breaths as he dealt with the pain across the top of his back and his lower legs. "No doubt tomorrow I'll have the bruises as evidence of the reality of my practical lesson, but what did that bastard say just before he hit me? I'm sure it wasn't 'excuse me could you move aside please, sir.'" At least he still had his sense of humour, even if the rest of his senses were not completely intact at that point.

"Err ... no, I think it was more like 'you fucking pig, do you think we want to be here because of you'. He was as scared as you and me, Tom, and that's just what it's all about. Fear is everywhere in this country and has been for forty years. It almost killed the hope, but not now. You saw for yourself how many people came tonight to demonstrate their opposition. Those Stalinist bastards can't kill the hope now." As she spoke her anger returned and her fear disappeared. "More and more people are starting to believe things can and will change. And the chanting, Tom, you heard the chanting on the march. In English it meant 'this is it, now is the time'. They can't control that. They can't stop it forever. They can't stop us and our voices anymore."

"These bastards corrupted our ideals and they've even taken away our public spaces, like they tried to do in Národni tonight, our places of celebrations and demonstrations. Well, now we've grown up. We're not children anymore. Ironically, maybe they've educated us too well. We'll show those bastards. Show them what real peoples' demonstrations and spontaneous marches are all about. They're our squares, our streets. They always have been. Now we're going to take them back. Most of all, Tom, it's our country, and we're going to take that back too."

Now, four-and-a-half years on from that night of 17th November 1989 on Národni in Prague and his sudden acquaintance with a rather large thick white police baton, the woman who had uttered those words of optimism, determination and hope was sitting opposite him in a Prague restaurant reminding him of the events of that night. Being a university lecturer though, his academic background taught him that history is not merely as it is usually portrayed, not merely about public events. It is also about personal inner events, in a man or woman's mind and in their actions. Tom's history, or at least the most recent and important part of it for him - the part concerning Jana - was a mixture of his personal experience and hope entwined with the experiences and hopes of Czechs and Slovaks, like Jana, that had grown and grown throughout that fateful year of 1989. The deadening thud and numbing pain of the police baton he'd experienced back then represented a reality of the fear that Czech and Slovak people had faced for over forty years, culminating in those 'November days of 1989'. The recollection of his pain that night was completely overwhelmed, however, by the personal reality that had grown inside him by the end of that crazy autumn – that the woman now sitting opposite him four-and-a-half years later was the one he was totally in love with then and was still now.

The mixture of the glowing warmth of his feelings for her and his recollections of the physical pain he'd suffered that night from the police baton were interrupted abruptly, however, by words from Jana that he believed were the signal about her feelings he was hoping to hear. The words that would send him off full of hope on his academic travels around the Czech Republic for the next ten days, "surely you know, Tom, because it was me who liked you, who really, really liked you."

They were out there in the air now. Singing to him in answer to his earlier question to her of, "Why your Englishman? Why was I your Englishman?" Now, at last, he had the confirmation he'd hoped to hear.

"Bubbles waiting to be burst," his friend Steve had cynically told him many times before. "It's the hope that kills you, mate," he was constantly warning Tom. "You get all expectant, all dreamy and misty-eyed, you think this is it, this is going to be the one, the love of your life. You start telling yourself you'll never want anyone else, be perfectly happy and contented. Then pop, the bubble bursts and she doesn't turn out to be quite the woman you thought she was, or more precisely, the woman you wanted her to be."

Tom had lost count of the number of times that he had been in a cafe or a bar in some continental city or other with Steve and had pointed out some charming, lovely woman to his friend, accompanied by the plea, "I just want one of them. If I had one like that I'd be happy and contented. There would be no more messing around, no more playing games."

"Yep, for two weeks you'd be happy," Steve would tell him. "And what was that word? Contented? Then you'd get bored and start to wander again," was always his friend's cynical response. Tom always protested, of course. He could be happy if he met the right woman. That was his persistent defence, usually dismissed with loud laughter and a shaking of the head from his drinking companion. But then that was Steve. Tom rationalised the cynicism with the thought that his friend always preferred it that way anyway. He had never really let himself fall in love. Steve had never done that in his whole life, so how would he know?

Anyway, who cares? Steve was wrong. Here was the confirmation at last, straight from Jana's mouth. As far as he was concerned she was the loveliest, funniest, wittiest, most elegant, classiest woman he had ever been able to make himself talk to, be at ease talking to. He'd seen plenty of that kind of woman, but had never got anywhere near them, let alone been able to string more than two words together and make intelligent conversation with any of them. They were too good for him, out of his league. But now here he was again, after four-and-a-half long years, talking to, smiling at, and laughing out loud with the 'woman of his dreams'.

Okay, maybe she wasn't the loveliest, funniest, wittiest, most elegant, classiest woman on the planet, but to Tom she was right now. He'd felt her dance into his brain constantly over those long years, usually when he was sitting alone at home late at night, or in the early hours of the morning, listening to music. Of course, he thought then of her smile, her wide brown eyes, but also of what he liked to think of as her slim 'tallness'. For some reason all the women he had been with, been lovers with, and the one he'd married, had been much shorter than him. He was six foot one, and always thought to himself that had he been advertising in one of those personals columns it would read 6'1", slim, fit, professional, 44 (he was forty-eight actually, but always thought he could get away with forty-four) requires… loving? Because he'd never felt he had been loved, really passionately loved. Although maybe, on reflection, that wasn't completely true. After all, he'd been married for sixteen years. He separated from his ex-wife when he was thirty-four and divorced a year later, but even so he accepted that they must have been deeply in love at some point. Maybe though that was a different kind of 'younger' love, he convinced himself. After all they were both only nineteen when they got married and his two kids 'came along' soon after. They were hardly kids now. Karen was twenty-eight and Jim twenty-four, although thankfully neither of them had yet made him a grandfather, so he wouldn't have to put that in any personals advert… 'Grandfather seeks, etc…'

So, now here was Jana, five foot ten, slim, definitely fit, in every sense of the word, and undeniably - in Tom's mind anyway - giving off suggestions that she wanted to fill the 'requires loving' bit of the ad. Her hair, a deep dark ruddy-brown mass that was constantly tossed to and fro by her movements, intermixed with the flick and sweep of her hand through it, was shorter than he remembered. As she told him earlier that evening, she'd had it cut even shorter two months earlier and it was still growing back. Nevertheless, it seemed to Tom that, at whatever length, it framed her longish face, wide mouth and full lips perfectly. Her optimistic, charming smile was still the same though, and still not broken by the cracks and lines of life which invade all our faces at some stage. Her dark-brown eyes were still sparkling and full of life. No doubt full of life because they'd seen plenty of it. No one who had lived through thirty years - or in Jana's case thirty-two of her thirty-seven years - under the Stalinist regime in what was then Czechoslovakia could fail to have seen life in all its aspects. The formalised and the non-formalised, the regimented and the sub-world that nobody really acknowledged or recognised existed.

Here she was and here it was, the moment. Not one that Tom had obsessed over during those past four-and-a half-years because he never really thought it would happen, but one he had secretly stored in those bleak inner reaches of his memory. It was there, but he dared not think about it too much. Too many dreams, too many hopes, too many bubbles Steve would no doubt say. Even now, especially now, were Steve there sitting at Tom's shoulder, he'd undoubtedly be muttering in his ear, "it's the hope that kills you, mate."

That is just what the email had given Tom. Well, a couple of emails actually, Hope, with a capital 'H'. Just a few quick, brief words to Tom from Jana's friend Monika before she gave his visiting students a lecture in Prague in March earlier in that year of 1994 had nourished his hope once again.

"Oh, by the way, a friend of yours says hi," Monika told him.
"Really, who?"
"Jana, Jana Sukova," was Monika's response.

He didn't know if any of his students or colleagues on his university's annual study visit - the third annual visit to be precise - noticed, but Tom's smile nearly took his ears off.

"Do you have her email address? Err ... I mean, does she have email? Can you let me have it?" he blurted out. "Perhaps when I am next in Prague we can meet up? All three of us," he quickly added knowing full well really just who it was he wanted to meet up with.

If that made him smile and kept him inwardly happy, for at least the rest of that day and night, it was nothing when compared to the effect of the reply he received to his first tentative email to Jana. "Great!" her reply on the computer screen screamed out at him. "Let me know when you are next in Praha and we can meet up. It is good to hear from you again, really!!! I am looking forward to seeing you in Praha. Got to run, but it's great to hear from you again!!! Love Jana."

He just sat there for what seemed like an age, staring at the screen until his eyes hurt with the white brightness of it, scrutinising every word, every punctuation mark over and over again. Exercising his so-called academic incisive brain in order to analyse and re-analyse every syllable, every word. What does that mean? What does "really" really mean? Just how many exclamation marks add up to an excitable consummate yearning? "She wrote, Love Jana," he muttered. "Love Jana," like he had to repeat it aloud over and over to convince himself, like it would give off some greater clarity, real meaning, if he said it aloud over and over. And three exclamation marks, three! He kept repeating it like it was some binding contract of intent between them and that his whole future with her was therefore sealed by three exclamation marks.

This wasn't some excitable southern European Latin woman this was rational, calm, Jana. Yes, she was an exciting woman, absolutely no mistake about that, but Jana's was an inner excitement, a composure that radiated charm. Now the exclamation marks were in Tom's head, in his thoughts, as he rushed headlong into a catalogue of conclusions, most of which of course, he had wanted to draw.

If that wasn't air to blow up some bubbles nothing was, he decided, again seemingly in an attempt to convince no one but himself. Suddenly his world was a million times brighter. Hope had returned, even if it could be the type that kills you. Who cares about that, for now there is hope again.

So, he emailed her back and arranged to meet for dinner at the start of his May visit. Now here he was having jumped straight in when he saw his testing opportunity to find out about her feelings. "Why your Englishman?" he had interjected as she recounted to him the phone conversation she'd had with her closest friend Dita about him prior to Tom's first ever visit to Prague in December 1988.

He'd met both of them, Jana and Dita, at an academic conference in Spa in Belgium in October of that year. Then, at the time Gorbachev's glasnost was spreading through East and Central Europe, Tom was scheduled to visit Prague in December 1988 for his research. So, he managed to contact Dita to ask her to try and arrange some academic meetings for him for his, "so important research," on the changes that were taking place inside the Soviet bloc in East and Central Europe. Well, he told her his research was, "so important," as he thought it might get Dita to like him more and help him. It might just persuade Dita that he really was a serious academic, that in truth he wasn't, well not in the Oxbridge, dusty books, faded old jacket with leather elbow patches and thinning hair sense of the word.

Dita Kralova was the more academically minded of the two women. In their fairly brief meeting in Spa it soon became apparent that was the case and that Dita was very single minded and totally serious about her work. They were both equally engaged in researching and studying for a Ph.D. - in sociology in Jana's case and history in Dita's - while also doing some teaching at Charles University in their home city of Prague. However, Jana seemed much more like Tom where academia was concerned. Whatever she did in that respect she didn't appear to believe it to be earth shattering, or about to produce any massive change in the fortunes of the planet or its inhabitants. Very similar to Tom's views about academia and its research. For him, far too many self-styled academics took their pronouncements and their, "so important," research, far too seriously. "Just like the Soviets, some academics believe their own propaganda," he remembered remarking to Jana in Spa.

"So, why your Englishman? Why did Dita call me your Englishman?" Tom blurted out in quizzical surprise to Jana, as he simultaneously tried to gulp down the spoonful of hot onion soup that he'd just put into his mouth, almost burning the back of his throat. While he reached quickly for the soothing cool Czech white wine in his glass Jana spelt it out for him and sent him the signal, the subliminal message. At least, that's the way Tom wished to interpret it.

"Simply because it was me who liked you, really, really liked you, so when Dita told me you were going to visit Prague at the end of 1988 she mischievously said to me 'Your Englishman is coming.'"

Now, finally, here in May 1994 he'd heard what he'd hoped to hear. His eyes were still smiling at that answer and in his mind his arms were both raised in the air while he raced off in a wide triumphal arc like some footballer celebrating a winning goal, when in the corner of his ear, above the crowd's adulation, cheering and applause, he heard Jana continuing with, "but when you split up with Dita I thought I'd never see you again."

Kerplunk!!

"Oops, that's tricky," Tom thought as the cheering subsided and the linesman stood there with his flag in the air signalling offside and disallowing his goal. To leap in now and express his undying love for Jana might not be greeted very well by her, to say the least. Not when she had moved on to speak of the 'dead'. Not that her best friend Dita was dead. Well, not in the physical sense anyway. What had passed away was the relationship he'd had with her for nine months through the spring, summer and autumn of 1989. This was going to be trickier than he'd thought.

"How is Dita?" he heard himself responding.

"She's fine. Working, working, working. You know Dita."

Yes, he sure did. That was more than true. He definitely knew Dita, very, very well, biblically in fact. Undoubtedly this was going to be even more difficult than he'd anticipated. Now he really could feel Steve at his shoulder, pin poised, waiting to join in as fate wielded the large pin followed by the massive pop!

Tom was still 'out there' searching for the eternal flame; the love and the light that would make all his angst, all his life, worthwhile. He now realised that he'd actually found it five-and-a-half years previously. Only trouble was he'd been confronted with choices and as usual, as always in his life, he made the wrong one. It wasn't that he didn't believe it when he said he'd fallen hopelessly in love with Dita. He did believe it. It was just that he now realised - too late, as many men do - that he'd fallen in love with the image he wanted to fall in love with, an intelligent and beautiful Czech woman who came across as very exciting in her long, swirling coat and beautiful hat, and who lived in the atmospheric city of Prague. Okay, that was unfair; Dita was a lot more than a Prague image he'd concocted. Even now he had to admit he had fallen in love with the clever, lovely person that was Dita.

The problem was that all the time this was happening, or he had convinced himself that it was happening at last, that he'd found his soul mate in Dita, an even greater reality dawned on him and grew and grew through the Autumn of 1989. By the end of that tumultuous year it was staring him in the face. His real soul mate, his actual perfect woman was in fact her best friend Jana. What now though? Just at the point where at last he had the belated and unexpected opportunity to tell Jana just how he felt she had brought Dita into their conversation. How was he going to deal with that? Steve, of course, would have had the answer straightaway, simple and easy. Just move on. That way you don't expect, and will not expect, too much. You don't get tangled up in the crap that is 'the hope', so most of all you don't get emotionally mangled.

Tom wanted the 'too much' though. Jana was what he wanted. If he could sort this mess out and be with Jana he would be happy and never need even to look at another woman. So, what now? How the bloody hell could he get around the 'Dita issue' and tell Jana how he felt? His head was spinning as he tried to continue to seem intensely interested in Jana's every word and at the same time search through the options about what to do that were whirring through the programme chips of his mind. How could he extricate himself from this without yet again losing all he had hoped for - to be with Jana?

He needed time to think, but he desperately didn't want her believing that yet again he wasn't interested. Most of all he didn't want her thinking her suggestions, the signs, the words he had waited so long to hear, were not being picked up on and were not being reciprocated. So, he did what most blokes do and delayed the moment of truth. Put things off. "Listen," he started to say, as if she wasn't, "I have to go to Liberec tomorrow, on to Brno on Wednesday, to Ostrava a week on Monday, then back here a week on Wednesday. I'd love to see you again. I really do need to. How about meeting up for dinner again then?" Enthusiastic enough he thought, with just a hint of a message for her there with the emphasised, "really do need to," delivered as he purposefully leaned forward on the table opposite her.

He needn't have worried. "Sure," she instantly replied. "That would be great."

See, there it was again. Her, "that would be great," response, another sign. It's okay, so far, so good. After all he did have to go to Liberec, Brno and Ostrava for some research work in the universities there. That would give him plenty of time to think through his 'grand game plan' and strategy during those long lonely hotel evenings in those cities.

"Here are my home and office phone numbers. Give me a ring next weekend and we can fix up something for the Wednesday night you get back to Prague," she suggested as she quickly wrote them on the back of one of the restaurant cards scattered on the table.

There's another one. Yet another good sign, both phone numbers, work and home. His mind and his senses were in overdrive. He'd try his luck once more and give her one more big hint before she left that evening. He looked straight at her, tried to look serious, and said as softly as he could, "I should have had these numbers ages ago, especially after what you told me tonight."

She just looked straight back at him though, straight into his eyes, grinned and although looking what he thought was a little bemused, simply said, "Yes." Was this another good sign? In time he would know. Anyway, she sent, "her Englishman," on his way with a quick kiss on his cheek outside the restaurant and, "see you next week," and she jumped into a somewhat battered looking old green Skoda taxi and off into the Prague night.

For Tom it wasn't a night for taxis. For some people Prague is at its best in winter, covered in the damp mists swirling off the Vltava River. He remembered vividly some of those days in November and

December 1989. That wasn't a time though for taking in some of the city's misty atmosphere. At that time the days of strolling by the river, or through the narrow little streets of the Old Town over the medieval cobbles with Dita, were very, very few. The three of them – Tom, Dita and Jana – were all too busy being swept along from demonstration to demonstration in the rushing tide of the 'Velvet revolution'. Now, in May 1994, this was a Bohemian crystal-clear warm Prague night, fit only for walking and going over and over in his mind the night's events and his conversation with Jana. Analysing every word, every one of her movements. Did she reach over and squeeze his hand at one point? Yes, of course she did. He remembered that well. Or did she? Was she smiling when she did it? What did that mean? Was it the smile of an old friend, or something more? Yep, of course it was something more. That was what he wanted to believe. He was right because it all fitted. Her actions, her words, what she told him tonight. It all fitted together and added up to just what he had hoped for. He just had to figure out how to deal with the Dita problem, but at least he had ten days travelling around the Czech Republic to work out that. Now he was outside his hotel and he could go in and rest easily, sleep well in anticipation of their meeting a week on Wednesday and the real start to the rest of his life.

Part Two: Tom's hope and 1989 beginnings

2
Recollections of earlier hope

The train slowly wound its way along the curve of the shimmering Labe River, a river that changed its identity to Elbe when it flowed across the German border. It was a hot Sunday afternoon and he was on the first train of his two train journey to Liberec anxiously reckoning that he wasn't going to make his connection at twenty past four at Děčín for the local train to Liberec. It was already ten past and his Hamburg bound Inter-City express should have been in Děčín a couple of minutes ago. No point in getting stressed about it though. Nothing he could do about it anyway. "Mmm ... that's a surprisingly relaxed approach," he mumbled. Maybe he was just slipping into the Czech way of 'well it will all be okay in the end, one way or another.' Or maybe it was the magnificent scenery through the train window; rolling hills densely covered with trees and forests sweeping down to the shimmering river. The green canvass was only broken by terracotta-roofed houses dotted invitingly in the hillsides. It could have been Austria, although no doubt nowhere near as clean, but then nowhere was as clean as Austria, apart from Switzerland of course. They were both so hermetically sealed you were almost suffocated. There was no way the Labe he was gazing at could be remotely described as clean. It was highly polluted, despite its tempting suggested coolness through the train window.

If the countryside he was surveying had made Tom forget the Stalinist past of the Czech Republic, or to be precise Czechoslovakia, its legacy suddenly hit him square in the face, literally concretely. As the train rounded the bend of the river just before Děčín his pleasant peaceful view was assaulted by huge concrete tower blocks, row upon row of flats, panelaks in Czech. A real eyesore and blot on the landscape. That guy Stalin sure is difficult to eradicate, he thought.

Eventually, slowly the train ground to a noisy screeching halt in Děčín station as what seemed like metal on metal brakes screamed their protest out for all to hear. And there it was, the connecting train to Liberec Tom presumed, waiting impatiently on the only other track in the very basic station. So that was what the ticket inspector on the inter-city express had been trying to convey to him in response to Tom's constant bleating in broken English, "but it will be late, the train," and, "miss connection." Now it was obvious. God knows just what it was in Czech that the inspector had told him, but the English translation was obviously, "they will hold the Liberec train until we arrive, you are not the only one making the connection you stupid English git!"

Anyway, so far so good he told himself as he descended the step from the express and strode along what passed for a platform and across the track towards the waiting local train. Děčín was virtually on the German border and Tom couldn't help feeling that the station reminded him of some of the frontier stations he had seen as a kid in John Wayne and Gary Cooper black and white American westerns. The platform consisted of planks of wood hardly raised off the ground and the only way to get from one train to another was across the tracks at the end of it. What was barely more than an enlarged shed on one side of the tracks passed as the booking hall.

Once he had climbed aboard with his bag he soon realised that the Děčín to Liberec train was certainly no air-conditioned, smart inter-city express. It was very much a Czech local train and there were definitely no first class carriages. Busy, hot, grimy and very noisy, were its main characteristics. At best it could be described as functional in the newly liberated post-revolution Czech Republic. Once he'd found a seat Tom casually surveyed his fellow travellers, soon realising that many of them had taken a keen interest in the man struggling through the carriage with his bag to find a seat. He was the only person in the carriage with even an overnight bag, let alone one as large as his. Not only that, but he felt that it was obvious to everyone else in the carriage that he wasn't Czech. Maybe he was just being self-conscious, but it was like he had a label round his neck saying 'foreigner with a large bag'. His self-conscious moment quickly disappeared as he spotted the usual number of sexily dressed young women in the carriage. Perhaps it was obligatory in every town, city and village in the Czech Republic. His eyes lingered on the slim, very dark haired young woman sat across the aisle from him. Her hair was cut quite short and looked naturally very black, very North Moravian. He guessed she was no more than eighteen or nineteen and was dressed in black cut-off canvass trousers, platform sandals and a black v-neck jumper with a white t-shirt beneath it. Despite the heat she exhibited no concern or sign of being bothered by it. She just looked totally cool, while in contrast he felt one or two beads of sweat start to form on his own forehead as a result of his exertions crossing the track and getting his bag up onto the Liberec bound train. He noticed she was reading what appeared to be an economics textbook. What optimism awaits her he wondered, some young boy waiting for her coming home at the end of the semester? Joy as they embrace as she gets off the train, hold hands, chatter, smile at each other, laugh with each other and enjoy one another's company in the early summer sun?

As he managed to tear his eyes away from the young woman he realised that the much older woman sat opposite him on his side of the aisle had been watching him and his staring. He tried a vaguely embarrassing smile, but her face remained expressionless and fixed on him in what felt to Tom like a mixture of contempt and disgust. Now he was getting even warmer, with embarrassment, even though the train had at last begun its journey and a very slight breeze was drifting into the carriage from the wide open slid down windows. As Tom removed his eyes from the fixed expressionless stare opposite he noticed the older woman was wearing a wedding ring. Her badly fitting sleeveless dark brown flowered dress looked distinctly like something from a second-hand shop, and a downmarket one at that. To complete her charming ensemble she had removed her flat white sandals and placed her white-socked feet on the grubby carriage floor. Tom guessed that the guy sat next to her was her husband, mainly because although there was the faintest of arm contact between them as they leaned on one another, there was definitely no conversation. One of her now distinctly blackened soled socked feet rested next to her husband's requisite bottle of Czech beer, which he had momentarily placed on the carriage floor while he munched on his sweaty salami and cheese baguette. Gambrinus Tom noticed, not a bad choice of beer in the new free-market Czech Republic. Tom had paid 175 Czech Krowns, about £3.50p, for a plastic cup of coffee and a soggy excuse for a cheese and lettuce roll on the recently disembarked inter-city express. "Christ, virtually the same as on British trains," he couldn't help remarking to the person who had served him. Anyway, the Czech husband opposite was seemingly enjoying his likely 8 krown, or 15 pence, bottle of beer, before no doubt later sampling the delights of his wife's effervescent un-socked feet once they got home. Undoubtedly the sun and heat of the day would add to the mystery of the aroma.

Tom decided to focus his thoughts, if only his fleeting glances, on the young dark haired woman across the aisle. She was definitely not wearing any socks, but now she did have a Czech-English dictionary in front of her. What an opportunity. Maybe the sun and heat had affected his judgement, made him slightly deranged in assuming a girl so young would want to talk to an old git like him, but in he ploughed, if only to pass the time of the journey. "Do you speak English?" he asked, knowing the answer full well. "Yes, of course I do dickhead, that's why I'm looking at a Czech-English dictionary!" is what she ought to have told him. Instead she settled for a much more polite, "a little."

"Do you know what time the train gets to Liberec?" was all he could think of to say next.

"At about six I think, but the conductor will know. You can ask him when he checks the ticket."

Tom wasn't sure whether this was a brush off, or just her being as helpful as she could. Meanwhile, he could almost feel the daggers from the be-socked older woman opposite him piercing into his body from her even more fixed stare. He decided to push on. "Your English is very good. Where did you learn?" He knew the answer to that of course. Everyone her age would have learned it in school after 1989, but he couldn't think of what else to ask.

"In school," was her expected reply. "We all learn in school now. I like to speak English. I watch American films and listen to American and English music. I want to go to work in England or America. I want to learn the language very much."

"Oh, I see. Well, good luck. I'm sure you'll do well," he reassured her.

He was tempted to look around the carriage to see just how many of his fellow travellers were now focussing on the conversation of the English stranger. Luckily for him it seemed that no one else in earshot could speak his native tongue. Those close by did appear intrigued by the sound of what was obviously a foreign language, but this was not Prague, fortunately for Tom, where many more Czechs spoke and understood English. This was a non-tourist area, at least a non-English or American tourist area. What second language was spoken and understood was German.

The faintest of smiles crossed the young woman's lips and she simply offered him a polite, "thank you, that's very kind of you. I must get back to my studies now. Perhaps we can talk later."

Taking the rather large hint Tom decided to just relax and try and cool off while staring aimlessly out of the carriage window. What struck him now was that this was the more industrial, poorer, and decidedly dirtier and grimier north of the Czech Republic. Reality was biting. Not only was this the more industrially downtrodden north, but also the reality of decision day with Jana was beginning to rush towards him. He had just over a week in which to work out his strategy. He thought the best place to start was to try and think about the good days with Jana that he remembered, the days when he first thought there was some spark between them. The times when he first started to notice her more and more as they got on so well. Maybe there would be some clues there about how to play it, how to recreate those fleeting good moments. The problem was, of course, that it all happened four and a half years before in the final months of the year of '89, a somewhat different, crazy, exciting time. Perhaps the bonding between them, if that was what it was, the fleeting moments when they seemed to be in each other's pockets, in tune with each other's mind, on the same wavelength even, were all at a time of high adrenaline and excitement. After all, the attachment between them and their friendship really took off during the 'November days' of that crazy year and on the demonstrations they went on together while Dita initially refused to go. Now the doubts were flooding into his mind, what if it was just that, a friendship.

What about the issue over Dita? It wasn't going to be easy to convince Jana that all the time she thought he was very much in love with her best friend he was, in fact, falling in love with her. Although he tried to reassure himself with Jana's comment that he was, "her Englishman," as far as Dita was concerned. Yet it had been Dita who had first smiled that sparkling, radiant smile of hers at him over lunch at the conference at Spa in late 1988 when the three of them had first met. The sun was streaming through the patio doors into the conference dining room and Dita, on the next table with a group of academics had turned her head, caught Tom's eye, and beamed a smile at him which was as warm and bright as the sun bursting through the glass doors. She followed it with a cheeky wink.

The Dita that Tom met in Spa was a very different East European woman from the stereotype that Tom carried around in his head. For a start she was more Central European than East European, and she would certainly say that herself. Indeed, as he was to find out in the future, she was always very offended to be called East European. For Tom, she was a cultured, charming, very intelligent, and darkly beautiful Central European woman. Throughout the conference she was predominantly dressed in black. One day in a nicely fitted black shirt and long calf length skirt, and the next day in black trousers and a plain black jumper. On both days though the dark colour of her clothes was set off against a quite bright small silver cross necklace and medium sized circular silver earrings. Mostly her clothes were simple, but somehow they conveyed elegance and style, although they obviously weren't expensive. She wasn't a tall woman, being around five foot six. Her charm, her intoxicating smile, and her demeanour had a striking effect on Tom and ensured that he noticed her, especially in a large group of boring academics. He hadn't misread the signs with Dita five and a half years earlier, or had he? After all her, "your Englishman," comment to Jana suggested now to him that Dita wasn't interested in him initially.

He decided that Dita had a presence. Yep, that was the word that best described the effect that she'd had on him in Spa. That described why he was attracted to her. So, during the coffee break in the afternoon session on the second day of the conference he plucked up the courage to approach her and mumbled some, what instantly seemed ridiculous, words about visiting Prague with his students. Dita wasn't impressed. Later in their relationship she told him that his mumbled excuse to strike up a conversation with her came across to her like some guy trying to use her to get some contacts in Prague for some bizarre student visit. Nevertheless, Tom did manage to obtain her Prague phone number and secure a promise from her that if he did indeed come to Prague then they could meet for a coffee.

That was mid-October. Two months later Tom was ringing her number from his hotel lobby in Prague. It was Saturday morning, around ten, and as he was also subsequently to find out during their relationship, ten on a Saturday morning was definitely not the best time to be ringing Dita. She was a night person. Late at night in her Prague flat she worked – read, wrote, drank coffee and smoked. In fact, at night was virtually the only time she smoked. It was not a habit she was proud of and always apologised profusely to Tom every time she lit a cigarette. Like most Czechs though, she liked her fag.

Eventually, after a considerable time during which he nearly lost his nerve and hung up, Dita answered with a very sharp Czech hello. "Ahoj," came abruptly down the phone line. Tom stammered a faltering and questioning toned, "err, hello, Dita?"

"Yes," she answered, with a strong hint of bemusement in her voice and with obviously no clue as to just who this idiotic, apprehensive Englishman was on the other end of her phone at the ungodly Saturday morning hour of ten o'clock.

"It's Tom, Tom, from England. We met at a conference in Spa, in Belgium," as if she didn't know where Spa was. "Do you remember?"

"Oh, err ... yes. How are you? Where are you?" she asked, more politely.

"I'm in Prague and I was wondering if we could meet up? I'm only here for the weekend. I have to leave on Monday morning," Tom ventured, in the hope that she would make some time for a meeting in her obviously busy weekend.

"I'm working on an article. I have a lot of writing to do," she answered, in what to Tom seemed a very calculated and disciplined way.

"Oh, err ... okay, but it would be lovely to see you," was all he could think of saying as he tried again. How could someone with such a sweet, radiant smile be so calculatingly hard he thought? When he got to know Dita more he realised that as far as her work was concerned and her writing very little came before it, if anything.

"Ring me tomorrow morning, Sunday," she suggested, "and perhaps we can meet for an hour for lunch."

"Okay. That would be great," Tom replied.

"Ciao," came ringing back down the line to him and with that he heard the click of the receiver and she was gone.

Looking back on that call, while the Liberec bound train clattered slowly on, Tom wondered how they ever developed a relationship. Obviously Dita thought at the time that Tom was merely out to use her for some academic ends, and in any case as far as Dita was concerned he was Jana's 'Englishman', as he had learned now from her best friend. So why was he bothering her? It could only be to use her for academic contacts.

Nevertheless, he did ring her again on the Sunday morning and she agreed to meet him at the Hradčanská metro station behind Prague castle. "Maybe a short walk and some lunch?" Tom suggested over the phone.

"Okay, maybe, but I have a lot of work to do later this afternoon and evening for Monday," was her qualified acceptance.

They met at the metro station booking hall, as she had suggested. A quite non-descript, communist era bland functionalist area. Tom was very early, not wanting to be late when she only had a limited amount of time to spend with him. Dita came rushing and bustling into the metro station ten minutes late. Tom had debated in his head, was she coming, wasn't she coming? Should he ring her from the metro station to see if she had got delayed? As he came to find out over the few months in which their relationship developed, Dita was always rushing to get somewhere on time and was very often not successful in that aim, even though she hated not being punctual.

They strolled around the streets behind Prague castle. The air was crisp with the sharp growing cold of winter and the footpaths were covered with seas of brown, crunchy underfoot leaves from the many trees that lined the pavements. They walked and talked and had, for

Czechs, an unusually light lunch. The hour she could spare him stretched into nearly three and it was past four o'clock on a darkening Prague winter late afternoon when they parted. The sky seemed full of snow clouds and as she left him Tom felt some light flecks of snow on his face. The dusk of the Prague sky seemed to perfectly match Dita's deep brown eyes. For Tom, her whole persona fitted perfectly with the surroundings, the time of day and time of year in the magical city they were in.

She had turned up at the metro station looking immaculate, even though she was so obviously in a rush. Not a hair was out of place and she greeted him with the smile that had so enchanted him in the Spa dining room. Although shorter than Tom, she had a stature and a charm which oozed through every part of her body. As in Spa, she was once again dressed all in black, and when the snow clouds gathered during the afternoon she produced a charming ruffled black velvet hat from her bag, which took Tom's breath away. Once more she'd made an instant impression on him. She personified his Prague, with her shoulder length dark brown hair and a long flowing black coat over a devastatingly simple black woollen dress. The coat just sitting above and skimming the top of black leather ankle boots, with just the right size of heel. A long dark grey woollen scarf was tied perfectly around the turned up collar of her coat. She was a picture of charm and beauty. She resembled everything that he thought was continental, both of the east and the west. Unfortunately it also represented everything that wasn't British. He found himself desperately wanting to see her again, but could only stammer as she was about to leave him, "err ... err ... the next time I am in Prague perhaps we could ... err ... meet for dinner?"

"Okay, we'll see," she told him, which filled him with hopeful positive conclusions. After all they got on very well, or so it seemed. She had given him three hours and not the one that she had told him on the telephone she could barely spare. What she did do though was put him in touch with a friend of hers who she told him could give his students a lecture on Czech politics, if he ever really did bring them to Prague. This turned out to be Monika who over five years later passed on Jana's, "say hello to Tom," message and begin his hopes rising again.

Coming to Prague in December 1988 to pursue and see Dita had been exciting for Tom, but November 1989 was an altogether different form of excitement. As the Czech train chugged sedately towards Liberec, seemingly stopping at a local station every five minutes, Tom recalled an argument he had read that the twentieth century history of the Czechs was marked by twenty-year cycles. Something vague in the back of his mind suggested to him that it was the Czech author Milan Kundera in his novel 'Ignorance' who identified these cycles and outlined them perfectly. According to Kundera, "The history of the Czechs in the twentieth century is graced with a remarkable mathematical beauty due to the triple repetition of the number twenty. In 1918, after several centuries they achieved their independence and in 1938 they lost it when their country was invaded by the Nazis. In 1948 the Communist revolution, imported from Moscow, inaugurated the country's second twenty-year span; that one ended in 1968 when, enraged by the country's insolent self-emancipation, the Russians invaded with half-a-million soldiers. The Occupier took over in full force in the autumn of 1969 and then, to everyone's surprise, took off in autumn 1989, quietly and almost politely. That was the third twenty-year span."

Tom's cycle of visits to Czechoslovakia, as it then was, began with Dita in December 1988, but it was the November 1989 visit that he recalled with most pleasure. Not only because of the revolutionary time and events, but because he now felt that was when he grew to know Jana much more. Now the young student across the aisle and the effervescent blackened white socks opposite him in the carriage were far away from his thoughts as he decided he'd search his memory for clues from the 'November days' of '89. Clues from the past about how to tell Jana just how he felt about her.

He would have to put those thoughts on hold for a while now though as the train finally rolled into Liberec station and came to a halt with a resigned screech of its brakes. A short five minute taxi ride from the station and by six-fifteen he was checking into the Hotel Praha.

3
A thought provoking pummelling

Whenever and wherever Tom arrived in a hotel room for the first time he was always struck by just how unnatural it was. Un-human, if that's a word? Too neat, no room he had ever lived in or worked in, in his office or his home, was ever that neat and tidy. Even the bed looked as if it had never ever been slept in. Sheets and bedspread, if there was no duvet, were always tucked in so tightly it seemed totally implausible that anyone could ever actually have got beneath them and into the bed. The bedside table had everything neatly arranged and stacked. The small writing pad and pen perfectly aligned just in front of the telephone. The room service menu, if there was one, strategically placed. The obligatory hotel stationery, with envelopes of course, was within easy reaching distance from the bed, or on the nearby writing desk. He wondered if anyone ever actually used the stationery, or even ever sat at the writing desk?

The room in the Hotel Praha was full of dark mahogany looking wood fittings. Although it was obviously not real mahogany, just some laminated imposter. No sooner had Tom put his bags down in the room and surveyed its dark and somewhat gloomy interior than the telephone rang. Despite the fact that he was not expecting to see or hear from anyone at the university until the next morning, he couldn't resist picking up the receiver and venturing a tentative and inquisitive sounding, "hello."

"Hello," said a female voice slowly in a Czech accent. "You want woman? I am very good. I come room now if you want."

Blimey that's a whole new version of room service and very quick and efficient too he thought as he was stunned into a five second silence. All he could think to stutter at the end of it was, "err ... no. Thank you. No." With that there was a click and the dialling tone was back. Perhaps it's their version of putting a chocolate on your pillow after the room had been cleaned each day he pondered with a smile.

Although declining the impromptu room service, he had noticed as he checked in that there was what he took to be a legitimate massage service available at a very reasonable price in the Fitness Room on the ground floor. So, he quickly unpacked and decided to treat himself to a massage before finding somewhere for dinner. It might also give him some more time to think about what to do about Jana while relaxing having the massage.

The masseuse turned out to be the stereotypical woman of East European Olympic shot putt proportions, with the regulation communist-era heavily lacquered big-hair do, and if your description was kind, a rose cheeked full face. Whatever she told Tom to do, even if it was in what to him was incomprehensible Czech, he did instantly, or at least he reacted in some physical way. If he got it wrong she firmly placed her large fat anvil-like hands on various parts of his anatomy and shifted him easily into the necessary position. This was usually followed by some more Czech and a brief smile, which remarkably for a Czech woman of her age exhibited the fact that she still had all her teeth. Tom instantly relaxed under her poundings and manipulations. His mind drifted back to Jana and his thoughts were of Prague and their proposed meeting in just over a week's time. How to play it? What to say, and how to say it, how to read, or worse, not misread the signs. Maybe it would help if he tried to recall his visits to Prague throughout the whole year of 1989 and how his feelings for Jana developed.

In March of that year he'd travelled by train from Vienna into Czechoslovakia. At that time it was easier to fly to Vienna than to try and fly directly to Prague, even though crossing into Czechoslovakia from Austria on a train was not exactly a simple procedure. In January 1989 Tom had read in the British press, and heard on the BBC, about the demonstrations in Prague to mark the twentieth anniversary of the death of Jan Palach. Palach was a student who had set himself on fire at the top of Wenceslas Square in January 1969 in protest at the Soviet occupation in August 1968 that had brought to an end the Prague Spring reforms of the Czechoslovak communist government.

The post-1989 post-communist Radio Prague subsequently reported that "The wave of suicide attempts by immolation that ran through the Czech lands in the first months of 1969 was a unique event on a world-wide scale, a result of the social atmosphere at the time. After Palach, twenty-six more people attempted suicide between January 20, 1969 and the end of April that year. Seven of them died. On Jan. 20, 1969 a large group of people gathered under the St. Wenceslas statue on Wenceslas Square and soon began to move in a silent procession, adorned with Czechoslovak state flags, black flags and enlarged photographs of Jan Palach. At the head was a sign carried by students that read 'We will stay faithful'. The procession that Prague doesn't remember, slowly, quietly moved on toward Mustek at the bottom of the square, from there it went to the Powder Tower (Prašna Brána, one of the gates that had formed one of the entrances to the old city) along Revoluční and Dlouhá streets through Old Town Square toward the campus of Charles University, where Palach studied aesthetics. In the hall of the Philosophy Faculty building the clocks were stopped so they showed the exact time of Palach's death (3:15). At 5.00 p.m. the entire square in front of the faculty building, as well as the surrounding streets, were full. On the building's balcony there appeared representatives of the faculty, students, workers and politicians. On the same day Josef Hlavaty burned himself alive (he died on January 25, 1969)."

The demonstrations of January 1989 commemorating the events of twenty years earlier, largely made up of students and intellectuals, were viciously broken up by the Czechoslovak authorities using water cannon, tear gas and police batons. With the new spirit of glasnost in Gorbachev's Soviet Union at that time though, such demonstrations in Prague were a sign that something was stirring. Indeed, Gorbachev had visited Prague in April 1987 and received a rapturous reception from the Praguers, expectant that changes were in the air. The Czechoslovak regime was, however, one of the most rigid and hard-line in Central and Eastern Europe. Not as totalitarian or as rigid as Ceauşescu's Romania, but authoritarian and rigid enough in its own way and definitely not the reforming kind.

Hearing of these events, and wanting to renew his acquaintance with Dita, Tom had decided he needed to try and get to Prague in

March during his university's Easter break. Although he was convinced by then that his acquaintance with Dita had become increasingly important, because of his work and research he was also keenly interested in what was happening in Central and Eastern Europe following Gorbachev's changes in the Soviet Union. These were indeed exciting times. He managed ten days. In truth, despite his good intentions very little work was done during the visit he recalled as the shot-putting masseuse pounded her anvil hands into his lower back. If not 'Ten days that shook the world', in the American journalist John Reed's famous phrase about the Russian revolution of 1917, his visit to Prague in March 1989 was certainly ten days that changed Tom Carpenter's life. He had written to Dita that he was coming in March, asking once again if they could meet. He had also sent her a postcard with a brief message after their short meeting in Prague the previous December thanking her for her help, saying how pleased and happy he was to see her again, and wishing her a happy Christmas. Very civilised he remembered thinking, cautious and pleasantly put, not pressurising or crowding her.

On arrival in Prague in late March 1989 he rang her as soon as he got into his hotel room. It was early evening, approaching six-thirty. Would she be there? Would she have even received his mail given the present situation in Central and Eastern Europe, and in particular in Czechoslovakia? If she was there he was determined to jump straight in and ask her to dinner that night. He would be insistent, and very firm. Wouldn't take no for an answer. After all he only had ten days and he was desperate to see her. As the telephone receiver echoed a ponderous heavy ringing tone in his ear he worried that as it was Friday night maybe she wouldn't be in? Maybe she had gone away for the weekend? That would be disastrous.

Then, a very soft, "Ahoj," came floating down the telephone line and into his ear.

"Err ... hello ... it's Tom," he responded, like some long-time friend.

"Where are you?" she asked him brusquely. She obviously hadn't got his letter, although at least she seemed to remember who he was.

"In Prague," he bleated out.

"Why? Why are you here?" She sounded confused.

That threw him and his well-rehearsed prepared text, not to mention his determined firmness. What fleetingly flashed through his mind now was complete indecision. Should he just blurt it straight out – "to see you" - in response to her, "why?" No, probably not the best approach. Although he'd only met her a few times it seemed to him that Dita was a very organised and private person. You didn't just announce to her on the telephone that you had travelled over a thousand miles and through numerous checkpoints on a train on the way into her country merely to see her. To some that would seem very romantic of course, but even after their brief acquaintances he judged that was not the way to do it with Dita. After all he didn't want to panic her and spook her.

"Hello, Tom? Are you still there? What do you want?" His indecisive silence was now appearing to annoy her. Not exactly the effect he had hoped for. Now he was panicking. All he could think to say was, "yes, I'm still here. Sorry, err … yes, I have to do some work here."

"Oh, I see," was her instant response, but just when he thought he was 'out of the woods' she continued with, "what work and where? It's not exactly very pleasant here at present Not exactly a good place to be a foreigner in, especially one doing research and asking awkward questions."

Oh bollocks! What now, he thought. From what he knew of her, from their few meetings, it wasn't that she was being abrupt or even that she didn't believe him, it was just that in her own matter of fact, direct way Dita always seemed to come straight to the point. She always sounded genuinely interested, especially where academic work was concerned. She was, indeed, a true academic. She took her academic work on Czech nationalism and culture very seriously.

Dita was fluent not only in English, but in French, Italian, German and Russian, besides her native Czech of course. She was straightforward and didn't suffer fools gladly, even if they had come many miles to pursue her affections. To Dita, such an act was foolish and irrational. To go many miles in difficult times to see someone you never really knew and had only met twice before was quite, quite ridiculous. So the last thing Tom wanted to do was to admit that to her right now, right at the start. He didn't want to appear stupid and ridiculous, which is exactly what he thought she would think of him if he admitted the truth of his visit. Later, many months on, of course he could, would, admit the truth. Then, he was sure it would seem very, very romantic, but not right now.

Tom decided the best form of defence was attack. He completely ignored her question and instead pushed on with his own agenda.

"Um... dinner... I was sort of wondering, thinking, I don't, err ... suppose-"

Useless, quite bloody useless, he thought. What happened to all that determination, that firmness? That won't take no for an answer crap?

While he hesitated and his proposal sort of tailed off he was put out of his misery by Dita in her usual forthright manner enquiring, "Tonight?"

"Well ... err," Tom attempted to continue, "I realise it is short notice, but I've only just arrived and I'm hungry. I was going to have dinner anyway, and I thought, well it would be nice to have it with ... erm ... someone as lovely and talented as you."

Ouch! What a prat! As soon as the words left his mouth he felt physically sick. God knows what she must have thought.

"Someone!" What anyone, "someone"? What a dickhead.

And, "someone as lovely and talented as you," yuk! What a complete idiot were the words that rushed through his brain. What is she some bloody tap dancer, or some all-round genius á la Michelangelo or Leonardo? Da Vinci that is, not di bloody Caprio!

Once again his misery was ended by Dita. Giggling down the phone she told him, "okay, Tom, sure. At eight, I'll see you at eight in Starométské náměstí, the Old Town Square, by the Horologe. Oh, and I'll bring all my talents."

"Great!" Tom punched the air with his free hand as he put down the phone. Now his mind was filled with plans and questions. Eight, I've got an hour and a bit. Only ten minutes to walk to Old Town Square from here. "Great!" he repeated.

Now he was excited, expectant even. Something he had planned was beginning to work. What to wear? Formal? Informal? Jacket? Leather jacket? No, don't want to seem like a biker or a Secret

Service agent. "Oh, shit!" he exclaimed loudly, followed by a quieter, "what the fucking hell is the Oar-loadge?"

He didn't even know how to spell it. How did it sound? "Oar-loadge?" He tried to recall just how Dita had pronounced it. He decided the best thing was to try to write it down phonetically. "That can't be right. That definitely doesn't look Czech." Now he was talking aloud to himself. Something he tended to do when panic was about to set in. His brain was already rushing down that track of self-doubt. What if I misheard her? Got it wrong? I'll never bloody find her. Old Town Square will be full of bloody tourists, even at eight o'clock at night, all standing there waiting for that bleeding astronomical clock in the square to do its fancy tricks.

Not that Tom ever really thought the clock was all that fancy, just a few figures that appeared from the little windows above it every hour as the clock struck. Nevertheless, it always drew a large crowd of tourists on the hour ready to gawp and ooh and ahh. Then he had what he initially thought was a flash of inspiration. He could, of course, ring Dita back and ask her, but he reasoned that would make him look an even bigger idiot than the one who only a few minutes earlier had told her she was, "talented". No, he would go instead and ask the receptionist in the hotel. Obvious! A good idea Tom old chap, he congratulated himself.

It was indeed a good idea, until Tom reached the reception. The old guy behind the desk, smartly decked out in his communist regulation style night receptionist uniform and proudly displaying the Order of Gottwald or Lenin or some such decorative ribbon and a multitude of other no doubt prestigious medals on his chest, could barely speak English. As Tom was soon to find out none of the medals were for linguistic prowess. "Hello," and, "Goodbye," seemed to be the limit to the old man's repertoire. So, even if he had understood just whatever Tom attempted to pronounce in order to convey what he thought Dita had said to him on the phone about where they should meet in the square the old guy was never going to be able to tell Tom what it was in English anyway.

Despite that somewhat obvious major difficulty Tom decided to plough on with his brainwave. "Oar-loadge, oar-loadge, oar-loadge," he exclaimed, his voice increasing in volume each time he pronounced the word. Such that by the ninth or tenth time he was screeching, and people were coming out of the bar to see just what was going on. "Oh for Christ's sake," not exactly a good expletive to be uttering in communist Czechoslovakia at that time, although nobody seemed to understand him anyway, least of all Gottwald's chosen son behind the reception desk.

"Oar-loadge, oar-loadge!" Tom tried again. "Why the fucking hell does he keep pointing to that bloody ancient timepiece sitting on the wall behind the reception desk?" Tom proclaimed quite loudly. "I know, I know," he screamed. "It's seven o'clock. I know the bloody time. That's not what I'm asking you. Look, I have to meet someone at eight o'clock in Starométské náměstí, by the bleeding oar-loadge!" Tom was now not only shouting but doing so very slowly, dragging every word slowly from his lips and over emphasising each one in true 'stupid English person speaking to a foreigner' fashion. The old guy just kept on pointing to the clock on the wall behind the desk.

"Okay, okay, yes I know the time. So maybe it is your time to pack up work and leave," Tom bellowed. "Is that what you're trying to tell me? Can't you just break the rules this once? Just tell me first, just in one mini-second, just contravene the great communist rule book about time-keeping for once in your god-forsaken life and please, please tell me what the bloody oar-loadge is!" Now Tom was ranting and had lost all control. Certainly not the sort of person to whom Dita would have been attracted.

"Look, look, I have plenty of Krowns, or pounds, whatever you prefer." Now he was not only resorting to bribery and the great capitalist mammon, money, but was also talking, or rather shouting, in pigeon English.

"I say, old chap, calm down. You'll have a heart attack or something. Burst a blood vessel. It doesn't do to get taken to hospital in this neck of the woods. Hospitals here are not very good old boy. Come and have a stiff vodka or something."

Tom wheeled around on his heels to see a well-rounded, rather chubby red faced man standing there in a so obviously English blue blazer with the obligatory gold buttons and grey flannels. His greying, thinning hair was swept back in the grand old style and he exhibited, of course, the necessary old school tie, although Tom hadn't a clue which particular school it was from. No doubt it was a good one, the school that is, the tie was horrendous, but at that particular moment Tom couldn't give a stuff. It was now ten past seven and his calm, well dressed approach to his appointment with the rest of his life – that is his dinner date with Dita – was looking somewhat under threat.

"Lancaster, Bill Lancaster," said the red chubby face and extended a hand. "I'm here trying to sell these people some second-hand machinery in the new spirit of glasnost and all that."

"Tom, Tom Carpenter." As the two men completed their perfect English handshake Tom couldn't help wondering why the English middle and upper class always put their surname first when introducing themselves, whereas the 'oiks', the working-class, always steamed in with their first name and sometimes never even bothered to utter their second.

"Clock, the clock," Lancaster attempted to explain.

"Yes, yes, I know," Tom replied, a little curtly. "It's rushing on and time is against me. You see I've got an appointment at eight and I can't seem to find out exactly where I am supposed to be meeting her. She told me where in Old Town Square, but it was in Czech and I haven't got a clue where she meant."

"Oh, a filly, I see, hope she's a nice one old chap," Lancaster interrupted.

"What? Yes, yes, bloody nice actually, and you see the thing is-"

Tom was stopped mid-sentence by a combination of Gottwald's well-decorated hero behind the reception desk pointing to the ancient timepiece on the wall, Lancaster pronouncing very, very slowly and deliberately, "clock, clock," and in a sort of instant Anglo-Czech friendship society both men smiling and knowingly shrugging their shoulders.

"The clock, old man, the one in Old Town Square, the Astronomical clock, that is what the Horologe is," Lancaster added smugly. "That's what this old chap on reception was trying to tell you."

"Oh right, thank you, thank you. I see now. Sorry, sorry," Tom apologised profusely to the old guy and his medals while he just stood there grinning, well with what few yellowing teeth he had left, and shaking his head.

"Oh Christ! Twenty past seven. Got to dash I'm afraid," Tom explained to his new English acquaintance.

"What? You sure you've not even got time for a quick stiff vodka? Touch of the old 'Dutch courage' old man?" Lancaster suggested.

"No, no, sorry, nice to meet you, thanks again, thanks a million for your help. Maybe bump into you again? Next time, we'll have that drink next time?" Tom extended his hand once again and dashed off up the stairs to his second floor room, not even waiting to take the lift.

Showered, shaved, suitably attired he was there at one minute to eight in front of the Astronomical clock in Old Town Square. This is ironic he thought as he caught his breath and tried to calm down, an Astronomical clock, all about the stars, the past, the future. Or was that astrology? Anyway, now he was calmer, or at least he was for ten minutes. It was now ten past eight and no sign of Dita. Had she changed her mind? She was always so keen on detail, but as he was to find out over the next few months timekeeping, or the lack of it, was one of Dita's few failings. Now though it was eight-fifteen and Tom was exclaiming, "Oh shit." What if he got the pronunciation wrong? Okay, oar-loadge was the Astronomical clock, but what if he'd misheard what she'd said and it wasn't what he thought it was?

He was now muttering and fretting. By now at that time of year the square was in relative darkness, although still quite busy. Some people sightseeing, or others just passing quickly across it on their way home late from work or off to meet friends in the city for the evening. Tom's composure was restored somewhat though when while constantly looking in all directions for the expected Dita his eyes were invaded by the sheer magnificence of his surroundings. Staroměstké náměstí was beautiful, a real picture of a mixture of architectural styles and periods. It was a quite stunning combination of Gothic, Renaissance and Baroque arches, porches, churches and buildings. Between these lovely architectural legacies, and somehow embedded as part of their charm, there was a constant movement of people. Framed by the darkness the whole scene was totally atmospheric. Somehow it was the complete embodiment of Mitteleuropa. How could anyone, even he waiting anxiously for the woman he hoped would turn out to be the love of his life, possibly get uptight in such a place? What a place to be meeting someone who you hoped would turn out to be the love of your life; very romantic. Nevertheless, this beautiful atmospheric scene was also full of people. He was beginning to wonder if he had missed Dita altogether and if they would ever find each other amongst all these rushing or staring bodies.

"Hello, sorry I'm late. I'm always late I'm afraid and I hate it. Hate it in others too. I'm always rushing." Suddenly, out of the darkness and the mass of bodies in the square she was there behind him. He hadn't seen her coming because he was looking in another direction. As soon as he turned round on hearing her voice though his eyes were met with that brilliant, dazzling bright smile that he had been so mesmerised by at the conference the previous October. It encompassed everything about her and blew away all his anxiety immediately.

"That's okay," he stammered, "only been here a few minutes myself."

Another stupid remark, which drew from Dita another cheeky grin and, "so, you were late for me were you? That's not very gentlemanly of you. I thought you English were gentlemen."

"Err ... no, not really. That is it's not that we are not really gentlemen. I ... err ... don't know. Erm ... no, I was on time. Just thought it was better not to make you feel bad. Just being a gentleman, I suppose." He extricated himself pretty well he thought.

Dita smiled even wider and this time the smile was in her eyes as well. She tucked her arm into his, gave it a little squeeze and said, "Come on, let's go and eat before you say anything else you might regret."

Now it was Tom's turn to smile. He began to feel even more relaxed. Good start he thought, promising.

This time she seemed immediately to be friendlier and less stand–offish. He began to think that she now believed he really wanted to meet her for her company and because he wanted to spend an evening with her, not because he wanted her to do something for him, like making an academic contact for when he was going to bring his students to Prague.

The meal was okay. A passable Czech attempt at pasta and sauce, though hardly 'bella Italia' cuisine. The more they talked, chatted, smiled and laughed, the more Tom was drawn into her. A few times she caught him staring inextricably into her wide brown eyes and for just a few seconds each time they seemed to gaze at one another. Or at least he felt she was returning his stare. Something was happening, something different. Maybe it was the setting, the situation, the ambiance of Prague. Maybe it was simply Dita's charm, and she was immensely charming, overwhelmingly so. It was an effortless charm. Whatever was causing it, something was definitely occurring. She was indeed a picture of elegance. Every detail was attended to. Unlike last time they met, on this occasion her hair was fixed back off her face with a clip and not even one mini-strand of hair was allowed to get loose. She wore very little make-up. She didn't really need it. Her complexion was already a darkish, glowing hue, perfectly complimenting her brown eyes, her immaculately groomed hair and that wonderful sparkling smile. She had a black polo neck sweater on and a long black skirt, just skimming the top of her black ankle boots. As on the last time they had met, over the polo neck she wore a simple silver necklace that matched her earrings, silver and round, and of just the right size for her face. What went through Tom's mind constantly throughout the meal was that he was sitting opposite, having dinner with, a vision of Central European beauty and charm.

She only asked a couple of times what it was he was actually doing in Prague. Each time he waffled on about research, Czechoslovak communist regime crisis, blah, blah. He didn't think he was very convincing and wasn't sure she really bought it, but it didn't appear to matter. Although she did make the point to him quite forcibly that it had all happened before in 1968 and that she was convinced nothing would really change as far as the communist regime was concerned. She did just seem very flattered that he wanted to see her and, dare he think it, he began to feel that she liked him and would be happy to see more of him.

That is just what they did; see a lot more of each other. In terms of the emotions Tom experienced those ten days seemed like a lifetime. Yet they appeared to flash by time-wise. They met every day. Hours were spent just walking and talking in parts of Prague he would never have found, but which Dita appeared to be able to conjure up at will. He lost count of the times she took him down yet another magical passageway or alleyway, or to yet another magnificent building or view over the city. There were what seemed like endless dinners, in what were not always the best of restaurants, but that didn't really appear to matter to either of them. They were getting lost in each other and lost in Prague. A couple of times, or was it three, there were drinks and dinner with Jana and Tom's acquaintance with her was renewed and fostered. In fact, looking back on it all, Tom now convinced himself that he increasingly had a rapport with Jana at the dinners the three of them shared over those few days. They all shared their laughter over silly Prague things and the Czech and English ways. Now, over five years on, he was persuading himself that it was Jana he bantered and laughed with most of all.

There was no doubt that of the two women it was Jana who was more interested in the developing political situation and in what was happening across the rest of East and Central Europe. It was the two of them, her and Tom, who talked most about that. For Dita it was as though all of that was an irrelevance. "Nothing will really change," she used to tell them over and over again. "I don't know why the two of you waste your time on it. The Russians will never really let it happen. It's all talk."

Despite his convenient, self-convincing memory now about his growing relationship with Jana he knew that at the time it was Dita who captivated him in that spring of 1989. In the late afternoon of the fourth day of that visit he decided he had to take the plunge. Nothing ventured, nothing gained, he told himself. After all what if he had ten great days in Prague with Dita and then left, went home, and nothing. He might hate himself for the rest of his life, regret saying nothing, not saying how he really felt and be haunted by it for the rest of his 'natural'. So, he decided he would pick his moment and tell Dita just how he felt, being convinced at the time of course that was just how he did feel. He was meeting her outside the National Library at the end of the Charles Bridge at four that afternoon. He was determined and this time he would be firm.

Dita was fifteen minutes late as usual. Seems the assistant in the library had kept her waiting some inordinate amount of time because she couldn't find the book Dita had ordered three days previously. The renowned communist efficiency even extended to libraries. In the National Library, as in all Czechoslovak academic libraries, a card index system for books was still employed. This required searching endlessly through cards in sliding box drawers in alphabetical order by author, filling in a form for the book required if you could find the index card and the reference number, and handing it in to a usually totally disinterested assistant behind the counter. No books were on show at all and the 'punters' were certainly never allowed to touch or peruse any books. In fact, if it weren't for the signs saying so you would never have known it was a library. Then three days later you could return and collect the book you had ordered, if of course it wasn't already on loan to someone else. However, no one ever told you the book you wanted was already on loan when you submitted the form. It was only three days later that 'punters' were informed of that and the whole process then had to start over again from the beginning. Archaic thought Tom, how did anyone ever get to read or learn anything?

Anyway, the library assistant couldn't find Dita's book and she would have to go back tomorrow she explained to Tom, while apologising profusely for being late.

"Stupid, stupid people!" She was angry and this made Tom a little apprehensive to say the least. His intended firmness was already drifting away.

"Let's go for a walk," he suggested, attempting to lighten her mood. "It's a lovely afternoon and the walk will take your mind off it all."

"I need the bloody book to work on tonight," she exploded. "How am I supposed to do that now? How will a walk help that?"

In truth it was a pleasant early spring day. The afternoon was mellowing nicely and promising one of those crisp, but clear early evenings that made it good to be out in the open air. Dita's mood though was definitely not mellow.

"I don't know Tom. I've got a lot of work to do and I've done very little of it since you arrived. I must get on, and what about you? What about your work? You don't seem to be doing much."

He sidestepped that one neatly, immediately responding with "oh, I did a lot this morning, skipped lunch and worked right on through till three-thirty."

As was often the case with Dita, what Tom thought to be a good response turned out to be double-edged.

"Oh great! So you've done lots of work. That's alright then," she stormed.

"No, no," Tom answered, trying hastily to defend himself. "It's not what I meant." This was not exactly a good start. Definitely not a good start to the next few hours that he hoped might well shape the rest of his life. He tried once more to retrieve the situation. "Look, you haven't got the book. You can't get the book until tomorrow. So you can't work tonight anyway. So why not just relax?"

If there was one thing Tom learned more than anything about Dita over the time they spent together during the next few months it was that she usually responded eventually to logic. "Okay, sorry. I will calm down. You are right, and after all I shouldn't be shouting at you. It's not your fault," she apologised, offering Tom one of her broader smiles which she was already beginning to realise he couldn't resist. "I just needed to get it out of my system, but you know I am starting to think you are quite a good influence on me, a calming influence, Tom," she suggested. Tom felt encouraged. However, as he was to find out and become usual with Dita, it was hard work. But then, conjuring up that old working-class protestant work ethic, if you have to work hard for something then maybe it's worth it.

Dita meanwhile had tucked her arm into his in what was becoming a bonding custom between them and asked "okay, so where are you going to promenade me on a Prague mystery tour?"

"Oh, err," Tom was stumbling again. He hadn't really thought that through, only that he wanted to end up on the Charles Bridge although he didn't intend telling her that right now. "I don't really know. How about if we go over the bridge and to the right? Then we can stroll in Malá Strana under the castle," he proposed.

"Well we've done that a few times before already," she pointed out, adding teasingly. "Not much of a calming magical mystery tour, Tom. But as you appear to like that part of my city and seem to eternally be a creature of habit – I know that much about you already – let's do that."

Another good sign, her, "I know that much about you already." One thing he'd learned about Dita almost straightaway was her liking for order. So, he concluded optimistically, what she described as his, "habit," was equivalent to her order.

They had crossed the Charles Bridge, turned to the right, and were by the Waldenstein Gardens when Tom attempted his first move in the grand chess game, or perhaps it should be the grand courting game. "So, tell me a bit about your past. I don't really know that much about you, Dita," he ventured. For three days they had shadow-boxed. Chatted, talked about their work, about friends, about Jana, about the future and where it would take her, what she hoped for, but nothing really about their pasts. He knew a little about her family. She was an only child and both her parents were in their mid-fifties, living and working in Prague. Nothing of any past relationships though. Now he was probing, or so he thought, although it was more like bludgeoning. "Relationships?" he suddenly blurted out. "Tell me, have you had any? Ever been married?"

Dita stopped walking, removed her arm from his and turned to look at him quizzically. It was as though he had held up a sign indicating in her mind that the conversation, and ultimately their relationship, was entering a new phase, going on to a different level.

"What are you asking me, Tom? Why are you asking that?"

He didn't know whether this was a good sign or not. Did she want him to ask that, or was he intruding on her private life? Should he plough on or back off and wait for later? Soften her up a little more? He decided on caution. "No reason, just curious. You are such a very lovely woman, and in your early thirties." Oops, bad move he thought, move on quickly. "I just assumed that there must have been someone special at some time. Oh, and I almost forgot, after all you're so talented." Yep, lighten it up a bit he thought.

She laughed and tossed back her hair, which she was wearing loose to her shoulders today. "Talented, yes of course, Tom, I remember the compliment," and she gave him a little mocking pat on the cheek. "But desired? No, it seems not. Maybe I am too difficult. Too set in my ways, too obstinate, too – what do you say in English – strobby?"

"Stroppy," he corrected her, "and you aren't." Okay he thought, maybe a little difficult would be a fair description, but he wasn't about to offer that interjection and opinion at that particular delicate moment. After all, thinking that you might be about to bare your soul to someone and that the next few hours might determine the shape of the rest of your life, you definitely don't tell that someone even that they are a little difficult.

"I was with someone for three years, but it ended two and a half years ago," Dita continued. "We just grew different I suppose. Do you say 'apart'? Is that right Tom?"

"Yes, that's the way we describe it, apart," he confirmed.

"Anyway, he is in Moscow now," she added, with a slightly lower, slightly disconsolate tone to her voice. "I haven't seen him for over two years, but I don't fall in love easily," she warned.

Tom thought her last comment was a little strange. A strange thing to say and he wasn't really sure how it was connected to her previous sentence. He decided there were good signs and bad signs in what she had told him. She was definitely opening up to him. Telling him things which for her, a seemingly very private person, were probably things she didn't often speak about. That was a good sign, but, "I don't fall in love easily," was clearly a warning. Maybe, if he was being optimistic, it was a challenge to him. Perhaps she was merely telling him if you want me you are going to have to work bloody hard. I'm worth it, but I don't come easy, let alone emotionally cheap.

By the time they had walked for over an hour in and out of the narrow hidden alleyways and arches of Mala Strana the Prague twilight was beginning to descend. A low dusky glow was starting to engulf the cobbled streets and lovely small houses of that magical part of the city and there was a growing chill in the air as the early evening twilight descended. Having wandered around in a large circle through the maze of streets they stopped for coffee in a cafe just underneath the Charles Bridge on the opposite side of the bridge to where they had met at four. Although in Tom's case he decided he needed a beer, even if only a small one, for some courage for what he was about to do. As they left the café and headed up the steps towards the bridge Tom glanced at his watch. Six fifteen. Now it was starting to get dark and the air was beginning to get even chillier.

"Do you have an appointment this evening?" Dita asked.

"No. Why?"

"I saw you looking at your watch."

"Oh just habit, an English one about time I suppose. No, no, I've nothing fixed. Maybe we could have dinner?"

"Yes, why not," she agreed. "After all I've no book to read, as you pointed out so rationally earlier Tom and you have definitely calmed me down. I feel much more relaxed now here with you." A small grin broke across her face, a further good sign. How many more did he want? It was now or never.

Soon they were on the first part of the Charles Bridge, passing the inlet that led down to a water-wheel. It was surprisingly silent around them. Neither of them were speaking and there were an unusually few number of people on the bridge, maybe twenty. As they reached the main part of the bridge he reached for her hand. She let him take it and he gave it a little squeeze, which caused her to turn her head towards him and gently smile. "You know, as I said earlier, Tom, you really are a calming influence on me. Two hours ago I was ready to tear someone's head off and now here I am strolling on this lovely old bridge with you." As was her way though she couldn't resist following the compliment with a teasing admonishment, "Of course you are also a bad influence on me because I should be working."

Now it was Tom's turn to smile. Then he took as deep a breath as he could without her noticing and plunged in. Held his nose and jumped straight into the deep end both feet first. He stopped walking and released her hand. Saying, "Your hand is cold, you should wear your gloves," he started to tuck her scarf inside her coat and button up the top part. She stood there looking up at him. This time it was not a quizzical look, but a look with a warm contented glow on her face. They had been together for just a few hours over the four days on and off and this was the first time either of them had really knowingly touched the other one. The first time she felt him doing something real for her and showing he cared. Tom finished buttoning her coat and ended the whole movement by returning to her scarf, tucking it into the collar of her coat and then lifting her wide collar up around her ears.

"You need your hat," he told her. "Where is that lovely hat that you wore when we first met in Prague last December?"

"I ... err ..." now it was Dita's turn to stammer. "I ... err ... left it at home. Anyway it is not that cold, Tom, not for us Czechs."

It was the first time he could recall her putting his name in a sentence in that way. Her voice was soft and low and he thought he detected a gulp in her throat as she spoke. She was staring up at him and appeared to be studying every part of his face, every line on it. It seemed that for the first time they were communicating without speaking, but for him Dita's eyes were definitely saying, "But I never realised just how caring you are and how much you care about me."

They stood there for what seemed like an age. In fact, it was probably less than a minute. Tom noticed out of the corner of his eye that it was long enough for some of the people passing by them on the bridge to glance over and give a knowing Czech nod about couples on the Charles Bridge. What to do next was the question filling his mind. Should he just blurt it out? Something like, "I really, really like you and would like to know you better," but that might frighten her off. In the end it didn't matter, she solved the problem for him. Leaning even further into his body and staring intently up at him she whispered, "Kiss me." This time he didn't make a stupid remark or attempt some jokey comment. He just leaned down towards her, placed each of his hands tenderly on her cheeks and slowly gently kissed her offered lips. It was a lingering kiss. It sent an overwhelming warm, contented, relief filled feeling rushing through him. Suddenly everything in the whole world was perfect. He had waited for and wanted that moment ever since he was intoxicated by her charming smile the previous autumn as it was framed by the sun streaming through the French windows of the dining room at the conference at Spa. It was relief that was now taking over Tom's feelings. Relief at overcoming all the tentativeness and all the apprehension, knowing that he had gambled, stepped into the unknown, and won.

As they kissed Dita's eyes closed slowly. As the kiss ended and Tom went to draw away she pulled him back closer and tighter into her, putting her arms firmly around his waist. A glow radiated from the whole of her face. The feeling between the two of them suddenly appeared to be lighting up the Prague early evening darkness. This was Tom's favourite time of day in Prague and now he thought it would definitely always be so. As she put her arms around his waist Dita leaned up and kissed him again. This time her wonderful smile appeared as she finished kissing him and opened her eyes, sending even more shock waves through every part of Tom's being. It was as if her eyes and her smile were linked by some mechanism in her face. In response all Tom could offer was a deep breath, "wow," but before he could say anymore she placed her index finger on his lips and said quietly, "listen." There were people walking by them on the Bridge and now they were certainly looking at the two of them entwined, but everything was silent except for the very low soft murmur coming from the water in the weir in the river fifty metres beyond the bridge.

They stood there for a few minutes more locked in each other's arms. Staring at one another, at Prague and up at the brightly lit castle on the hill above them. "Listen," Dita repeated.

"I am," Tom told her.

"No, Tom, this time listen to me. It is said that if you kiss someone on the Charles Bridge you will always return to Prague, but if you kiss that person twice on this bridge not only will you always return to Prague but also to the person you kiss. That is why I kissed you after you kissed me. That is why I didn't let you go."

Tom had his answer. Now he really did know how she felt about him.

Eventually they strolled off the bridge into the Prague low light, through the narrow cobbled streets, up Karlova, across Old Town Square and up Celetná towards the Powder Tower marking the old entrance to the city. They exchanged very few words, merely glances, smiles, hugs and squeezes of each other's hand. Dinner was on the agenda, although at that precise moment neither of them seemed to care where or when. Three-quarters of the way up Celetná they heard shouting and the heavy footsteps of people running. Their seemingly carefree, trouble less, sealed off world inhabited only by the two of them was suddenly shattered by the reality of life in communist Czechoslovakia. "Quick, under here," Dita pulled Tom by the arm into the darkness of some arches. Just as she did four young people, three boys and a girl looking no more than eighteen or nineteen, came running around the corner from the direction of the square behind the Estates Theatre. They were all breathing heavily. Out of the darkness Tom could see that one of the boys had a nasty looking gash above his left ear from which a considerable amount of blood was pouring, staining part of his short cropped hair a vivid dark red. As he passed where Tom and Dita stood the bloodied boy stumbled on some loose cobbles, half-fell and was trying to regain his feet when Tom stepped forward to offer him a hand. Dita forcibly yanked the Englishman back under the arches.

"Are you crazy, Tom?" she angrily whispered to him while looking incredulously straight into his face. "Do you hear those shouts and those other heavy footsteps? They are the Secret Police with their big boots and large sticks. Do you want a lump on the side of your head like that boy has? Leave it!"

Tom stepped back and the boy ran on. A few seconds later around twenty men came charging round the corner, some in police uniform and carrying long fierce looking batons. One, who was obviously the officer in charge, paused slightly on seeing Dita and Tom, barked something in Czech to Dita and she pointed in the direction of the Powder Tower, the opposite direction to that which the boys and the girl had gone.

As the police disappeared in pursuit of their prey she rounded on Tom. "My God, are you mad? Sometimes, Tom, you seem so rational, so calm and normal, and then suddenly you do something completely crazy. So irrational! I don't understand. They were obviously students who had been on some demonstration or other broken up by the police and you were going to help them!" She was no longer whispering and the tone of her voice was rising by the second. He was stunned by the combination of her display of fear and her immediate anger with him.

"I was only trying to give him a hand. He looked really hurt," was Tom's attempt to rationalise his actions and calm her down.

Dita was having none of it. "You do what you want, but just remember that I am here. I have to live here when you've pissed off back to England."

It was the first time he had heard her swear, although he would find that it wouldn't be the last. "Oh yeah, they'll give you a bump on the head and maybe a night in the cells. That'll be good for your research! Then they will throw you out of the country. Me, I will still be here, with no job. They'll take that away from me. Well, no job to speak of. They will put me ticket checking on the trams or working in a dead end job in a factory. Then where will I be? You have to think about what you are doing all the time in this country, Tom, especially now. You really don't understand do you just what it's like to live in this country? You don't 'just give someone a hand'. Not without first of all thinking about the consequences of just who you are helping and what these bastard communists think of them."

Dita was in full flow. It was also the first time Tom had recognised and seen, experienced first-hand, the insidious fear day in and day out that people lived with in Czechoslovakia, even during the days of glasnost in the Soviet Union. He might have had the answer he wanted earlier in terms of Dita's response to his soul baring and how she felt about him, but now he had observed first hand a whole new set of questions, issues and problems about where she lived and how she and the rest of the Czech and Slovaks lived their lives. Things weren't as simple and straightforward as they'd seemed an hour before in their own incubated cosy world on the Charles Bridge.

Despite what for Dita was a moment of madness by him, he now at least knew for sure that she obviously liked him. So much so that once she had calmed down a little, over dinner that evening she invited him for dinner at her apartment the next evening. "I will cook for you," she told him firmly.

Her rented apartment was in the north-west part of the city in Dejvická in an old building that was probably constructed in the nineteenth century during the Habsburg period of Austro-Hungarian rule. It had been converted into twelve apartments at some point and Dita's was located on the top floor, the fourth. The stairwells were dark and bleak, clean but badly lit bare concrete broad flights of twelve steps at a time and no lift. The outside of the building was a badly faded yellow colour, but one that gave it a pleasant character and feel as you approached it. It was located in a short tree-lined street that had a quite open, bright and airy atmosphere. Dejvická, behind the castle, was one of the nicest parts of the city.

Behind the heavy solid dark wood door to her apartment Dita had liberally covered the pale lemon walls of most of the rooms with various framed paintings and prints. None of them appeared to be of much value. Their purpose was clearly purely one of brightening the plain, drab walls. Once she had greeted him with quick kisses on both cheeks Dita insisted on giving him a guided tour of her whole apartment, of which she was seemingly very proud.

In the hallway and in one corner of the lounge were some pot plants. The three in the hall were small, but one of the four in the corner of the lounge was quite large, so much so that it appeared to be taking over that part of the room as its own. Tom definitely wasn't a gardener, or even a pot plant keeper, so he had absolutely no idea whatsoever just what each of these predominantly green specimens were and at no time, then or in the future, did he feel the slightest inclination to ask Dita about them. Apart from the pot plants there was a brown wood circular hat and coat stand in the hall and what looked like a quite old brown leather three-seat sofa in the lounge. It had obviously seen better days, but Tom found it quite comfortable when he eventually got to try it. One other wooden-armed low chair with a beige seat cushion and back was placed in another corner of the room and behind it was a tall metal pedestal lamp. As he was to subsequently find out, Dita much preferred the room dimly lit and would always put on that light rather than the main ceiling light. During the day light was provided through two large windows that almost covered the length of one wall in the lounge and in the spring and summer sunlight streamed into the room through them. Although not a large room the lounge engendered a feeling of space and light, not least through the effect of the high ceiling, a feature and style of all the rooms in the apartment. The floors throughout were polished natural wood, covered with a number of small and larger rugs of various shades and quite bright colours, which added to the general feeling of warmth and comfort throughout the apartment.

The kitchen though was very small, no more than eight feet by six. Dita described it as, "very practical," and it had an old four ring gas cooker in one corner next to a small fridge and a stainless steel sink and drainer along the length of the opposite wall. There was a very small window almost at the top of the far end wall of the kitchen that provided some natural light, although it was no more than two feet square.

He was a little taken aback when the tour continued into the bathroom and then Dita's bedroom. She was, indeed, immensely proud of what she had done to her flat to make it, "her home," as she put it and was determined to show the Englishman every part of it on his first visit. A top loading 1960s style washing machine was situated in the bathroom alongside one end of the bath. The bathroom was larger than the kitchen, but not by much. The bath had the usual Czechoslovak shower fitment that consisted of a chrome hand spray nozzle which you had to kneel and use if you wanted to wash your hair. Even after only a few visits to Prague Tom had learned, and become used to, that routine as in none of the hotels he'd stayed in would anyone over three foot tall been able to stand and apply water from the shower nozzle to their head.

Her bedroom was even larger than the lounge, a good twenty feet by fifteen he reckoned, with a large six feet high glass fronted bookcase stretching completely along one of the fifteen feet walls. Naturally, as Tom was to fully understand when he got to know Dita better, it was crammed full with books, mainly academic texts. Once again the walls of the bedroom were a faded lemon colour adorned with yet more artistic prints and a couple more pot plants stood on the floor in a tray in one corner. Her bed was large, a good King-size, with a crisp white sheet neatly folded back over a plain dark green thick blanket and topped with two large white pillows. The pillows were almost square, as was the Czechoslovak custom, rather than the more oblong rectangular ones he was used to at home.

She certainly seemed pleased to see him and welcome him to, "her home. Well, you wanted to know more about me, Tom," she told him as she finished her guided tour. "Now you have seen where I live and sometimes even where I do some of my academic work and writing."

"Yes, yes, it's very nice, very homely and comfortable. You must be very happy here," he told her as he followed her to the door of the kitchen while she found a vase to put the flowers in that he had brought for her.

She turned out to be a good cook. Cooking for a man, their man, was something Czech women took great pride in and Dita was no different. Nothing was too much trouble and the man always had to be overfed, not to mention 'over wined' or 'over beered'. It almost seemed like a matter of great honour for Dita, and most Czech women he'd ever met, that he had more than enough to eat and drink. Looking back on it now, five years later, it was indeed a very nice comfortable evening. "A good beginning," he remembered muttering as he descended the stairs from the flat just after eleven-thirty and dashed off towards the Dejvická metro station to catch the last train back to the city centre and his hotel.

Thump! Tom's fond Prague recollections of the expectations and anticipation that come with meeting someone new of the opposite sex were rudely, or to be more precise almost brutally, interrupted by the Liberec masseuse smacking his arse somewhat intimately and announcing what he assumed to be, "finished." At least that's what he guessed and hoped she'd said. The trouble was that when he tried to stand he could barely move. He had been so relaxed in his fond recollections that he hadn't noticed the pummelling his body was taking. No doubt he would feel the benefit tomorrow, but for now he somewhat circumspectly shuffled his way back to his room to briefly inspect for signs of bruising. As it was now just gone seven-thirty he figured he could lie down and nap for an hour before exploring Liberec and finding somewhere for dinner. Deciding not to try to strengthen his upper arm muscles by wrestling with the clamped-on sheets and bedspread he flopped down on top of the bed covers, kicked off his shoes and drifted into an almost instantaneous sleep.

4
At Liberec

Waking in a hotel room for the first time with the evening gloom flooding in through the open window is a disorientating experience. The unfamiliar dark wood furniture was shrouded in the growing darkness from the world outside the Hotel Praha room. As he woke from his nap Tom could hear faint traffic noise from the street below and the clatter of a passing tram. It was as if the street noises were muffled by the dark that had descended upon Liberec while he was sleeping. In reality the muffled sound was just the effect of Tom's slumbering senses slowly coming to life. He felt as if he'd been asleep for ages and in his disorientated state he had no idea of the time. A check of his watch showed that in fact he'd only been asleep for just over an hour. Now it was time to get on with the usual hotel evening ritual, unpack some clothes, jump in the shower, shave and get out and look for somewhere half-decent to eat. Although half-decent might be a bit of a problem from what he had seen of Liberec in his taxi ride from the station, and from what he recalled from his previous visit five months earlier at the end of 1993. Not too many beers though, he didn't want to show up at the university the next day with a hangover.

As he stepped out of the hotel lobby and on to the street at just gone nine that evening Tom was instantly reminded that he was in the more industrial north of the Czech Republic. It's the smell, that's what made the atmosphere so different. It wasn't an 'in your face' stink, not that kind of smell, not that strong. It was a sort of stale, but not pungent, smell. You could almost taste it in the air. A mixture of dust and grime and a kind of faded oldness smell, as if an old well-worn sticky carpet was spread above the whole town. Despite that Liberec was a pleasant enough country town, at least in the centre, although the locals he'd met at the university would always insist to him it was not a town but a city. It had the usual nice Town Square just to the side of his hotel. The square was dominated by the imposing town hall, apparently a replica of the New Town Hall in

Vienna according to the blurb in broken English in the Town Guide pamphlet in his hotel room that he'd stuffed into his pocket. A much more recent addition to the square's characteristics was the McDonalds, now obligatory in the Czech Republic since the collapse of the communist regime in 1989.

He couldn't be bothered to traipse around peering through windows and doorways to try and find a restaurant where the food might look inviting and vaguely edible, so he settled for a *rybí sendvic* and *velké hranolky* – fish Mac and large chips – washed down with a coke in the 'house of the golden arch'. As this was right next door to his hotel at least he filled his stomach before setting out on his anticipated pessimistic exploration of Sunday night Liberec. While he stuffed his fries into his mouth he glanced through the rest of the description of the town in his hotel room pamphlet, learning that Liberec was famous for its cloth production begun in the Middle-Ages by Flemish weavers. This tradition apparently led to tremendous prosperity in the middle of the eighteenth century, when a succession of textile factories was established. From what Tom had seen from his previous visit though that prosperity had long gone. A glance around now in McDonalds at his very few fellow diners, predominantly seemingly sixteen and seventeen year olds, showed him that any textile industry that remained obviously didn't produce quality clothing. The place was dominated by very cheap looking, mostly out of shape and faded from washing, t-shirts. Jeans were prominent of course, but again very obviously from the cheaper end of the market. While the couple of youngsters who seemingly felt the cold on what was a warm evening sported the latest Liberec fashion in acrylic, out of shape, interestingly patterned baggy round neck jumpers.

In the event, Tom's pessimism about anything resembling nightlife on a Sunday in Liberec was entirely justified. He wandered aimlessly around the darkened, dimly lit, almost empty streets in the centre of the city, stopping occasionally to peer into hardly cramped full shop windows exhibiting old cd's, shoes or some men's clothing. There was some western brand-name shops, like Benetton, which seemed fairly recently opened and at least had some colourful well-stocked windows. Wandering leisurely down the hill of the pedestrianised street leading from the town hall square he noticed a branch of the Czech shoe company, Bata. The company originally produced shoes in the Czech city of Zlín, quite close to Brno in the south-east of the country where he was headed in a couple of days. Bata himself left Czechoslovakia during the communist period to live in Canada, and Bata shoes were quite well known across the world now, not least in England. Reckoning that he could do with some new shoes, Tom made a mental note to try to get to the shop sometime during his following day at the university. Directly across the square from him as he reached the bottom of the hill was a fairly large Tesco's store. He'd seen one in Prague. Obviously, like McDonalds, they were 'breeding' across the Czech Republic. Like the others he'd seen though this was not just a supermarket but was more of a department store, although from its size it wasn't the sort of department store you'd spend hours in, maybe an hour at most.

At one point he did come across a small square with a building in it exhibiting a barely lit sign above a very silent doorway that stated, "Irish Pub." A push of the door and a quick look inside showed him that there were just two rather overweight men in the pub sat on bar stools creaking under the strain of their ample bodies. Neither of them looked Irish. They looked decidedly Czech and not very friendly as they turned awkwardly to see who the stranger was invading their inner sanctuary. Tom also noticed that there didn't seem to be an Irish beer tap in sight, just the usual Pilsner and Staropramen. Not a sound emanated from inside the pub, except the creak of the challenged bar stools as the men turned to look at him peering round the door. He hastily dragged his nose and face out from the half opened door and retreated back into the Liberec evening. Eventually he convinced himself that the stroll had been good for him and that he really didn't want to find any nightlife anyway. Combined with the alcohol free evening, the stroll and a relatively early night would put him in good shape for his day at the university on Monday.

Running parallel to the pedestrianised hill street he'd strolled down was a similar street taking him back up to the town hall square. After a brief wander around the 'Tesco square' – what an exciting evening he thought – he sauntered back up the parallel street towards the square and his hotel. As he reached the top of what was much the same non-descript street something took his eye on the right-hand side of the front of the Town Hall. Striding now more purposefully over towards it he realised as he got closer that it was some sort of memorial. It was in the form of a part of a tank track. From what he could understand from the Czech inscription it was a memorial to eight people who died in August 1968 trying to fight against the Soviet tanks invading Czechoslovakia to crush the 'Prague Spring' reforms. Tom mumbled ironically, "mmm ... no doubt these people died trying to stop the Soviet tanks as they rumbled into Liberec from across the nearby Polish border letting loose their shells supposedly in a move to liberate the town's population and the rest of Czechoslovakia from the 'corrupting agents of capitalism' seeking to overthrow the communist system according to the Soviet leadership."

He stood there trying to imagine what it must have been like for those people who died trying to stop Soviet tanks that had presumably rumbled into the square from one of the two streets he'd just walked down and up. Probably their only weapons were cobblestones dug up from the street itself. How could anyone imagine being so scared, yet so desperate, as to face tanks with stones. No doubt though they had an unshakeable belief in something different, a different way of life to what was about to be re-imposed on them by the Soviets.

Throughout history Czechs and Slovaks have believed that in their position in the centre or 'heart' of Europe they had a unique role of providing a bridge between the civilisations of East and West. Civilisations in both of which they shared. On those days in August 1968 it must have seemed inconceivable to them that Czechs and Slovaks could possibly share any civilisation characteristics with their unwelcome invaders from the East. All that those who died sought was political liberty and social justice.

Four and a half years previously in November 1989 Tom had been caught up in events shaped by those Czechs and Slovaks once again seeking political liberty. Even if only briefly and at what proved to be the beginning of the very end of events, he'd experienced the fear known by those being attacked for trying to struggle for their beliefs and for a different way of life. It wasn't Soviet tanks he'd faced, and at no time did he think he might die, and of course he'd had Jana there by his side at the time. It was a time though when he first believed he saw a different way of life for him and realised that he felt something different happening between them - his own personal 'revolution'? As he stood there staring at that tank track memorial in the square at Liberec in the early summer of 1994 he convinced himself that somehow changes in his life were caught up in events and changes in Czechoslovakia at the end of 1989.

The period that came to be known as the 'November days' was the climax. Indeed, talk to most people, and not just foreigners but even many Czechs and Slovaks, and they will tell you that the 'November days' were when it all began. It didn't of course. The culminating events of that momentous year of 1989, the beginning of the end, really started nearly a year earlier. Although some people will tell you that the 1989 crescendo, when the building blocks of communist East and Central Europe came crashing down one by one, really had its origins twenty-one years earlier in the attempted reforms of the Czechoslovak 'Prague Spring' of 1968. That was when the particular Czechoslovak great socialist hope that its experiment in the use of human reason to transform society in its entirety might succeed had been crushed under the wheels of Russian tanks rolling into Prague and the rest of the country, including Liberec.

Tom had heard rumours when he was first in Prague in December 1988. "Things will change. Things are changing," Dita's university friend, Monika, had told him. At that time those rumours were commonplace across East and Central Europe. Things were always about to change. Tom had heard it before from many different people. In Poland *Solidarność* (Solidarity) supporters had been saying the same thing for nearly ten years by then, ever since the Gdańsk shipyard strikes of 1980. In the East German part of Berlin 'The Wall' was always about to come down.

Nothing ever seemed to change though. The more people in East and Central Europe told themselves things were about to change the more they could survive the tedious and monotonous parts of their lives, which for most of them was by far the largest part of their daily, weekly, yearly lives. It made it easier for them to go on day after day. This, after all, is what Dita always told him throughout the coming months of their relationship in the summer and autumn of 1989. As he was to find out, Dita was the ultimate sceptic, or maybe he thought in moments when he gave her the benefit of the doubt she was merely a realist. Who was he to question her lack of optimism? It had not been him who'd had any shred of optimism ground out of his character through thirty-odd years of existence in communist Czechoslovakia.

In true Czech fashion the 'November days' really began in January 1989 with a relatively small demonstration on the fifteenth of that month at the top of Wenceslas Square. It was estimated that around four thousand people, mostly students but also some intellectuals from the dissident organisation Charter '77, gathered at the statue of Saint Wenceslas, the patron saint of Czechoslovakia. This was the place where on the 16th January 1969 the student from Charles University in Prague, Jan Palach, dowsed himself in petrol and set himself on fire in a protest against the Soviet invasion and crushing of the 'Prague Spring' on the 21st August 1968 and the subsequent so-called 'normalisation' process which was imposed after that in Czechoslovakia by the Soviets. The Soviet troops came in under the guise of the Warsaw Pact, claiming to be protecting the so-called socialist states of East and Central Europe from counter-revolutionary elements propagating the 'Prague Spring' reforms in the Czechoslovak government. They claimed to be protecting the Czech and Slovak people, even if that meant they had to kill some of them in the process, as the Liberec tank track memorial testified.

In fact, Palach dowsed himself in petrol and set fire to himself on the steps of the National Museum across the road from the Saint Wenceslas statue at the very top of the square. He then staggered across the road and collapsed by the statue, subsequently dying from his burns. So, to commemorate the twentieth anniversary of the event, on the 15th January 1989 Palach's contemporaries gathered by the statue to continue to demonstrate against the oppressive communist regime. The demonstration actually took place the day before the twentieth anniversary of the event in order to highlight the hypocrisy of the Czechoslovak government, who on that day were signing new human rights accords at a meeting in Vienna of the

Conference on Security and Co-operation in Europe. Amongst the demonstrators was Václav Havel. In characteristically heavy-handed and over-reactive fashion the Prague State riot police charged the crowd and dispersed the demonstration with tear gas and water cannon. Over a hundred people were arrested and many more were injured. For the next five days the demonstrators returned to the square and the police battled with them in the streets of central Prague. Little did the police, or their political bosses, realise that they couldn't wash away events that were pushing against their version of history. Over the five days the crowds of demonstrators gradually increased. Havel was one of those arrested. He was sentenced to nine months in prison for 'anti-social behaviour'.

Reading about it in his English *Times* newspaper and watching the scenes of the January 1989 demonstrations on a very brief low key BBC television news report, it seemed like just another demonstration in another Central European country for Tom. After all the people in Prague who he now called his friends had consistently told him, "nothing will change." If they, at the 'front line' so to speak, believed that then who was he to believe otherwise. Also, from his visit to Prague just a month earlier in December 1988 he had been surprised to find that it seemed that quite a few Czechs looked upon Havel and the intellectual dissidents of Charter '77 as just a small bunch of troublemakers. It appeared then that the hope in Prague had died twenty years before in 1968.

Tom came back to Prague three months later in March 1989, in effect to pursue Dita. By the time he came again though to see her at the end of June he sensed and felt a very different atmosphere in the city. Mikhail Gorbachev had visited Prague in April 1987 and since then his pronouncements on the Soviet Union's policy towards its East and Central European 'Soviet Empire' states like Czechoslovakia had become progressively more and more liberal. His famous 'Sinatra doctrine' statement – or rather that made on his behalf by his press secretary Genadii Gerasimov in 1986 – began to look more and more believable by the middle of 1989. When asked at a press conference in 1986 after a summit meeting with US President Reagan what the Soviets intended to do about the countries under their influence in East and Central Europe in the context of their policies of *glasnost* and *perestroika* in the Soviet Union Gerasimov told the world's press that they would apply the 'Sinatra doctrine'. When pressed he explained that it was a reference to the Frank Sinatra song 'My Way', and as such the countries would be allowed to do things 'their way' without Soviet interference. It did seem to Tom that by the middle of 1989 that was what was happening, at least in terms of any open Soviet military interference. Things had moved on swiftly in Poland in terms of challenges to the communist regime and there was no sign whatsoever of any Soviet threat of military interference on the surface at least. Also, of course, things were changing rapidly in the Soviet Union itself and the politicians and the military leaders there, not just Gorbachev, had enough problems of their own to worry about without concerning themselves too much with Czechoslovakia's or Bulgaria's or Poland's problems, or those of the rest of their satellite states in their East and Central European 'Empire'. Something was definitely happening across East and Central Europe. By the end of that summer of 1989 the pace of those changes would be raised to a multitudinous thunderous gallop.

By June people in Prague were talking more openly about the possibility of change. There were still plenty of rumours everywhere, just like there always had been, but now they were more intense and seemingly more expectant. One of the most prominent was that Gorbachev was going to make sure that they had a 'Czech Gorbachev'. Somewhat ironically though, it occurred to Tom that even then they anticipated the Russians making the change for them. The forty years of being a Soviet satellite state had indeed left its imprint, even on the non-conventional Czech psyche. Once again the Russians would replace their leaders for them, just as they had done in 1948 and in 1968. This time though it would be more peaceful and much better. At least, that is what some Czechs seemed to believe.

Dita's friend Monika had heard just such stories and rumours in her department at the university and if the academics and intellectuals believed it, expected it to happen, then of course it must be true. At least, that was Dita's sarcastic 'take' on it and she wasn't slow in making her views known on the rumours to Tom. That was one thing she definitely did have in common with him, total disdain for some fellow academics and their bloated self-importance. By August in the hot, sticky, Prague high summer such rumours could be heard everywhere. By then it seemed that even Dita, the acutely excruciatingly sceptic Dita, was beginning to believe just a little bit that something was changing, that something might happen. Although, she argued it would not necessarily be for the good as it would probably end in another disaster and the communists would react by clamping down even harder.

The January demonstration on the twentieth anniversary of Jan Palach's death had been put down quite viciously by the authorities. Although the students continued to protest, becoming increasingly aware of events elsewhere across East and Central Europe, in the Soviet Union, and even in Tiananmen Square in Beijing in May and June 1989. The intellectuals of Charter '77 also continued to weave their webs of dissent. They were a relatively small group, but their voice outside Czechoslovakia in the West was a growing and disproportionate one.

Monika had been told by someone in her department at the university, who knew someone whose brother knew him well, was a friend supposedly, that Zdeněk Mlynář, one of the leaders of the 'Prague Spring' reform group expelled from the Czechoslovak Communist Party after the events of 1968, had been meeting with Gorbachev regularly for years. Mlynář studied at Moscow University with Gorbachev in the 1950s and they had remained good friends. "Gorbachev wants Mlynář to be the 'Czech Gorbachev' and lead Czechoslovakia to a new more liberal form of socialism," Monika said she had been told, and one night over dinner in August she wasn't slow in repeating this excitedly to Dita, Tom and Jana. Dita was far from convinced when she heard this from her friend. "It doesn't matter who's in charge the bureaucrats and the self-seeking parasites in the system will just continue to control and operate things in their own interests. Nothing will change. Mlynář, Husák, Jakeš, or a Czech Gorbachev, nothing will be different for most people," she pronounced to the three of them on that warm August Prague evening.

"Well, look what's happening in Poland," was Jana's response.

"Yes," Monika waded in to support Jana's optimism. "Free elections, and there's talk of a *Solidarność* victory and a non-communist government."

"There is always talk," Dita dispassionately replied. "Talk, talk yes, and rumours, always rumours, but nothing happens, and a non-communist government, really?" She waived her fork in the air in her right hand contemptuously like a magician's wand, not fashioning a magical dream but dispelling and dismissing what she obviously believed was an extremely fanciful idea. "Those nice Russians, you know the ones with the rather large amount of tanks, bombs, guns, and the huge army, they will never let that happen. They almost went into Poland in 1981 at the very height of *Solidarność's* popularity and support. Their tanks were on the Polish border ready to go in. It was only Jaruzelski's declaration of a state of national emergency and the imposition of military rule that stopped the Poles seeing the same bloody shits in red star Russian tanks that were on the streets of Prague in August 1968. Gorbachev can say what he likes, but the Russian Generals and the KGB have a different fucking agenda."

Tom was taken aback by the depth of her cynicism, as well as being somewhat shocked by the strength of her language. Dita was in all other respects a clever, intelligent, optimistic and rational woman. When it came to the topic of any possible change to the existing way of life for Czech people though, even in her the sparkle of life had been extinguished by years of Soviet occupation. An occupation not only of the Czech lands but even of the Czech minds it seemed. For many Czechs it produced apathy of course. Life was the way it was. Day to day survival was the first priority. To get food and drink, sometimes simply just to try and find it, and. to get through each day of the often mesmerising, mind numbing work. These were the priorities, the main pre-occupation of most Czechs. For Dita though all this didn't provoke apathy in her thoughts. It brought anger. Anger borne out of her frustration Tom reckoned, frustration at her own situation, academically and personally. Frustration at the system, with its bureaucracy and corruption, but most of all frustration at what she believed was an ingrained apathy in the majority of the rest of her fellow Czech citizens. "Most Czechs don't give a shit!" she was fond of telling all who would listen and especially Tom, Jana and Monika. It was a strange kind of frustration Tom thought. It had worn her down so much that she was now convinced that there was no point in trying to do anything - demonstrate or protest – as there would not be any mass support against the regime. She clearly wanted things to change and hated the corrupt communists who ran the country. Her hatred though had been overtaken, overwhelmed, by her cynicism about the apathy of her fellow citizens.

Jana and Monika usually went very quiet when Dita held forth on all this. She was forceful, and her thoughts, her voice, and her gestures portrayed an unshakeable certainty. They wouldn't nod in agreement and never muttered a 'yes', but equally they never voiced or displayed their disagreement with her, at least not in front of her. She was unquestionably the dominant personality out of the three of them.

On the rare occasions when Tom found himself alone in Jana's company or in Jana and Monika's company the tone was different. When they discussed the current Czech situation in Dita's absence Jana's optimism was infectious and in stark contrast to Dita's resignation. Jana's thoughts and utterances seemed to exude a certain appealing logic, even if on reflection over four years later they probably amounted to an appeal mixed up with Tom's other developing feelings about her.

"Charter '77 and the dissidents are not a very large group really," Jana pointed out to Tom over lunch with him and Monika one bright Prague August day in '89. "They are a diverse group of people from different backgrounds and with different views on many things. What unites them is their opposition to the system and the corrupt communists in control," Monika added.

"Yes, the way they choose to display their opposition is by what they call 'living in truth', whatever the consequences," Jana continued. "They have maybe a dozen or so real leaders and one who seems to be at the centre, not so much dominating as uniting the various strands of opposition, Havel. Unlike the plain speaking *Solidarność* leader Wałęsa in Poland, Havel is an intellectual, a writer, a playwright, and he likes to think of himself as a bit of a philosopher, but definitely not as a politician."

There was a certain element of cynical distrust and disdain that came through in Jana's voice as she mentioned the word 'politician'. Tom hadn't heard that tone from her before. It was a new side to her that he hadn't seen previously, although it was a distrust of politicians and a disdain for them that he had heard from many people the world over.

Monika voiced her agreement with her friend, although in a tone that didn't sound quite so cynical. "Havel is seen here as more of a moral force than someone who is likely to overthrow the existing communist regime and form a government. I think he is more like, seen as more like, Jan Hus the fifteenth century Czech church reformer. You know, Tom, one of our historical Czech national heroes," Monika suggested. "I don't think he is really, or can really ever be a leader of some mass opposition movement like Wałęsa in Poland, or even our Tomáš Masaryk who built and led the first Czechoslovak Republic at the end of the First World War."

"Havel writes about the, "mysterious multiformity," and about the, "infinitive elusiveness of the order of being," and his plays go on about, "the modalities of humanity in a state of collapse," but I'm not sure what use those phrases would be in action in attempting to overthrow the communists or what use they'd be with a large police baton searing down towards his head," Jana's scepticism intervened. "Still, to be fair," she added, "like Wałęsa he does seem to have a profile and be a sort of focal personality for the dissidents, as well as being someone who seems to appeal to all the opposition groups. And he has suffered house arrest, forced exile and prison for his beliefs, so he can't really be criticised in respect of his beliefs and his consistency, or even his bravery. So, we shall see." With that still relatively open mind and open-ended statement Jana's summary and assessment in August 1989 of the personality that was Václav Havel was complete for the moment.

In fact Charter '77 consistently denied it was any kind of formal opposition. It was instead a group of people, a relatively small group as Jana had pointed out, who held a wide range of viewpoints but who were united by a common moral approach and attitude. Havel's eloquent ability to express this moral dimension of 'living in truth' made him a natural leader of an inherently leaderless initiative. The group's supporters ranged from Trotskyists to practising Catholic clergy, and a wide range of perspectives in between. The differences among the group demonstrated that the strength of Charter '77 lay not in a specific ideology or ideological perspective, but rather in its moral conviction that the existing communist regime was totally false and corrupt. This belief bound the group together, as well as the conviction that overt political opposition would be pointless in the face of the communist regime's repression, backed as it was by the Soviets. Instead these wide-ranging dissident activists encompassed their differences under the general umbrella of the focus of Charter '77 on human rights.

Whatever the appeal of the theory of 'living in truth' Dita was right when she was never slow to argue that for most Czechs the reality was that it was far too difficult to overcome the fear that the communist regime had generated among the vast majority of the population, including most of the intellectuals and so-called intelligentsia. The problem for the small group of supporters of Charter '77 was that the theory of 'living in truth' was both its greatest strength and its greatest weakness. It was its greatest strength because it left the communist regime powerless against those who practised the theory. As much as anything they 'practised it' in their heads, in their minds, but it was also its greatest weakness because for the overwhelming majority of Czechs and Slovaks such a way of living was far too difficult and impractical, and therefore left the regime unchallenged. Indeed, Havel himself recognised this paradox. In his 'Letter to Husák' he asked rhetorically, "Why do people not protest the obvious and daily injustices they suffer?" In his 'The Power of the Powerless' he answered himself that if they do not conform the regime will, "spew them from its mouth," and most people did not want to be spewed.

In 1988 the antipolitical opposition of Charter '77 began to turn to more active political confrontation, at least in Prague. A regular underground newspaper called *Lidove* (People's News) began to appear and Tom remembered hearing from some of his academic colleagues in England that some of the dissidents had established the East European Information Agency, which liaised with other dissident agencies in Hungary, Poland and the Soviet Union. Through these channels, and others, information about what was happening on the ground throughout the Eastern bloc was passed on to foreign radio stations like Radio Free Europe, the Voice of

America and the BBC, and then relayed by them to the Soviet bloc countries through illegal radio broadcasts.

Despite Dita's continuing scepticism these developments made Tom realise by the late summer of 1989 that things were definitely changing. That realisation, and of course his developing relationship with Dita, had brought him back to Prague once again in early November. From what he heard and saw then he realised that the strategy amongst some sections of the dissident opposition had shifted from the simple advocacy of human rights into outright political activism, and to what he anticipated would lead to a position of inevitable confrontation with the communist regime.

He recalled that by the late summer of 1989 over another lunch with him and Jana in Prague Monika's mood had stepped up a gear and she could no longer restrain her optimism, especially as Dita was again absent. "The old communist government politicians, the dinosaurs we call them now, will not be able to contain the mounting tension and anticipation for long," she'd told him and Jana. "The more people hear about *Solidarnosc's* successes in Poland the braver they will become here. Even the dissidents are now getting more and more support, and are changing their strategy towards a more political approach. Havel and four others put out a document called 'Just a Few Sentences', calling for the immediate democratisation of Czechoslovakia, an open media, freedom of assembly, and free speech. In just a short time over twenty thousand people signed it. It is the first time such a document has received such widespread support outside the narrow circle of the small group of dissidents." Now Monika was sounding as optimistic and convincing to Tom as Jana had, although not of course as appealing personally.

The autumn climax to the year of change began in early September when over five thousand East Germans took refuge in the grounds of the West German embassy in Prague. At that time Czechoslovakia was one of the few places in the world East Germans could travel to without needing to get documents and permission from their own country. In August of that summer of 1989 the Hungarian government had decided to relax controls along the Austrian border and thousands of vacationing East Germans had decided to turn their holiday trips to a fellow communist country,

Hungary, into permanent departures. They sought to make it to what they believed was the more prosperous and freer West Germany by way of Austria. By early September the wave of the exodus had reached the West German embassy in Prague as thousands of East Germans holidaying in Czechoslovakia made for there and set up an impromptu refugee camp in the embassy grounds.

Jana phoned Dita when the West German embassy events started to gather pace and word spread throughout Prague. "Have you heard that the FDR (West German) embassy is under siege from thousands of GDR (East German) refugee tourists camping in its grounds and wanting to leave for West Germany?" she asked her friend down the phone.

"Yes, I've heard the rumours," was Dita's typical low key reply to any mention of rumours.

"Well, let's go and have a look," Jana suggested.

But, as Jana expected, Dita was not interested. "Why would I want to go and gawp at a load of East Germans deluding themselves?" she responded.

With that her friend instantly gave up, knowing her well enough to understand that with Dita it was pointless to try and shift her when her views and decision were so firmly conveyed.

It turned out though that the East Germans were not deluding themselves. The refugees in the embassy grounds were eventually allowed to leave for West Germany through an unprecedented agreement between the East and West German governments. Over five thousand of them left Prague in special trains bound for West Germany, although much to the concerns of the refugees the trains were first required to go via East Germany. It seems that the East German government expected that the exodus would taper off, but for the people of the East and Central European countries, not least in Czechoslovakia, the decision to let the East Germans leave was seen as a clear sign that things were indeed changing.

For Jana, who called Dita once again when she heard the news that the East Germans were being allowed to leave, it was another reason not to give up hoping that things in her country would eventually change, but as she told Tom in September before he left to go back to England, "it's not changing like it is in Poland or in

Hungary. Not that fast, and not everything or everyone in the government is changing all at once, and it's not changing from black to white as you say in England, Tom. But definitely ..." – and she hesitated, seeming to want to convince herself as much as Tom – "slowly and surely it's changing from black to a Prague dark grey. I think you say a murky or is it foggy grey," she added with a grin.

"And," she continued before he could agree or disagree, "people are saying that the government is going to make some concessions on travel, as well as on religion and some cultural things. Adamec and his reform communist supporters are pushing for those things."

At that time in the late summer of 1989 little did she know that by the time winter was upon her country and snow on the ground the year's events in that fateful November would increase Jana's optimism even more, sustain her beliefs, and eventually give her and millions of Czechs and Slovaks what their 'hope' desired. They dared, initially some of them at least, to continue to hope for the unthinkable, for the impossible.

5
To Brno

It was another warm morning and the open windows in his taxi taking him to Liberec railway station gave him some relief from the growing heat as they allowed the breeze from the movement of the car to blow into his face. The more he thought about his evening to come with Jana in a week's time though the warmer he became, and the palms of his hands started to get clammy. What if by constantly taking him back to the past four-and-a-half years ago his mind was telling him to leave it and not pursue Jana? Telling him to leave everything as it was, as it had been. After all how many times had his friends told him about one woman or another, "never go back. Never try and look up that old girlfriend. It would never be the same." Now his brain was filling up with nothing but negative thoughts. What if it really all was a big mistake to even be having dinner with Jana again? What if much of what he remembered and recalled about that summer and autumn of 1989 was just him looking at that time through rose-tinted glasses? Looking at the little things he had done with Jana, the little things she had said to him, completely wrongly? Was he just putting far too much emphasis on them because that was the way he wanted to see it? What if she saw it completely differently? What if for her it was merely all wrapped up with the excitement of the time? What a bloody disaster he would be creating then by completely misreading it all, by steaming in and telling her how much he liked her and had fallen in love with her back then in the autumn of 1989.

No, no, he was convinced - as the taxi did a u-turn across the tramlines and the main road into the lay-by outside Liberec station - his constant recollections of 1989 were a positive process. What if his mind was really just trying to tell him to search there amongst his memories of 1989 in order to find the best way to 'play it' in a week's time? Telling him to search in amongst the events and the moments they'd shared that had drawn him towards Jana by the end of that momentous year. That was a far more attractive proposition for him, much more positive. No contest really as to which argument he preferred, or which he would convince himself of most.

Liberec station had its fair share of 'communist realist' architecture and corrugated iron. It was quite small and clean. Nevertheless, it still wasn't exactly a place to be recommended for pre-train snacks and didn't exactly exude an ambience that would induce any traveller to wish to linger for too long. It was fortunate for Tom then that his train to Brno was on time, and as he had only arrived at the station twenty minutes before it was due by the time he had bought his ticket and found the platform he had only a few minutes to while away taking in the spartan splendour of Liberec main station and its bare platforms.

Even though almost everyone he'd spoken to at the Technical University Faculty in Liberec had told him it was better to go to Brno by coach, Tom had still preferred the train. This was mainly because he always reasoned he could get more work done on a train than a coach, or bus as the Czechs called it. There was more room and he reasoned that he was less likely to have to be sat next to someone on the train than on the bus.

He'd had a pleasant enough two days of meetings at the university, interspersed with coffee breaks and lunch, and more than decorated by the usual 'academic sights' of secretarial short skirts and long legs strategically introduced into his view so as to prevent him dozing off from boredom in the meetings. The visit was rounded off on Tuesday evening by the obligatory dinner with the Faculty dignitaries and some academics, some of which, the women at least, were pleasant company. He'd been dispatched on his way back to the hotel with requests that he must come back for a longer visit soon.

At the Faculty dinner Tom had been sat opposite Daniela Baránková, a lecturer who taught both Economics and English at the university. She was around late thirties Tom reckoned and about five foot ten in the not-too-high heels she wore. Daniela had a longish, thin face and swept back dark black short hair. Tom put her in his 'category' labelled 'quite strikingly attractive'. It was not that she was what could be called naturally beautiful, but she had quite sharp features and high cheekbones, which, together with her closely cut black hair and her slim figure, definitely qualified her very well for that particular category of his. On the relatively few occasions that Tom had seen her previously, either in the university or at the functional dinners, he couldn't fail to notice that Daniela's seemingly near-perfect figure was always exhibited to its best in her very smart 'wardrobe'. She was always very well dressed, at least that had been the case every time he had seen her at work in the university or in the evening. Immaculately dressed, in fact, everything matched, right down to the smallest detail. Earrings, necklace, jewellery, not to mention her various dresses, suits, skirts and blouses, usually finished off with a striking complementary silk scarf tied loosely around her elegant quite long neck. On this evening she'd opted for a royal blue quite high neck dress, drawn in at her slim waist with a thin white belt with gold buckle and set off with a vivid blue and white silk scarf around her neck.

Tom had first been introduced to her at a conference in Liberec the previous December. He couldn't deny that he'd been impressed not only by her good looks but also by her elegance and charm, as well as her obvious intelligence. Her English was almost perfect and seemingly at times much better grammatically than his own he thought. As it turned out, and as she told him when he complimented her on her English the previous December, she'd spent a year in Britain in 1992 travelling all over, as well as a year in the United States. Like many Czech academics, as well as Central and Eastern Europeans in general for that matter, her accent was sort of Americanised, sometimes what could be described as slightly mid-Atlantic. Even though he'd had only a few real conversations with her Tom soon realised that Daniela was a very forthright, determined and ambitious woman. At some of the dinners at the conference the previous December and in a couple of conversations with her in various bars with the group after the dinners Tom had sensed that she was taking a particular interest in him, and he wasn't thinking it was his academic work that intrigued her. Just one or two tell-tale glances and eye contact between them suggested to him that she might be 'interested'. Also, he noticed that she always seemed to be sat next to him or opposite him at the conference dinners. Now there she was again doing exactly the same thing. He'd not seen her at the university during the day but she'd turned up at the evening dinner, obviously invited by the 'powers that be'. When the group moved from the bar of the restaurant to the long table for dinner Tom had been one of the first to sit down. Daniela quickly made a determined move to get the seat opposite him and then spent the whole of the meal engaging him in face to face conversation, accompanied he felt by some pretty determined full on eye contact.

Once the dinner was over and the party adjourned to the bar for coffee it again seemed to Tom that she was monopolising him, so much so that he felt people were beginning to notice. They probably weren't of course, but he did think he was beginning to feel self-conscious about not mingling. But he just couldn't force himself to move away. As they sat there at one of the tables in the corner of the bar drinking their coffee she was now increasingly patting his arm as she chatted to him and at one point rested her hand on his thigh as she leaned forward to make a quieter comment to him about one of her colleagues. For Tom her hand, with its long fingers and finely manicured nails, seemed to stay there for an age before she leaned back and moved it away.

Okay, he reasoned, some people get off on cars, or drugs, or booze. Me, I get off on having intelligent women show some sign of interest in me, and especially foreign women, especially Czechs. Or at least I get off by convincing myself that they're interested in me. So, when after all the signs he reckoned he'd read so well – sitting opposite him at dinner, monopolising the conversation with him, the constant eye contact, the touching over coffee – Daniela suggested to him quietly as they finished their coffee that just the two of them go on to another late night bar where there was music he was amazed to hear the words, "no, I can't I'm afraid," coming out of his mouth, followed by, "sorry, but I've got a really early start in the morning for my journey to Brno, maybe next time?"

He could see in her face that she was not best pleased, but, maybe hedging her bets for that next time she simply quietly said, "Okay Tom, I do understand. But I can see from your face that if you didn't have to leave tomorrow early for Brno you would like to go on to the music bar just with me." Changing her facial disappointment to a tempting smile, she added, "it's a pity, but next time for sure, and we'll go out and have dinner first, just the two of us. Let's keep in touch then with email and try to arrange your next visit soon."

Totally amazed at his own newly found self-control Tom had said his goodbyes – not only to Daniela, but to those members of the Faculty still lingering in the restaurant bar – and quickly made his way across the main square and upstairs to his hotel room. So, he'd had a good refreshing eight hours sleep and he'd even managed to find an empty first class compartment on the train to Brno as it pulled out of Liberec station on time on that Wednesday morning. "Okay," he muttered as he sat down in the compartment seat next to the window, "time to do some serious thinking about just how to approach dinner with Jana in a week's time." How to tell Jana just how he felt about her, what approach to take, dive in or work around to the subject slowly? Raise it early over the starter and risk a very difficult atmosphere over the next couple of hours, or maybe a very pleasant time if she feels the same, as he obviously hoped she did. Or, wait and raise it late on, over coffee, once she, and him, had got a fair bit of wine inside them? As long as she didn't think it was the wine 'talking' of course.

So, a chance to gaze out at the Czech countryside on the four-and-a-half hour train journey and once more ponder his tactics and prospects with Jana next week in Prague. His thoughts were almost immediately interrupted by the ticket inspector though. "Okay sir, Brno half-past two, we hope," he informed Tom in broken English as he clipped his ticket.

Just how he knew Tom was English was a mystery, but then who knows how most foreigners could identify the English at a thousand metres or more. Perhaps the English have an aura, an effervescence of fish and chips, permanently embedded in their clothing. How awful Tom thought, and he immediately started sniffing his shirtsleeve in a somewhat strange manner, which caused the inspector to look at him more than a little circumspectly as he slid the compartment door closed. No doubt this merely confirmed what the ticket inspector thought about the English anyway and was simply another way of identifying them from afar – through the stupidity of some of their actions.

Tom stopped sniffing and tried to act normally, removing some papers from his briefcase. The train seemed to be endlessly running alongside countless different short stretches of water. What seemed like small streams or rivers? Or maybe just one stream winding its way close to, away from, and back again to the side of the railway line. At times the stretches of water were covered in a polluted green slime. Yet, in the late spring sunshine it conjured up an image of idyllic rural simplicity, although one which undoubtedly didn't exist. The kind of stuff the nineteenth century Russian writers used to conjure up. A green, pleasant, warm, simplistic existence in the North Moravian countryside, Tom imagined. Chekhov would have been proud of him. Even the polluted stretches of water seemed to reflect life itself. At times beautiful, if sometimes a strange unexpected beauty, yet forever scarred with the imperfection and damage always there. Always just around the bend, but still nonetheless lending to the beauty and experience.

Now, as he stared out of the train window, the scenery had changed. Miles and miles of flat shimmering open plains. The image was of a flat landscape with few contours, strangely reflecting his thoughts about calmness. Was Jana going to finally be his calm and contentment with real peace he pondered? His deep introspection was interrupted by something he realised about the passing Czech countryside. What's missing? What is it that is so different from the English countryside? Then it came to him. There wasn't any livestock in the vast expanse of green fields. No cows, no sheep, not even one pig to be seen from that great mass of them that so obviously kept the Czech pork plates brimming to overfill. He later found out that it was because the livestock was mainly kept inside. They didn't see the light of day until they hit the plate, followed closely by the Czech stomach.

Enough of this sightseeing out of the train window and mind wandering, time to focus on the real issue in his life and how to approach his meal with Jana in a week's time? He decided to again try to systematically go over everything he could remember that had happened between them back in that year of 1989. Recollections of the start of his 1989 'November days' visit to Prague always brought a smile to his lips. He'd come to see Dita again of course, but that wasn't the reason for his amusement. It was the question, "why are you here, Mr. Carpenter?" and what followed at Prague airport in early November 1989 that always amused him. Funnily enough that was a question he'd asked himself a vast number of times in various crazy situations he'd got into in different places across the world. They mostly involved women in one way or another. It was a question that usually prompted him into making a flippant answer. This though was not a time for a flippant answer. This was a time to concentrate and be serious, and think carefully about his answer. This was a Czechoslovak StB Secret Police officer asking the question in quite good English and in a very serious manner. Although as his mind drifted off slightly he wondered if there was such an 'animal' as a non-serious StB officer?

Concentrate and don't be stupid, Tom's brain warned him, bringing him back to focus. These are tricky times. The whole of Czechoslovakia is on edge, the whole of East and Central Europe really. Right now was a time to act like who you are supposed to be, a serious academic.

Instead of his previous relatively smooth, even if somewhat bureaucratically protracted, passages through Prague airport passport control this time he had been taken to one side and detained. This was a very different time from before though. This was early November 1989. Now here he was in a small room in the airport faced by two rather large, long black leather coated men, the stereotypical East European secret police officer in equally stereotypical 'uniform'. Tom always found it coincidentally interesting that after the revolution, and certainly by the time of his 1994 visit, the leather coated 'uniform' had passed on in Prague to, or been taken over by, such salubrious characters as the Czech and Russian mafia. These two prime examples of the original model at Prague airport in November 1989 had very courteously explained in quite good broken English that they were members of the department of the Czechoslovak police responsible for interior state security. They even offered Tom a coffee and told him that they hoped that they would not delay or detain him for long, a sentiment that he echoed wholeheartedly.

"According to the visa stamps in your passport you visited the Czechoslovak Republic a lot of times in the past year, Mr. Carpenter. You must like it here in our country?" The same black leather coat continued even before Tom could answer the initial enquiry about why he was here now. The talking questioning black leather coat descended from a neck the thickness of which Tom decided he'd probably never come across before in his life. The neck sat beneath a round, almost Mongol looking face with narrow, barely open eyes, a small black goatee beard and very short-cropped jet black hair. Tom guessed there might be some Russian in there somewhere, although he couldn't really tell from the man's accent and he certainly wasn't about to ask. The second leather 'uniformed' man remained silent and just stared intently straight into Tom's face while leaning casually with his back against one of the grubby magnolia coloured bare walls. There were not even the photographs of Gorbachev or the Czech Communist leader, Husák, which usually adorned the walls of rooms that were officially part of the 'State apparatus'. The silent StB man was bald and shiny on top. Maybe it was shaven? Who knows Tom thought, and again probably not the time to really care. Quite a thick neck, although by no means in the same league as his questioning colleague. A much thinner elongated face that the Englishman couldn't help noticing was ornamented on each side with extremely unusual protruding, almost pointed ears, very reminiscent of Mr. Spock on Star Trek. Tom wisely concluded that he probably also had the same sense of feeling as the Star Trek character – none whatsoever. Spock in the leather coat's ears were totally the opposite of his interrogating colleague's which had obviously seen combat and were well and truly cauliflowered. Both men obviously gave some weights in a gym some serious attention. He just hoped their brains were not as well developed as their biceps.

For an instant Tom thought about contradicting his interrogator and pointing out that his visits to Prague over the last year could hardly be termed, "a lot." His brain wasn't exactly working at full speed on that particular detail, but he reckoned this was his fourth visit, although no doubt the Czechoslovak Passport Control stamps in his passport that was now firmly grasped in the stumpy fingers and quite menacing looking fist at the end of one of the leather coated arms would confirm that or not. Then again were four in a year a lot he wondered? Maybe to the StB officer at these particularly dodgy times it was.

Before he could think any further about entering into a debate as to whether four constituted a lot one of the StB leather coats offered him some advice and a warning. "These are dangerous times here in Prague," the thickest neck continued. "There are many counter-agents, bandits and criminals who have come into our country and into our beautiful city of Prague recently, and they want to make trouble."

The man's English was improving by the second and now Tom was beginning to get really worried. This was a more intelligent thick neck than he'd initially reckoned. He began to feel himself get a little warm and was desperately trying not to start sweating. That might be seen as a signal of some kind of guilt and that he had something to hide.

"Naturally we would not want any proper, legitimate foreign businessman from the West to be put in danger in these difficult times. So, as a precaution the government has decided to warn foreigners, businessmen such as yourself, of the dangers, for your protection of course."

"Or are you a journalist?" the other leather coat leaning against the wall menacingly intervened in a definitely raised tone. What was most worrying for Tom was that this was the first time the second officer had spoken. They were clearly a well-rehearsed 'act' in checking and trying to catch people out.

Tom was now fully alert, definitely at his politest and on his best behaviour. He quickly realised he would have to be at his most proper and decided to try to use his status as an academic, if not to impress them, then to try to convince them he was harmless by giving off an aura of naivety bordering on the eccentric. He knew full well that academics were not exactly above suspicion in Czechoslovakia at that time as many of them were active in the dissident movement. So, just playing the 'academic card' wasn't going to get him out of the room and the airport quickly. Consequently, he decided upon the 'naïve English eccentric academic' approach.

"Oh, I'm not a businessman," he interjected. "Or a journalist, I'm an academic. I'm actually here to continue my research on part of the history of your lovely and very important country, in the nineteenth century, and of course of the great part that the people have played in that history." He thought that might be going a little over the top - people's history, great struggle and all that – but he reckoned that just the academic tag alone wouldn't impress them and was hoping that the people's history and struggle stuff would appeal to any semblance of so-called communist instincts which might be hidden away somewhere in those huge frames of muscle. Everyone knew it was the middle-layer intellectuals and academics that were most involved in the challenges to the Communist regime. They were in the forefront of the supposed troublemaking that the leather coat had just warned him about. So just saying he was an academic was not going to get them off his back. But he couldn't lie as they probably already knew just who he was and what he did and the worst thing he could do he reckoned was start with a lie. Anyway, technically he hadn't lied to them. It was just that he was more interested in the history being made right then rather than the nineteenth century period he had identified as his research interest to the 'leather coats'.

Trying to sound as boringly proper and correct as possible he waffled on with as much historical stuff as he could muster. "I'm researching and studying Czech nationalism, the origins of the Czech national revival during the Habsburg Empire period." Again not a complete lie as there was indeed a good deal of Czech nationalism present in some of the strands of the dissident movement involved in the events of 1989.

"You know, the period of the Austro-Hungarian Empire, mostly the nineteenth century. Jolly interesting time," he added, trying to sound as eccentrically British as possible, although now he really was beginning to wonder if he was going completely over the top and embellishing it a little too much. Maybe best to just shut up now he thought briefly. His interrogators by now looked completely nonplussed. By then Tom was gambling that your average StB goon who had been put on airport duty wouldn't exactly be all that high-powered, let alone super-intelligent. He was hoping that these two 'leather coats' were just that, your average StB goons, despite what appeared to be their improving by the minute English. So, instead he decided to take a chance and ploughed on.

"I work at a university in England. Well, I'm a senior lecturer actually, a Doctor of Philosophy. In your country I'd be the equivalent of a Professor." He thought that would impress them as he tried to sound both suitably pompous and ramblingly ineffectual at the same time. Offering them his university business card he decided to make just one more push and overload them with as much information as possible in the hope that they would be so busy trying to sort through it all that they would forget some of the more difficult questions that they might ask him.

"Yes, I was here in March with some of my students. They loved it, especially the pivo, the beer, eh. The best in the world I'm told and very cheap for them of course." That at least drew a small chuckle from the two men. Now he thought he really was beginning to sound like an ineffectual eccentric Englishman.

"Then I came back in June for my research, but I had to go back to England at the beginning of September to see my boss. He's a bit of a stupid arsehole really." Tom thought attacking the boss would always go down well, and especially well with two guys who'd no doubt been stuck out on airport duty all day by their boss.

"Anyway, I wanted to ask him for a sabbatical. You know" – they plainly didn't –" time off, a term off from lecturing, so that I could finish my research here and surprise, surprise, the arsehole actually agreed to it. Just like that. Crazy these bosses sometimes. You just don't know what they want you to do, or how they will react from one day to the next." That drew a slight nod in agreement from one of the 'leather coats', even if it was one that was accompanied by a somewhat bewildered look on his face. A look that was no doubt induced by Tom's non-stop rattling machine-gun delivery of volunteered verbal information over what seemed like an age, but was probably only five minutes or so.

He had indeed requested a sabbatical at short notice from his Head of Department, but his 'boss' had only eventually given in and agreed when Tom pleaded that now really was the time to be in Prague as far as his East and Central European research was concerned. Not because of research into the nineteenth century though. It was the closing years of the twentieth century that interested him most, especially the quickly developing events in the closing months of 1989. That was what his research was really about and why his boss had given him the sabbatical.

"So, he's let me come, my boss. I wanted to come much earlier, but it took much longer this time to get a visa. I guess it's because of all the stuff you talked about. What was it? Oh, yes, crime, troublemakers. Well, I'm not interested in all that. Don't want to go anywhere near those bloody lunatics." To emphasise the point he tapped the side of his head with the index finger of his right hand and rolled his eyes. He was now certainly going completely over the top. He felt his voice getting even quicker and higher. Taking a deep breath he tried to slow down and ended with, "I won't be going anywhere near them, those people. Just want to get into your libraries and some of the Czech national archives. You know, to have a look at some of your important unique historical documents and records; can't see them in England. I'm only here for six weeks, from now till just before Christmas. Oh, I don't suppose you celebrate that. Anyway, I will be leaving on the twentieth of December. I expect it will be bloody cold here by then. Still, better than all the rain in England, eh?"

The twentieth of December was when his visa was due to expire. Little did Tom realise then that by that time no one in the country – bureaucrat, StB border guard or otherwise – would really be bothered about visas and a whole new era would be beginning for Czechoslovakia and its people, including the two thick necked leather coats.

With his what he reckoned was a normal English comment about the weather Tom decided to shut up. The two StB men had just stood there staring at him dumbfounded all through his machine-gun type explanation. When he finally did shut up they just virtually repeated what they had said before about being careful about troublemakers and making sure that he didn't go anywhere near them. They were obviously so confused by his ramblings that they even forgot to ask him where he was going to be staying. This was something he had thought about while he was bombarding them with his story about his, "arsehole boss." He knew it would be an extremely tricky question to deal with. He was sure they would ask him. They would expect him to be staying in a hotel. To tell them he was staying with a Czech friend, Dita, would not go down well at all, either with them or for that matter Dita. Czechs just didn't have western friends staying with them at the best of times, let alone at the time of the unstable situation in Czechoslovakia then. Indeed, in stressing the delicacy and danger of her own situation and association with him Dita had said a number of times that the secret police always, "went for female contacts of westerners." All Tom could think to do if he was asked was to try and bluff his way through it by cloaking it in the fact that it was an academic friend he was staying with, a fellow researcher. Amazingly though they just didn't ask him. It was early in the evening and maybe they had had a long boring day stuck out at the airport and just wanted to get rid of the rambling eccentric Englishman as quickly as possible, get home to their knuckle of pork, dumplings and large amounts of good Czech beer. Who knows Tom thought as he sat relieved on the bus to the city centre from the airport? Anyway, they'd obviously swallowed his story. They even apologised, sort of, for any delay to his arrival and then sent him on his way, wishing him good luck with his work and with his, "arsehole boss."

By the time Tom arrived at the door of Dita's flat forty-five minutes later he'd decided it was best not to tell her about his airport experience. She was a worrier at the best of times and he didn't want the very start of his six weeks with her buried beneath what he believed would be an over-reaction by her. After all at that time he was genuinely looking forward to seeing her. Just as he had been every time he had come to Prague since their first meeting. Usually she would have come to meet him at the airport, but as it turned out it was just as well that she had a meeting in work late that afternoon and couldn't get away, telling him in their last phone call before he left England that she would meet him at her flat and would make sure she was there by the time he arrived from the airport. If she had come to the airport no doubt the StB men would not have been so easily put off. Her usual way of greeting him was to throw her arms around his neck and give him a long kiss accompanied by that broad, white smile of hers. That would have attracted attention at the airport at any time and certainly would have done in the tense circumstances gripping the country at that time. A foreigner, who had become quite a regular visitor to Czechoslovakia throughout that unstable and unpredictable year, being hugged and kissed by a Czech woman in such a public place would definitely not have been missed by the 'leather coats'. Tom still got his long kiss, a hug and the broad smile as soon as Dita opened the door to her apartment, preceded by a quickly high pitch squealed, "you're here," and followed by a soft deeply sincere, "I've missed you very much, Tom."

Suddenly his pleasant reminiscences of Dita in 1989 were interrupted by, "Brno Hlavní Nádraží," over the train's public address system. Tom couldn't comprehend the rest. His Czech didn't exactly extend that far, but he knew from a glance at his watch that it must have meant the train was pulling into Brno. It was twenty-seven minutes past two in the afternoon. Not bad, the ticket inspector had said they would arrive around two-thirty. Time for a nap at his hotel, then shower, shave, and explore for the first time the offerings of downtown Brno.

Part Three:
1994 - The Czech Republic five years on and the hope of the Czech people

6
At Brno

There was Petr waving and shouting, "Ahoj, Tom," on platform eight of Brno station as the Englishman manoeuvred his bag down from the train. "Let me take that," he suggested as he offered him his handshake. "Good journey?"

"Yes fine," Tom replied. Although given what had been going through his mind about Dita for most of it he was tempted to add very interesting, very instructive, and I learned a lot about myself.

Petr was a sociologist who worked in the Faculty of Social Studies at Masaryk University in Brno. He was a tall, slim man, slightly taller than Tom at around six foot three. He wore those wiry type glasses. Not really 'Lennonesque' as they were bigger and rounder, but the same sort of thin wiry frames. He was prematurely bald for his age, 42, although he still had the usual hair on each side of his head going up to about a couple of inches above his ears. It was going a little grey, as was his stubbly short beard. It wasn't really 'designer stubble', more like scruffy stubble. It just looked like he constantly needed a good shave. This scruffiness on his face was completely at odds with the rest of his appearance. Tom always thought Petr managed to look smartly dressed, which somehow seemed to fit in perfectly with his slim appearance. It was a simple smartness though, nothing extravagant, and usually in black or grey. Brighter colours didn't seem to figure in his wardrobe, or at least in the clothes Tom had always seen him wearing. Today they were black jeans and a simple, plain black polo shirt. Petr was an outwardly calm, often quite serious man. He gave off a vibe of complete outer calmness. Nothing seemed to fluster him. Or at least, nothing Tom had seen him react to. Maybe he was just good at thinking rationally and holding it all inside. Perhaps inside he was really a seething mass of discontent and anger. If he was though, he certainly knew how to control it. Petr took his work, and especially his research, very seriously. He was a real academic. Despite that, surprisingly Tom liked him and got on well with him from the moment they first met, and it seemed the feeling was mutual.

Brno station was bustling with people heading home into the suburbs of the Czech Republic's second largest city. It was the sort of station that you would expect to see in an Orson Welles black and white movie based in Central Europe - one with all those dark alleyways, arches and passageways, with people chasing each other in the shadows. It was typical old-style Central European. There were huge high quite ornate ceilings in the booking hall, tall arches and doorways, and a great mass of humanity swarming through the whole building. Petr proudly proclaimed it had been the recipient of the first ever train from Vienna in 1839. Tom wondered just how many souls, largely of Central European origin, had passed through the station's quite impressive, if in need of a good clean, entrance hall over the previous one hundred and fifty years or more. For him it had the sort of ambience he had expected and liked about Central Europe. It was his first visit to Brno and already he thought he would like it, even if not all of it was readily appealing to the eye.

The main building and station booking hall exhibited a charm which managed simultaneously to be in conflict with the general grime of the place and yet at ease with its nineteenth-century 'Old World' elegance. Its appearance immediately struck Tom to be one leftover from a long bygone age and not from the period of Marxism-Leninism and the great 'communist experiment'. Most of it was much more distinctively representative of the middle of the nineteenth century.

He only had one holdall type bag and a shoulder-strap briefcase, but as Petr struggled up the exit stairs with Tom's holdall the Englishman reflected that the great 'communist experiment' obviously had not extended to anything as grand as escalators in the main railway station of what was by now the second city of the new 'young' country of the Czech Republic. What was immediately visible was that the large number of people who were flowing through the station in the same tide of humanity as Tom and Petr on that particular Wednesday afternoon were seemingly quite 'down-at-heal', with lowered eyes, and many wearing shabby, cheap, generally grubby clothes. Tom's quick first impression was that these people exuded a general feeling of hopelessness that comes from the struggle of everyday life in a whole range of situations; the general tiredness and weary look of overcoming the difficulties of just getting through the day. It seemed that for these people nothing much had changed in their everyday lives following the events of 1989 and the 'Velvet revolution'. The world had moved on, just like it had for Brno station since its opening in 1839, but for the 'Brnaks', for many if not most of the people of Brno Tom glimpsed scurrying through the underpass below the station it appeared that the world and its changes since 1989 had passed them by. They had seemingly missed their new 'capitalist train', or at the very least they were travelling way back in the rear of the baggage carriage. This was of course an initial perception that was to change a little over the next few days. And after all, he reminded himself, where in any major railway station in the world do you find a good environment? Don't they always seem to be inhabited by their fair share of 'less well off, 'down at heal' looking people'?

What also struck Tom as he and Petr made their way through Brno station was that many of the people they passed had embraced the all-encompassing 'label' capitalist mentality of the west. These though were not designer labels that caught Tom's eye. They were different names that he didn't recognise and had never heard of. They were obviously much cheaper, down-market names. In some cases they were just 'rip-off' slight variations on the more famous sportswear labels such as were common in many parts of the 'new and extended capitalist' world now. Maybe these were just another component that now came as part of the self-assembly kit for major railway stations of the world. Well, the new Central and Eastern Europe capitalist world anyway. These were indeed so obviously poor copies of the real thing. These people had the jeans and the trainers – well, some of the younger ones did – but they weren't Levis or Calvin Kleins or Nike or Adidas. Tom was to see people wearing those later in his visit in more salubrious surroundings. What these 'main railway station people' were wearing could immediately be seen to be poorly made, poorly fitting, badly put together shabby copies. It fitted with much of the Central-East European and Czech copy of western capitalism and liberal democracy since 1989. The people were impressed by the 'image', but they hadn't quite got the 'idea' yet. They'd 'got' the concept of capitalism, of liberal democracy, or of trainers, jeans and the 'lifestyle', but it didn't quite work, didn't quite fit. The substance beneath the surface of the supposed style – of the quality of the clothing or the quality of the democracy – wasn't really there yet. Maybe eventually though the 'copies' would turn into the real thing.

"I have my car outside," Petr informed him as they strode through the main booking hall of the station, "and your hotel is only a few minutes away, the Best Western International, yes?"

"Yes, Best Western," Tom confirmed. "Is it okay?"

"Oh, very, very classy," came the answer, with an accompanying grin and, "far too good for you, Tom."

The two men had first met the previous December, at the end of 1993, at the university in Liberec. Petr was one of a group of Czech academics dealing with Tom's modules on the European Union that he had written for four universities in the Czech Republic as part of a joint EU-Czech Republic education project focused on European Studies. Vaclav from the Technical University in Ostrava – the next stop on Tom's journey - was also there, and the three of them became good friends. For some reason though Petr and Tom struck up a more relaxed, less formal, instant rapport. Their background and general outlook on life was very similar, and over seemingly endless Czech beers late into a couple of December Liberec nights they became the best of friends. Petr slapped Tom on the shoulder as they left the station and emerged into the Brno afternoon sunshine. "So at last Tom Carpenter comes to Brno. It is good to have you here. We will have some beers and a good time. Some work of course, but not too much," he promised his English friend.

Five minutes later Petr deposited Tom at the hotel, checked his reservation was okay and then once again smiling broadly told him, "We are meeting my Faculty Dean for dinner at eight. You have some time to rest my friend before Czech dumplings and pivo await you." After his many visits to universities in the Czech Republic, and before that the former Czechoslovakia, Tom had by now got used to the obligatory Faculty 'welcome dinner', although Petr did add, "and after we, just you and me, can explore my city's nightlife."

After being on his best behaviour and surviving dinner with the Dean of the Faculty Tom was ready by ten for Petr's promised exploration of Brno's Wednesday nightlife. Initially it turned out to be pubs and bars and a considerable number of glasses of good tasting, although very heavy, Czech beer. Beer drinking, Czech beer drinking and Czech pubs in Brno were very much still the male preserve, just like throughout the Czech Republic. This was not your local Brno 'Fleece and Firkin' or 'Weatherspoons'. Not much chance of meeting any totty in a Czech 'ale house'. So, quite quickly his expectancy turned into no more than that of a Brno Wednesday boys' night out with Petr. For most of the evening that was what it was. From one smokey, male saturated pub to another, until just after midnight Petr proclaimed, "okay my friend, time to introduce you to Charlie's."

"Charlie's?" Tom repeated inquisitively. "What's Charlie's?"

"Charlie's is the most famous club in Brno, Tom. Everybody who comes to Brno has to go to Charlie's at least once. Although once people have been there they usually can't stop going back."

"Where is it? Is it far?" Tom was feeling decidedly uneasy about the word club, and especially one called 'Charlie's' given the word's slang connotation where he'd grown up. Even though he felt entirely at ease with his relatively new friend he was somewhat uncertain just what sort of establishment Petr was proposing they visit now.

"It's right in the centre of the city, Tom. Just off Náměsti Svobody, a couple of streets from here." Sensing his friend's unease Petr added, "And don't look so worried. It's not a striptease club or a nightclub. Charlie's, well to give it its full name which nobody ever uses though, Charlie's Hat, is just a club for some drinking, some dancing and hopefully meeting some nice Czech women. The students use it as well. So I might get to introduce my very important Professor friend from England to some of my students as well. Just introduce you, Tom, nothing more," he warned.

"Oh, I see. Okay, sounds interesting." Tom was now more relaxed about it and even showing some keenness. "Why is it called 'Charlie's Hat' in the middle of a city in the Czech Republic?"

"After your famous English compatriot, Tom, Charlie Chaplin, you'll see when we get there." With that brief explanation Petr emptied the last remnants of his beer glass saying to Tom, "come on let's show you Charlie's. I guarantee you will be hooked afterwards, Tom." He couldn't resist a chuckle as he added, "I will turn you into a Charlie's addict."

Quite what association the establishment in the middle of Brno had with the famous silent screen film star comedian was by no means apparent to Tom. What was certain though was that Charlie's definitely had a character all of its own and what could only be referred to as a very novel ambience. The two men entered through a single door from one of the main streets off Náměsti Svobody. It immediately struck Tom that you would never find this place if you didn't already know it was there. The doorway, with an almost grudgingly small 'Charlie's Hat' sign above it and definitely no mention whatsoever of the word 'club', was set back a couple of yards between two innocuous looking shops, one selling decidedly plain cheap looking clothes and the other rows and rows of basic plastic kitchen utensils. The highlight and feature of that particular shop window was a rather neatly stacked pyramid of bright red plastic colanders. Obviously the 'star buy' of the week Tom chuckled to himself as the two men nipped through the doorway and into a very grubby, and definitely not salubrious, passageway about twenty yards long. The entrance to Charlie's instantly reminded Tom of one of those not very nice men's toilets that used to be situated all over London. The ones for which the entrance was usually surrounded by iron railings and that you had to go downstairs and underground to use, with their grubby beige tiled walls and overpowering smell of urine and bleach. At the end of the passageway and what Tom already thought was a not so inviting entrance to Charlie's they turned right and he followed Petr down a flight of narrow stairs. They emerged into another passageway below ground of similar length and standard of lack of cleanliness. A strong whiff of urine flooded into Tom's nostrils and he muttered, "this smells nice Petr. Just exactly where are you taking me?" Maybe it really was an imported London underground toilet he was being taken into.

"It's the toilets, Tom. For future reference they're there, in case you feel the need." As the Czech pointed to the toilet entrance and the stench wafted up Tom's nostrils he determined that he was definitely going to try to avoid feeling, "the need".

"I thought we were already in the toilet. Smells like the whole place is a toilet," was his swift response to Petr who greeted the comment with a wry smile and, "well, one thing you should learn straightaway about Charlie's, Tom, is that you should always go to the toilet before you come here. But it will get better, you'll see."

At each end of the corridor was a door and as the two men joked with each other about Charlies' distinctive aroma the one to their right opened and a tall young woman in tight denim jeans, an equally tight black T-shirt and with long straight blonde hair down to the middle of her back strode purposefully towards what passed for an impersonation of the women's toilet. Tom, whose attention was immediately shifted from the stench in his nostrils to something far more pleasant, guessed she was in her early twenties. "Mmm ... twenty-two, twenty-three maybe," he rhetorically enquired of Petr followed by, "let's go and look in that bar then."

"No, no, Tom. That's just a small bar. The largest bars and the most women, my friend, will be this way. Follow me." With that Petr set off down the corridor to the left. When he opened the door at that end of the corridor the two men were immediately cast into a crowded bar occupied by what, from a quick glance around, Tom calculated to be seventy per cent women. The bar itself was about twenty-five yards long and faced the door. In front of it were some bar stools, all occupied, and opposite it were tables and high benches along the back wall. These were full of groups of people of all ages, from what Tom again reckoned were early twenties through to mid-forties. He immediately noticed that two of the tables were occupied by groups of women, five on one and six on the other. One of the groups was obviously women in their early to mid-twenties. The women in the other looked like they were in their mid-thirties. The overwhelming majority of the women in both groups – blondes, brunettes and one darkish redhead – were lovely. Simply dressed, mostly in jeans and t-shirts or shirts, they seemed instantly to exude both style and sex appeal for Tom. He decided immediately that two of them in the younger group were absolutely gorgeous. They had a beauty that was natural, one that gave an impression it was produced without any effort whatsoever on their part.

"Stop dribbling and close your mouth, Tom, and tell me what you want to drink?" Petr interrupted his staring.

"Oh, a beer thanks Petr, Starobrno will be fine."

"They don't do that here, Tom."

"No, no, sorry, I didn't mean to stare. Didn't realise it was such a big deal with the Czechs. Nobody anywhere in the world likes you staring I suppose, sorry, Petr."

"Not the staring, Tom. The beer, they don't do Starobrno here," Petr informed his friend with a chuckle. "How about Velvet, it's not too bad and quite smooth?"

"Okay, if you recommend it Velvet will be fine thanks, but what about all these women? You never told me about this place before. Is it always like this? And it's only Wednesday night."

"Always," the Czech confirmed over his shoulder as he managed to find a space at the bar and get the attention of the barman, "and on Fridays and Saturdays it's really packed. You can't move in here."

Tom found that difficult to believe. He could hardly see how you could fit many more people in there. Around the walls were various pictures and posters of the little comedian who gave his name to the place. The walls themselves were a somewhat grubby off-shade of creamy yellow. No doubt stained that way by the years of cigarette smoke. Tom was going to ask his friend why it was called 'Charlies Hat' rather than just the 'Charlies' by which he came to learn everyone referred to it. What was the fixation with the little man's hat? He decided there was really not much point. This was the Czech Republic and even if there was a reason – most unlikely, and most likely the answer would have been simply, "why not?" – it would have been forgotten long ago. In any case such inquisitive thoughts were erased instantly from his mind as a slim young woman with shoulder length jet black hair and dark smouldering eyes said something to him in Czech and pushed her way to the bar between him and Petr just as his Czech friend was about to pass Tom his beer. Tom couldn't resist a, "who's your friend Petr?" while nodding his head in the direction of the dark-haired woman.

"You are English," she immediately interjected.

"Yes, that's right. Are you from Brno?" was all Tom could think to say in trying to make himself heard above what seemed to be the increasingly loud music.

"No, I'm from Opava in northern Moravia."

"Yes I know where that is," Tom told her, and in a desperate attempt to try to keep what passed in his head for a conversation going he added, "It's near Ostrava. I'm going there on Monday. I arrived here this afternoon. What do you do here? What is your work? Where did you learn your English?"

In a now desperate attempt to keep the woman engaged in conversation Tom was nervously rattling out questions. His enquiries stalled though when she told him, "I'm a student at the university, Masaryk University. I'm studying Bio-chemistry. I learned my English at school, but it's not very good I think."

"No, no, it's fine. Very good in fact," was Tom's attempt at flattery, which he followed rather pathetically with his usual standard response of, "it's much better than my Czech."

"I like to speak English," she told him. "I was there for six months as an au pair last year. I love it, especially London. Speaking English is like a drug to me. The more I speak it the more I want to learn and go on speaking it."

Tom couldn't resist blurting out what he thought on reflection later was probably the most cringing chat up line he had ever used. "Okay, so let me be your drug dealer," he spouted out, followed by the completely disconnected statement of, "I was born in London."

While the girl giggled slightly Petr let out a loud roar of laughter. So loud it could even be heard across the bar above the thumping music emanating from the large loudspeakers hung somewhat precariously on the wall at each end of the room. The Czech had been amusing himself behind the young woman's head pulling faces at Tom's attempted chat-up. When Tom descended into the depths of the inane he could prolong his silence no longer. Leaning over the woman's shoulder he deliberately told her in English so Tom could hear and understand, "my English friend here is a Professor, visiting the university, the Faculty of Social Studies, although you wouldn't think so given his appalling pathetic use of language. I'm just giving him a tour of the highlights of Brno, including our wonderful nightlife. It's his first time in Charlie's, although I don't think it will be his last. Now, if you'll excuse us, I still have to show him the rest of our wonderful famous club."

With that he pulled Tom away from the bar by the arm, nudging him in the direction of some more stairs downwards at the left-hand end of the bar.

"What are you doing?" Tom asked him somewhat agitatedly. "I was in there."

"Yes, yes, of course you were, Tom, that's why I dragged you away. She's a student; remember I said earlier I'd just introduce you."

"But she wasn't one of yours, she's doing Bio-Chemistry," Tom protested, "beautiful and clever."

"Beautiful and clever," Petr repeated, aren't you always saying that's the most dangerous combination, Tom? A student's not a good idea, my friend, believe me, even one that is not taught by me, and anyway I think I saved you from melting into all that sickly goo that was gushing out of your mouth," he added sarcastically. "Plus I really do have more to show you, including plenty more women, follow me."

The two men descended the flight of stairs further into the dark bowels of the Brno earth and emerged into a dimly lit room reminiscent of a long curved roof tunnel forty to fifty yards long, a veritable cavern. From what Tom could make out in the dim light it was made entirely of red brick, although no doubt in a brighter light the bricks would be heavily coated with a thick nicotine stain. At one end of the tunnel stretching for half its length was the dance floor, compacted with a mass of swaying bodies exhibiting their style to what was now even louder music – a mixture of Czech and western popular music. There were more packed tables taking up most of the end of the tunnel into which Tom and Petr had descended. While desperately trying not to spill his beer and with a shouted, "come on, Tom, this way," Petr led him through the gyrating bodies on the dance floor and up more stairs to yet another bar, the atmosphere of which was decidedly more smoke than air. In fact as they started to make their way up the dozen or so stairs Tom's attention was immediately drawn to what seemed like a layer of smog resting on top of the slightly clearer air below. It was like a cloud sitting on the top of a mountain, although he was sure this was not going to be an as clear and refreshing an experience on his lungs. He definitely wouldn't be standing at that 'Charlie's summit' taking deep breaths of the clear fresh air around him. At every part of this new underground treasure that Petr had brought him to Tom's eye was caught by good looking women, young and not so young. The drinking, dancing, having a good time clientele were overwhelmingly women. At one point Tom shouted in Petr's ear above the loud music in the lower bowels of the club as they struggled, pushed and weaved their way across the packed dance floor, "Where are all the men? Why are there so many women?" To which Petr's only response was, "are you complaining Tom? It's always like this here. I have no idea why. I'm only a sociologist, my friend. I don't understand people or society, least of all Czechs." Said, of course, with irony and a grin and followed by, "of course if you really want to go to a place where the women outnumber the men overwhelmingly, even more so than this, you should go to Aloha a couple of streets from here. But you should go there much earlier in the evening. Between seven and nine o'clock is usually best."

"What's Aloha?" Tom instantly asked.

"It's a cocktail bar Tom," Petr shouted to his friend above the almost deafening music and through the thickening smog.

"I don't do cocktails," was Tom's snapped reply.

"Neither do Czech men, Tom, that's the point. They drink pivo, only beer, Tom," Petr told him through his broad smile. "But Czech women do. The place is always full from around seven till nine o'clock, full of Czech women and virtually no men."

Logging Aloha in his memory bank for a future early evening visit Tom's introduction to the place owing its name to the baggy trousered one's headgear stretched to around three a.m. Then finally, after much staring and a couple of futile attempts by Tom at conversation with women, they staggered and swayed out of a still throbbing and buzzing packed Charlie's. A place that Tom was certain he would return to again and again on his visits to Brno.

"Yep," he told his Czech friend as they surfaced into the clearer, quieter Czech night air on the street outside, "you were right, Petr. I am now officially a Charlie's addict."

"Just got to introduce you to Livingstone's now then, Tom, and you will have been to the best two clubs in Brno."

"What, now? It's three in the morning, Petr."

"No, not now, Tom. We'll save Livingstone's for another night, but I'll need to take you or you'll never find it even though it's only just on the other side of Náměsti Svobody. And the toilets there are an even better 'experience' than in Charlie's, my friend, although so is the beer."

"Dobrou noc, Tom, or as you English say, good night,, Petr bid him as he helped his friend out of their taxi with a gentle push at the entrance to Tom's hotel. "I will pick you up at nine in the morning and take you to the Faculty."

"Oh great," Tom muttered as he swayed into reception, "probably manage five hours sleep. That'll make me feel nice and fresh for a day of Czech academia."

7
The seventy-two year-old man and the seventeen year-old girl – can't wait to be old!

"So, Tom, this is Lenka. She will show you around the Faculty while I have my meeting. I should be finished by eleven-thirty. Look after him well, Lenka, treat him gently. This morning he is a little delicate from too much Czech hospitality last night and an introduction to Charlies."

It was nine-thirty and just minutes before these introductions by Petr and the passing over of Tom to his guide for the morning the Englishman was struggling somewhat with a Czech beer laden stomach. Struggling with that and with his throbbing head and his eyes, which appeared determined to close up completely. Tom had managed to hide the disobedience of his eyes by employing his sunglasses, which as it was a bright sunny Brno morning did not seem unusual. Although inside the Faculty he had drawn a few strange glances, as well as a whispered, "bad head?" question accompanied by a smile from Petr as they entered the building. "Don't worry," the Czech added, "I have something, or rather someone, who will cure that hangover for you and wake you up. Your eyes will be open wide in a few minutes believe me."

Tom wasn't sure what the hell he meant. All he could think of was that he had managed to gulp down two cups of coffee at what passed for breakfast in the hotel before Petr arrived. Now he realised just what his friend was on about. Lenka was the special Czech kind of paracetomol which Petr had told him a few minutes earlier would cure his headache and the rest of his hangover. Lenka was a twenty-four year old Ph.D. student of Petr's. Bloody charming, Tom thought as his eyes tried to widen. He removed his sunglasses and smiled. Attempting for the moment to ignore the searing, aching pain in his temples on the side of his head he ventured, "Dobry den, I'm very pleased to meet you."

"I've heard so much about you and your work," the increasing in charm by the second Lenka replied.

"Oh, I'm sure Petr has flattered me far too much. Exaggerated," Tom protested. Petr, meanwhile stood behind his student, just out of her vision, grinning broadly over her shoulder at Tom's instant recovery and adding a wry, "yes, I probably have." His hangover cure prescription seemed to be working, although Petr asked Lenka to get Tom some more coffee to help his hangover before she took him off on his tour of the Faculty, adding, "Although I'm not sure he needs it so much now. He seems to be immediately improving."

Once Lenka had left his office to get the coffee a still grinning broadly Petr couldn't resist a "well, there you are an instant Czech hangover cure. We should bottle it and market it. We would be Czech Krown millionaires don't you think? You see what a good friend I am to you."

Tom could only protest, "yes, but you've only given me two hours with her."

"But, Tom," Petr interrupted, "I've seen you at work in Liberec last December remember? Normally I wouldn't leave the poor girl with you for two minutes let alone two hours, but I have to go to my meeting." With that he once again apologised for having to go and left his office just as Lenka returned.

Lenka was quite tall, around five foot eight or nine. Slim, delicately slim was the category Tom would put her in. He always seemed to have 'categories', although he was never quite sure what he really meant by them. They were just expressions of his perceptions and impressions for his own benefit really. Lenka's immediate impression on him was one of gentle charm. Her slimness was nevertheless exhibited in a nice, well-proportioned figure. Her hair was bobbed and very dark, framing a pair of big deep dark brown eyes and a seemingly quite natural - so natural that she didn't appear to have the slightest clue she was doing it – pout across her slightly pale rouged lips. Her lips were those that immediately look soft and barely kissed. The clothes she wore were not those of a well off, or even a reasonably well off person. After all she was a student. Nevertheless, those she was wearing were very simple and quite elegant in a certain fashion. One thing she didn't look was cheap. She had on a short-sleeved black silk-like - although it obviously wasn't – blouse and a mid-calf length dark grey skirt. The slight mascara lining her eyes highlighted their sparkling clarity perfectly. She exuded a wide-eyed innocence and yet a worldly charm. Tom immediately realised that she was very intelligent. Even their brief introduction had told him for instance that her English was excellent. For some reason he found the whole 'package' was magically wrapped up by her Czech-English accent. She had that overall effect of charm, elegance and an innocent beauty that instantly reminded him of Jana. For him that was so peculiarly Czech. He fleetingly wondered if this was how Jana was at twenty-four.

Apologising profusely for it being from a machine she gave him the coffee, which he gulped down gratefully before they set off on his tour. They spent two hours together, although in fact only about thirty minutes were spent showing Tom around. The faculty was a new building that was, "opened", as Lenka put it, "less than two years ago." There was quite a lot of light grey stark concrete, although it was a much more modern looking, open, airy and bright building with a large amount of glass than the grey soul-less socialist realist monstrosities of the communist era that Tom had seen more than his fair share of in Czechoslovakia and other parts of East and Central Europe in the past. From what Lenka showed him and told him it had, "all the latest and most modern facilities and technologies." She showed him a couple of the lecture theatres that exhibited a good amount of sunlight streaming through the large windows that stretched almost from floor to ceiling. This particular feature gave her the chance to demonstrate the automatic modern electronic operation of the window blinds, something she was particularly proud of it seemed. Tom had to admit it was a darn site more modern, light, student and lecturer 'friendly' and conducive to study than most of the lecture theatres in which he was required to try and 'educate the masses' back at his UK university. In fact, although he definitely thought it he luckily restrained himself from commenting to Lenka that, "it pisses all over the sort of shit-hole I am expected to try and lecture in back in England." Maybe she wouldn't quite appreciate that sort of comment, or that in fact it was a compliment to her university. All in all though he quickly came to the conclusion early on in his tour that this was a very nice environment in which to work or study. Light, open, clean, modern and full of seemingly keen, friendly students and people, not to mention of course some stunningly beautiful young female students. Most Czech students studied for five years from eighteen. Except for a very small minority they all went on to do a Master's degree immediately after their Bachelor degree. So some of these lovely girls that he feasted his eyes on throughout his faculty tour with Lenka were in fact women and could have been twenty-two or twenty-three.

They 'did' the library. It was a little sparse, although at least there were now books on show and accessible to students, unlike in the past in Czechoslovak libraries before 1989 with no books to be seen and the process of ordering them from index cards at least two or three days in advance. Then he was shown the 'computer centre' as Lenka described it and as it was labelled on the door. It was really just a room with around twenty or so computers in it, each machine furiously occupied by seemingly keen students. For some reason beyond Tom's comprehension towards the end of his thirty-minute whistle-stop tour he was shown the Faculty Administration office. He was afraid his clear lack of interest in the Faculty administration might have shown, not only to the office staff but also to his guide, although he did manage to remark, "intensely interesting," as they left the office. This was met with a slight smile across her lips and, "you are not really that interested are you," delivered in a very Czech matter of fact way. Tom had come to understand that for the Czechs such a remark was merely a case of let's not waste time, let's be straightforward about it, be blunt even, although not exactly rude. Before he could answer Lenka suggested, "Let's go for another coffee. There's a quite nice cafe across the road, and we can get out of the Faculty for a while at the same time." Although he was by now almost swimming in the 'dark black stuff' Tom quickly agreed, not wishing to give up any chance of the full two hours of the charming female company present given to him by his friend Petr.

"So, tell me about yourself," he asked as he stirred into his coffee his second lump of what he thought was badly needed energising sugar.

"Well, I'm in the second year of my thesis on the sociology of business development and management techniques in Brno," Lenka replied. "It's looking at the changes in business management and business management culture being made here in companies in Brno after 1989 and in preparation hopefully for the Czech Republic to join the European Union."

"That sounds interesting," Tom offered, despite thinking anything but and that he was now heading up a blind alley. To ask more about it would probably bring even more boring information and definitely not the direction he wanted the conversation to go in at all, especially with his still slight headache. But not to ask more would be rude. He really meant his, "so tell me about yourself," question to be answered with more personal rather than academic information. In the event he settled for, "what will you do with that thesis when you finish?" Trying to find out what she thought the future would hold for her and hoping that would bring her on to more personal stuff.

"I'll go into business management in one of the newly developing enterprise sectors, maybe in Brno, maybe in Prague. But only for a couple of years and then I definitely want to start my own business, working for myself, probably a management consultancy." She was very definite and clear about what the future would hold for her. There was not a doubt in her mind it seemed.

This was a very single-minded, determined twenty-four year old; charming, intelligent, bright and beautiful in a stylish sort of way, determined and very, ambitious. For a fleeting moment he caught himself picturing her in about six years' time as she approached thirty and in a tight black short-skirted business suit, white shirt open to the cleavage, and big padded shoulders. Now he was having great difficulty through the distraction of this vision, and his lingering dull hangover headache, in motivating his supposed academic brain that he was trying to intellectually engage and at the same time maintain concentration. He found her very sexy even now. Christ knows what she will be like at thirty, he thought.

Without engaging his brain he blurted out, "you are a very intelligent and good looking woman, Lenka. There must be lots of Czech boys chasing you?"

Initially she was taken aback. No doubt thinking where did that come from? They were talking about her academic position and future career prospects and suddenly Tom had thrown into the conversation something very personal, something someone might find very intrusive, especially someone as sensitive as he took her to be. She paused, looked a little strange at him, and then smiling replied, "oh yes, Petr told me about you."

What the bloody hell does that mean he thought, but before he could think of just how to respond she continued. "He was joking with me I think." Her eyes seemed to open even wider and an inquisitive look came over her face. "Petr told me be careful of him, Lenka. He is a charmer."

No, surely his friend wouldn't do that to him having sent her as a 'charming guide gift' to him. Now he was really confused, but while he was still bemused at how to respond she carried on.

"He warned me about your English charm, your, how do you say, your golden tongue?"

Tom stammered, "err, it's err ... silver tongue actually, but I get the point." Just as he was about to try to extricate himself verbally – although at that moment he hadn't a clue how - from what he thought was an extremely embarrassing situation, he noticed she was grinning from ear to ear. He realised she wasn't offended at all by any of this, wasn't even embarrassed by it. In fact, she seemed to take it as a huge complement. Just as many other Czech women he'd met had. It wasn't a problem for them. They liked it, even got upset if you didn't flatter them and flirt with them. Not like English women. They wouldn't have taken it quite like that at all. It would have been something more on the lines of, "you patronising git," and a slap round the face, and if you really picked the wrong one your balls would have been ritualistically cut off and mashed up in front of you.

With Lenka there was no such problem and she went on to try and answer Tom's question. "Well yes, some Czech boys do chase me, but they are just stupid boys. Unfortunately most Czech males are boys, even when they are older, even when they are in their thirties, at least those that are not drunks by then. I prefer men, older men. Although I have to say I haven't really been out with many. I just find them easier and more interesting to talk to."

The temptation did briefly cross Tom's by now very attentive brain, but fortunately he dismissed it. Don't even consider it old man, he told himself. Even if she's sincere, it just wouldn't be a very clever or good thing to do. She's Petr's Ph.D. student for Christ's sake. To leap in at such a seemingly blatant opportunity and ask her to dinner would just not be wise, and Petr would certainly not be happy. This was definitely one of his students, unlike the biochemistry student in Charlie's the previous evening and after all Petr had even warned him off her.

"For some people it is strange, not normal," she continued, "although for many Czechs it is accepted more I think than in other countries like England, for instance. But I find older men fascinating, more interesting, more worldly-wise and experienced, and definitely more romantic I feel. I don't see what's wrong with that. It's the way I feel, and why shouldn't I? Is that very wrong?" Her voice was now firm and raised in a kind of self-defensive fashion.

"No, no, not at all," Tom agreed, although finding this a total agony, torture. He never realised that he had such self-control, such willpower to refrain from jumping in with both feet and even ask her for an evening drink.

"There is a story in this part of southern Moravia, a romantic legend, a fairy tale? I'm not sure how you describe it in English," she continued.

This time Tom didn't correct her or help her out with her English. He didn't really care what she called it or how it was described in English. He was transfixed and was not about to interrupt her as she continued, "it is about a seventy-two year old man, an artist, a painter who falls in love with and pursues his seventeen-year-old model. He woos her. I think that is how you would say it?" Tom, mesmerised, could only vacantly nod. "Constantly, romantically he woos her. Eventually she falls deeply, deeply in love with his charm, with his intelligence and with his artistic talent. After they are together for six years, inseparable and deeply in love with each other, the artist dies. The girl, now twenty-three, is totally distraught. Her life is suddenly completely empty without him. It has no meaning and no future. According to the story she lives the rest of her life of sixty more years deeply in love with him and his memory. She never loves or goes with anyone else. She feels that she found real true love with the artist and can never ever love another. Any other love or relationship would be meaningless for her. I think it's a beautiful story don't you, Tom?"

As she finished the story and expressed just how she felt about it Lenka's voice lowered almost to a whisper and she fixed on Tom's eyes with a piercing stare. All he could do was gulp visibly and think crudely, Christ she is even a romantic. Some lucky bastard Czech guy is eventually going to get all this for himself. Hope he appreciates it more than his beer!

"Yes, that is very lovely," was all he could pathetically think to say to her, barely able to get the words out of his mouth.

"Yes, I really think so," was her calm, almost serene reply with her eyes still staring firmly into his face.

Tom decided that if he'd 'read' this correctly and this really was a 'come on' then he had passed the test with flying colours unfortunately. A few years ago he would have jumped straight in. He didn't know though whether to be pleased with himself for his self-restraint, or whether to be sad that he seemed to have lost the urge and was beginning to realise and feel his age. Petr had warned him of the demographic divide in the Czech Republic. Not only were women of Lenka's age, and up to thirty, particularly unimpressed by most Czech men but they also outnumbered them by around three to one. In some cities it was seven or eight to one at the present time. Tom thought that he vaguely remembered Petr telling him one beery, memory-clouded night when they first met in Liberec that Brno was one of those cities. Not surprisingly though his recollection was somewhat foggy on that. He did recall more clearly that Petr had told him that for women in academia after they reached twenty-six there was very little chance of meeting a suitable Czech male. His Czech sociologist friend had explained that it was a known fact that most people meet their future marriage partners in work. In Czech academia, however, most of the men were old, sometimes very old, professors. Or at least the personnel in Faculties were heavily biased in that direction age-wise.

His recollection of that 'research' information which Petr had communicated to him over Liberec pivo was interrupted by Lenka's reminder that Tom was supposed to be meeting him now. Lenka brought him back to reality with, "we'd better go back to the Faculty and find Petr. He will think I have kidnapped you."

Chance would be a fine thing, he thought. In the current morose state that her romantic story, and as far as he was concerned her advances, had brought him to he would probably have ended up suggesting a game of dominoes or cards rather than anything he hoped she might have in mind. An event that had perked him up and put his clouded hangover head in the bright clear sunny clouds of optimism a few hours earlier - being introduced to Lenka - now ended by bringing him down to earth with a bump. "It's the hope that kills you, mate," he could hear his friend Steve reminding him in his head. Somehow, the charming, lovely young Lenka had inadvertently made him very, very aware of his age and mortality. She had made a happy man feel very old. Although he consoled himself with the thought that maybe all he had to do was wait until he was seventy-two, come back to Brno and take up art. "Bound to find a lovely seventeen year old then," he murmured. At least that thought raised a chuckle inside him.

8
The Brno early evening and the time of day he both loved and hated

Another two-and-a-half hour lunch with Petr. More fatty pork and dumplings covered with the sort of deep dark brown thick greasy gravy that struggles to move about on the plate, and of course all washed down with a couple of Czech beers in the smoky faculty cafeteria. One more meeting with the Dean of the Faculty followed, but thankfully only to exchange pleasantries otherwise Tom would definitely have struggled to stay awake if anything remotely resembling academia had been involved. Then by four-thirty he was back out on the streets of Brno heading back to his hotel. He strolled through the expansive open space that was the very pleasant square in front of the university's medicine and music faculties, Komenského náměstí, pausing briefly to admire the imposing statue of T.G. Masaryk, the first President of Czechoslovakia, after whom the university was named. Masaryk was someone whose spirit, willingness and courage to write and express unpopular views directed against Czech myths and prejudices during the time of Habsburg rule over the Czechs was seen as an example to future generations of Czechs.

The square was almost in the centre of the city and yet it felt very open with plenty of trees in full leaf. It gave off a real feeling of light and space, especially on what was a lovely sunny late spring afternoon. The strong bright sunlight, the fresh air, and the impression of space was an immediate vivid stark contrast to the tobacco brown stained walls and ceiling and the thick smoky atmosphere of the faculty cafeteria. The square was full of people passing through it and across it to their many mid-afternoon destinations. A large number of them were students scurrying to their classes or to the university libraries, or just sitting on the low walls round fountains or on the few benches with their books. The procession of trams rumbled their way through the centre of the square constantly disturbing the silent relaxed feeling.

The Czech early starts were beginning to take their toll on him though. He thought briefly about going straight back to his hotel for a nap. Refresh himself for the evening's task of exploring Brno's Thursday nightlife, after all he'd have to check out if it was any different to Wednesday's. However, he couldn't resist what he'd come to know as the late afternoon Czech cafe society and its seemingly unique atmosphere, with its groups of people chatting over coffee after work. It seemed like a tradition. Rather than the beer and the pub of the English the Czechs went to the cafe. He'd go back for a sleep in an hour or so he decided, but firstly find a nice cafe.

Sitting outside one in a street just off the square he decided that it was that time of day that he both loved and hated. It was especially poignant when it heralded the fall of the cloak of dusk late on an autumn or winter afternoon, and somehow, for some reason, Saturday afternoons always had an even more magical feel. This though was late spring or early summer and not Saturday but Thursday. There was not the same chill in the air. He was sitting outside in the still warm sunshine and not inside with its very traditional dark wooden tables and chairs, its wood-panelled walls and its big picture windows onto the street, not to mention its obligatory intensely smoky atmosphere. There was not the same autumn and winter creeping cold crispness or the same warm gratification of being inside peering out at the passers-by through some slightly misted up large cafe window. Not quite the same late autumn afternoon self-satisfaction of mooching around a small bookshop dipping into different books that took his fancy, but that he knew he would never read even if he bought them. The act of browsing through them made him feel academically pure though. It helped convince him that he was still interested in new ideas, new arguments and new information, new to him anyway. It was a kind of self-satisfying, self-gratifying even, comfort blanket. Academic and intellectual masturbation at its most refined.

Despite it being a different time of year from his autumnal comfort blanket there was still a pleasant glowing feel to it. It was an atmosphere that he felt in most cities after around four in the afternoon. For some reason it was always a different much deeper warmer glow in the cities of Central Europe he visited. He couldn't explain it, couldn't put it into words very well. It was after all a feeling. It never lasted very long, just those fleeting couple of hours at that certain time of the day in the late afternoon and early evening. It was a very personal experience, a personal thing. It provided memories only he knew; memories that only he would recall and share with himself. They evoked an even stronger feeling when they were memories of that time of day spent in the company of a special woman – in a cafe, or just strolling through the streets or browsing in a bookshop.

That was what he loved about that time of day, how it made him feel good. Warm and self-satisfied, smug even, in a peculiar sort of way. It was a kind of self-contentment. All was right with the world and he had no worries. Yet simultaneously he could hate this time. Just when he had convinced himself he was enjoying it alone it seemed that everywhere around him there were couples enjoying that time of day together, enjoying the comfort of being engulfed in one another. Everywhere there were women walking with their arm tucked inside their man's. Or they were sitting in cafes smiling and pecking one another's cheek, or just sitting and gazing into one another's eyes and holding hands. They seemed just glad to be together and in one another's company. They were so completely at one with each other. He saw it at other times of course, but at this time, and in Central European cities, it seemed even more intense and even more commonplace. Maybe it just drew his attention to his own lack of a partner to squeeze and hug, or to peck on the cheek at that particular time on those fast fading Saturday afternoons. Maybe it just spotlighted even more the gap in his life. Conversely, the spotlight and that gap always seemed to grow stronger and fiercer as the daylight faded and dusk descended. A period when the warmth, glow and comfort of the time of day needed to be shared in order to experience it fully. Anyway that is what he told himself. Only very,

very rarely though – a few times with Dita – had his actually been the hand being squeezed or the cheek being pecked.

His alarm went off at seven. When he got back to his room he decided he'd read for a while before a nap. His reading lasted about fifteen minutes and then he'd dozed for around an hour-and-a-half. Instead of doing as he usually did, rolling over for another fifteen minutes, he roused himself straight away for a shower, a shave, and a clean, as yet unused on the trip pale blue shirt. "Dita always preferred me in a light blue shirt. What will Jana prefer next Wednesday?" he wondered as he checked himself out in his hotel room mirror, followed quickly by, "well, Tom, old mate, next Wednesday is next Wednesday and this is this Thursday, and time for a night out in downtown Brno."

By just after seven-thirty he was striding out of the lift, across the lobby and out into the still quite bright and warm Brno early evening sunlight. His first thought was to get some food inside him. Take the precaution of putting something in his stomach to soak up the possible impending alcohol just in case it turned out to be a long night. From his past experience of nights out in Czech cities there could be a lot of bar and club-hopping ahead. That could mean a lot of beers. So, food was an essential prerequisite. Mash potatoes would be ideal, but unlikely in Brno or virtually anywhere in the Czech Republic. So, in true trashy out on the town drinking session tradition he aimed straight for the 'Golden Arch' and the 'big M'. A 'Big Mac' and a large fries later he was belching his way across Náměstí Svobody.

Only eight o'clock, still a bit early to start boozing he thought. He was usually a late starter when it came to drinking on a night out, preferring not to get stuck into the beers much before nine if he could help it. Then again he was also invariably a late finisher too, or often an early morning finisher. "Yep, definitely too early," he muttered, "especially in this country, where the serious drinking doesn't seem to get off the ground, or onto the bar stool for that matter, until the early hours way past midnight." He settled instead for an early evening stroll and taking in some of the sights and buildings of what appeared to be a pleasant enough city. Maybe a coffee or two in one of the pavement cafes if it stayed warm enough? That would pass away an hour or so.

Brno was now in that twilight time, the time when in most city centres the workers had almost all made their way home and left their offices and shops. Meanwhile the drinkers and party animals had not yet arrived in large enough numbers to take up occupation of the city centre. It was a strange, empty time, but one that he again always found very pleasant.

Tom's mind was miles away, feeling very smug, pure and pleased with his philosophical self-musing on the finer points of life when he was rudely awakened to the fact that not everyone wasn't working in that twilight world he'd conjured up.

"Sex, you want sex?"

In broken English it was the phrase of the international language of sex.

"Oh Christ, is that the standard issue phrase to every prostitute in the Czech Republic?" he voiced straight into what were very young girl's eyes. Having seemingly exhausted her English vocabulary she now looked extremely perplexed by Tom's reply. Although she understood his facial expression enough to know that he was less than happy and certainly would not be taking up her offer.

Through his wanderings and self-obsessed musings quite without realising he'd strolled onto the edge of the Brno red light district and into a very different kind of twilight world. The early evening 'street girls' were out plying their trade, largely to the very few passing motorists. There were three of them. Their combined age would have been pushed to reach fifty. Looking very thin and with clothes that were decidedly downmarket they hardly cut an attractive proposition. How could they possibly ever get any 'business', Tom wondered. Nevertheless, one of them, with quite bright obviously dyed blonde hair, was engaged in some bartering, leaning into the passenger window of a very battered looking old Skoda. Her arse, barely covered by her very short white skirt, was cocked up strategically, arched almost at right angles to the top of her body and her rigidly locked at the knees long high-heeled legs. She at least was obviously attracting some attention, not only from her potential customer but also from the very few pedestrians passing by, now including Tom.

Tom politely declined the offer from her fellow worker. "No, no, děkuji," he told her, even politely including a Czech thank you.

Undeterred she renewed her offer. "Very, very good sex," and on seeing Tom's gaze at the cocked arse leaning in the Skoda window somewhat to his surprise she extended her English vocabulary adding, "nice arse. You can have two if you like, sisters, very young, for only two thousand."

Two thousand Czech Krowns, about fifty quid. Quite a good deal, Tom fleetingly calculated, although with no intention whatsoever of taking up the offer. Well, a good deal in monetary terms anyway if not in quality, definitely not in quality. These were street urchin girls. No doubt as dirty as hell he reckoned, and he wasn't referring to their sexual experience. The financial attractiveness of the deal came with 'conditions' and consequences that he thought could be lethal. Despite his initial thoughts on who on earth would ever take up the offer of sex with these three particular specimens of humanity even he was realistic enough to know that some low life punters would have done so, thereby contributing all sorts of concoctive diseases to these girls' particular 'fluidic' mixture. After all they hardly gave off an effervescence of Chanel, let alone looked as if they had seen anything that passed for soap in some time.

Two out of the three were very dark in complexion, even allowing for what Tom took to be a lack of soap. He guessed they were Romany. Judging by the very dark rings around the eyes of the one trying to engage Tom in a deal it definitely looked as if substances other than natural ones, or those from their clients, had entered their bodies. The one propositioning Tom had on what he took to be the standard uniform for her trade, a very cheap, brittle looking plastic short coat. All three of them exhibited their thin, less than attractive spindly legs to the ultimate limit, covered only very marginally by a handkerchief-size passing impression of a skirt. The girl offering her services to Tom was probably no more than fourteen or fifteen he reckoned. Her hair was dark black, very long and very matted. It was obviously her turn to wear the shiny black plastic coat that night. Not easily deterred she continued to attempt to block his path, and then began to rub with her hands what appeared to be very small excuses for tits – obviously not yet fully developed – through her grubby black T-shirt underneath her plastic coat. This process was accompanied by further words of encouragement informing Tom that they were, "very, very nice, and very good." Not that nice, not that good and not plastic tat, thank you very much, Tom reasoned. With that thought he briskly finally dodged past her and headed off back in the direction from which he had come, contemplating that particular social aspect of the brave new free world in the Czech Republic five years after the 1989 'Velvet Revolution'.

A glance at his watch told him it was now just gone eight-thirty. Sod the coffee I need a beer he decided. Darkness was now beginning to descend on downtown Brno and the party go-ers were coming out of their darkened rooms and onto the city streets. It was still quite pleasantly warm. Warm enough to sit at one of the lit up pavement cafes and watch the world go by, with hopefully some members of it wearing an excuse for a skirt, high heels and sticking their chest out, although preferably not street prostitutes. This wasn't Italy though, where he knew from experience that you can sit for hours at a street cafe watching the superb passeggiata, or at least the female part of it. Nevertheless, Brno had its moments and a quite considerable number of its female inhabitants could hold their own in the 'sticking out of chests and bums' and 'exhibiting long legs' stakes.

Strolling down the main street, Česká, through the centre of the city he passed an Irish pub. Every city, everywhere in the world must have one now, it's globalisation he jokingly reasoned. A Ronnie MacDonalds and Rosie O'Shaginans, or some sort of similarly named Irish alehouse, in every city. This particular one, labelled Molly Malone's, didn't exactly look full of Irish men or of flame-haired Irish women for that matter. Even in a down-market, spit and sawdust sort of way it didn't look particularly inviting or salubrious. Tom declined and strolled on.

Unusual that, usually it was the sort of place he would have dived into without a second thought, downed six pints of Irish beer and staggered out two or three hours later farting and belching, convinced he was immediately attractive to every bloody woman in the world. Convinced that all he would have to do was smile at them and they would come running.

He was still very sober now though. No drink had yet passed his lips that evening and it was nearly nine o'clock. So, he headed for a street cafe back in Náměstí Svobody and settled for a medium beer – medium for the Czechs was about a pint, large was at least a litre – whilst surveying the world passing by and contentedly musing on his reasonable state of calm contemplation. Indeed, soon after he sat down it struck him that Náměstí Svobody - Freedom Square in English - was itself a Czech and Brno conundrum. It wasn't a square at all. More of a triangle than a square, but little details like that never bothered the Czechs.

Perhaps his calmness was due to the fact that he kept reminding himself that his meeting with Jana was now less than a week away. Less than a week to work out a strategy yes, but also less than a week to what he hoped would be the start of something different in his life. A new perspective and everything in his life would be calm after that. No more of this chasing around searching for something special. He would have something special, Jana. No more looking for hope, looking for signs. He wouldn't need to because he would have the reality of being with Jana. He decided that it was all this that filled him with this new found inner serenity. Not a phrase that he often, if ever, associated with himself. He was much more likely to usually be filled with some mixture of alcoholic liquids when he came to ponder his life and various romantic disasters. For now at least though, just like many elements of the country of the post-1989 Czech Republic he was in, he was filled with optimism and hope for a brighter future.

9
The 'Titanic' of romantic disasters

While he was trawling through his forlorn past history with women Tom's calm optimism was shattered by thoughts that entered his head about his greatest romantic disaster, Sandra. She'd been a mature student, starting her degree at thirty-two. Although studying at his university in England she wasn't a student of his, and virtuously and professionally he could hold his hands up and say truthfully nothing had occurred between them while she was studying. It had only been after she'd graduated that he bumped into her one evening in a pub in 1984, by which time she was thirty-six, two years younger than him. Besides her brain of course her best attributes were her shoulder length curly black hair and tight little arse. Like many women of that age in the mid to late 1980s, especially married women and single parents, she had returned to education once her younger years had passed. For various reasons these women had never pursued higher education in their youth. They either got married young or got pregnant young. Many of them became either pissed off with their husbands or with their life in general, or both. Seeking new interests, new challenges, they returned to education looking for access to knowledge and an opening up of their minds.

Sandra was one of those women, and she also fitted the pattern of Tom's women perfectly. The women he had become romantically entangled with - shortish, five foot four, emotionally erratic, irrational, completely unpredictable, and indecisive, totally unable to make a decision until circumstances forced it upon her. Once he got to know her he realised, or assumed, some of these traits were due to her 'little habit'. She found it difficult, if not impossible, to let even one night go by without a joint to put her to sleep. She told him she loved him right enough, but this was usually only after the combination of a joint and an orgasm. Love, for Sandra, meant need, her need. Why the fuck, how the fuck, did I ever get involved with her he wondered with a wry grin and a shake of his head as he sat in the street café in that Brno square in the middle of Europe. Maybe he had just supplied the answer from his own mouth – a fuck. It wasn't even a question of whether or not she was a good fuck. It was just a question of a fuck. It was there, so he was there. Although searching for some self-justification he reasoned she was very attractive, her darkish complexion perfectly set off by her curly black hair. She also always had some sort of a tan, although not that garish orange that many women got from a bottle or an overused sun lamp. Sandra's always looked more natural and generally it was, and her figure was good, a nice firm body, Tom recalled. It was her personality, no doubt related to her 'little habit', along with the baggage of her ex-husband that was the problem.

Like many of the women of that age who had returned to education at that time once she had graduated Sandra was left with nowhere to go, except back to the home, which she obviously resented intensely. Not least, because her home was also inhabited by her real dickhead of a husband. Having been married to him for what must have been twelve excruciating years, by the time she reached her early thirties she was well and truly over him. She had definitely outgrown him mentally. Not difficult that though since he had all the intelligence of a block of wood. Once Sandra had graduated she was cured of the particular form of 'stupidity disease' that the dickhead dispensed liberally verbally to any audience he could capture. He was a 'gonna be', as Tom labelled that particular type, a real 'Del boy', full of hair-brained schemes, although definitely without the charm or wit of 'Del'. He was a worker alright, "a grafter," as Sandra would always tell Tom. He couldn't be faulted in that respect according to her. It was just that whatever he did, whatever he turned his hand to, he simply trod water, and sometimes came very close to drowning. He always spent more on the outlay of his wonderful scheme than it was possible to make in profit. He didn't have any clue whatsoever that the words budget and costing existed, let alone their meaning. So long as at the end of the day – usually in the pub in front of what he thought was an interested audience – he could stand there with a wad of twenty pound notes in his hand it didn't matter that all the bills still had to be paid out of that cash. It made him, Dave was his name, feel important and he could boast about being successful to anyone daft enough to listen. That was what he got off on, made himself feel good. That was his 'little habit', although from what Tom heard he also had a similar 'little habit' to Sandra's and at times a considerably stronger one that shared its nickname with the black fizzy drink Tom usually mixed with his Jack Daniels.

Tom had only come across the future millionaire twice, completely by chance after he started seeing Sandra and a year after she'd finally managed to divorce the waste of space. Not surprisingly, from what he had already heard from Sandra about him, Tom took an instant dislike to the guy. It wasn't so much Dave as an individual that he disliked - although if he was honest it was also that - it was just the type that 'Del boy Dave' represented that he couldn't stand. Because he was self-employed he managed to wangle it so that he paid no tax whatsoever. He always transacted in cash according to Sandra. Yet on the two occasions that Tom met him Dave was only too ready to pontificate on the lack of government spending on the NHS and on education. He pointed out that, "his kids deserved the best education." Presumably, as he knew that Tom worked in education he thought that would impress him. And of course, Dave couldn't resist outlining this very impressive scheme that was going to make him, "extremely well off within the year." Tom could only respond with, "Better not tell the tax man then." A comment that went straight over 'Del boy's' head, if he even registered it at all as he was in full flow with his self-importance and out to impress approach at that point.

Initially his arrangement with Sandra suited Tom. She lived on her own with her three kids and wanted to take things slowly because of them. Increasingly though their relationship got more and more intense. Eventually the kids accepted him and he spent more and more time at her place. He felt more and more at ease, even comfortable with his life. Maybe, just maybe, this is it, he told himself. This'll do for me. For him it wasn't though a case of this is as good as it gets. For a while he thought this was better than it gets, perfect. He was happy, very, very happy.

Then after two years of being together, although not totally living together – she didn't want to yet, Tom was increasingly happy to – the nightmare final year began. Suddenly Sandra got the 'fear', fear of the impending menopause. It wasn't that she actually got it. But, as Tom came to cynically realise, like many women of that age she had decided that the proper procedure was that first she had to get herself completely worked up, fuck up her life and everyone else's around her, simply through the fear that one day she would get it. "After all," she was, "approaching forty," she would scream at Tom and he just, "didn't fucking understand." This would usually be followed by, "it's alright for you. You've been there, done it. What have I ever done? I want to be seen as an individual, as me, not as part of some fucking couple."

By the time her anger got to that point Tom knew that they would definitely not be a, "fucking couple," that night anyway. And he presumed that when she was screaming at him about him having, "been there," and, "done it," she wasn't referring to him and the menopause. Because of all this she decided that she, "needed space." It wasn't about shagging other people. It was just about, "being seen as an individual, having time for herself. Doing just what she wanted when she wanted."

As he took a rather large mouthful of his beer sitting outside the cafe in Náměstí Svobody he recalled being a bit confused by this last piece of logic. He always found that trying to rationally understand Sandra made him need to take a long large gulp of some sort of alcohol or other. After all, "he had given her loads of bloody space," he remembered screaming at her during one particularly vehement exchange of views. He rammed home his point with, "we don't even live together, but thirty miles apart for Christ's sake." As for the, "it wasn't about shagging other people," argument, well, he smugly smiled to himself as he took another gulp of his beer, strangely enough it turned out it was indeed about just that. It wasn't just that she did eventually go off and shag someone else, although that had devastated him, it was why couldn't she be honest about it? Honest about what she wanted to do. She'd always said that men couldn't help themselves. They just followed their dicks. Why couldn't she just admit that having been married for twelve years and faithful and then only after that been with Tom, she wanted to see what shagging was like with a few other people? It would still have hurt him of course, but at least she would have been honest about it and he would have known where he stood. He wouldn't have had to go through all the months of anguish and argument when she almost destroyed him each time she came back to him. That typified everything he found most contradictory, most frustrating, most annoying in Sandra. Her need to try always to morally justify everything she did in some way or other. She always needed to take the moral high ground.

Although if he was being completely honest to himself what pissed him off just as much, if not more, was that she eventually went off and first fucked a waiter, and a bloody German waiter at that! One who had unbelievably pushed a note through her letter box one night apparently, saying, "Fancy a drink sometime?" or the German equivalent no doubt of, "fancy a fuck?" She then went scurrying off to the cafe where he worked; supposedly, "just to see what he looked like," which even a blind German waiter could see meant, "eh up Fritz, get the towels down on the sunbeds I'm up for a shag here!" So, Tom had been well and truly fucked over for a German waiter. Sat now in the street cafe in Brno he recalled subsequently somewhat bizarrely recounting the story to an Irish barmaid late one night over a lonely pint in a bar in a small town in southern Italy. "A waiter? Hmm ... very classy!" was her sarcastic remark. Tom thought at the time blimey what does it mean Sandra must be like if even a barmaid in a no hope Irish bar in southern Italy takes the piss out of it as, "very classy." After all aren't barmaids supposed to go for waiters, especially Italian ones? Mind you, he remembered the barmaid did also offer sarcastically, "well, I suppose waiter service is better than self-service."

After the 'German front' episode Sandra had come scuttling back to him. Offering nothing that even carried a whiff of an apology of course. She didn't, "feel guilty," she told him. She had, "nothing to feel guilty about. After all they were on a break." The fact that Tom reckoned they'd made love eight days before she first went and shagged Fritz – pulled his 'Bratwurst' – didn't seem to matter to her. Does eight days constitute 'a break' Tom remembered thinking at the time? Obviously to Sandra it did because she had rationally convinced herself it was and that was all that mattered. Everyone else would just have to accept it and she could still feel pure and morally correct. Of course she would reinforce this reasoning with her cynical form of manipulation, such that Tom was usually left with an option that in fact left him no option but to agree to what she wanted all along. In the last throes of their relationship this was always accompanied with, "if you agree, Tom, it's your choice." A sort of 'Pontius Pilate' approach, only it was Tom who was the one getting crucified.

Even when she did eventually scuttle back to him and he surprisingly agreed to try again it was still to be on her terms and her conditions. Not least of course because she had nothing to feel guilty about according to her. That particular logic was beyond Tom, even beyond his supposed Ph.D. intellect. Anyway she still wanted and demanded her space. She would see him when she could, but she exclaimed, "She had a busy life." Just what precisely she thought other people with a job, home, kids, etc., had Tom never really fathomed out. He recalled thinking at the time ironically, Christ if everyone is so busy, as busy as Sandra, how the bloody hell do any relationships ever last or even get started? But there he went again, trying to think logically and rationally. A big, big mistake with Sandra, unless you first of all had her 'logic key', which meant knowing precisely what she really wanted all along and sod everyone else. Even then, even if you thought you had acquired her 'logic key', you still had to deal with her 'Pontius Pilate' impression.

He took one more swig to finish his beer as he thought about how their relationship stumbled on for another six months or so after the 'Fritz-shag' episode, and about her eventual revelation to him that, "she had made a big mistake," and wanted them to get back together. He began to wonder if this was just how he now remembered it all. Was this simply what he told himself about it now? Maybe this was just how he now rationalised his actions through it all, as the innocent party, but what if he wasn't he began to ask himself. What if it really was all his fault; some things that he did, or didn't do, to make her feel secure or insecure, sure or unsure about him?

Any fleeting thoughts in his mind about any of these doubts were quickly erased by a recollection of something Sandra had told him about Fritz, or whatever his real name was – Tom always referred to him as Fritz, which constantly managed to annoy her. Even after she had come scuttling back from her 'German period', Sandra still tried to defend Fritz. Not what had happened, but him as a person. After all she had to convince herself and others that he was a really sincere person or she could never have liked him and been with him. She had to convince everybody, including herself, especially herself, that Fritz was a suitable person for her to be with. Well, to shag at least anyway. This particular recollection of her defence of him to Tom always made him chuckle. This time was no different as he sat in the growing darkness of Náměstí Svobody. In fact this time it made him laugh so loudly that he drew strange looks and glances from the other customers seated nearby outside the cafe bar.

The source of his regular amusement was the great line that Fritz had so remarkably easily sold the so-called intelligent independent minded Sandra. Even when she repeated it to Tom after they had got back together she still apparently seemed completely convinced of it and of Fritz's sincerity. It went something like, with of course the German accent, "I am afraid of commitment because I was in a relationship before - it turned out that he had been in at least four over the previous two years and all with women in the same town that Sandra lived in, and often at the same time although he forgot to mention that - but I went off and slept with another woman which really hurt the woman I was in a relationship with and living with at the time. I don't want to do that again. I don't want to hurt someone again, so I am not looking for commitment." Err, doh! Tom remembered thinking and not being able to stop himself from saying when Sandra quite innocently it seemed relayed this particular 'pearl of wisdom' to him. Well, "Err doh!" and sarcastically applauding. That pissed her off no end.

"What's your problem, Tom? That too sensitive for you is it?" she glared at him.

"Too sensitive! Too fucking sensitive!" He couldn't stop himself laughing as he said it. "It's fucking brilliant! Brilliant! Must write that down," he told her sarcastically. "Who knows when it will come in handy?" Looking angrily straight into her eyes, trying not to lose it completely he spat out, "let me translate that for you Sandra. Not from the German, but from the female into the male."

But he was indeed rapidly losing it. He charged on full throttle into enemy territory, right through German enemy lines. "Hey, you say to a woman before you shag her, or maybe even as you are shagging her – who knows when is best, maybe we could consult our Blitzkrieg expert – you say, don't look to me for commitment, because I don't do commitment. Because I know I will only end up shagging someone else and hurting you in the process. So, I am only thinking of your feelings and caring deeply about you by not promising you commitment that I know I will not keep. See, I am a really caring, sensitive person, but I'd still like to shag you. So, can I get in your knickers now please?" Tom recalled that at that point he was actually laughing and holding his sides, and with a mixture of tears of laughter and anger streaming down his face. It was like Brezhnev sending the Soviet tanks into Czechoslovakia in 1968 because he was sensitive and cared about the Czechs and Slovaks so he didn't want to hurt them.

"Oh yeah! You would see it like that with your warped brain you insensitive bastard!" Sandra bawled at him. "Bloody typical! Not every man is like you, you know!"

"Oh, I know that full well, especially after what you've just told me," he stammered as he smothered a laugh deep in his throat. "It's obvious that's the case. This guy's fucking good, brilliant in fact. No wonder we always lose to them on penalties. He's technically superb, knows just where to place the ball, which corner of the female net to put it in. And you swallowed it, swallowed it hook, line and glockenspiel." She tried to respond, but he wasn't letting her in. He ploughed on voice raised and not giving an inch. "You are supposed to be a bloody intelligent woman. To Fritz you must have seemed like some bleedin' turkey voting for Christmas. You say to him, Sandra, 'I am an independent woman, with a busy life so I am not looking for a relationship,' and he says to you – no doubt rubbing his hands with glee or some other part of the wanker's anatomy – 'I don't do commitment, because being a sensitive, caring person I don't want to hurt you. So, I'm not looking for a relationship'. Fuck me I've won the lottery! he must have thought. The guy's a wanker, but a very good, first class wanker!" With that he stormed out of her house with only a parting, incisive shot of, "but you wouldn't see that Sandra because he is a manipulator. He made you feel that he was letting you decide what you want. Made you feel that it was your decision and so any consequences would be yours, and that's why you can't see it. He's a manipulator, just like you fucking are! Only he's even better at it than you because he's got 'vorsprung durch technique'!"

The nightmare romantic disaster that was Sandra drifted on, or rather galloped out of control at times, for a further three months until Tom finally realised he didn't need the anguish or the bloody madness of it all. It was like some very bad romantic comedy movie, or should that be 'black comedy' he thought now? Anyway, it definitely should have gone straight to video and not been released to the general public, or at least to Tom. He was finally convinced that he wasn't the problem, she was, and why did he need a problem like her? He decided eventually that she just wasn't worth it. He always thought now that his whole relationship with Sandra could be summed up by a couple of lines in a Cher song. The title eluded him, but it wasn't 'I got you babe', although for some reason he always remembered the lines. Maybe it was the pain, anguish and bloody waste of time of the whole 'Sandra roller-coaster' that made him remember, "so you feel misunderstood. Baby, have I got news for you. On being used, I could write the book." To think that at one point he'd been convinced that she was 'the one', that this was it. That being with her would do for him. Now just thinking about it put him into a cold sweat. "Phew, lucky escape," he muttered. Anyway he cut his losses and left her dangling. Where was she now? Who knows and who the fuck cares he thought as he tried to catch the eye of the somewhat evasive Czech waiter so as to get another now badly needed large Starobrno beer.

Bollocks to all that. Why the bloody hell am I wasting yet more of my life thinking about that mad cow while I'm sat here in this nice square on a lovely warm Brno night. In the end all that had done was make him angry, even now. What about Jana next Wednesday? That was a much more positive thought and a much more pleasant use of his brain and time. Although what to do about, and how to deal with the question of Dita, was perhaps not quite so pleasing on his brain. Just how was he going to get round to securing the emotions of the best friend of the woman he had spent months supposedly deeply in love with in Prague five years earlier? Tricky! Maybe he should employ the 'Sandra approach'. Employ the 'Sandra logic' and the 'Pontius Pilate' killer punch. Something like, well Jana, I love you deeply, and I realise you are Dita's best friend and that I definitely messed her up emotionally, but I love you in a different, more meaningful and caring way than I did her. But - and here comes Pontius – if you choose to love me and hurt your friend it will be your choice, not mine. So don't blame me, and Dita definitely can't blame me, because it will be your choice. Can't see that working, don't think I'll have much success with that approach. In his usual fashion he decided to put off trying to solve the difficult problem for a while longer. Best get stuck into a few more beers and maybe that will loosen up the thought processes. Maybe then a solution will magically appear through the powers of Starobrno. "Clever bloke like me must be able to figure out something. Surely I've learned something from my past experiences with women, especially Sandra," he told himself.

Tom's meandering thoughts were brought to an abrupt end by a voice from immediately behind his café chair and a firm hand placed on his right shoulder. "Your papers! Vere are your papers," boomed down on him in broken English. He straightened up from his relaxed slumped seated posture and for a miniscule moment the brief thought went through his mind of oh shit, you are supposed to carry your passport with you at all times and mine's in the hotel room. When he eventually dared to turn his head though, he saw Petr standing over him grinning widely.

"That worried you, my friend. I was just on my way home to my flat from a late night working in the Faculty and I thought I might find you hanging around here at this time looking at the short skirts, or rather what they are barely covering," the Czech goaded him.

Tom was beginning to think that Petr was getting to know him a little too well.

"So, how many is that?" he asked Tom, pointing to the newly delivered Starobrno beer.

"Oh, only my second and the previous one was only a medium one." Although why he found the need to be so defensive about it Tom was not really sure.

"Bloody hell, Tom, this is the Czech Republic. It's nine o'clock and you're only just starting your second beer. You will not make a very good Czech, my friend. You need some more practice." With that Petr waived his hand to beckon the reluctant waiter, ordered a large beer for himself and added, "Come on, old man, now I'll show you a Brno Thursday night."

Blimey Tom thought, is a Brno Thursday night likely to be much different from the Brno Wednesday night he had only just recovered from? He was determined it would be, certainly in terms of far less alcohol. "Not too many beers tonight please, Petr. I'm bloody tired," he pleaded to his friend. His somewhat unpleasant reflections on life with Sandra seemed to have brought back his tiredness and had rather diminished his desire to go chasing around bars in Brno with Petr looking at women.

10
A Brno Friday afternoon and reflection

Unfortunately Tom's optimistic plan of not too many beers was soon destroyed by Petr's enthusiasm. Although he did manage to limit his alcoholic consumption to five or six beers, he reckoned his Czech friend must have had around eight or nine. In reality Tom lost count as they drifted in and out of four, or was it five, very smoky Brno pubs and bars, the highlight of which was Livingstones. Yet another tucked away down a passageway club that you would never find if you didn't know it was there. Right in the centre of the city, just off Náměstí Svobody, but on the opposite side of the square to Charlies, Livingstones was more student orientated in its clientele. What Tom liked most about it though was the music the DJ played, predominantly from the 1960s and 1970s, together of course with the very cheap Starobrno beer. Although he was once again bemused as to quite what connection the Scottish explorer David Livingstone had with Brno, and when he asked Petr the response he got was just a look of total bewilderment that he should even think to ask such a question.

Livingstones though was a considerably much more dimly lit and darker place than Charlies, although unlike most of the clubs and bars Petr took him to in Brno it wasn't below ground. Its décor was a weird mixture of what appeared to be some African wooden sculptures and what to Tom looked merely like American Indian totem poles. Bizarrely there was an old wooden hand plough hanging from the ceiling in the middle of the club. Quite what that had to do with David Livingstone either Tom was unsure, although he did have some vague recollection that as well as being an explorer he might have been a Scottish farmer. He guessed it wasn't actually David Livingstone's own original plough though. The bar, which always seemed to be three or four deep with people trying to get a drink, ran all along the far wall from the entrance, but unlike Charlies which was a much narrower place, it was a good forty feet or so from the entrance door. Immediately to the left of the entrance was a raised wooden dance floor with a wooden hand rail that didn't seem to have one inch of it that was not taken up by glasses full of various forms of alcohol, while the dance floor itself was a constant jammed seething mass of gyrating bodies struggling to find room to exhibit any of their best moves. The floor of the whole place was wooden and covered from the evening's various forms of spilt alcohol in places, the sort that at times made the soles of your shoes slightly stick to the floor. Tom instantly liked it, not only because of the music but most of all because of the whole feel and atmosphere of the place and the people in it. It was packed, and it wasn't exactly salubrious in its décor and furnishing, but immediately he could see that everyone in there seemed to be having a great time and was enjoying themselves to the full. Within a matter of minutes he pronounced to Petr, "This is the best, my favourite in Brno. I'm sure I'm gonna like it here and come back again and again."

To which Petr just smiled and told him, "Yes I was sure you would Tom, and you always will. Everyone comes back to Livingstones over and over again."

The Scottish explorer's place closed at 3 a.m. and the evening was rounded off for the two men with a decidedly dodgy looking very dark brown Czech sausage on dry brown bread and lashings of mustard from a fast food place that was really no more than a hole in the wall. Just the thing to induce the perfect chronic heartburn as it infiltrated the beer sloshing around in Tom's stomach. Sure enough it reminded him of that at a point in the early hours of the morning as he stumbled in darkness from his hotel bed and groped his way to the bathroom to empty his bladder. It felt like someone was conducting a chemistry experiment in his throat and had turned the Bunsen burner up to full power. He grabbed some anti-heartburn tablets from his wash bag, threw them down his throat with a glass of water and staggered back to his welcoming bed to snatch some more sleep.

His peaceful slumber was disturbed by a ringing noise in his right ear. Very, very gently turning his head on its right side he realised it was the phone and grabbed at the receiver. He only succeeded in knocking it off the bedside table, sending it flying to the floor.

Stretching over the side of the bed he managed eventually to lay his hand on the receiver and gently put it to his ear.

"Dobry den, Tom, are you ready?" It was a somewhat indecently full of life Petr. "I am in reception waiting for you."

"What? ... What bloody time is it?" Tom abruptly enquired of his friend in very non-academic terms, becoming acutely quickly aware by doing so that any sound emanating from his what seemed like sawdust filled mouth was likely to cause an instant reaction of a sharp pain to the side of his head.

"Nine-fifteen, our meeting is at ten," Petr informed him.

"Oh shit," followed by, "ouch," came out of Tom's very dry mouth, although he couldn't really quite figure out how he managed to get anything out of it.

"I'll be up in ten minutes," Petr added. "Get in the shower now, Tom. You really are out of practice Czech beer-wise aren't you, my friend."

As Tom slowly circumspectly emerged from the bathroom and his shower he was greeted by Petr's tap on his hotel room door. "Here you are, Tom, orange juice and coffee, very good black coffee, rolls and some cheese." With that Petr attempted to hand Tom the tray as he entered the room.

"No, I think you'd better bring it in," Tom told him. "My hands are a little shaky. I think you'd better pour the coffee as well."

How Tom got through Friday morning he really couldn't work out. He felt as though he was on autopilot, although Petr was very kind to him and only arranged one morning meeting, followed by lunch. In the middle of the meeting though he found he'd switched off and his mind was drifting. Just how many nights could he take like this? At this rate he wouldn't exactly look great for Jana next week. Certainly his mind wouldn't be at its sharpest and it definitely needed to be if it was going to perform the mental and emotional gymnastics needed in order to not only convince Jana of the way he felt, but also convince her that everything would be alright between her and Dita. At this particular point in time he hadn't the faintest clue about how to do that, and didn't exactly feel in the right physical condition and mental frame of mind to dwell too long on that question at all.

At least by two in the afternoon Tom's stomach lining felt as if it had recovered. Now he fully understood just what all those stodgy Czech dumplings were really for, to soak up the previous night's beer. He still felt pretty knackered though. So initially he thought it would be wise to take an afternoon siesta back at his hotel rather than take up Petr's prescribed cure of the 'hair of the dog', or in this case the 'hair of the rather large Czech dog masquerading as more beer'.

"Come on, Tom. It's a tradition to go for a beer or two on a Friday afternoon at the end of the week's work. It's the same all over the world isn't it? Don't you do that in England? Well, it definitely is here, my friend," Petr argued.

"I'm knackered and I really don't think I can face another beer at the moment," was Tom's apologetic reply.

"Okay, then what about a stroll on a nice sunny afternoon instead and I can show you the best parts of my city? That will clear your head on a Friday afternoon," Petr suggested.

Tom let the guilt get to him, and decided it would just be rude not to take up his friend's invitation, even if he was knackered. Also, a stroll might actually clear his head and help him focus later on the major issue looming in his life that he would confront next week - Jana. So, the two men set off to wander the Friday afternoon streets of central Brno, or as Petr put it whilst trying to persuade Tom, "to wander on an end of the week Friday afternoon, to talk of life and of work and some possible future project collaboration, and of course, to talk of women."

"Very profound," Tom mumbled to his friend, followed cryptically by, "I thought you were a sociologist not a philosopher."

On such a sunny Friday afternoon Brno was emptying for the weekend. As the two of them sauntered slowly through the narrow back streets of Brno discussing the city and its history, the merits of short skirts versus tight jeans, everything and anything, stopping occasionally to face one another and wave their hands in friendly disagreement over this or that point of major importance in life's great concourse, other people were making for the railway station or for their cars to go to their weekend cottages in the South Moravian countryside. For Tom, even though he had only known Petr a relatively short time, it did indeed feel that he was with a good friend and spending what was turning out to be a pleasant Friday afternoon. As they walked and talked, laughed and argued, his tiredness slipped away. He felt more relaxed than he had done for some time. All the stresses, trials and tribulations of the angst over women, over relationships, loneliness and age, seemed to fall gently and effortlessly off his shoulders as he walked and talked leisurely and freely with his Central European friend. Who knows, he thought in a moment of rare silence between them, maybe it is something in the relaxed thoughtful and clinical Central European philosophical academic mind and psyche reflected in Petr's words that somehow magically soothed his problems. Anyway, whatever it was all his problems and issues just didn't seem so important anymore, or at least they didn't at that particular time in the beautiful cobbled back streets of Brno on a bright sunny Friday afternoon.

Some of the very narrow cobbled streets were flanked by a variety of old buildings, mostly of a character and beauty that seemed to even draw out some peculiar quite different character and charm of their own from the proximity of the occasional badly placed newer bland Stalinist grey ones nearby. Tom and his Czech guide soon found themselves in the narrow lanes surrounding the sv. Petra a Pavla (St. Peter and Paul) Cathedral. A towering structure with spires that had been darkened by centuries of weather and which imposed itself on the whole of the Brno city landscape, as Tom couldn't help noticing when he arrived on the train on Wednesday. Like so many homages and monuments to this or that God – and in this case it was firstly a catholic God – the cathedral dominated the Brno panorama. As the two men wandered past, with Petr outlining the history of the building and of the church as an institution in Brno, a christening party emerged from the cathedral. The small baby was cradled in its mother's not exactly well-dressed arms, and she was flanked by what were obviously the child's father and grandfather. These two men were both equally quite sadly attired in what seemed to be the obligatory ill-fitting, poorly cut and badly designed Central and East European suit. The colour of the two men's suits, a rather strange brown and an equally unusual thick light and dark grey stripe, also unfortunately fitted perfectly the stereotypical Central and East European suit.

Petr and Tom smiled and nodded to the christening party, offering and exchanging the usual Czech 'good day' of, "dobry den". Petr, in Czech, added his congratulations to the mother. The Englishman, obviously feeling more relaxed and by now in a more light-hearted Friday afternoon mood, attempted to point out philosophically to Petr the coincidental symbolism of it all. "Ah, a new beginning, a new life, just like in Czechoslovakia after '89 and the 'velvet divorce' from Slovakia in 1993."

Petr stopped walking, turned towards him and grinned, "Tiredness gone then, your old brain cells starting to function again? Better get you to a cafe for a beer before you start to think too much." Borrowing a phrase he had heard Tom use many times he added with a smile, "that would be really dangerous for someone as educated beyond his intelligence as you, my friend."

Tom couldn't even kill the moment by offering his usual expletive. All he could manage from within his new found Central European street calm was, "okay, that's good of you to offer." Although even then he couldn't resist adding sarcastically, "I wondered when you would finally get around to getting your Krowns out of your pocket and buying me a bloody beer for a change. First of all though, in my new found mood of spiritual calmness, I want to briefly look inside this little church of yours."

As they entered the cathedral Tom picked up a pamphlet about it from a stack of them just inside the large old wooden doors. Before he could look at it though, Petr started to tell him a story about the church. "There is an interesting and unusual story about the cathedral bell, Tom. How do you describe it? A legend I think you call it. It is unusual because the cathedral noon bell always rings now at eleven o'clock in the morning, one hour early. It is a reminder from the time of the siege of Brno by the Swedes in the middle of the seventeenth century. The Swedish commander besieged Brno with his army, which was many times larger than the Brno garrison. He boasted that his army would defeat and destroy the Brno garrison within three days. But despite a huge bombardment the city bravely defended itself for three months. After that time the Swedish soldiers began to complain to their commander. He told them they would make one last attack the next day, and if they did not conquer the city before the cathedral bells rang for noon they would retreat from the city for good. The next morning the Swedish canons bombarded the city once again, and the larger Swedish army managed to eventually break through the city walls. It finally seemed as though the city would fall. The cathedral bell-ringer watched the scene of the destruction of his city from the hill on which the cathedral stood. Watching the Swedish army charging into his city and watching the smoke rise above the city brought tears to his eyes. He wondered how an old person such as himself could help. In his despair he grabbed the rope of the cathedral bells and began to ring it with all his strength. Of course, he didn't know the effect it would have on the Swedish army. It was just a big coincidence, but the ringing of the bell stopped the battle and the advance of the Swedish army as the Swedish commander believed that it was the noon bell that was ringing. So he gave the order to retreat. Legend has it that what he apparently thought was what sort of leader would he be if he didn't keep his word to his troops. So the city was saved, and it was still one hour before noon because the time that the cathedral bell-ringer had rung the bell in his desperation was exactly eleven o'clock. Since that time the noon bell at the cathedral has been rung at eleven o'clock every day."

"You're an excellent guide. That's a very interesting story. I'm learning so much about your lovely city," Tom thanked his friend. After a quick stroll around the inside of the cathedral he suggested, "it's only fair after such a comprehensive guided tour and all that talking that I refresh your no doubt very dry throat. As your tour has been completely free of charge I'll use my Krowns to buy the beer instead," he added sarcastically.

As they sat this time with small beers outside a cafe close to the cathedral Tom started to once again look at the pamphlet he had picked up as they entered the church. The statement across the front of it immediately caught his eye. It was not only in Czech, but also in Italian, French, and the English that he carefully read out to Petr.

"We can call the Christian cathedral in different ways: oasis of silence, jewel of culture, dominant ... In fact it is a place of meetings. The past meets the present, man meets the man, but first of all the man finds himself because he has the opportunity to meet his Creator and in the same time to realise his greatness and nobility of the mankind.

Therefore we wish you not only to get rich in your knowledge but we would like to help you find the sense and the aim of your life as well by the visit to this cathedral." (Church Administration of the Cathedral)

The brief thought went through Tom's mind that the statement was very apt for him in many respects at this point in his life, especially in attempting to find the sense and the aim of his life, with Jana. He didn't want to get into that too much now though. That was far too heavy on such a sunny pleasant afternoon. He was feeling much more light-hearted and relaxed after Petr's perfectly prescribed stroll in the Brno sunshine. So, he decided to pursue the light-hearted approach. "It's everywhere in this part of the world isn't it, the past, Petr. The whole region is a historical theme park. If you could find some historical Central and East European Mickey Mouse or Donald Duck you could make a fortune in Czech Krowns."

"But we had them, Tom. They were all in the Politburo and the Communist Party Central Committee. The trouble is they tried to re-write history, but their version of history wasn't like Disney's, at best it was boring, but it definitely wasn't funny, my friend." Petr was now shaking his head vigorously. "Not in the least bit funny, thankfully though people didn't believe them. It might seem like a Disney-type 'make believe' period now to you, Tom, but those of us who were here can tell you it certainly wasn't a fairy tale. At times it was very depressing and sometimes quite frightening."

Petr was now becoming seriously agitated. This was a side of him Tom hadn't seen before. Usually he was all calmness and control. Tom thought he'd better try and change the subject. Maybe the statement across the front of the cathedral pamphlet and the chord it struck with Tom about his own life would calm Petr down. Get him back into a calmer and safer conversation.

"Nevertheless, even allowing for the broken English this little musing by the Cathedral administrators strikes a chord with me, Petr. All that stuff about the past meeting the present, man finding himself, finding the sense and aim of your life, hits the spot for me and my life."

The still slightly agitated Czech jumped in with, "Tom, if you stopped looking for long enough you might just find yourself."

"Blimey, that's a bit profound on a sunny Friday afternoon. Not exactly what you promised me on this walk of yours, Petr." With a grin Tom added, "That's a bit too Czech for me. Let's go and see this so called castle of yours. Seems a bit small to me, nothing like the proper castles we have in England." By way of trying to lighten his friend's mood a little more he offered him a wink as he finished his sarcastic comment.

From the cafe nearby the cathedral they made their way across the street of Husova with its Friday afternoon bustle of packed trams and busy traffic, and then went up the hill through the wooded green park to the entrance to the Špilberk Castle. Once again in the warm sun life felt easy, good, hassle free for Tom. "Perhaps," he told Petr, "Brno is good therapy for me, my hassle-free zone, my place of spiritual relaxation in the heart of Central Europe." He was convinced that he was experiencing a Central European feel to the afternoon, some kind of indescribable, almost atmospheric quality. Surprisingly, maybe it was actually really just the academic in him flowing out, something he definitely always tried to avoid admitting. Whatever it was though, strolling with his friend in such a place, this city at the heart of Central Europe, was having an effect on him. Clearing his head and making his mind operate fully once again, and it certainly made him think and talk. Something he shared with Petr when thanking him for being so insistent on the walk and for refusing to let Tom slope of to his hotel bed at the end of their morning's work.

"It's something men find difficult talking about and sharing with other men you know, Petr. Life and all its trials and tribulations. At least they certainly do in England. I don't know about in your country, but from what I've seen and learned about it I'm guessing it's the same here." Now he was getting really philosophical and deep. Fortunately, before his Czech friend could confirm or deny the anal-retention of the Czech male, Tom managed to remember where he was and stop darkening the mood. "But hey, on such a lovely sunny afternoon nothing really matters that much."

Even though he was after all a sociologist Petr was clearly getting a little uncomfortable with all this introspective therapy and sharing that Tom was getting into. He was rescued from his embarrassment by two good looking youngish women, in no more than their late twenties, who unusually offered the two men a, "dobry den," as they passed them by on the path in the park up to the castle. As Tom stuttered out in his surprise a courteous, "dobry den," reply Petr couldn't help laughing. He slapped Tom on the back, asking him, "What is it with you my friend? I don't know what it is you have, but can I have some please? That is most unusual. It has never happened to me before, women who I don't know suddenly saying 'good day' to me in the park. Incredible! Do you have a woman magnet, Tom?" With that he burst out into even greater laughter, much to the bemusement of the two women who were still within earshot.

Now it was Tom's turn to get serious. "You don't understand do you, Petr".

"Oh, I think I do," his friend interrupted.

"No, no, I don't mean what you think I mean. I'm not thinking about sex here. I'm thinking about me."

Once again Petr let out a huge laugh and could hardly contain himself as he spluttered out through his laughter, "but ... but ... they are your two favourite subjects, Tom, you and sex, and always connected in your thoughts I think. I thought that was what your Ph.D. was on." Now the Czech was holding his sides with laughter at his own humour as he mocked his English friend's attempt to be deadly serious.

Determined not to be diverted from what he thought was his deep philosophical analysis of life Tom tried once more. "That, that which has just happened is the stuff that makes life worthwhile for me. It makes life smile for me. Here I am a stranger in a city miles and miles from my home on a sunny Friday afternoon and two lovely young women walk by, smile and say hello."

"Actually, Tom, it was 'good day', and I don't think they smiled," Petr protested.

"Okay, okay, whatever. You said yourself it was unusual. So don't split hairs."

"What? I don't understand. What does that mean, Tom?"

"Look, Petr," now it was Tom who was getting agitated, "you're side-tracking me. It doesn't matter what it means. It's an English saying. The point is, the point I am trying to make to you, my friend, is that it is the surprise, the expectancy of the unexpected, or should that be the unexpectancy of the unexpected? Anyway, it's the wisdom of the uncertainty, the possibility of the chase, the sheer possibility of the possibility, the sheer bloody hope that makes all life worthwhile as far as me and women are concerned. I reckon it is the same for many men like me, and probably even those unlike me. It's not the sex."

Petr laughed loudly. "Oh no, of course it isn't, Tom, it's the ... what was it ... unexpectancy of the unexpected, whatever that is?"

"Well, okay Petr, it's also the sex, but it's not only the sex, and at first it's not the sex, or even the thought of the chance of sex. It's the recognition of me, the recognition of self if you like, if you want to get academic and philosophical about it. Surely in the Czech Republic - Kafkaesque, Havelesque Czech Republic - you can understand that. The sheer unexpected excitement of that happening, a simple 'good day' from a pretty young girl, as meaningless as that probably was, makes life worthwhile for some of us. Not to mention, of course, the smile that accompanied it."

"Nor the largish, stand-up, protruding chest and nice arse, although I'm still not convinced there really was a smile," Petr once again mischievously interjected with a chuckle.

"Look," now Tom was getting agitated. Here he was trying to be serious, bare his soul to his friend even, possibly get some advice or help, but his friend was just making light of it all. "Look, Petr, strange as it may seem, one very small tiny event, one small happening like that, makes me happy, and fills me with a nice warmth. It may be a kind of madness, the whim of an ageing man, but for me now, today, that occurrence means more to me than the girl's body. Okay, I know, it's crazy. It was only a pleasantry, a 'good day', but maybe, just maybe, it was a recognition. Anyway, it was for me, a recognition of me. That's the way I take it, will take it, and will hang on to it. I don't lust after the girl's body, well, okay yes maybe I do a bit, but most of all I long to have her, or what I mean is okay not her, but someone like her, love me. Someone to love me, be pleasant, care about me, walk in the park with me on a sunny Friday afternoon, or a Saturday or a Sunday morning. That girl's 'dobry den', her 'good day', makes me feel good. It allows me to dream of having her love, not just her sex and her body. Anyway, the best sex only comes with the best love. Casual sex, even the sort that is bought and sold, is just that, casual sex. It's not love, and that's what I really want. That's what I've been searching for, not casual sex, but love."

Petr was left almost speechless. His only offering to his friend was, "I think I understand, but in a way I think it is quite, quite sad."

"I know, I know," Tom agreed, "too right it's sad, but there is always hope, Petr, always the hope that one day it will happen," reminding himself again of his upcoming dinner with Jana.

As they strolled on through the park the green spaces were full of groups of people sitting on the grass, chatting, drinking, and even reading, some out loud to their friends. "It's that time of year," Petr said, "when you know summer has arrived, because the city is full of young girls in t-shirts and because men like us start to feel very, very old."

After all their philosophising the two men eventually found themselves walking through the entrance to Špilberk Castle. Petr gladly changed the subject and turned into a tour guide once again, talking about the castle and how it had been founded in the second half of the thirteenth century by the Czech King Premysl Otakar. "Between 1277 and 1278, to be exact," he told Tom. He reminded his English friend of his earlier story about the legend of the cathedral bell and how in 1645 the fortress – or rather the soldiers within it – had resisted the siege of the Swedish army for three months, together with the town of Brno. "Their resistance," he pointed out to Tom, "contributed greatly to the outcome of the thirty years war in Europe." He couldn't resist adding, "So you see just how important we people from Brno are, Tom. We helped to save Europe for you English, and after all it is a Europe that your people love so much," he added sarcastically.

"Yes, yes. I get your point, Petr. You are very important people here in the centre of Europe." With a wry smile the now once again more relaxed Englishman added, "And where would we be without you?"

They went straight to the top of the castle so that Petr could show off the wonderful panoramic view of the city from what was its highest point. Brno lay before them. Its historical glory bathed in warm clear sunshine. The Czech pointed out the different architectural make-up of the city, each building and area of it reflecting a historical period. From the Gothic and the Baroque to the Stalinist socialist realist row upon row of blocks of concrete grey flats dominating another hillside above the city.

"We call it 'concrete city'. Have you ever seen so many ugly monstrosities in a row as those blocks Tom?" Petr rhetorically enquired on seeing Tom's gaze fixed on the hillside blocks of flats. "Look, over there, Tom," the Czech continued. He was pointing to a yellowing, quite large low building set in some nice parkland. "It's a convent now, but it used to be the offices of the Academy of Sciences." Petr's academic interests were never far away, unlike Tom's. "The Department of the Academy dealing with Ethnicity and Religions," he added.

Tom nodded courteously, attempting to show some interest where there really was very little. He was really quite happy to just stand there in silence observing the sunlit city shimmering below them. The terracotta roofs of many of the buildings in the older parts of the city offered a cool calming beauty. What could possibly be wrong with Tom's world on such a day as this, on such a relaxing afternoon?

He was soon brought down to earth, however, by Petr's continued Brno information session. Not everyone, it seemed, had always had such a 'golden' impression of what lay below them. Petr told him about the former Stalinist city council's plan to build a wide Parisian type boulevard connecting the Trade Fair and Exhibition Ground in the south-west of the city with the older parts of Brno. "Of course," he ironically pointed out, "the Stalinist madness meant that most of the old buildings in the city would have had to have been flattened."

"That's progress for you," Tom suggested sarcastically. "Stalinist progress," and they both smiled once more and shook their heads in unison.

"I wonder just what history will make of all that forty years of madness in a hundred or two hundred years' time?" the Czech asked rhetorically and growing more serious by the minute. "Who knows?" was his answer.

"Talking of history," Tom interjected, "just what happened here in 1989, Petr, in November and December, compared to what happened in Prague?"

"There were demonstrations here," the Czech told him, "just like there were in all the large cities and towns all over Czechoslovakia. Not as large as Prague of course. They were the same sort of people demonstrating here though as in Prague, mainly students, intellectuals and artists at first. From the university and from the theatres, and of course the media soon followed. Then workers joined them, from the brewery and the factories. Of course, the workers at the brewery made sure the beer was still produced." This last comment was made with a chuckle.

Tom couldn't help adding, "Naturally, that goes without saying."

"After the large demonstration in Prague on 17th November and the one here that day the demonstrations just went on and on every day. It was a very strange, but exciting time, Tom. I don't really know how to describe it. You always felt, I always felt, something different was happening. Different from what we had lived through for years and years, but it was peculiar. Because although you felt something was happening, something was changing, at the same time there was this lingering fear – I think you say nagging away – that it couldn't quite be true. Even right up until it all collapsed, the communist government and the whole system, you still thought it might all be a trick. A dream, and that at a stroke the whole protest thing would fail and it would go back to the way it was. I was quite young in 1968, just sixteen. Maybe because of that it was easy to think nothing would really change. It is hard to describe to someone who was not here in November and December 1989, did not live through those weird and wonderful days, how you can feel optimistic, frightened, and cynical all at the same time. It is hard for someone to understand I think. To live your life in a particular way, a rigid fearful and soulless way in many respects, for many, many years. Yet at the same time those years were still years of certainty. A certainty of no expectations and no hope yes, but also there was an element of security in the 'rigidity of less'. Even in the dull, meaninglessness of it all there was some peculiar certainty and security. Then, in a flash everything was turned upside down. Not that you didn't want the removal of those bastards. Not that you didn't want the dumping of that corrupt system, but it was a leap into the unknown, a leap into uncertainty. You knew your soul would be better off, freer, but your wallet, your place to live, place to work? There were lots of fears about those things and the future."

"You see, Tom, everything we did, or were supposed to do, everything around us in our lives every day up until it all changed at the end of 1989 was supposed to strengthen our collective identity as 'good communists'. That was the way it was supposed to be according to the government propaganda. The way we were supposed to live our lives every minute of every day." Initially Tom thought this was just the sociologist in Petr coming out, but as his friend continued he soon realised it was just the humanity in him that Petr was relaying.

"Whether it was the literature we read, the music we listened to, what we watched on TV or at the cinema or the theatre, where we lived and the architecture all around us, even where we walked in our cities, the urban space, the squares and market places, and where we were born, got married and died, they were all shaped, organised and designed to produce and strengthen our collective identity as 'good communists'. In sociology it is called an attempt at creating what in English is the 'storehouse of collective memory and identity'. Really it was just a huge social engineering experiment. But you can't just manufacture something if people don't want it, Tom, especially something so oppressive and soul destroying as we experienced."

Once again Petr's comments touched a nerve with Tom as the Englishman went off on his personal tangent. Was he trying to manufacture something in his mind about what Jana really wanted? Manufacture an interpretation of the signs he believed he'd seen from her? Did he have a selective 'storehouse of collective memory' as far as what he believed happened between him and her in the huge wider turmoil of the events of the autumn of 1989 in Prague?

Tom's drifting self-obsessive and self-centred thoughts were brought to an abrupt halt as Petr realised he had turned their relaxing afternoon into something much more serious. "Sorry, Tom, it's one of those things I can go on for hours and hours about. I get quite heated up about it," he apologised.

"No. No, it's not a problem at all, Petr. It's fascinating for me to hear it. I think you are the first person I have talked to about it in this way, or rather listened to, since those November and December days I experienced in Prague of 1989."

"What? You were there, Tom, in Prague then?" The Czech was shocked.

"Oh, it's a long story Petr, and of course it involved women."

Once more Petr let out one of his guffawing belly laughs. "My God! Only Tom Carpenter could find himself in the middle of one of the great revolutionary situations and stories of the twentieth century and say it involves women. In November and December 1989 my whole country's future, the future of the whole of East and Central Europe, the people in my country's way of life, is being turned upside down, is in turmoil, but for my friend Tom it was all about him and women. And presumably, as you use the plural, Tom, it was more than one!" All Tom could do was shrug his shoulders and frown. Without waiting for Tom's answer Petr added, "of course. No need to ask really, bound to be more than one!"

"It wasn't just about women," Tom uttered in his defence. "I was there for academic work and I just got caught up in it. Alright, I was involved with a woman, Dita, but I found myself falling in love with her best friend." Petr was still grinning broadly.

"Bloody hell, Tom, this is more complicated than the 'November days' and our revolution. Maybe you should have got Havel to help you sort it out! After all, at the time he surely wasn't too busy to sort out Tom Carpenter's love life! Maybe he could have formed an organisation like Civic Forum. How do you call it, an 'umbrella' organisation?" Without waiting for Tom's confirmation of his English he went on, "an 'umbrella' organisation of all the 'interested parties', I mean women of course, and you could have reached some agreeable settlement, just like we did through Havel and Civic Forum with the bloody communists in our country." Petr's smile had broadened right across his stubbled face, amusing himself not only with his friend's re-told 1989 Prague predicament but also with his analogy between his country's 'Velvet Revolution' and Tom's love life.

"Okay, okay, Petr, enough. I told you it was a long story, and complicated, and it's still going on. I saw one of the women for dinner last weekend, Jana, and I'm meeting her again next Wednesday. I haven't seen her for almost five years. I missed my chance then. As usual I made the wrong choice. No, not the wrong choice, it seemed the right one then. It seemed, at least I thought initially, that I was in love with her best friend, Dita. I suppose it was just that there was another one, a choice that would have worked out better. Was better, someone I was more in love with, or that's what I think now of course. Maybe Prague will give me a second chance when I meet Jana for dinner next Wednesday. That's what I'm hoping for. Anyway, I was in Prague in 1989 and not here in Brno. As you said, if you hadn't lived here through the forty years of communism, or even some of it, most of it, like you had, you couldn't really experience the feelings of the time, as someone like you did. I may have been there in Prague but I was an outsider. I experienced the excitement but I couldn't really feel all the emotions you went through, and I guess most Czechs and Slovaks went through. Don't worry, Dita made that point quite clear to me many times through those 'November and December days' in 1989. Now forget about my bloody love life for five minutes and tell me a bit about what happened here. I've told you about my hope for next Wednesday and Jana, now you tell me all about you and your country's hope in Brno at the end of that incredible year of 1989."

"Okay, looking at it now, Tom, besides the uncertainty we all felt, and the disbelief and fear that it might all be a dream, the funniest thing is the bastards in charge – the communists in charge, not just here in Brno but all over the country – didn't have a clue what to do. For years they had passed laws and made rules about every part of our lives. They thought and believed they controlled everything. Everything was, how do you say, regimentated?"

"Regimented," Tom corrected him.

"Yes, regimented, but when one little part of that whole process was challenged, at first only by the students and the actors, their whole world fell apart easily and their regime collapsed. As Havel said, 'it was built on sand'. I can only say what happened in Brno. Of course, I saw what happened in Prague and in some other cities on TV, but in Brno the communist administration just didn't understand the situation. So many people demonstrating and standing up to them all together was like another world to them. In their cosy, make-believe world those sorts of things just didn't happen. At first they couldn't even recognise what was happening. They believed their own propaganda. So, if some people were demonstrating then they must be just a few troublemakers. Or else, it was a few troublemakers, a few criminals as they called them, just stirring up others and leading them on. When it finally sank into their tiny brains that wasn't the case they just didn't know what to do, didn't know how to react. They'd not really faced anything like it before on such a scale. Not in Brno, and not across the whole of Czechoslovakia. The last time anything like it happened, in 1968, the Russians came in to save them, but their vodka drinking, borsch eating Russian comrades weren't going to ride in on their tanks to save them this time."

Tom was sure that the Russian comrades of the Czechoslovak communists Petr was referring to were not the ones who would have been riding in on their tanks anyway. It was the poor sods in the Soviet conscript army, frightened to death, who had driven their tanks into Prague in August 1968. They were so frightened that they had fired on the very imposing National Museum building at the top of Wenceslas Square in the mistaken belief that it was the Czech and Slovak Federal Parliament building. The repairs to the marks of the shells and bullets had been visible on the building for the past 25 years. Meanwhile, the Federal Parliament building next door was undamaged and was never attacked. The particular Russian comrades Petr was no doubt referring to were the Soviet leadership and Tom was sure they might well have been swigging vodka, but were also more likely to have been tucking into smoked salmon and caviar amongst other 'Stalinist' delicacies, rather than borsch.

Petr was in full flow though. "That nice comrade Gorbachev," he added with a large dose of sarcasm, "wasn't going to send in the Red Army to help the bastards this time. He'd said as much. Told the world he wasn't going to send in the tanks like Brezhnev did in sixty-eight. Even though Gorbachev was after all a communist and people still had their doubts, it did seem that the world was a different place in 1989 than it was in 1968. So, even though we were never completely sure right up to the end, still had our doubts that the Soviets wouldn't ride to the rescue, in some ways people seemed more optimistic about it all. And the more it went on through November and into December with the demonstrations growing and the Russians not coming, and because we'd all heard about what had happened in other countries like Poland and Hungary, the more optimistic and less fearful people became. So, the demonstrations here were peaceful, just like in Prague, but they just grew and grew. More and more people came and demonstrated until eventually things changed. Looking back now it is strange to be talking about those days in such a peaceful, matter of fact way, but that is pretty much the way it was. We kept thinking the violence might come, but it never did. Kept thinking and wondering when the army, our army, the 'people's army', would move against us, or the Russians would come in. Strangely none of that at any time looked remotely likely to happen, even though we feared it might. There was never any sign of it. It's all very Czech, I suppose. At least that is what your world outside it, in the West, has said about it, Tom. The 'Velvet Revolution', mmm … yes, very Czech, but I never heard a Czech call it that at the time. It never seemed like that at the time, never seemed very 'Velvet'. As I said, instead it was a time of great uncertainty and fear, and hope, of course, but even right up to the end you could never be sure it would happen. Never be sure our hope would be realised. Also you never really knew who to trust. There were Secret Police informers and infiltrators into the dissident movement everywhere. People who were not what they seemed or pretended to be, so you had to be careful what you said and who you said it to all the time."

At that point Petr's reminiscences just tailed off and came to a quiet end. It was like he had exhausted himself through thinking and talking about it. He just stopped talking and looked out over the Brno landscape. The mood enveloping the two men was now very different from that when they set out on their Friday afternoon Brno stroll. Now it was much more serious and sombre. After a couple of minutes silence, as the two of them stared out over the Brno rooftops Tom offered an apology for what Petr had obviously interpreted as his thoughtless light-hearted flippancy an hour or so before in the cafe opposite the cathedral. What Petr had just been telling him about his feelings in 1989 made Tom's previous remarks seem even more tactless. "Sorry about earlier, Petr, I wasn't taking what you had to experience up to 1989 lightly. Sorry if I annoyed you. Now it must seem as if before 1989 was a different world."

For Tom life in the Czech Republic now in 1994 meant a kind of pleasant isolation, wrapped in a kind of sparse simplicity. Yes it was a complicated and quite difficult existence, where nothing came easily. Shopping, working, travelling to work, the everyday chores of human existence, all came with an added expansion of effort. Yet for him all this seemingly was made simple through the very lack of alternative, lack of great choice and of opportunity that produced choice.

"You don't really understand, Tom do you? You think you do, but you don't." Petr's voice strained a little. He was a little, just a bit, annoyed again and his voice betrayed his frustration at his friend's romanticism about his country.

"Of course, yes, it may be very romantic and nice to you, Tom. It might all look like it is nicely wrapped up in some blurred, misty, pretty, nostalgic romance from the past, like an old brown coloured photograph."

"Sepia," Tom interjected, but Petr ignored him and went on.

"For those of us who live here it is still hard work. Just to go and try to buy something simple like a washer for a leaky tap, or a part for a washing machine or a car, if you are lucky enough to own one, can take a whole day, sometimes two, sometimes a week. Look around you, Tom. In your eyes you see simplicity, a fall back to something of the West of fifty years ago, long gone, long lost, and now romanticised. Well, open your eyes wider, Tom, this traditional Central European post-communist theme park we live in here, just like the communist one before 1989, is definitely not bloody romantic! It is not fucking fun and far, far from fucking simple even five years later!"

Petr's mild frustration had now turned to anger again as he spoke about it. His voice had gradually got louder and louder, almost to the point of screaming. People nearby were beginning to turn and look. It wasn't really anger with Tom it was more anger with what he had lived through. What he'd had to put up with for all those years before 1989 and even since then. It seemed as if all of Petr's pent up frustrations and anger of his forty-two years had suddenly been released and were now verbally gushing out of him. He was giving Tom a real personal insight into the harder aspects of life in the new post-communist Czech Republic nearly five years after the 1989 revolution.

"What is worst off all, Tom, is that while it appears so much has changed, for most people in their ordinary, normal shitty everyday life nothing much has changed really. You try and find me a fucking washer for my tap in Brno!"

"Err ... mmm ... got your drift old man," was all Tom could offer. "Mmm ... a washer, let me see?" With that they both let out loud laughter, Petr realising that it wasn't after all really his friends fault and acknowledging the ridiculousness of his 'washer' moment.

Petr though was still clinging briefly to his retrospective philosophical moment. "I suppose in the end we're all where we are, where we are now, Tom, because of choices we've made in our life. Choices we've made at the crossroads of our life. Like yours over your women in Prague in 1989. But for a long, long time people in this country had no choices to make, no choice whatsoever. They could make no choices because there weren't any available to make. The opportunity to make any wasn't there. Of course Czechs and Slovaks tried to make some in 1968, and the choices and opportunity were almost there, and then 'our comrades' the Russians came in with their tanks and crushed our choices and opportunity. Saved us from ourselves it seems so they said, or at least saved us from some so-called supposed subversive elements in our society. So, when another hope and opportunity unexpectedly came along in November and December 1989 Czechs and Slovaks took it. Fearfully and still full of uncertainty we made our choices. So, this is your Czech sociologist friend offering you a philosophy lesson, Tom; giving it to you as a Czech gift from Brno during your first visit to my city." Smiling a wry smile through his greying stubble Petr added, "My philosophy lesson gift is this. When you get the opportunity always choose wisely, especially if, like you next Wednesday, you get a second opportunity. After 1968 we got our second opportunity in 1989. But remember, the choices you make take you down a certain path, a certain road, and ultimately of course lead you to more choices, but also, my friend, to more opportunities, and it is very, very seldom that you get a second chance, a second opportunity, and a chance to go back. So, choose wisely, Tom, but be careful what you wish for, especially where women and you are concerned. "

Tom listened intently to his friend's philosophy lesson. He knew he had made his choice back in the summer of 1989. He chose Dita, but as Petr had pointed out to him, he'd got a second chance, a second opportunity, and a chance to choose Jana now he hoped. He could go back to his crossroad and choose again and he was determined to do just that the following Wednesday.

They hadn't actually seen anything of the castle interior itself when a few minutes later, while Tom was still reinforcing in his mind his determination to take his opportunity with Jana next Wednesday, Petr glanced at his watch and informed Tom he was sorry but he had to go. Between them they'd certainly talked about a lot of history – that of Petr's city and country, as well as their personal history - while they walked, even if they hadn't got round to talking about much of the history of Špilberk Castle. But it was now approaching five o'clock and Petr had another family gathering to attend that night, his sister's birthday.

The Czech left Tom with an, "okay, my friend, I've had my outburst and my communist philosophical cleansing. Good for the soul you know. Tomorrow I'll pick you up at ten and we will have a day at Slavkov, a very interesting place. We will have a real Czech sobota, a Czech Saturday, Tom."

"Okay fine, thanks, but why Slavkov, where's that and what's there?"

"Slavkov, Austerlitz is what I suppose you know it as, Tom. To us it's Slavkov because it's Czech now, always has been for us I suppose. You know don't you? It's where the battle of the three Emperors happened, Napoleon and the defeat of the Austrians and the Russians. More history, it's a very interesting place. You'll enjoy it and we can have a few beers. Well, you can, as I will be driving. See you at ten tomorrow. Make sure you're up, and no hangover,

Tom." With a wink and a smile Petr left him at the entrance to the park surrounding the castle and rushed off towards an arriving number five tram.

Tom had forgotten for a moment that in Central Europe everywhere was history. Every place was historically important in the great Central European theme park. Well, they were to the Central Europeans at least. History, in a part of the world that had changed its national borders like others change their socks, really did seem to hold a special importance for many of the people who lived there; people whose lives had been shaped and affected by it many times over down the years. "Bugger the future for now then," he murmured as he watched Petr board his tram, "least of all sorting out my own with Jana next Wednesday night. Let's go and look at some more of the past instead. Who knows, it might give me some inspiration about just how to play next Wednesday night with Jana. Yep, Napoleon, he was a great strategists wasn't he? Maybe he can help. After all, his strategy seemed to have worked with Josephine."

11
To Slavkov, with Napoleon, Josephine, magical mirrors and thoughts of Tom's Waterloo

Saturday turned out to be what Petr described as, "Brno's hottest day of the year so far." It was blistering. Even in Petr's not exactly pristine Skoda it didn't take long to cover the thirteen kilometres or so to Austerlitz, as Tom kept referring to it, much to his host's annoyance. By ten-thirty they made their first stop on the grand historical 'theme park' tour at the hill from which Napoleon apparently surveyed the battle, and commanded his troops to victory over the Russian and the Austro-Hungarian armies. A large bronze plaque, about a metre and a half square and fastened to a stone plinth showed the outline of the battlefield and the positions of the troops of the various armies. Petr meticulously pointed out to his English guest the corresponding points of the armies' positions on the panorama that stretched out before them. From the hill the land spread out endlessly across a grassy rolling plain that was already shimmering in the heat that bounced off the land and rose in waves in the distance before them even though it was only mid-morning. It was, indeed, some view and it was immediately understandable why Napoleon chose it to try, and eventually succeed, to control the battle.

"This plaque looks quite new," Tom suggested.

"Yes, it's a replacement. The previous one, the original one, was stolen by gypsies last year," Petr informed him.

Tom let out a little chuckle, adding, "Well that's the brave new capitalist entrepreneurial world you've entered into now my friend. In the new spirit of capitalism and individual free enterprise in this country of yours who could really blame someone or some group of people, for realising that such a large piece of copper had a nice market value as a commodity?"

Joining in the relaxed banter Petr couldn't resist, "but Tom, in the past in this country we were always taught that a great philosopher once wrote that all property is theft."

"Past life, that's a past life, back in history, old man. You have to forget those old communist ways of yours you know. The world has moved on, things have changed," the Englishman sarcastically replied. Although he couldn't help simultaneously thinking to himself that if something was stolen it was still the gypsies who got the blame, guilty or not, just as it seemingly always had been. If it were true though, it was ironical that the record of Napoleon's great victory was purloined by gypsies, that great mass of nomadic owners of Central and Eastern Europe.

Next stop was the museum at the other side of the battlefield and time for a bread roll, some cheese, and a late morning bottle of beer that Petr had thoughtfully brought with him just in case Tom needed revitalising. For him it was just some orange juice. He never drank alcohol when driving. In the Czech Republic the limit was zero, no alcohol at all when driving, and Petr wasn't the sort to risk it. It was one of the very few rules that most Czechs didn't try to bend or get around. The two men sat on the grass outside the small building that housed the museum of the battle and once more gazed out over the scene of the conflict. Just below where they sat swigging their drinks and munching on their cheese rolls was a very small wood. Not much bigger than a copse. Petr, continuing his tour guide mode, pointed out that some of the heaviest fighting had taken place there on that second day in December in 1805 when thousands of soldiers from the three great armies had lost their lives. He told Tom that some of the bones of the soldiers killed were still being found there to that day.

"In English, Slavkov means 'place of fame', Tom. It is, indeed, a place of fame for so many reasons. You know that it is featured in Tolstoy's great novel 'War and Peace' and is regarded as Napoleon's greatest victory. Austerlitz, as you like to call it my friend, was a clever and brilliant trap that destroyed the armies of

Napoleon's enemies, the armies of the Russian and Austrian Emperors. He tricked his opponents into thinking he was weaker than he actually was and then called in nearby reinforcements." Tom was impressed by his Czech friend's detailed history lesson as he continued to outline the famous battle. "At first Napoleon met the combined Russian and Austrian army of 85,000 men and around 300 guns with just 66,000 men. He deliberately abandoned a strong central position on the higher ground of the battlefield and left his right flank weak Tom. The Austrian and Russian army moved forward to occupy the higher ground Napoleon's troops had abandoned and then weakened their own forces in the centre in order to crush the French right. But once the bulk of the Austrian and Russian troops attacked Napoleon drew up more troops that he'd held in reserve, unknown to the Austrian and Russian commanders. Then, with more and more Russian and Austrian troops sucked into the attack, Napoleon launched an assault that took back the higher ground he had previously abandoned and that completely split the enemy. So, he drew them into a trap. Is that the way you say it, Tom?"

"Yes, yes, that's right, Petr. Go on, it's very interesting. What happened then?"

"After some fierce fighting the French crushed the Austrian and Russian armies. Thousands of their troops drowned when a frozen lake split under the weight of men and guns as they tried to get away from the advancing victorious French, and it is said Napoleon ordered his troops to fire at the ice to split it open. It's estimated that the French lost around 8000 men, while the Russian and Austrian emperors, who were present at the battle, saw more than 27,000 of their troops killed, wounded and captured. So, it is indeed a place of fame, my friend, but also I think a place of sadness. Quite a history lesson eh, Tom? That French self-proclaimed Emperor was quite a strategist. Who knows, maybe you can learn something here about strategy that will help you with how to deal with your woman problem in Prague next week, Tom?"

Although Petr finished by trying to lighten the mood on what was now such a lovely sunlit day, Tom wasn't reacting. He just sat and stared out over the whole now peaceful panorama. He dwelt on how extremely calm he felt on what, as Petr had promised him, was a very pleasant Brno sobota, or more precisely, a Slavkov sobota. It was strange that sat in such a place, steeped in the death of so many thousands of young men in such a violent arena almost two hundred years before, he should feel such calmness and tranquillity. The two friends sat in silence for almost half-an-hour, each obviously drinking in not only the liquids in their particular bottle but also the sheer magnitude of what had occurred at that place. A place that now in the brilliant golden heat of a beautiful late May day seemed so serene. Perhaps it all really just reflected our mortality, Tom conjectured silently. As soon as we are born death is there waiting for us. For some poor sods here, in this place of so many deaths almost two hundred years ago, it was a death of supposed national honour, of national pride. A violent, horrible death, but maybe still followed by a calmness, a serenity, an ending that comes to us all. Whether our death is violent or non-violent and peaceful, whether we are with someone and deeply, totally in love with them – and by this he meant himself in love with someone like Jana – we all die alone, very, very alone.

Suddenly Tom felt a chill briefly come over him on that very hot day. The strange beauty of the place and the calmness it had produced within him had gone. Dissipated by his own thoughts and fears. He could always spoil the moment, even when it was his own. And when he was with a woman he could always spoil a serious, deep, meaningful moment by making some flippant, jokey remark, usually denigrating himself.

He finally broke the silence with, "thank you Petr."

"For the beer? You're welcome, my friend."

"No not for the beer, Petr, for bringing me here. You're right. This is a very important place historically. I feel like I am right in the centre of Europe, right in the middle of Europe here." Tom was now letting out his academic side. "This place, the great mass of humanity, the soldiers of three great armies locked in combat in a struggle over the control of the whole of Central Europe right here nearly two hundred years ago. It's an immense thought. And five years ago another equally great mass of people, the people of large parts of Central Europe, engaged in a struggle over the nature of control over their own lives in this their part of the world. This time though in a much more peaceful combat, a much more peaceful battle. Maybe, just maybe, we have learned something over the past two hundred years, Petr, maybe?"

As he finished his philosophical musing Tom turned from gazing at the landscape to see a wry smile on Petr's face. "I knew you would find something here, Tom, something interesting. I wasn't sure what it would be; something for you personally, something for your work? I'm not sure the Romanians in December 1989, or even some of our light-fingered gypsy friends, would agree with you about a more peaceful combat or that we've learned something over the past two hundred years. Maybe though you are right and there is a significant connection in this part of Central Europe. After all it was the Hungarians opening their border with Austria in the summer of 1989 that really opened the floodgates and started the great tide of humanity flowing out of the communist east towards the west. That started the final part – the end game I think the Americans call it - of the events of 1989."

"I was with Dita then," Tom informed Petr. "That summer, at the time the Hungarians took down the fences. It was weird really. As I told you yesterday at the castle, I was in Prague. Right in the middle of huge events which were unfolding, but I was wrapped up in her."

"Not unusual for you, being distracted by a woman, Tom," Petr interrupted. "But you must have been one of the few foreigners from the West in Prague at that time, at least one of the few foreigners who were not from the media. Now that was unusual."

"I was virtually oblivious to the August events. Of course, I became more and more interested as that incredible summer and autumn unfolded, especially in what went on in Prague in November and December. Dita was very, very cynical about the whole thing, believing nothing would really happen. Nothing would really change. A relatively few awkward people would be allowed to leave, but that's all that will happen, she would say. That's the way it always happens she kept telling me. We spent long, hot, summer Prague days walking and sitting in parks. Long lovely Saturday and Sunday afternoons just walking, talking, and holding hands through endless Prague cobbled backstreets and tiny squares, and climbing up and down long flights of steps. Up behind and above the castle, below the castle. Across the Charles Bridge, God knows how many times across the Charles Bridge; around and through the narrow streets by the St. Agnes Convent. We drank bottomless cups of coffee, or stuff masquerading as coffee, in Christ knows how many coffee houses and cafes. Sometimes we just sat for hours without needing to say a word. Just wrapped in each other's arms or lying in each other's laps. On park benches, on benches by the river or sometimes just in her apartment listening to music and reading, with the windows flung wide open, the sun streaming in and Beethoven's violin concerto or a Chopin piano concerto streaming out. We just enjoyed one another, were part of one another. I lived with her in every part of my senses. Her simple beauty and charm that always brought a smile to my face when I looked at her. Always made me think then just how lucky I was and that life really couldn't get any better. I smelt her freshness everywhere we went, a distinctive, indescribable smell that for me was just her, a mixture of her and what her beauty made me feel. Every time I was near her that distinctive beautiful smell that was her, her being, came flooding into my senses. We got inside one another's soul so completely it seemed it could never end. I suppose to some extent it was all wrapped up in the romance and the soul of that city, Prague. But, Petr, she was a very, very intelligent and strikingly charming beautiful woman. I thought that was it. I really did. I really thought that was it, 'the one'. I'd found 'the one' and didn't need to hope anymore."

Tom's voice broke slightly as he betrayed his emotions; emotions of regret more than those of disappointment. Really he was talking to himself. His regret was over his own shortcomings, his failure to be happy with his situation and be contented. Now could he ever be? Would he ever be and not feel some strange stupid need to continue and enjoy the search. Maybe it was the search and the chase that he had become engulfed by, and so could never really be satisfied with what he had. Maybe he just loved the chase, was in love with the chase, but he continued his self-justification.

"I really did believe at that time, through that summer of 1989, that my whole life had been leading to that particular point in time.

Hungarians opening the border? What border? What Hungarians? Like I said, I was almost oblivious to it. I didn't care. I only cared about one thing. Had one thing in my mind – her, Dita. And you know what, I really, really think now, believe now, that I was the main thing in her mind. The thing, the person, she cared about, thought about most, and you know what else, Petr? In true Tom Carpenter fashion, true to form, I fucked it up. I did. No one else did."

Once more Tom's voice broke slightly. Maybe it was the atmosphere of the place he was in, of the surroundings in which he found himself. A place where thousands had lost their lives, probably without the opportunity to examine what would have been their short time on the planet; a place of death and of history, a place with a solemn air hanging over it, even on a hot sunny summer's day. Whatever it was though, now Tom was clinically dissecting his existence. Philosophically examining his life, or at least what he believed to be key points in it, and for once in his life he seemed to be taking responsibility. But that was an unusual place for him to be in and it was definitely painful, hurting even. They were his mistakes he was talking about, "his fuck-ups, no one else's," as he so eloquently told Petr. His language always deteriorated when he got angry with himself. He felt his eyes begin to moisten and tried to brush the moisture away with his index finger.

Looking straight at his Czech friend he told him, "oh, of course, I tried to convince myself there were other reasons to end it. Convinced myself it was because she wanted children and I didn't, convinced myself that I wouldn't be able to get a safe and secure job out here, especially given my age. Convinced myself that at my age it was too much of a gamble to give up my job in England and take some temporary post out here, even if one were to become available. Any reason and every reason, you name it and I found it. But they weren't the real reasons. I guess, looking at it now honestly, being honest to myself at least, it was some sort of inner fear of fucking up yet another relationship. Something inside me – maybe some safety mechanism, a self-protection mechanism – a fear of ballsing up something that was so good. How could it get any better than it was at that particular time? It could only go downhill from there. Maybe that's what I told myself. Maybe because the search and the chase were the things I liked most, enjoyed the most, I convinced myself that everything after them would only be less exciting, less interesting, would make me less happy. How could things possibly get any better than they were right then and there in Prague in that summer and autumn of 1989? Given the time, all those momentous events of the time, it was like I just didn't believe in my own personal 'revolution', didn't believe that I could accept change and that things would only go on getting better in my life. I guess a lot of Czechs and Slovaks felt that way eventually about their 'revolution' in that year. I know Dita did eventually. Initially, she was always so adamant that nothing would change in her country, but eventually she became wrapped up in the events of the autumn of 1989 and what was changing. In a way I guess it's like your fear during the events of 1989 that you were telling me about yesterday, and your worry of uncertainty and change. Well, it's not the same as the massive changes that were happening in your country obviously, Petr, but I suppose it was the changes that I was facing in my life then relating to my growing relationship with Dita that worried me and made me uncertain."

"So, what did I do, me, a supposedly intelligent, well-educated man? Well, of course, I protected myself, as well as Dita I convinced myself in self-justification. I protected both of us against eventually fucking it all up by fucking it up then and there, fucking it up sooner rather than later. That was the brilliant Tom Carpenter intelligent logic I applied, Petr. Does that make any philosophical sense to you?" he asked rhetorically. "Crazy eh, bloody crazy, and all so fucking hopeless." At this point the question flashed into Tom's mind as to whether he wasn't sounding a little like Sandra's 'Fritz' and his logic on commitment, but he couldn't 'go there'. That would be just a little too deep and scary for him, even at that profound philosophical moment; too Sandra-logicesque.

"But it was even a little more complicated than that, Petr. You see I had also eventually by the end of that crazy year of 1989 was convinced that I'd chosen the wrong one and was really in love with Dita's best friend Jana. So that was another justification for fucking up my relationship with Dita."

Petr interjected just a little sarcastically, "yes, that's definitely a little more complicated, Tom."

"Okay, and maybe now it's just hindsight justification, whatever that is, but you know what, Petr, I really do believe now that ever so slowly throughout those Prague 'November and December days' of 1989 I found myself also falling in love with Jana. So, and this is even more crazy, for a time I felt I was in love with two women at the same time. I couldn't stop myself. Not that anything happened between me and Jana physically of course. But my emotions at that time were swept along just like the tide pushing your country's revolution forward, and like that revolutionary tide my feelings for Jana just grew and grew. Maybe it was just that. My emotions and growing feelings for Jana were linked to my being caught up in all the turmoil and upheaval that was going on in Prague at that time. Who knows? But I never believed it possible to be in love with two women at the same time, until it happened to me. Bloody stupid eh, my friend?"

Petr had listened in total silence and was still trying to come to terms with Tom's introspective self-evaluation - the sheer complexity and contradiction that was his friend's personality – when the Englishman threw the final part of the puzzle at him; a part that would have tested Freud, let alone the Czech sociologist that Petr professed to be.

"Anyway," Tom continued, in what he thought was an attempt to lighten the mood by being a little more flippant about the final even more ridiculous element in the equation that was his love life. "Here's the conundrum now, and I'm sure an intelligent sociologist like you can help me with it there not being a psychiatrist around here at the moment. I'm sure you can come up with a very rational Czech 'how to get round the rules' answer so as to suggest the best way for me to proceed." At the end of those few ironic sentences Tom took a deep breath and his expression took on a much more serious side once more. "As I told you yesterday while you were giving me your very informative tour of Špilberk castle, next Wednesday I will go to meet and have dinner with Jana. It turns out that when I first met the two of them five and a half years ago it was Jana who really fancied me, who really liked me. I was, "her

Englishman," apparently. This is what she told Dita after the three of us first met and just before I first came to Prague at the end of 1988. Jana told me this when I had dinner in Prague with her last Saturday night, having not laid eyes on her or spoken to her for four and a half years. Now, of course, being Tom Carpenter, I have fallen in love with her all over again, or really I have always been in love with her since those exciting days at the end of 1989 but had thought my chance had gone. Well, I'll certainly see next Wednesday whether my growing feelings for her in November and December 1989 were all about the excitement of the events we were caught up in or whether now, in your new calmer democratic Czech Republic, Petr, four-and-a-half years on my feelings are the same and it really was all about her. After having dinner with her in Prague last Saturday night, and admittedly only seeing her for a few hours, I certainly don't think my feelings have changed about her. So, I'm convinced, and I'm thinking what a mistake I made five years ago. I chose the wrong bloody one, as usual. I think I really did fall in love with Jana all that time ago through those crazy autumn days of the incredible events of 1989. I guess that was the real reason why eventually I knew I couldn't love two women at the same time, and so I fell out of love with Dita. Okay then my clever Czech friend just what should I do next Wednesday over dinner in that magical city of yours? Exactly how do I tell her of my undying love and convince her of that so we can spend the rest of our lives together? While at the same time, of course, explaining that yes, it's true, I did have an undying love for her best friend five years ago, but that was different. It was not the same as the way I feel about her."

Tom smiled wryly at Petr, took a last swig at his now quite warm beer, and finished his extremely long self-examination with, "Napoleon defeating the Austrians and the Russians? That was easy compared to this, my friend. So what would the old one-armed, one-eyed Emperor lover have done do you reckon? What sort of grand strategy would he have come up with? What would you do to ensure my 'greatest victory'?"

Unfortunately Petr's response was to let out his usual deep laughter at Tom's love life predicament. "Oh great!" Tom exclaimed. "Very constructive, thanks a bunch. I knew I could count on you for instructive advice and concerned help."

Through what had now moved on to a giggling fit Petr attempted some sort of coherent response to Tom's obvious annoyance, "Tom, I'm laughing because..." The Czech was finding it hard to spit out what he was trying to say. The more he tried the more his amusement grew, until almost his whole body started to shake with laughter. Slowly, as Tom's scowl and lack of amusement grew, he managed to compose himself enough to splutter, "I'm laughing because only you, my friend, could reduce the solemn and sombre atmosphere of this place, the monumental historical importance of what happened here, to a question about your love life. I'll tell you what my answer is to your dilemma. It's let's go to the castle. Or I suppose you would call it, like the French, a chateau, and I will show the room there where Napoleon fucked Josephine and no doubt one or two other women in the vicinity. He didn't seem to bother with explanations and deep examinations of his inner-self, Tom. He just got on with it. Just got on and did it."

"Oh yeah," Tom grinned at him, "but he was a fucking Emperor, in every sense of the word. No one questioned him, least of all his women. He didn't have to look inside himself. He could do whatever he liked."

"You know, Tom, there is a story that Napoleon claimed that after making love with him Josephine had just one thing to say to him – do it again! Those were the days, eh?" Petr suggested with a sarcastic glint in his eyes and a shake of the head. "Still, as you said, Tom, perhaps we've come a long way in two hundred years."

As they walked back to Petr's car Tom reflected that he couldn't recall ever talking to a man, or a woman for that matter – although that would have been different – in such a way about those things before. He couldn't recall ever being so open about his feelings, and certainly not to the ever cynical Steve, his mate back in England. Tom would have got a real blast of, "pull yourself together, mate. Just get on with it and see if she's up for it." The Napoleon approach I suppose, Tom thought.

Petr was right, the castle was indeed a chateau. It was that, now very familiar to Tom, post-1989 Central European mixture of old interesting buildings and elements of western plastic theme park. For sure the chateau and most of its contents were old and authentic enough. According to Petr, doing his guide bit again, it was built at the end of the seventeenth century. And Tom did indeed see on the official guided tour the room and bed where Napoleon slept, although the guide never actually mentioned him fucking Josephine in it. Even though the tour was in Czech Tom reckoned he would have picked up that sort of phrase from the faces of the very serious and intensive looking small band of eight others in that particular guided tour group. The 'plastic' part of the place hit Tom straight in the face though as he entered the chateau with Petr. Everyone entering and queuing to buy a ticket was greeted by young women and men dressed in what looked like very downmarket, left over from some cheap 'Carry On' film, early nineteenth century period costumes. The guides for the tours wore similar costumes. The whole thing seemed just slightly off-key and somewhat tacky, and Tom couldn't resist a, "see, it's a theme park, like I told you yesterday, Petr."

The only consolation in all this slightly sad manifestation of history, or at least the Czech interpretation of it, was that the particular guide for his and Petr's tour was a rather pleasant and lovely looking young girl of no more than eighteen or nineteen. She had her very long blonde hair tied back and platted in a pigtail that dangled halfway down her back. Much to the delight of Tom, and no doubt the other male tourists in the group, she had the quite pleasurable consideration to push her two best attributes to the front, or rather the top, of the bodice of her low cut costume dress. In fact Tom immediately pointed this out to Petr in what he thought was a whisper, although why he was whispering he couldn't quite figure out as he assumed no one else there understood English. Leaning over to Petr's ear only a few minutes into the tour, in true 'Carry On' tradition he offered his instantaneous character assessment of, "nice tits mate, and she knows how to make the best of them. I'll have five hundred Krowns with you on them popping out of the top of her dress before we get right round this place and finish the tour. I bet Napoleon would have given her one."

Two of the women in the tour group looked round sharply at Tom, and Petr glared at him a "shussh!" followed by a quietly whispered, "what happened to the serious, philosophical, what is life really all about Tom of half-an-hour ago?"

"Oh him, I try and keep him locked away. He only comes out when there are women problems and I feel age creeping up on me. So that Tom only pops out on very rare occasions, unlike her tits I hope."

With that Petr placed one hand firmly over Tom's mouth and shook his head vigorously in a sort of 'I give up with you' fashion.

Twenty minutes into the one-hour tour the philosophical, in turmoil Tom returned. The tour group entered a fairly small room of about four metres by four. It was obviously some sort of dressing room. Petr, who was translating as much as possible of the tour guide's Czech, explained to Tom that it was the dressing room of a Duke in the Kounic family, who initially had the stately home built. In the corner of the room, near one of the doors leading to what Tom presumed was a bedroom, a large, ornate, gold leaf decorated floor to ceiling mirror hung on the wall. The guide spent some considerable time talking about it, smiling constantly and seemingly quite taken by it. For Tom, from her tone of voice and facial expressions of pleasure she seemed totally wrapped up in what she was telling the group about it, although he obviously couldn't understand a word of what she was saying. It was seemingly an object that gave her great pleasure and made her smile. Petr waited until she had completely finished talking and as the rest of the group moved on with the guide he translated what she had said for Tom.

"It is what I think you call a myth, Tom, a legend that has been passed down over two hundred years. A story I suppose. She told us that it is said, believed even, that if you stand in front of this mirror and make a wish out loud, not only will it come true, but you will always be rich, always be handsome, and always be loved."

Petr followed the rest of the group through into the next room. Tom hung back by the mirror though. Petr returned to look for him and found him standing in front of the mirror just finishing muttering something in a very low tone.

"So, that other Tom has popped out again. What were you wishing? Let me guess. It wouldn't have something to do with a Czech woman called Jana by any chance? Something like Napoleon's Waterloo for you, Tom?" Petr teased him.

"I hope not," Tom interrupted. "Waterloo wasn't exactly a success for Napoleon was it, Petr?"

"Anyway," Petr continued, "your lovely friend the tour guide has just told me in the next room while you were doing your wishing in the mirror that she is a student ... of English, Tom, and she said to tell you that 'no they won't pop out. They never pop out, and certainly not for a perverted old Englishman!' She also said to tell you that she 'would never have shagged a one eyed, one-armed bandit like Napoleon, even if he was an Emperor'. Now, my educated academic friend, she seems to have pushed those best attributes of hers, which you were so keen to point out to anyone within earshot, right down the front of her dress. In fact, they are so far down I think they must be around her waist! Oh yes, before I forget, and she said you owe me five hundred Krowns, or will do by the end of the tour."

"Oh, piss off," was all Tom could think of in terms of a deep philosophical reply.

At least that embarrassment had the effect of shutting Tom up for the rest of the tour. After Petr had made him aware of the young girl's English ability he listened attentively to everything she said, even though he couldn't understand a word. He even tried some peace offering by constantly nodding his head as she spoke and occasionally muttering, "Mmm ... interesting." This did have the effect of bringing a smile to her face though, followed by a tilt of the head in Petr's direction and a raised eyebrow as she knew that Tom didn't have the faintest idea what she was talking about. At the end of the tour Tom thanked her profusely, going somewhat over the top, and finally gave her a hundred Krown tip. "No harm done. She seems fine," was his attempted self-convincing comment to Petr after he bid her his finest Czech goodbye of, "Nashledanou," and the two men emerged back out into the still hot sunlight. Although he did have to suffer her final embarrassing comment, said with a lovely accompanying smile, of, "thank you for the one hundred

Krowns tip, but don't forget the five hundred Krowns that you owe your friend."

"Yes, Tom, no harm done I suppose," Petr agreed. "In fact, a very entertaining afternoon thanks to you. Life is never dull when spent in your company is it, Tom," was the Czech's amused sarcastic response. "But tonight I am going to have to leave you to your own devices again in Brno. I know it could be frightening, for Brno I mean, not you. God knows what messes and tricky situations you will get yourself into. Anyway, I have promised to visit my parents at their country cottage tonight and tomorrow and I can't really put it off. You could come too if you want."

A cottage in the Czech countryside with a couple of sixty year olds plus on a Saturday night wasn't exactly Tom's idea of a vibrant night out, let alone a Saturday night. "No, thank you for asking me, Petr, but I wouldn't want to intrude. It's family and all that after all. No, it is okay I'll just have a quiet meal and a couple of beers. Be nice to have a quiet night, just wandering about exploring your city's Saturday nightlife."

"That's just what I'm worried about, Tom. You exploring Brno's Saturday nightlife," he warned the Englishman with another smile. "But okay, if you're happy doing that, that's fine. I'll be back in the city early tomorrow evening, so we can have a beer before you leave for Ostrava on Monday, but not too many, honestly. You know what you should do tomorrow? You must go for a stroll in Lužánky Park, the oldest park in Moravia and Bohemia, and then walk up Schodová, 'the street of steps', to the Villa Tugendhat. It is all very beautiful and the Villa is a UNESCO World Heritage site, one of the fundamental works of international functionalist architecture, built in 1930. You can't leave Brno not having seen it. The hotel will give you a map for those places. Now, let's show you the gardens of this chateau, find a cafe for a beer for you and we'll leave here about four-thirty. That will give me plenty of time to drop you off back at your hotel before my drive into the countryside to be at my parents place for seven, and for you to have a sleep for an hour or so before you go out for your quiet night."

12
Janácek and a different type of tune – the music of youth

It was still bloody hot in Brno, touching thirty-two degrees and only the end of May. He hadn't exactly got up with the lark, or whatever the Czech equivalent of it was, or even with the hot sunrise. More like he'd come home with it. It was five-thirty a.m. when he dragged himself out of the music-thudding exotically named Bolero club into screeching bright new daylight. It's funny how when you are in these places, usually below ground, you always think life outside stays the same and that time stands still, light or dark. This was especially the case in some of the more salubrious club-type establishments in the Czech Republic in which Tom had found himself on a number of occasions. Some of them were very, very dark, both physically and psychologically.

He'd stumbled back to the hotel, not drunk exactly, but merely comforted by the friendship and acquaintance he had renewed that evening and into the early hours with his American associate, a Mr. Jack Daniels. However, luckily another American element, Coca-cola, had been present in such fairly large quantities, together with the stuff that sank the Titanic, so that JD had been diluted considerably and his presence side-lined.

It was just past noon when he drew back the fading blue curtains of his eighth floor hotel room and surveyed, or at least squinted at, a shimmering Brno. A couple of paracetomol, a shower, shave and a bottle of water later he was sauntering down Masarykova street heading for breakfast masquerading as lunch.

As it began to regain its senses his mind was wandering. Is every street and square in the Czech Republic now called Masarykova or náměstí Masaryk he aimlessly wondered? The first leader of the new

Czechoslovakia in 1918, Tomas Masaryk, had obviously replaced Lenin and the 'great' Czech communist leader Gottwald in the Czech A to Z street guide, no doubt signifying the final triumph of liberal democracy over Marxism-Leninism. After all, Czechoslovakia was a place that had witnessed an almost revolving door of name changes of its streets and squares with each change in the nature of its ruling regimes. From his research Tom knew, for example, that in April 1920 the government of the newly established post-first world war Czechoslovak state had issued a decree banning names of streets and squares which the government saw as not being able to be, "placed in harmony," as they put it, with the history and external relations of the Czechoslovak nation. This was to be especially so in relation to the names of any streets or squares commemorating, "persons who showed hostility towards the Czechoslovak nation or allied nations." In fact, the re-naming of streets and squares started after 1918 and created something of a precedent. Every subsequent regime – Nazis, communists, and now the post-1989 liberal democrats – continued the re-naming process and thus ensured a brief boom in the employment of street sign-makers, although each boom was somewhat short-lived and thankfully interspersed with years of inactivity. Nevertheless, it was a wonder the Czechs and Slovaks ever really knew just where they were, especially with so much beer inside them, he chuckled.

His breakfast imposter was an omelette, washed down with plenty of coffee and orange juice, and eaten very pleasantly under the shading parasol of a pavement cafe. What now on this warm Sunday afternoon? He had to go to the railway station to buy a train ticket to Ostrava for his journey tomorrow, but that was hardly going to take up the whole afternoon. Go for a stroll in the park Petr had told him about the day before maybe? "Lužánky Park, the oldest park in Moravia and Bohemia, and then walk up Schodová, 'the street of steps', to the Villa Tugendhat," that was what Petr had suggested. Sounds something worth seeing he decided, and maybe take a book, sit in the sun in the park and do some reading, if he didn't instantly fall asleep in the sunshine.

As he finished his orange juice and ordered a third coffee memories of the long night before came into his mind. Funny how when you've had a good drink the night before you start to recollect things in disjointed pieces. Start to remember bits and pieces of the previous evening's entertainment, like the woman who he thought was a very, very good dancer, a bloody good dancer. She wasn't short, but not too tall either. Five foot six or seven maybe. He reckoned she was early thirties, thirty-two maybe? Slim, with a nice trim figure. It looked well cared for. Probably went to the gym regularly. Her hair was blondish and shoulder length. Bobbed? Was it bobbed he wondered as the waitress brought his new coffee? He was never sure just what that meant. Anyway, if it meant trimmed and cut neatly into her face, then her hair was definitely bobbed. Dirty blonde was the other term he was looking for, as he recollected someone, somewhere, although he had no idea who or where, telling him in the past when pointing out to him a woman with similar colour hair. It was the smile of the woman the night before and her dancing that captivated him though, transfixed him in the Krokodil Club at the bottom of Kounicova. She could definitely dance. It wasn't that she had extravagant movements. It was just the opposite in fact. Her movements were minimal, subtle and seamless. She danced like she felt it, like she felt the music inside her, flowing from her. If he was in another age, in the past, in years gone by, he would have called it graceful. But it was more than that. Fluid, yes fluid, maybe that was the word that best described it, although even that was perhaps too harsh a word to use. Anyway, he was convinced it wasn't something you could, or even should, describe. It was more of a feeling, and a very nice feeling at that. Just watching her move was a feeling, an experience of someone really enjoying being herself doing just what she wanted. She exuded charm and seemingly total confidence, not only in her dancing, but in her whole self.

At this point he realised he'd never seen Jana dance, and wondered if the charm about her that so mesmerised him would be exhibited in her dancing? That was, indeed, a nice thought to ponder on sat outside a café in Brno in the warm sunshine of an early summer Sunday afternoon.

After his mind's fleeting visit to the possible image of Jana dancing, he returned to his recollections of the night before and his captivating dancer. Her charm was what came across in her smile he remembered thinking at the time. It beamed, with her lips slightly apart and shining teeth. Her smile betrayed just how much she enjoyed dancing. He then remembered though that she was dancing with a guy with long, dank, greasy looking shoulder length black hair, or at least initially Tom thought she was. A guy who looked like he belonged to one of those Peruvian Indian flute playing groups that seemed to exist in every town square in every part of the world he'd ever visited. He looked somewhat younger than her. Maybe only five years or so, but he acted considerably younger. Or perhaps she wasn't as old as Tom thought and it was just that she exuded a cool, classy charm and grace – there was that word again – way beyond her years. Although now he thought about it, Tom recalled realising quite quickly that the South American Indian flute player was not so much dancing with her as seemingly pestering her and her real dancing partner, her female friend. She appeared to be politely, but firmly, having none of it. As far as Tom could see she wasn't telling him directly to piss off, which was strange. At times she seemed intrigued by him, interested even. At other times quite cold. Why did so many of the beautiful and charming Czech women he'd ever seen appear to be with, and sometimes enraptured and fascinated by, men who were dorks? Blokes who they were obviously with as a couple, but who appeared to treat them terribly and at times almost ignore their existence even though they would be stood only a few feet away looking immaculate and totally gorgeous. Meanwhile many of the men would be just wearing grubby black t-shirts and jeans. It was as if they had been slumped in front of their Czech TV with their beer, and in many cases beer bellies, when their woman had appeared, gorgeously dressed, and simply said, "right let's go out for a drink," and the man had just roused himself, plonked on his scruffy shoes or old pair of trainers and walked out the door. Very weird that. Maybe that's the way Czech men are and the women just accept it. Maybe that's where he had been going wrong.

It was just like the country though. Just like the Czech Republic, he remembered starting to convince himself the night before as he sat pawing over his beer, watching the charming captivating dancer, her friend, and the 'Peruvian musician'. It could make you feel happy. Make you feel great, feel really good. Then in an instant it could make you feel really sad. Sad for him meant reflective. It, the Czech Republic, could seem like one huge fairy tale at times, as he'd recently suggested to Petr, although there never seemed to be a happy ending for Tom. Not yet anyway. It seemed that everything that was good about this country for him – its beer, its women, its feeling of evoked contemplation – eventually always just ended up causing him to reflect on everything that was sad in his life and everything that was missing from his life. Caused him to reflect maybe that he'd never yet found the one real woman, the love of his life he'd been searching for, caused him to reflect on all the missed opportunities on that front and the wasted, aimless, drifting days, weeks, months and years. Maybe now it was too late anyway, too late because of his age and probably more the case, too late because of his cynicism.

Eventually, around midnight, the captivating slim, dirty blonde dancer, a Kateřina or a Tereza perhaps, who knows, left, taking with her, much to Tom's satisfaction, not the South American flute player, but just her smile and her female friend. He consoled himself with the fact that at least her image in his mind, the classy characterisation of her he had manufactured from afar, was not soiled or damaged by her leaving with the long haired dork younger man who had tried so hard to force his way into her dancing, and no doubt hopefully into her pants. Her love of dancing, and who knows her love of life, was gone from Tom's life in an instant, out of his life forever; a lost opportunity for him? Who knows?

Now, as he sipped away at his coffee the next day watching Sunday afternoon strollers and passers-by and thinking about all this from the night before, the self-doubts were flooding into his mind again. As he thought it all through, went over and over the previous evening's events, constantly returning to the image of the captivating dirty blonde dancer, he began to wonder whether maybe that was really all he wanted, lost opportunities. Did he thrive on them? Relish them? Or was it really a youngish slim blonde with a joy of dancing and life, and a great smile, that he sought? But would he be forever happy with her if he had taken his opportunity and ended up just that, with her? Or was this just another illusion, another false ideal with which he deluded himself? After all she was just another fabricated image in his mind. He never even knew her, had never even spoken to her. She might have been a great, self-confident and happy dancer, but what about her personality? How could he possibly tell just what sort of person she was from the way she'd danced? Really he'd just fallen in love with her dancing. Not exactly much on which to try to base a relationship. Anyway, after a few months with her would he be bored, as his friend Steve always insisted? Be searching for new excitements, new challenges, and new tall slim brunettes perhaps? Maybe he was simply so messed-up emotionally after all these years that he was incapable of being happy with anyone, or rather any one woman? Incapable now of the word he could no longer even say aloud – commitment. He might go on from day to day deluding himself that he was searching for the 'Holy Grail', that special love of his life, but again perhaps it was just that, the search, which provided him with the most excitement. Was it that in reality which he liked most of all? So, he didn't really want to find the 'one special woman' at all. Really didn't want to actually find 'the love of his life', because then he would have to give up the exciting search. Now that really was sad. Even sadder than the fact that by the time he left the bar where the captivating dirty blonde haired dancer had exhibited her talents so well the only people left in the place at around one a.m. were him and a well-built dodgy looking guy sat in one of the corners with his eyes fixed solidly on his half empty glass of pivo.

Despite his recollection of his around one a.m. leaving time, the overall time span of all of this was still foggy in Tom's Sunday afternoon mind. He did seem to vaguely remember thinking that given the place's by then lack of clientele it was definitely time to leave, and take his thoughts of his slim, dirty blonde haired dancing image with him, keeping them pure and untainted by any association whatsoever with reality. It was time to wander around downtown Brno finding a much more populated club, hopefully with better scenery to look at than his dodgy looking male bar companion sat in the corner. That was when he'd stumbled upon the Bolero Club on Česká while on his way to Livingstones. He'd quickly decided to abandon going to Livingstones, for a while at least, and first of all give the Bolero a try.

At that point on a sunny Sunday afternoon though he decided that was quite enough reflective introspection for the moment. He caught the eye of the waitress, paid the bill, and set off briskly towards his hotel to collect something to pretend to read as he dozed the afternoon away in the sunshine in Lužánky Park, after visiting the Villa Tugenhart.

As he collected his book from the bedside table in his hotel room he noticed amongst the assorted debris of Czech bank notes, coins and receipts from the night before a scrap of paper with a phone number scrawled on it accompanied by the name Beatrix. Another recollection from the previous night hit his brain hard. Beatrix had been sitting diagonally opposite him at the Bolero club bar. The scenery in the Bolero, although certainly more densely populated than in the Krokodil Club he had just left, was by no means eye-catching, either in respect of the clientele or of the ambience of the establishment. It was definitely downmarket in both respects. Shabby was the word that came to mind as Tom had made his way down the flight of a dozen or so steps into the basement constituting the club. Old sticky feeling carpets, no doubt from years of spilt alcohol, signalled that he wasn't exactly entering an establishment where a tie would be required apparel for gentlemen, even in the unlikely event there were any real gents in there. As he made his way through what was a smallish ante-room with a couple of very sorry looking old red velvet settees and two equally sorry looking couples of what could be described kindly as older men and women sat on them deep in conversation, he wasn't exactly filled with optimism that the night's entertainment could go anywhere other than further downhill. The walls of the larger room he entered next, with a square bar in its centre and a small dance floor at one end, had paint flaking from them, visible even in the dim light. It might be called subdued, but that would be too kind. Strangely for a club called Bolero, there were large images of what looked like Egyptian pharaohs painted on the walls. That at least had brought a brief smile to his lips. Most of his fellow late night downtown Brno clubbers in this establishment were far from well dressed. There was a profusion of cheap looking bri-nylon type shirts and heavy duty poorly cut jeans amongst the men. The chosen 'Saturday night finest' of the women was dominated by black or blue trousers and skirts and equally cheap looking blouses or tops. The odd man, and even some of the women, wore jumpers reminiscent of those diamond squared ones that Val Doonican had once sported and made his trademark, although again of nowhere near the same quality or fit.

Beatrix was with one of the very few more expensively looking, though still badly dressed men in the place. Even in the dim light, it was immediately obvious to Tom that her male companion was considerably older than her, looking well into his sixties. His hair was so grey it visibly glowed in the dull club light, especially when the rotating ultra-violet light from the dance floor caught the corner of the bar where he perched on his bar stool. Tom's greying speckled mop looked positively black in comparison. Even though the lower part of his body was hidden below the counter of the bar, it was still apparent that the guy had a significant beer belly, which considerably stretched the fabric of the black roll neck jumper he was wearing beneath his forced wide open large grey check jacket. Beatrix was what might kindly be referred to as nicely rounded, some might unkindly say plump. Her best assets were proudly exhibited in a tight fitting black silk looking – though it obviously wasn't – blouse tucked into a white knee length skirt. Her mid-forties looking face was heavily made up and framed by her blonde peroxide shoulder length hair.

She quickly made eye contact with Tom not long after he perched on his bar stool and ordered his first JD and coke. Tom's pleasant surprise was cemented with what he detected as the faintest of smiles of recognition from her. Ten minutes later, after a couple more glances exchanged and further eye contact made, she mouthed something to him behind the man's back. Tom had no idea, of course, what she was trying to indicate or say to him. He couldn't lip read in English, let alone Czech. When, though, a few minutes later her male companion disappeared to what Tom assumed was the toilet, no doubt to empty his colostomy bag he told himself, she quickly, very demonstrably waived her hand in Tom's direction and motioned him over. As soon as he got within arm's length though he was unceremoniously told in very broken English, "you no sit." Simultaneously the scrappy piece of paper with her phone number now lying crumpled on Tom's hotel bedside table was thrust into his hand, followed by the phrase, "I have no English, only a little Deutsch. You ring tomorrow." Tom took that to be a request rather than a question and quickly retreated back to his bar stool and his mate JD. As he sat there, still making the occasional glance in her direction and feeling a little smug, he started to reflect on the linguistic challenge of him speaking very little German and not a great deal of Czech. As she informed him of her linguistic limitations he had fleetingly thought of responding, "It's alright, luv, Christ I don't want to talk to you." However, he restrained himself, although she obviously wouldn't have had a clue what he said and he guessed it certainly wouldn't have mattered anyway as far as she was concerned.

Choices, now he had choices on a hot Brno Sunday. Sunbathe and read or choose the mystery of Beatrix's phone number and all that might lay behind it. Maybe it was the influence of all his previous introspection over the past couple of days, including his philosophical discussions with Petr at Slavkov and during their Brno Friday afternoon stroll, but he found himself screwing up the piece of paper and dispatching it to his hotel room rubbish bin. "If I'm serious about Jana I don't want to be messing about with someone who was so obviously a prostitute," he determined.

"Oh shit! Jana, yes Jana," he exclaimed, "I was supposed to ring her over the weekend to confirm and fix up Wednesday night. No worries, it's only early Sunday afternoon, definitely still the weekend." He reached to grab the bedside phone, scrambled through his diary to find her number, took a deep breath and dialled it. She seemed very matter of fact.

"Yes, yes, Tom, I remember what we said," was her answer to his tentative, "we said about meeting for dinner again this Wednesday."

"How about at eight at the clock in the Old Town Square?" she suggested.

Tom readily agreed, and with a brief, "I am looking forward to it. See you then, bye," she was gone.

As usual his immediate reaction was to try and analyse her response. "Hmm ... she's looking forward to it. That's good," he found himself muttering. "But she definitely was very matter of fact. Maybe she just had something else on her mind and was busy with something else. Yep, that'll be it. Still, she said she remembered and suggested somewhere to meet straightaway." With that he consoling though he grabbed his book and set out to explore the places Petr had suggested.

City centres during the day at weekends are strange, barely inhabited places he thought as he wandered across Náměsti Svobody. Not all of them, of course. Those like Prague, Florence or Rome that are packed with tourists could hardly be described as uninhabited, but they are the exceptions, the tourist cities. Most cities are generally empty in their centre at weekends. Even parts of London, in the financial districts and the City of London office areas he remembered being deserted at weekends. They were empty of the weekday bustling, rushing workers, scurrying back and forth to their offices, their lunches or sandwich bars and the shops. He always preferred those times in city centres at the weekend. Maybe it was the space and the relative solitude. Maybe it was a feeling of connection with the few other seemingly equally lonely souls wandering through the empty city centre streets; a lonely city solidarity perhaps? For sure he could see more of the city and relax more at those weekend times.

After about ten minutes of gentle strolling, observing, and letting his mind wander aimlessly he was entering Petr's, "oldest park in Moravia and Bohemia," Lužánky Park. The wide areas of grass were littered with people taking advantage of the hot afternoon sun, reading, picnicking or just sitting in groups and chatting. As he walked across what was a pleasant enough expanse of greenery right in the middle of the city he noticed what appeared to be some sort of pavilion used for exhibitions and events and in one corner of the park were some tennis courts that were in full use that day. Having crossed the park and a fairly busy road he entered Schodova street under an impressive arch that was obviously a nineteenth century legacy from the days Brno was part of the Austro-Hungarian Empire and immediately began a climb up what were an equally architecturally impressive five flights of steps to the main part of the street. He didn't bother to count them but reckoned there were over a hundred and fifty as he struggled a little for his breath as he reached the top.

From there in a couple of minutes he was outside the Villa Tugenhart and luckily just in time to join a guided tour. From the side he had entered, the Cernipole road, it looked far from impressive bland grey concrete. Once inside on the tour though he soon realized why Petr had suggested he visit it, and why the people of Brno were so proud of it. The Villa was full of light and gave off a real feeling of space and air through the huge glass windows that ran floor to ceiling all along the side of it facing the city, with fantastic views out over a shimmering Brno. Realising Tom was the only non-Czech person in the group, the tour guide kindly provided some English commentary, after firstly apologizing for what she described as her, "not very good English," although in fact it was perfectly good English, as Tom complimented her later. As Petr had told him the day before, she explained that the Villa was a UNESCO World Heritage site and one of the fundamental works of international functionalist architecture, built in 1930. Judging it was well worth the visit, and much more virtuous than spending the afternoon with a prostitute, Beatrix, he congratulated himself on his new found better judgement and purity.

An hour and a quarter later, back down the steps, across the park having decided against sitting and reading there, and a short stroll and he was in the small piazza in front of the Janáček theatre. Well, it could hardly be called a piazza in the Italian sense. It was more of a concrete laden square, on one side of which was a small park. Even though it was now quite late in the afternoon, approaching five, it was still warm and there wasn't a cloud to be seen in the clear blue sky.

The Janáček theatre was one of those 1950s and 1960s type communist grey concrete and glass constructions of which the regime had been so proud. It resembled any number of 'Palace of Culture' soulless buildings Tom had seen across Central and Eastern Europe and in the Soviet Union itself. Outside it, to one side of the square, was the obligatory huge statue, towering twelve feet or more above its surroundings. At first he thought it was some actor whose immortality had been honoured for his contribution to the magnificent cause of socialism through his interpretation of socialist realism. On checking the inscription though he quickly realised that it was the man after whom the theatre had been named, Leoš Janáček. The huge image of the Czech composer had obviously seen better days. The stone had turned mouldy green in places, mostly in long wide streaks down the composer's coat, waistcoat and trousers. No doubt the result of years of heavily polluted communist industrialized Moravian rain. His head and hair had clearly been visited on numerous occasions by the local pigeon corps, who had left their customary deposits. The statue had obviously not been cleaned for years, if ever.

The rest of the square had also seen better days. Years of neglect had taken their toll on this great communist cultural achievement. The pipes that once obviously supplied water to a long defunct fountain in the centre of a large rectangle pool were now completely rusted over. The water in the empty pool had now been replaced by various items of junk, as if to reflect the debris of the great Stalinist human and architectural failed experiment of the past.

As he sat there on one of the concrete benches around the square and watched the early evening Central European life slowly pass him by Tom thought of the contrast between the city of Brno in Southern Moravia and that of Liberec in the north of the Czech Republic. Brno appeared a more pleasant and greener city. An even more stark contrast, however, was that with Prague. Obviously there were fewer inhabitants in Brno, but hardly any tourists, well no British ones at least, just some small groups of Germans and Austrians. It was just much, much quieter, and far more peaceful than most of Prague. Sitting there in the centre of the 'second city' of the Czech Republic he could feel the silence. Only very occasionally was it punctured by the distant low rumble of the Sunday schedule trams. In Brno though they weren't called trams, for the people of Brno – Brňáks if they were men and Brňačka if they were women - they were called 'šalinar'. They even had their own different name for the tram, the staple form of transport in Central and Eastern Europe.

For Tom, on that Sunday at least, Brno was a city at peace with itself, a city that had found itself. He decided that peace came from the mixture of all the ingredients of Central Europe that made Brno the city it was. Indeed, a city that Brňáks and Brňačka claimed was at the very centre of Europe, 'Mitteleuropa'. Here was a city with not just a history, but a soul that was its history. Maybe this, the peaceful city of Brno, was 'his Jana', the image of Jana he held in his mind; a woman always seemingly at peace with herself, and contented with herself and her life, while bustling, frantic Prague had maybe been 'his Dita'.

As the sun dipped lower in the sky and the light began to fade Tom noticed an old, quite smart Czech man, dressed in his best, probably his only, suit and tie sitting almost opposite him on a bench on the other side of the dilapidated waterless fountain pool. The man took a comb from his pocket and carefully, methodically, combed back his already immaculately groomed white hair for three or four minutes. His careful combing set Tom's mind wandering. Perhaps the old man was so meticulous about his Sunday best appearance just in case that very afternoon he might meet the woman of his dreams, of his life. Or maybe he might even meet for just one more time his reincarnated dead wife. Who knows just what the man's hopes could be. Seeing him sat there going through his combing ritual, while the Englishman opposite speculated about his hopes, was quite a poignant moment. The whole run down concrete square symbolized an era of hopes and dreams of Stalinist false expectations and glories. Eventually, after he had finished combing the man got up from his bench and strolled slowly and deliberately around each side of the empty fountain pool. Tom wondered briefly if he'd been transported in some time-machine back to 1960s or 1970s Czechoslovakia. Watching the old man pass him by he couldn't help muttering, "is this it? Is this as good as it gets? You have fleeting moments of hope that you cling to, and that bring you a sense and feeling of happiness. Then you get old, and all you have are the memories of youth and memories of expectations."

All this deep self-introspection reminded him of a story he'd heard about the man commemorated by the huge dirty statue towering above him as he sat on the uncomfortable concrete bench.

Nothing constructed by the communists was ever meant to be comfortable. Suffering and being uncomfortable was a way of life, in order to build the 'great communist world of the future' where everything would be better.

In July 1917 Janáček met and fell in love with a young married gypsy woman, Kamila Stösslova. He was sixty-three, she was twenty-five. A few days after meeting her Janáček launched himself into composing a song cycle about a young peasant farmer who was seduced by a gypsy girl and ran off with her. It is said to be a watershed in his artistic career. In the song cycle the farmer embarks on a sexual liaison with the girl, who as a gypsy was a social outcast. Janáček called the piece 'The Diary of One Who Disappeared'. The songs were based on a group of anonymous poems published in a Brno newspaper in May 1916 and for Janáček they were about celebrating personal freedom; a personal freedom to cross class, ethnicity and culture in search of attaining completeness of one's self through love. And presumably, although it appears that Janáček never had any sexual liaison with Kamila Stösslova, a personal freedom to cross social taboos about age differences between lovers. In his own current situation one of the most striking things about the story for Tom was the songs' identification and demonstration of the dilemma of on the one hand finding and attaining complete happiness through love of another individual and on the other hand having to accept the sadness and heartache of what has to be given up in order to achieve that fulfilment – to be subject to the condemnation of society and the pain which may be caused to others in one's life. Would his love for Jana now cause pain, not only for Dita but also ultimately for Jana in destroying the close friendship between the two women? In the song cycle the peasant farmer suffers an immense feeling of loneliness as he gives up and says goodbye to his home and family in order to pursue his gypsy love.

'The Diary of One Who Disappeared' was a dramatic musical expression of Janáček falling in love with Kamila Stösslova, a musical representation of the obsession of an older man for an attractive younger woman. Given the story about an older man and a younger woman that Petr's student, Lenka, had told him a few days before, Tom began to wonder if it was something in the air, or maybe 'in the water' in Brno that produced these type of relationships?

Janáček, who was born in the village of Hukvaldy just outside Brno, reinvented Kamila, whom he called 'his Gypsy', as his muse. She became the inspiration for his music and work over the next four years. From their meeting in a pub in the spa town of Luhačovice until the time of his death Janáček wrote four operas, two string quartets, two symphonic works and a Mass. It was said that Kamila was his inspiration for all these works. She provided him with the context and atmosphere within which he could interpret his emotions in his music. He wrote over seven hundred letters to her and in one of those in 1927 he wrote to her, "everything for you." Janáček hadn't had a very happy life with his wife and eventually he divorced her. Their two children had died. Despite the divorce though they continued to live in the same house, although living very separate lives, even though his wife continued to cook for him and generally look after him. For much of his life Janáček was in fact a marginal, quite provincial musical figure in his homeland. It was only with the successful premiere of his opera Jenufa in 1916 that he became more widely famous.

By 1928 Janáček's imagination about his relationship with Kamila had completely taken over his life. It was a relationship based though only on the infatuation of an elderly and ageing man for a much younger woman. As far as any intimacy between them was concerned, the whole thing, their relationship, took place only in his mind. Turning all this over in his mind Tom wondered quite what another famous Moravian, Sigmund Freud, would have made of Janáček's obsession with his Gypsy. Was it a yearning for a lost youth, an attempt to stave off the toll of the passing years and old age, or just the imagination running wild of an elderly man in his later years? Or perhaps, Tom preferring out of self-interest to be more charitable in his judgement, it was simply the fact that we only really appreciate true beauty and truly beautiful things as we grow older. Our understanding and appreciation of beauty grows as we do. As he sat in that run down square in front of the theatre he convinced himself that these Moravian stories about older men and younger women should give him yet more hope in his pursuit of Jana. After all there were fifty-five years between the old man and the young woman in Lenka's story, and thirty-eight years between Janáček and his Gypsy, Kamila Stösslova, but between him and Jana there were only a mere eleven years. "Should be a piece of cake," he mumbled as he rose from the bench and set off slowly across the square.

He made his way out of the square, through Moravské náměsti and across the centre of the city to the Špilberk gardens and park under the castle that he had visited with Petr on Friday afternoon. Soon he was sitting on another bench taking in the early evening warm air, watching the sun sink slowly out of the sky and observing yet more Sunday Czech life pass him by.

On the next bench sat two young Czechs of seventeen or eighteen maybe. The age of expectancy, of hope and surprise he thought as he watched them out of the corner of his eye, all the time pretending not to. Even though he was seated Tom could see that the boy was tall, well over six foot, already quite broad shouldered and was wearing shorts, an off-white t-shirt and the obligatory western cultural image trainers. The girl was also tall and slim, though not as tall as the boy Tom guessed, and she was still the kind of young innocent girlish slim that would 'fill out', probably quite nicely, in a couple of years. At this age though her faded blue jeans barely clung on to her very slim hips and her pale pink t-shirt exhibited her jutting shoulders almost like a coat hanger had been left in it. Her longish blonde hair was tied back in a pony-tail. The two of them just sat there barely touching each other, but enough to let each know they were there, and staring out at the Brno skyline. After ten minutes or so they got up to make their way back down the hill and through the park. As they passed Tom on his bench the girl stopped opposite him to smell the scent of the lavender on the bushes beside the path and then encouraged the boy to do the same. He made a cursory pretence to do as she suggested and inhale the scent, followed by what was obviously a glib remark in Czech to his young love. Her response was to lightly jab him in the ribs, obviously a reward for his glibness. A brief exchange of knowing smiles between them followed and she wrapped both of her arms firmly around his waist as they strolled on down the hill totally and utterly enwrapped in one another's being, totally and utterly in love on a beautiful still warm early evening.

Two good looking young people enjoying the early summer and enjoying each other's feelings and hope completely in the new post-1989 Czech Republic.

Through his observation of those smallest of actions and things the world was a lovely place again for Tom. How lovely were those fleeting moments in those, for him, long gone quickly passing years. Yet those two young lovers will not realise right now just how fleeting those times are. How quickly those lovely days of innocence and hope pass. Is youth really wasted on the young, as the saying goes, he pondered? Can those little touches and actions – the faintest of innocent touching of hands, the gentle playful loving tap in the ribs or on the arm – can they never be reproduced by 'forty-somethings' like him? Or are they the property of the young? Have those moments long gone for him, never ever to be revisited? Maybe he should dash after the two young lovers and tell them to make sure they enjoy it completely now. Explain to them just how brief and fleeting it really is. They would never be convinced of that at this point in time of course, this lovely moment on a glorious sunny day; that the way they felt now would ever change or could ever be lost. No doubt Janáček could tell them, but he, like Tom, was humming a tune from a different age to their present golden sunlit world in the new Czech Republic.

13
To Ostrava – the shortages and the excesses

He spent a reflective remainder of Sunday evening alone over a meal in his Brno hotel, followed by a comparatively early night. A lift to the station in Petr's struggling Skoda, hearty goodbyes and a, "see you soon, my friend. Now you've been to Brno you'll want to come back many more times I'm sure," from Petr, and he was clambering aboard another Czech train with his bag bound for Ostrava.

Just under three hours later, around mid-day, he checked into the Hotel Imperial, which claimed to be the best hotel in Ostrava. His first impression on entering his fourth floor room was that the furniture was somewhat IKEA-ish. Pleasant enough with a lot of light wood and seemingly newly furnished. The maid had thoughtfully left the air conditioning on so the room had a welcoming coolness compared to the mid-day heat outside in the dusty Ostravian streets. His first meeting at the Technical University wasn't until two o'clock so there was time for a refreshing shower in what turned out to be a very modern bathroom with a smart walk-in shower.

"Jesus!" Tom's mind screamed, "is there a shortage of dress material in this country?" True, it was late May and getting hotter, but even in his nineteen-sixties' youth he couldn't remember ever seeing skirts so short on young girls as he was now 'socially scientifically observing' as he strode through the main square, Masaryk Náměstí, on his way to the university. In bloody Ostrava! Not exactly a city Tom had ever heard of as being world-renowned for its good looking females. What was it his Bristol University friend Bob, who had been there a few times, had said to him about the place when Tom called and asked him what it was like?

"Oh yeah, Ostrava, have you ever been to Port Talbot on a wet Wednesday?"

Some wet Wednesday. It was Monday and the only wetness he was starting to feel on his first visit to Ostrava had nothing whatsoever to do with raindrops falling on his head, or anywhere else for that matter. It was very warm and getting hotter, and Tom's wetness was from perspiration rather than rain.

"Maybe it's like coppers," he told himself, "as you get older they start to look younger. Maybe as you get older so the skirts start to seem shorter. Who knows?"

He was so busy musing over these finer philosophical points of life, and simultaneously fixing his eyes on the post-1989 Czech Republic's obvious chronic shortage of clothing material, that he almost walked straight on down Sokolská třída and right past the entrance to the Economics Faculty. Or he would have done, except that there was a whole gaggle – just what is the collective noun for young girls in short skirts he wondered? – of arses, long legs and micro skirts bouncing towards the doors at the entrance to the Faculty building. Strutting in to study economics, "no doubt it would be micro-economics," he chuckled.

Christ! Who'd be a lecturer here, and at this time of year, in such heat? All these nubile young things and all about to become high-powered Czech market economists no doubt. Frightening, quite frightening!

"Ahoj, Tom, dobrý den," were the words that punctured Tom's meandering brain. Even after many years, every time he heard the Czech hello of 'ahoj' it always made Tom smile; because of its pronunciation as ahoy he always got an image of a sailor approaching in his head. This was no sailor though this was Václav, a Professor and the Head of the Department of Macro-Economics in the Faculty. He was a short and quite stout man with black thick-rimmed glasses, who like most Czech men loved his Czech beer. Quite serious about his work at times and a man who gave the impression that everything had to be done correctly, everything had to be in its place. This was no doubt a legacy of his period spent growing up and living under the regimented regime of communist academia pre-1989. He also possessed a quite dry sense of humour. Tom liked him. Maybe it was his dry sense of humour, maybe it was his enquiring mind. Václav was always quizzing Tom about this or that in Britain, and for a Czech economist he was fascinated by British, particularly English, history. Maybe it was simply Václav's love of, and intense knowledge of Czech beer that endeared him most to Tom. Whatever it was, he was looked upon as a friend. His dress sense was very much sober, conservative Central European. Tom often went to conferences and meetings in the Czech Republic and elsewhere in an open necked shirt and sometimes without a jacket. Václav, however, would always have a jacket and tie on, and predominantly it would be a suit he would be wearing even in the hottest weather like today. After all, that was what was proper and correct. Today it was a sort of light and dark grey, fairly wide striped suit. The sort Tom had seen in plenty of Czech menswear shops. It was accompanied by a white shirt and a dark blue tie, exhibiting boldly in gold in its centre the university crest, the image of an owl inside a circle. No doubt the owl signified wisdom Tom was reminded as his two days of meetings, intense serious discussions, and heavy Czech lunches and dinners were about to begin in earnest. So, he thought it might be wise to get those long legs and short skirts right out of his head and clear his brain for some work.

As it turned out the afternoon was pleasant enough. In the Czech way of things the scheduled meeting time of two o'clock did not actually mean that work and meetings started at that time. This was the Czech Republic and first there had to be káva and voda – coffee and mineral water. This was followed by seemingly endless tours of offices and introductions to everybody from the Vice-Rector of the Faculty to the various secretaries of departments. Names, names, and more names, all Czech of course. Some of which Tom could distinguish, like the Monikas and the Lenkas, or the Kateřinas. Some of which he had no chance with, like Bohanka and Drahomira, but most of which he would never remember or recall. Or probably even need to throughout the two days of his visit, let alone beyond it on his next visit to what was by now a very hot and sunny Ostrava, and which was beginning to seem a million miles away from that Port Talbot wet Wednesday.

He'd made sure he registered and remembered the Vice-rector's name, of course. Also he made a definite point of remembering and logging in his brain the particular name that was appended to what were yet more quite magnificent and delightful long legs, seemingly in their mid-twenties and barely skimmed by the shortest of short pale pink skirts. Could a skirt get any shorter and have any point in existing at all, he wondered? These longs legs, in what he determined won the prize for the 'shortest skirt of the day' he'd seen so far, belonged to one of the two departmental secretaries in the outer office from the one in which Tom would be having most of his meetings throughout the two days. Hmm ... Michaela, that was locked into his brain cells and safely filed away under the one's marked 'Important' and 'short skirts', or should it be 'wide belts'? Anyway Tom made bloody sure he didn't forget it, and that she was made well aware that he had well and truly registered her, what was for him oh so important existence, by constantly using it over and over at every opportunity throughout his two days in the Faculty. The long legs were just the most striking part of what was a slim, tall, very fine body, topped by bobbed natural blonde hair.

"Thank you for the kava, Michaela, Oh, and thank you for the voda, Michaela."

"Dobrý den, Michaela, jakes se máš? – good morning, Michaela, How are you?"

"Yes, Michaela, thank you I would like some káva."

"You look very well today, Michaela. Your dress is very smart, Michaela."

It became embarrassing, such that Václav started smiling every time Tom went into his pathetic routine. Just before Tuesday lunchtime, as Michaela brought into the meeting some pre-lunch káva and voda, the Czech Professor grinned at his English guest, winked at him, and barely stifling a laugh, said, "well Tom, your Czech certainly seems to have come on magnificently over the last two days, especially your mastery of the pronunciation of Czech female names, well one in particular anyway."

Tom offered him a wry, slightly embarrassed grin and spluttered, "thank you, Václav, that's very kind of you to say so." Not content to leave it there though he excruciatingly followed that with, "what do you think, Michaela?" At that Václav let out a loud and very deep guffaw. Michaela, unfortunately, was at that time pouring out the coffee. She turned a very deep shade of pink, far deeper than the colour of the excuse for a skirt she had been wearing when Tom was first introduced to her the previous morning, and she almost succeeded in pouring the hot coffee into the lap of one of Václav's colleagues. All she could utter was, "yes, your Czech is improving all the time," which caused Václav to let out another almighty laugh.

Once Michaela had left the office, while they drank their coffee Tom ventured, "I think she likes me, don't you, Václav? Does she speak much English?"

"Well, she certainly knows your name, Tom, and I guess she understands that you certainly know hers," Václav replied, followed by another chuckle.

In fact it was gone three-thirty on the Monday afternoon before Tom eventually sat down in Václav's office with his host and two of his colleagues to discuss some new courses which he had helped to write for the university, as well as a future joint research project the Czechs had proposed on their country's long term preparations for entry into the European Union. Tom amazed himself. He actually found himself taking a keen interest in the discussions and participating enthusiastically, and only found himself struggling to keep his mind focused for a very few minutes. Not once did images of the shortest of short skirts and the longest of legs they skimmed enter his consciousness. He didn't know whether this was something he should be pleased about or worry about. Bloody hell he thought during his late afternoon fifteen minute walk back to his hotel, am I becoming a serious academic?

By just before five o'clock Tom's arduous Czech working Monday was over and he was taking a leisurely stroll back to his hotel, once again taking in the sights of sunny Ostrava, especially the short ones. The new consumer led Czech Republic was a very strange free-market economy mix now post-1989. You only had to look in the various shop windows in a place like Ostrava to see the vast differences in wealth and poverty in the new Czech liberal democracy. A row of four or five shops with pretty tacky, poor quality goods, especially clothes, in their windows would suddenly be interrupted by a very expensive shop. Usually this was one selling expensive western sports clothing or brand-name clothing such as Levis or Wranglers. Brand names were the new dogma for Czech youngsters. They'd replaced the communist party slogans that used to be displayed thirty feet high or more on the side of buildings imploring the people to work harder for the glory of communism. Adidas, Levis, Nike, etc. had become the communist wall slogans now and the 'party cards' of the nineties. Ostrava had fewer of them, but that was probably a reflection of its local economic problems. It had been the centre of the Czech old 'smokestack' industries. The sort, like steel and coal, that Margaret Thatcher had either attacked or restructured in the early to mid-eighties in Britain, depending on your political persuasion. Being close to the Polish border Ostrava had suffered greatly from competition from cheap Polish coal and the local heavy goods vehicle factory at nearby Vítkovice was now threatened with closure, being unable to compete effectively with German and Japanese imports.

So, as he strolled back to his hotel Tom thought that Ostrava had the air of a city struggling to survive in the new climate of capitalism in the Czech Republic. It was looking a little shabby and frayed at the edges, like an old comfortable jacket who's inhabitant, the communist system, had long since passed away. Fine in late May and the sunshine, but don't think I would like to be here in the freezing cold of November, December or January, he decided. The city, or at least the city centre that Tom saw, did though seem to have the usual East European layer of dust that had settled everywhere, which made it appear like it needed a very large hoover employed over the whole place. It was a layer of dust that in autumn and winter when mixed with rain and snow would no doubt turn into messy muddy grime.

It was around five-fifteen when Tom reached his hotel room. With another Czech gastronomic feast to come at seven-thirty in the shape of dinner with the Dean of the Faculty and other members of the department he decided maybe a nap was in order. While he was undressing for his nap he noticed something which was obviously a hangover from the old communist days, and which made him chuckle. On the back of the door to his room was a notice headed 'Fire Safety Precautions'. The old communist bureaucracy was alive and well and 'living' in this directive which stated in its first paragraph:

"According to the Act of CNR # 133/1985 Sb., on Fire Protection, in wording of subsequent regulations (complete wording #91/1995 Sb) on fire protection, no.17, for the sake of protection of property, health and lives of citizens against fire, citizens are required to behave in the way not to cause any *change* of fire and to contribute, as much as they can, to appropriate fulfilment of tasks in the fire protection."

Not having the no doubt lengthy and wordy appropriate Act and the relevant sub-sections to hand Tom smiled, thinking he wasn't quite sure how he was supposed to act so as, "not to cause any *change* of fire." Further down the same notice he read, under the heading, "Basic duties of hotel *quests* in prevention of fire and in case of fire," that he should "refrain from smoking and ***manipulation*** with open fire," and that he should not, "carry out any incompetent repairs," nor, "overload electrical circuits by connecting electrical appliances." Just what, "*manipulation* with open fire," was amused him, as well as the fact that the notice seemed to imply that he could by all means carry out competent repairs to the electrics of his room, but not incompetent ones, and certainly could not under any circumstances use an electric razor, that being an electrical appliance. The notice concluded by warning him that, "Failure to comply with the above Fire Safety Precautions is a criminal offense according to the Act#91/95 Sb. On Fire Protection, no.78." "Mmm," he muttered as he slipped into bed, "better be real careful there then."

14
A Marlboro manoeuvre

As it turned out the dinner with the Dean of the Faculty was okay. Somehow lunches in the Czech Republic always seemed much worse, and for this dinner Tom chose salmon, figuring that even the Czechs couldn't do much wrong with that. It turned out to be a good choice. Plain and simple, except for the obligatory dollop of foamy whipped cream on top, but not too dry or over cooked. It seemed that someone in the post-1989 revolution Czech Republic had discovered cans of foamy whipped cream and it was now being applied to everything, sweet or savoury, from pancakes to soup. The company was bearable and outside the restaurant at just after ten o'clock he thanked his hosts and, as it turned out, somewhat over optimistically strolled off to explore the Ostravian Monday nightlife.

His 'Ostravian Port Talbot wet Wednesday' friend Bob had said that except at weekends the only nightlife worthy of the name existed in the bar of the hotel Tom was staying in, the Imperial. Even labelling it that could be liable to prosecution under the trade description act, according to Bob. Most of the larger hotels in Central and Eastern Europe had an obligatory so called night club and casino rolled into one. Generally they had their 'tame' prostitutes, who obviously paid for their 'space' or 'plot' at the bar and were not slow to make eye contact and utter the obligatory, "hello". This was usually followed by what little English or German they had, and pretty soon after by the universal language phrase of, "you want sex?" That aspect of Czech life had quickly caught up with Western Europe in its post 1989 revolution world, but somehow the central and eastern European version felt even seedier.

As Tom made his way back to the hotel the streets of Ostrava were deserted even though it was only just gone ten o'clock. It was the by now familiar scene to him of the dimly lit sparsely populated streets of a Central European city. The two bars he passed were either empty or occupied by one or two very drunk looking, scruffily dressed, middle aged Czech male forlorn souls. Ironically he noticed that both these advertised themselves as 'Herna' - 'non-stop 24 hours bars'. Why on earth should they want to stay open for 24 hours? There is next to nobody in them now and it's only ten o'clock. Do all the trendy party animal Ostravians suddenly come flooding into town on a week night at three or four in the morning desperate for a drink at a 'non-stop 24 hour' bar? Somehow Tom doubted that.

He decided to lift his head above the depressing 'Herna' bar level as he continued his stroll back to the hotel. Tom always tried to remind himself to lift his head and eyes above street level in the Czech Republic. There was always something interesting around every corner. The top parts of some of the buildings he passed now were quite unique and beautiful in their design. Yet they were interspersed with quite bland, typical communist period grey functional ones. It was, indeed, a strange mixture. The stark, grey, blandness of the communist period buildings contrasting with the sometimes quite striking pastel shades of light pink, yellow and blue of the older buildings from the period when the Czech lands were part of the Hapsburg Austro-Hungarian Empire. It produced a peculiar contrasting beauty in some of the streets.

Masaryk Náměstí was empty, except for a couple of young sounding voices chatting somewhere across the other side of the square. As Tom turned into it he could hear them echoing across the large square despite the fact that he couldn't see anyone else there. It felt a little eerie and again peculiarly Central European. The darkness of the poorly lit square, and the deserted nature of the place at a relatively early hour of the night in what was after all the third largest city in the Czech Republic, gave it a particular atmospheric quality. The arched passageway in the corner of the square, and the sound of voices emanating from some distant out of sight bodies, was very familiar, and for him very typical of the mystery and intrigue of the whole Central European region.

"A beer in the hotel bar then," he told himself. "Then bed and maybe even some reading for work." He was still feeling virtuous after his meetings earlier in the day and from his revived academic self. His academic persona soon disappeared though as he entered the Hotel Imperial bar and casino. He couldn't help but smile at the predictability of it all. Indeed, had there been a special place on the roulette table where you could place a bet on the strategic positioning of the prostitutes in the bar he would have cleaned up. Three sat perched on the high stools at the bar. They were perfectly strategically placed on alternate stools so that no matter where Tom went to sit at the bar – or any other punter for that matter – one of them would be sat next to him. Her, and at least one other of her fellow business associates, would then be able to catch his eye in the mirror directly in front of him running the length of the back of the bar behind the bottles of drinks and optics.

The place itself had about twenty people in it besides Tom and the three prostitutes. Two other prostitutes, as he reckoned them to be, were sat individually at a couple of tables with two groups of four and five guys who looked like German businessmen. They wore the suit that was the 'uniform' that gave them away.

It felt very strange. It wasn't that he was likely to do anything; enter into any monetary business arrangement with the women. Engaging the prostitutes in conversation though, the 'preamble to trading', he somehow found extremely exciting. He was like some naughty schoolboy about to do something wrong which he knew he shouldn't do, but couldn't really resist.

These were 'professionals' in every sense of the word, who had learned their trade over many years. No doubt under the pre-1989 communist regime when the party bosses used to get their 'perks' as and when required in what were then special communist party hotels. The three seated at the bar he estimated to be in their early thirties. As he levered himself up onto one of the bar stools he immediately sensed the women exuded a confidence, even to the point of going way past self-confidence to a clinical hardness. It was fine-tuned, honed down to the minutest detail. After all this was their business. Clothes, hair, shoes, even the obligatory lighter tossed casually on the bar in front of them alongside the packet of cigarettes and the sunglasses on the top of the head, all were immaculate and precisely placed in the environment of their business 'office'.

The one that first caught Tom's eye in the mirror behind the bar was sitting on his left. Almost as soon as he sat down she immediately applied what he had observed many times before in Central and East European hotel bars, the standard 'Marlboro manoeuvre', as he'd come to label it. First, demonstrably picking up her cigarette packet and lighter, plucking out a cigarette carefully and deliberately between her long well painted fingernails then gently sensuously placing it between her glossed ruby red full lips in the most provocative manner possible. Next she flicked open the top of her lighter, lit the cigarette and took a long slow draw. There was nothing overly sexy about all that, except that every part of the procedure was conducted with her eyes firmly downcast until the very final part. As she sucked slowly in, puckering her perfectly formed cheeks through her long endless draw on the cigarette, she slowly raised her eyes and fixed a long, consuming, piercing gaze straight into Tom's eyes in the mirror running along the back of the bar. This was followed as she exhaled by an emerging, ever so slight smile as somehow she allowed the tips of her sparkling white teeth to just show themselves through those perfect full red lips in complete unison with her widening eyes.

Even though Tom had seen a 'Marlboro' so many times before – in Bucharest, in Budapest, in Prague – he didn't think he had ever seen one executed so perfectly. There was no haze of smoke to obscure her first contact gaze as she exhaled. Instead there was just a long horizontal perfectly controlled tube of smoke at the level of her mouth. There was certainly no hint of a cough. That barking, off-putting cough that was so often exhibited by women smokers of a certain age in Central and Eastern Europe was not about to burst forth from her mouth into the air of the hotel bar. The 'draw' was long and slow. The pace perfected, so as to excite an air of expectancy in the subject of her subsequent gaze. She knew she was being watched and studied, so there was no need to rush. Indeed, the delay would only make success more certain. Equally, the raising of the eyes was timed to perfection, as was the co-ordination between her smile and eye contact with Tom through the mirror. It was a 'Nadia Comenech perfect 10' of a 'Marlboro', truly a performance of Olympic gold medal winning proportions. So good was it that Tom felt his stomach turn over nervously, and he was reduced to almost melting in the intensity of the gaze of her brilliant wide eyes and the smile just brushing across her full lips.

Without moving his stare, frozen like a rabbit in car headlights in the mirror at the back of the bar, or even attempting to turn his head, he found himself stammering, "would you like a drink?" As for virtually the whole of the time that prostitutes in hotel bars like these sat there with never a sign of a drink in front of them – certainly never one they bought themselves, except the occasional mineral water – her answer was obvious.

"Yes, I will have vodka martini, and with ice please. Thank you," she said slowly and deliberately in almost perfect English. Something else for which no doubt the timing and delivery had been honed through much previous practice, after all it was the finale to the manoeuvre, the equivalent of the seamless gymnastic dismount. Without giving Tom the time to think she volunteered, "My name is Susanna."

That was another characteristic of the prostitutes in the Central and Eastern European hotel bars such as the Imperial, most of them spoke quite good English or German, depending on what was required. That meant you could at least just talk to them. For Susanna though it was not about talking, even if that was all Tom believed he wanted, someone to talk to.

"Room number, sir?" The barman interrupted Tom's thoughtful mesmeric appreciation of Susanna's execution of her Marlboro performance.

"Sorry?" Tom asked.

"Your room number? To charge the drink, sir," the barman repeated.

"Oh, err, four two two."

"And another drink for you, sir?" The barman was persistent; after all he wasn't going to go away while he thought he could get some drinks sold. Maybe he thought that Tom, in his mesmerised state, was going to pay less attention to monetary matters as far as drink was concerned and make the barman's night by spending some serious money. Tom had noticed that the barman was not exactly rushed off his feet selling drinks. Not that this was unusual in hotel bars like this in this part of the world. It was the prostitutes who were the real trade of these bars. That was where the hotels made their bar profits, from a rake-off from the girls' business transactions. It was a sort of equivalent to rent, only in this case it was usually rent for a bar stool or a designated reserved table near the bar. Anyway, the barman was disappointed. He clearly wasn't going to send his bar takings rocketing through Tom's beverage consumption habits that night.

He did ask for another beer though. He didn't really need another one. He'd hardly touched his first one. Strange that too he thought, got to order another beer, can't have the woman thinking I don't drink. Not macho enough. Strange, because this particular woman he was so concerned about creating the right impression with was a prostitute, who wouldn't give a monkeys whether he liked a beer or two or not. In fact, she probably preferred it if he didn't have too many beers. Anyway, she was definitely not interested in his liquid dietary habits. She was interested in only one thing, what was in his wallet. So, why the hell did he need to do the big macho man thing?

"I am funny to you?" Susanna interrupted his thoughts that were provoking a slight smile on his lips.

"No, no, to me you are very beautiful," he replied, now turning on his bar stool to face her head on and at the same time thinking that was a stupid thing to say, and a bit forward maybe? Bloody hell Tom, his brain screamed at him, there is a beautiful, sensuous woman sat six inches from you with her tits hanging out, what the fuck is all this shit going through your mind about was that a bit forward? She's a prostitute for Christ's sake. She doesn't give a stuff if you're a bit forward.

Susanna's whole body language was by now doing a 'Jerry Maguire' – show me the money! She had crossed and uncrossed her legs what seemed about half-a-dozen times in a minute. Each time Tom caught a faint rustling sound. A mixture of the friction of her dark stocking clad legs and whatever particular piece of satin underwear she had covering her lower body, which in turn was rubbing against the lower part her very tight fitting slit-side satin turquoise dress.

Tom guessed she was around five foot eight in her heels. A very flat stomach, nice full hips, tight nicely rounded arse, and pushed up and out very full rounded tits. The upper part of them protruded proudly out of the top of her bright satin turquoise dress, which was supported over her shoulders by two very thin straps that ever so slightly exhibited the strain of supporting her two fine upper assets. Her hair was full and thick, put up in clips, but which he guessed would fall at least to her shoulders and maybe further when released. It was that colour which was so common and popular in Central and Eastern Europe, a dyed blonde. This though was a dyed blonde that had been done very well, and not the almost white variety which was clearly over-peroxided and exhibited black roots. Her eyes were brown, just above a perfectly formed nose and those full, ruby red lips. As he was to find out later, according to her own description she was, "just a typical Moravian woman."

What to say next to keep the conversation going? He was frantically racking his brain trying to think what to say. Clearly, "do you come here often?" was not appropriate. Hang on though, this is a prostitute for fuck's sake, he reminded himself. She would be practiced at it, and it slowly dawned on him that he wouldn't have to think about how to keep the conversation going. He wouldn't have to do anything, except sound interested. She would lead, that was her 'business'. All he had to do was relax; a sort of verbal equivalent of laying back and thinking of England.

Tom's relaxed mood was rudely interrupted by a very coarse sounding, "Hello, I'd … like … to buy you … a drink." It was hammered out slowly and deliberately in that usual English way of talking to foreigners, slow and loud. Worse still it was in a bloody scouse accent. He quickly realised though that as it was in the form of pigeon English that most English people seemed to think was a universal language for foreigners the offer was not directed at him. Instead it was aimed at one of the other two prostitutes sat at the bar. The one sat immediately on his right, and who seemed slightly younger than the others. Maybe if he kept quiet the 'scouse git' might not realise he had a fellow Englishman to latch onto and bore all night like some long lost friend. The problem was though what to do about Susanna. Just how could Tom continue combat and engagement without talking, especially as he was still convinced that was all he wanted to do? The scouser perched himself on the stool next to the younger prostitute, two stools to the right of Tom, and was leaning on the bar sideways on still trying to engage her in conversation. This also meant he was looking straight down the bar to where Tom and Susanna were sitting.

The scouser was short and squat, around five foot two and almost as broad as he was tall. He had the required scouse thick dark curly hair and the obligatory small dark moustache, which Tom thought rested on his top lip like some dark dead caterpillar. He sat there in his designer label pink shirt and black trousers smelling like Henry Cooper's armpit soaked in some foul smelling concoction resemblant of Brut.

"My ... name ... is ... Kenny," was his next piece of sparkling repartee. The younger prostitute looked quizzical initially, and then quickly looked completely mystified. The 'scouse git' had managed to hit on what was probably the only prostitute in the place with no or very, very little English.

"Meine ... namen ... ist ... Kenny," he tried again, obviously to the limit of his German. A smile crept across Tom's face. Perhaps the scouse didn't know which country he was in, or where he was exactly. His smile broadened as he decided that as the German's had stolen, 'liberated', or whatever you'd like to call it, part of Czechoslovakia in 1938, given the scousers' world class fame for 'liberating' things Kenny should feel well at home with German. Also, Tom couldn't quite see what Kenny thought he would achieve by conveying his name. Even if the prostitute eventually understood, would that suddenly transform her mastery of English and did Kenny then think they would be able to converse in perfect English? Just where was he going, or more to the point where did he think him and the prostitute were going with this name business?

"I make you smile again. You are making fun at me," suddenly Susanna reminded Tom she was still there. What to do now though he thought. Belying his academic prowess and supposed intelligence he too resorted to German, reasoning that Kenny would continue to ignore him if he thought he was a German.

"Nein," he tried to say to her as quietly as possible. This also required him to lean towards Susanna from his barstool in order to whisper directly into her ear. Although she looked more than a little perplexed at his use of German, she took his movement closer to be a sign of encouragement and immediately placed her finely manicured right hand on his inner thigh, gently squeezing her blood red nails into the very top of his leg. This was accompanied by, "I can make you smile very much if you want," whispered extremely sensuously and softly directly into Tom's left ear. Her warm breath accompanying her whisper, her thigh squeeze, her deep soft voice and her magnificent effervescence almost caused Tom to fall off his barstool. All he could do was gulp, take a deep breath, and all this intoxicating atmospheric presence of Susanna caused him to completely forget scouse Kenny's proximity and respond with, "yes, we'll see."

"Eh, eh, you're English." Tom's cover was well and truly blown as Kenny waded in full throttle on overhearing Tom in his moment of weakness.

"Err, yes," was all Tom could think to say.

"Kenny, Kenny Swain's the name, from Liverpool," as if Tom hadn't guessed. "And yours?"

"Tom, Tom Carpenter."

"What you doing here then, Tom? Meself, I'm sorting out some engineering machinery for these dick-heads. They couldn't figure it out themselves. Stuff they bought cheap from us two years ago, that's the company I work for. They never seemed to have got the hang of it. Haven't got the nouse you see, couldn't organise a piss up in a brewery."

And thereby Kenny had written of the entire Czech nation, not discounting the fact that given their beer drinking prowess – the Czechs drank more beer per head of population annually than any other country in the world – they obviously most definitely could organise a piss up in a brewery, and make a bloody good job of it. Kenny though was into overdrive and was not allowing Tom to get a word in edgeways. Not that Tom really wanted to, as he now found himself embroiled in the very conversation and situation he wanted to avoid. Kenny never waited for Tom's reply to the first part of his question anyway. He obviously wasn't really interested in what Tom was doing in Ostrava, and in any case Tom preferred not to tell him too much. In fact, Tom preferred not to talk to him at all.

"So," Kenny rattled on, "help me out here pal. You don't speak the lingo by any chance do yer? See, I'm trying to, like, make some headway with this young gel here, and I ain't getting very far."

That was an exaggeration, he wasn't getting anywhere. By now the younger prostitute was way beyond looking mystified and was looking distinctly disinterested. So much so that she was scanning the rest of the bar to see if her radar could pick up any sign of other possible punters. Kenny could have just stepped straight out of a space ship from Mars for all she cared. He made as much sense to her as someone from another planet, and his increasingly animated gestures with his hands as he firstly tried to communicate with her and then explain to Tom, certainly made him look 'out of this world', or at least out of the world of a Czech prostitute.

"No, I don't speak Czech," was Tom's reply. Then he whispered something in Susanna's ear, who had obviously understood most of Kenny's diatribe, even through his thick scouse accent. "Okay, let's help our new friend, Kenny, out. How much for your friend?" he asked her.

Susanna's brilliant white smile got broader. Tom also noticed a hint of mischief in it dancing across her lips in a sort of cheeky grin and growing all the way up to a sparkle in her eyes. This was no ordinary Czech hotel bar prostitute. This was a clever, intelligent woman, with a wicked sense of humour. As her smile broadened she raised her eyebrows slightly, looked Tom piercingly straight in the eyes, then leaned further forward to softly blow sweet smelling air into his ear and said, "she is cheaper than me, because she is not so good, or so beautiful, yes?"

Susanna then said something in Czech to the barman, who was discreetly pretending not to take any notice of the whole procedure. Taking a pen from him she proceeded to write on a beer mat 3,000 Czech Krowns, followed by 250 DM, which Tom took to obviously mean Deutsch Marks. Next to American dollars the Deutsch Mark was the currency that the 'working girls' most wanted. It would open far more 'doors' for them than Czech Krowns, especially if their dream was to one day leave the Czech Republic.

"She is this, or this for Deutsch Marks," Susanna breathed in Tom's ear, pointing to the figures with one of the long red nails of her left hand. Having finished writing the price on the beer mat those on her right hand were back quite tightly wrapped into the upper inner thigh of his left leg, and she finished off yet another perfect manoeuvre superbly by gently placing her full ruby lips on Tom's cheek, drawing back, again fixing his eyes with hers, then just again faintly raising her eyebrows and smiling slowly. What very little clarity that was left in his now foggy brain had him fleetingly reckoning that the price for the girl almost certainly included the hotel's 'top slice'.

Susanna's even closer proximity while showing Tom the girl's price on the beer mat, not to mention her even more intense piercing eye contact, made him gulp again. Only this one was harder and deeper, and almost audible. Susanna obviously saw it, and it made her smile even more. She knew full well the effect she was having. She was reeling him in. Sensing his discomfort over her close proximity – by now she was almost sharing his stool and her effervescence was cocooning him nicely – made Susanna move in for the kill. She tightened the grip on the inner thigh of his left leg with her right hand even more, such that Tom felt like she was going to slit straight through his trousers, and simultaneously turned more towards him on her bar stool, leaning across to place her left hand at the very top of his inner right thigh. This meant she was now firmly resting the full weight of her body on his thighs and not much was left to Tom's imagination, even if his by now intoxicated brain had still been working. What did flash through his hazy, mashed up brain though was an instant message that said she is good, bloody good I bet!

He took another deep, deep breath. He was now almost gasping for air, waiting for one of those oxygen masks that are supposed to drop down from above his head on a plane in the event of an emergency, and this definitely felt like an emergency. He tried to look calm and composed as he turned to the waiting Kenny and told him "three thousand Krowns, or two hundred and fifty Deutsche Marks."

"Sorry?" a confused looking Kenny replied.

"Three thousand Czech Krowns, or two hundred and fifty Deutsche Marks if you have any German money, they prefer that. I don't know, but you may get it a bit cheaper if you've got the Deutsche Marks. Anyway, that's what she'll cost you for an hour", Tom explained.

"You alright pal?" Kenny responded, completely going off track. "You've gone very red in the face and you're sweating. I mean, it's not that hot in here and there is air con, like."

"Yes, yes, I'm fine." Tom was getting more and more agitated, thinking how the bloody hell did I get embroiled with this scouse git when I should be having a very nice and intimate conversation with this gorgeous woman sat on the barstool on my left. Now he was beginning to lose it. He started to raise his voice. Now he was the one talking slowly and loudly, but the foreigner he was trying to make understand came from north of Watford.

He tried once more, slowly and deliberately, and certainly not very quietly. "Three thousand Czech Krowns or two hundred and fifty Deutsche Marks that is what she will cost you for an hour!"

The penny dropping in Kenny's brain was almost audible. It was the mental equivalent of Big Ben chiming on the hour, or more resonantly, of Lennon and his pals screaming out at the tops of the voices on 'Twist and Shout'.

"Christ! I don't want to shag her, pal! I just want to talk to her." Now it was Kenny who was almost shouting as he reacted indignantly.

"I'm sorry," was Tom's rapid, exasperated, wits-end reply. "I didn't get the price for that, but I suppose she will have to build into the price the cost of scouse lessons for herself and you'll have to allow for the price of the tickets for your return journey here in six months when she has completed the course!"

Tom's patience had completely run out. He was now attempting to swat the irritation that was destroying his evening with what he thought was a mixture of wit and intelligence.

"You taking the piss, pal," was Kenny's intellectual reply. "You want to come outside and then maybe you can get to find out just what the Czech NHS is like!"

Tom backed off, not least because Susanna's grip on his thighs had tightened and out of the corner of his eye he noticed her move her head to attract the attention of the not inconsiderably sized barman and his waiter colleague. If they weren't careful both he and Kenny would find themselves involuntarily checking out not only the Czech health service, but also out of the hotel.

"Look, she is a bloody prostitute," he defended himself to Kenny in an almost whispered tone. "Even if she could talk perfect English, or even scouse – he still couldn't resist it – even then she wouldn't be interested in merely talking to you. She is working."

Although he was speaking in a much quieter way, Tom was still annoyed. He couldn't resist spelling it out forcibly, even if relatively quietly to Kenny.

"So, either let her work, become a paying customer, or piss off!"

Tom's anger spilled out again as he almost spat that comment at Kenny. He was angry because his unreal dream world conversation with Susanna had been punctured. Although it was also party that he never did much like scousers.

With that last outburst to Kenny though he thought he was beginning to sound just like what he imagined the girl's pimp would sound like. "Look, she's working ... become a customer or piss off," or whatever was the Czech equivalent. Anyway, that was a statement he didn't expect to hear coming out of the mouth of an English university lecturer in a hotel bar in darkest Ostrava.

At least it forced Kenny to back off. "Okay, pal, just being friendly like. No need to lose your cool. Only came in here for a quiet beer and some polite conversation," he offered in his defence.

Oh Christ!" Conversation? Don't make me laugh! Is there anyone in there, Tom wondered? It walks, it talks, although God knows what language? The lights are on, but no one's home and what comes out of his mouth appears to emanate from a vacuum masquerading as a brain. Someone probably left it somewhere. Put it down for a few minutes at Lime Street station in Liverpool, like one of those hearts that are transported for transplants. Along ambled Kenny, looked at it, tilted his head to one side and said, "Looks like a brain. Someone's left it there. Obviously they don't want it. I'll have that, and off he went with it."

"So, what is it that we are doing then? Am I not working too, or are you just looking for conversation?" Susanna had seen and heard her chance from Tom's outburst and was now whispering her query into his ear in a provocative way that she had obviously practiced to perfection. She took her opportunity well and once again her timing was perfect, just as Tom's defences were at their weakest, clearly pointing out the contradiction between Tom's statement to Kenny and his own activities, or lack of them, with her.

"Oh, err, yes, sorry, I got distracted."

"Well, I can do that very well. I am sure you will enjoy my distractions," Susanna interrupted him, once again with perfect timing. She stared straight into Tom's eyes, took a deep breath, drew up her, "distractions," until they looked as though they were going to burst right out of the top of her dress, and at precisely the right moment she dropped her eyes downwards to fix on them at their full bloom and then raised them slowly to once again gaze into Tom's eyes.

"Err-" Tom started, but didn't get to finish. She did it for him. "Normally it would be 3,500 Czech Krowns, but especially for you, Tom, it will be the same price for me as for my young colleague here, 3,000 Czech Krowns or 250 Deutsch Marks, for one hour, but I am much better don't you think?" Now she was deliberately using his name, and lowering her voice to an exceedingly sexy breathless whisper she added, "She is only a young girl, not a woman like me. Or maybe," she hesitated and leaned forward once more, "for you, another special rate, 10,000 Krowns or 800 Marks for the whole night."

Tom gulped hard. His brain was now completely mashed and numb. For what seemed like an eternity he just stared into space, unable to utter any sound. But it didn't matter Susanna was now on full throttle as she charged on in for the kill.

"I am very good. You will like it very, very much, and when you come to Ostrava you will always want to come to see me your Susanna. You will never forget. Room four, two, two, right? Of you go. I will be up there in five minutes." He was like a little boy as she whispered it very slowly into his ear. Each sentence finished off with a soft warm blow of breath into his ear and accompanied by the overpowering effervescence of her perfume. She helped him off the bar stool by the arm and as he stood facing her ready to give her a kiss on the cheek she slipped her arm around him and squeezed his arse to send him on his way, very much like a man would do to a woman he thought. His new scouse 'friend' Kenny was now trying to engage another of the prostitutes sat at one of the tables in the bar in conversation as Tom passed him by heading for reception and the lift.

15
The panelak and two different lives in the new post-revolution Czech Republic

For Tom even a prostitute could become part of the dream, the 'hope'. Not just to shag, but to fall in love with, to 'save'. How many men thought just that he wondered, doubting his motives? That was exactly the road he very briefly went down with Susanna. Not content with an hour on the Monday night he had arranged to meet her the next day, insisting that they meet for a late lunch. He rushed through what few meetings he had in the university that Tuesday morning. Then he said his goodbyes and thank you to Vaclav and his colleagues, and a very special goodbye and, "I hope to see you again very soon," to Michaela and what seemed her even shorter skirt and longer legs of that day.

By twelve-thirty early in the afternoon he was back in his hotel changing his shirt, spraying his armpits with deodorant and slapping on far too much after-shave. A bit of a strange thing to do considering he was about to go and meet a prostitute, he thought. As he stepped out of the lift into the hotel lobby Susanna was there waiting for him. "Ahoj, Tom." Her eyes sparkled as she greeted him with a smile. This was a different Susanna. More relaxed looking, although still very well dressed in a light beige suit over a pristine white shirt, unbuttoned just far enough down to show off her fine "distractions" that she had been so proud of in the hotel bar the previous evening. A thin silver chain ran down from her neck and nestled gently in her cleavage. The whole image was beautifully framed by her long flowing blonde hair. Tom had forgotten quite how tall she was. As she was wearing quite high heels she was almost the same height as him.

She gave him a soft kiss on the cheek and then completely to his surprise suggested that they go to her flat for lunch. She would prepare it for him she told him. As he hesitated, and seeing his surprise, she insisted, "It is no problem, really I want to do this for you."

He was taken aback and for a moment lost for words. Whizzing through his brain were lots of questions. Did she do this for all her clients? Was this just part of her routine, all part of the service? Or was he special? And where was it she would take him? He didn't know Ostrava, only a very small part of the centre. She seemed okay, someone you could trust, but he had only spent a couple of hours with her the night before, and a fair bit of that wasn't exactly taken up with talking and getting to know one another. In fact he knew next to nothing about her, and it would somewhat spoil the moment to ask her to write down her address and give it to the hotel receptionist if she genuinely just wanted to cook for him and show him where she lived. Then his positive, optimistic, hopeful side kicked in. Maybe she just did really like him. Now he was off on his Czech dream again, only to be interrupted by Susanna grasping his hand with that firm grip of hers he so remembered from the night before.

In fact, what he was to experience and see over the next few hours was a real insight into life in the Czech Republic and Czech society post-1989 and the revolution. A whole kaleidoscope of differing, contradictory, and most of all confusing emotions and perspectives emanating from what he saw of Susanna's life, how and where she lived it, her hopes, and his struggle to make sense of it all and understand it. It was not quite what he expected. It was a strange, newly free but empty world of some women in the Czech Republic after the 1989 revolution. Initially it had been a new life of hope, but from what Tom saw now it was a life of isolation and loneliness for many women like Susanna. A fragmented, somewhat sad existence encompassing a whole range of different identities, and a life lived within a perspective from which things appeared somewhat different from the actuality of their life to many of the individual women. The events of 1989 may have offered the optimism of a social revolution, but from what Tom was about to see from his experience with her it was a revolution that had gone backwards socially into a strange void of bleak meaningless existence for some women like Susanna.

"Don't look so worried, Tom, I am a good cook, I will not poison you. And I will let you go." She hesitated slightly, and flashing one of those lovely mischievous smiles of hers, added quietly, "… eventually. Come, we will ask reception to get us a taxi. It's not far. I do not do this with every man I meet here at the hotel, Tom, but I like you. You are a nice man. You made me smile last night when you were trying to avoid talking to that other English man."

Thank God, he thought, that she added the last bit of that sentence. That it was the episode with the scouser, Kenny, in the hotel bar that made her smile and not his performance elsewhere in the hotel a little later. And did she, did she really like him? His Czech dream was back in focus and he squeezed her hand saying, "Okay, thank you, yes, let's go," and they walked towards the reception desk where she ordered a taxi.

As he occasionally glanced out of the window of the taxi he decided he had never seen so many blocks of flats. Well, not these grey dour looking blocks; row upon row of them. He'd seen more blocks before on his way into Moscow city centre from the airport, but they were not as drab looking and soul destroying as these. These Ostravian versions were even more sad and forlorn. The Moscow blocks were undoubtedly depressing in their own fashion, in their stark isolation, a kind of 'people farm', but they looked cleaner, on their outside appearance at least. They were a whitish grey. These Ostravian blocks were a dark yellowing grey. True, some had been painted on the outside, obviously a development since the fall of the communist regime. Those were few and far between though and consequently stood out as exceptions. Row upon row of the rest of the numerous blocks looked remarkably similar in their depression, however.

How did people remember just which one they lived in? Even the buses and trams encircling the vast estates looked the same. It was a kind of 'never, never land', rather than the anticipated communist future utopian wonderland. No wonder Ostrava was the most densely populated part of the Czech Republic. Three hundred and twenty thousand people piled high on top of one another in these depressing grey boxes, like piles of baked beans tins in a supermarket, although certainly not the Ostravian supermarkets that Tom had seen briefly. And, he guessed, not in the very occasional run-down looking small supermarkets dotted between some of the blocks that they passed in the taxi.

Ostrava was a 'satellite' city. The former communist regime had constructed most of the housing accommodation outside the centre, which was mainly given over to business offices and shops From his academic research work Tom knew that when they moved into these concrete monstrosities the people saw it as part of the 'great leap forward'. It was something better than they had ever had before. On the inside the 'panelaks' – the flats – were very well heated, even over heated. Usually this was from massive coal burning, environment polluting and blackening, centralised city heating plants. The flats were functional enough though. The new scientific socialist panacea reality at work Tom recalled, from the many former regime pre-1989 communist propaganda sources he had read in his work.

Eventually the taxi shuddered to a halt and the driver stopped fighting with what seemed the non-existent gears. A fight he was clearly losing overwhelmingly judging by the constant grinding noises emanating from beneath the car. Tom motioned to pay, but Susanna quickly told him, "no Tom, it is okay, leave it to me please. It is my treat."

The taxi left them outside one of the more depressing looking blocks, if one of these monstrosities really could look more depressing than another? Tom looked around briefly and realised that he really had no idea where he was or what was the way out of this huge concrete maze. Susanna opened the entrance door and again firmly clutching his hand led him up two flights of stairs to her front door. What Tom noticed instantly once they were inside the entrance door to the block was just how spotlessly clean the entrance hall and concrete stairway were. Not a speck of dust in sight and a complete contrast to the grimy and untidy outside area surrounding of the block.

Then quickly he was inside Susanna's panelak, standing in her hallway just inside her front door. She was removing her shoes, putting on slippers and motioning him to remove his shoes. In his anxiousness to take in his surroundings he had completely forgotten the Czech custom of removing your shoes when you go into someone's house or flat. He stooped down and removed his, offering Susanna a nervous, "sorry, I forgot". This drew another reassuring, "don't be so nervous, Tom," from her followed by a flippant, "relax, I am not going to bite you. Well, not yet anyway." He let an apprehensive smile slip across his lips in response.

On the inside Susanna's flat was somewhat more than the 'functional' that Tom had expected. She told him that she had used money from her work to modernise the flat and have a brand new kitchen fitted. Liberally scattered around the walls of the lounge were various cabinets. The type of 1970s style dark wood-like covered chipboard cabinets. Some had glass doors, behind which were the obligatory tea sets or ornaments, reminding Tom instantly of his own old Aunt Julia's flat. Somewhere he would be taken to on a visit five or six times a year and would always wonder, even as a kid, just how much of her life his aunt invested in regularly cleaning all the ornaments. Susanna told Tom she only worked for two weeks out of each month in the hotel. The rest of each month she spent in her panelak, presumably to do just that, clean her ornaments. Fleetingly he wondered just how much she made in working for two weeks in the hotel. It must have been a relatively tidy sum for her to spend the rest of the month off. Well, relatively tidy for a Czech woman in Ostrava, anyway. She certainly seemed to be content in the little hideaway world of her flat. Although perhaps her life had little else to it other than preserving what she had obtained through her 'hard labour'.

The whole place engendered an almost surreal feeling in Tom. Whilst it all seemed very western 1970s and dated it would undoubtedly be better than what many of Susanna's neighbours had, unless of course the whole of the concrete jungle of blocks of flats was inhabited by prostitutes. A sort of huge Ostravian brothel maybe, Tom chuckled to himself. Even Susanna's 'mock wood' kitchen would have been a vast improvement on the kitchen in most of the other flats. She was obviously very proud of what she had. She had bought the flat from money from her previous work in Prague, she said. He was somewhat stunned though, although he tried not to show it, when she proudly proclaimed to him that she had been paid 120,000 Czech Krowns, about £3,000, for one week's work as an escort for one particular foreign client in Prague. Top academics in Prague only earned an average of 10,000 Czech Krowns, about £250 a month, he recalled and that was in universities in the capital city. Susanna had earned what was a year's salary for them in one week In that respect, what Susanna did was extremely well paid. In Ostrava, though, her life seemed a very empty one. To Tom it matched the surroundings of the bland, characterless grey tower blocks. He asked her just what she did with her life during the two weeks each month when she wasn't working at the hotel. How did she pass the time?

"I watch TV, mainly movies," she told him. She had some cable TV it seemed, one station of which merely repeated its schedule four times a month. "Sometimes I just sit in front of the TV day after day. I have seen the movie 'Chaplin' six times. It is a very good, very nice movie I think. I like it very much. Have you seen it, Tom? You know, Charlie Chaplin? It is his life story and all about his lost love, very romantic, but very sad."

Blimey, that guy Chaplin gets around he thought. A club named after him in Brno, or at least his hat, and now a prostitute in Ostrava constantly watching a film about his life. He's obviously very popular in the new Czech Republic. "Yes, I've seen it, but only once. It's good, but like you say, a little sad," he rather vacantly responded. He was briefly tempted to point out that no, he didn't actually 'know' Charlie Chaplin, although he did grow up near to where the little comedian grew up and had drunk in 'his' pub, well the one named after him anyway, many times at the Elephant and Castle in London and of course recently in 'his hat's club' in Brno. Knowing the Czech sense of humour, however, and certainly the way it differed to the English in terms of irony and double meaning, he decided such a remark would be lost on Susanna. Anyway, his mind was elsewhere, trying to fathom out the point of this 'sleep walking' twilight existence of hers. Materialism was the only answer he could come up with. But how could he, or most other people, understand or comprehend this mind-numbing existence Susanna was experiencing now in order to strive for some materialistic better future life if they themselves had not experienced the sort of mind-numbing existence that she, and millions of others, had lived through most of her life under the communist regime in Czechoslovakia up to 1989. Maybe that was just it. The years of living under the communists were the answer to the basis of her present beliefs and principles of working towards a better tomorrow. Working for a better future for herself. How many similar slogans to that had he seen written in huge letters on the side of buildings in the communist states of East and Central Europe prior to 1989, and especially in the Soviet Union itself? Slogans that urged the people of those states to, "labour and work for a better tomorrow and a better future." Of course they were meant to extol the virtues of working for a better future collectively for the whole of the communist societies, for all the people, for the glory of the great communist society. Susanna had merely adapted it to a, "better future," for herself, obviously taking a more individualistic approach. Also, she was certainly applying a different type of 'labour' to that envisaged by the former Marxist-Leninist leaders who had framed the slogans.

"My life here in my flat is a quiet, calm one," she continued. "I like to be quiet and I have my flat to look after, to clean." Ah, yes, the ornaments and the tea set, Tom remembered. "And I go shopping to the local supermarket or the new big Tesco store and supermarket that we have now here." With that she proudly pulled back her net curtains to show Tom, "the new big Tesco," just across the main road at the back of her block of flats. "I can walk there from my flat and can see it from my window. I go there once a week, sometimes more often. They have some nice things. I like to cook, so you can get some nice things there. I have bought some Pstruh – I think you say Trot – for lunch, Tom. I remembered you told me last night that you like rybí, sorry, fish," she quickly added. "Is that okay for you?"

"Yes, that will be very nice, thank you, but it's called trout in English," he briefly corrected her. Although he was actually thinking at the time that he was sure that he had never had anyone tell him before that they could see the Tesco supermarket from their window, and so proudly.

"I am sorry my English is not very good. Thank you for telling me," she apologised.

"No, no, your English is very good," he complimented her, followed by his standard, "somewhat better than my Czech."

"So, I like to relax here in my own little home. My life at work in the hotel, and occasionally when I still work in Prague, is not like that. It is, how would you say it, unusual? I work from ten or eleven o'clock at night until five or six in the morning, sometimes in Prague even from eleven in the morning until five in the next morning. Then I sleep most of the day and if it is in Prague I sleep up the stairs in a room above the nightclub where I work. I am not like some of the girls at my work, I am not with drugs. Quite a lot of them are, then they are on the hook, I think that's how you say it. They depend on the drugs. I suppose that you think that mine is a strange life, but it's what I do, Tom."

Her English was by no means perfect, but he knew what she meant. Anyway, on this occasion it wasn't the time to worry about correcting her grammar, so he opted instead for, "well … err … yes, I suppose it is unusual." He was struggling. He didn't really know how to answer. If truth be told he thought it was bloody strange and even somewhat sad, not least the way she referred to it as work in a very matter of fact way. He wasn't about to go down that particular avenue though. That wouldn't be very productive in terms of what he could see in the focus of his eye line at that particular moment – the outline of Susanna's superb figure as she stood sideways by the window of her flat and the sun streamed through highlighting her very full breasts straining against the tight crisp white shirt, now fully exposed as she'd removed her jacket. Tom quickly tried to re-focus. To get his mind back on the conversation, at least for a short while over the lunch Susanna was off to the kitchen to prepare for him.

So, she barely went out in Ostrava other than to work or to the Tesco supermarket. What about men? Men outside of 'work', he wondered? Men in Ostrava who were not clients? Where did they fit in, if there were any, in her strange almost hermit-like Ostravian existence? Should he ask? Why was he even thinking about asking? Why did he feel he wanted to know about other men? Was he getting swept along by all this, a lovely, beautiful Czech woman taking him to her home? After all, as she said, it was her, "quiet place." She had not asked him for anything, any money for the afternoon, and now she was cooking him lunch in her own, "quiet place," which was separate from her work. His mind was racing on and he couldn't stop himself asking as they entered the kitchen.

"But is it all just that, Susanna? Is it all just work and a quiet life here for you?" he continued, deciding to take a chance, throw out the question and see what happens. "It is a little unusual and strange your life. What about men outside of work? Don't you have any male friends, a boyfriend?"

"A boyfriend?" was her bemused reply. "A little strange? Thank you, Tom" She was a little agitated, but before he could explain she continued, "I don't think it is strange. It gives me money. More money in a month than I could get in a year in a factory here or in most other jobs. It is not something I want to do, will be able to do,"– she let out a little laugh – "forever. These will droop, Tom." As she said that she put both hands under her breasts on the outside of her shirt and lifted them upwards. "The hotel is a busy life. Prague, when I work there, is a busy life. That is work. My flat and here is for relaxing. My flat is a quiet life because there is no sex here for me."

Blimey! That last comment caused Tom some concern to say the least. Was he not going to get his leg over later was all he could think of at that particular moment. Surely she could make an exception to that rule. Although he thought it best not to raise it or enquire at that particular moment as she was in full flow extolling the virtues of, what now seemed to Tom, her 'double life' and split personality.

"I don't want a man outside of work," she continued. "Not that I mean I want one inside work, you understand?" But she didn't wait for his response to that enquiry. "I don't want or need sex, and for sure because of my work not a man. And especially not," she raised her voice a little, "a Czech man!"

Tom was now completely confused. Here was a very beautiful Czech woman. Okay, he thought, she does what she does in the hotel because she wants the money and consequently a better life for herself, and as she had told him before, for her sisters and mother who she helped support financially. He couldn't help thinking though, not without some self-interest, where was her real need being fulfilled? She had told him that next year she could stop doing what she did now. She would have enough money then and would go back to a normal job, in an office maybe. So she was calculating in that respect. Yet, unless Susanna was different, it was common knowledge wasn't it that prostitutes fake it. All those 'oohs' and 'aahs', and the panting, are like a very bad 'B', or should it be 'Z' rated movie or video. So, if there was no man and no sex for Susanna – and she wasn't telling him either that she had a special woman friend in Ostrava, wasn't saying she was a lesbian – just where and how did she get her 'rocks off'? Maybe, it dawned on him, she was the archetypal anal-retentive, and she got her 'rocks off' from cleaning. Maybe this is what Czech women were really about and he had found the key as to why Czech men loved their beer so much. Or maybe the answer was simply that Susanna had a self-help hobby and an 'electrical friend'. Who knows? It just all seemed very sad and bleak, just like the grey, bland tower block in which she lived, and all the many other ones around it.

What was clear already from this limited excursion into Susanna's private life was that the world of the Czech prostitute was a clinical one. Or at least, the world of this particular Czech prostitute. For Susanna there was a clear cut distinct division between her two lives, and not just in the way she lived them. To Tom, one was decidedly grubby and seedy, even allowing for her glamour and beauty, and the other in her flat was cleaner, scrupulously clean in fact, fresher, and where Susanna exhibited a more natural, clean beauty. It was a contradictory light and shade existence where rather sadly the most pleasing sunlight for her seemed to shine from the new Tesco supermarket that she could see from her flat window.

Her clients were therefore also easily put on one side of the divide, her work side. Quite where this left Tom he wasn't sure. She told him that, "For sure, some of the men she met in her work fell in love with her. Many men do fall in love with prostitutes, Tom." She was teasing him, smiling and winking at him in a manner which even in her kitchen as she washed trout he found incredibly seductive, much to his surprise. He resisted the temptation to get to his feet there and then and, even with her hands smelling of fish, show her just what sort of effect she was having on him. He guessed she knew that very well though, after all as he had found out the night before, she was well practiced at it.

"Of course, like most people I am romantic. I mean I am a romantic," she explained. "Romance and the dream of it, of one day meeting the real man for me is everything for me. One day I will, one day I will, Tom." She repeated it as if she was trying to convince herself as much as she was him.

So that is how she clinically dealt with what she did, he reasoned. That is how she got through the constant laying on her back, making the requisite noises, while some man – any man who could pay, young or old, handsome or ugly – got what he wanted. She had her hope.

"I know that one day it will be all perfect," she interrupted his train of thought. "I just have to get through doing what I do so that I can get enough money to live how I want. Then I will have more chance to meet my right man, Tom. Anyway, sometimes it is not so bad doing what I do. Often, very often, it is only a few minutes work." She laughed out loud and went on, "a few minutes of effort, a few minutes of making sounds he wants to hear and ten seconds of gratification for him. That's not so bad is it?"

Once again he was wondering where he came into this picture she was painting. Where did last night fit into all this? Surely it was more than ten seconds, but before he could ponder that little dilemma too long she reassured him.

"Of course, I am not talking about you, Tom. Don't look so worried." Again she was grinning, now as she was bending down to put the prepared dish of fish in the oven. Although Tom's concern over just where his performance the previous night ranked in all this drifted away as he glanced right down Susanna's cleavage as she bent over and placed the dish on the oven shelf. His eyes definitely weren't focusing on the oven bound trout, but instead fixed on something must more appealing as they made their made their way down her perfectly arched back to feast on the magnificently formed cheeks of her arse proudly straining against the cotton of her light beige tight skirt as she locked her long legs straight and bent forward.

She briefly glimpsed his stare, winked at him again and gently scolded him. "Tom, are you listening to me? Are you concentrating on what I'm saying? Or is your mind on other parts of me?"

"No, no, erm, I mean yes, yes, of course I'm listening to you. Do go on," was all he could think to say, turning slightly pink in the face.

Mischievously enjoying his discomfort, she continued, "Your face has gone a bit red, Tom. Maybe it was the heat from the oven when I opened it? Anyway, as I was saying, for the boys, the eighteen, nineteen or twenty year olds, it is never the full hour that they have paid for and it is the same for many of the others. Once their ten seconds of heaven has come and gone they are done, empty. Mostly then they want to get away as much as I do. So, I tell them to shower, shower myself, and then leave them and go back down to the hotel bar if it is in Ostrava, and if it is Prague and the night club I take them gently downstairs by the hand to the bar for another drink before sending them on their way and looking around for another 'ten seconds' and 3,000 Krowns."

She told him some of the older men, a few, wanted more. Some fell in love with her. At thirty-two she was the right sort of age for the forty-somethings and even the fifty-somethings. She was undoubtedly a fine looking woman, one of some style, with a great figure and good dress sense. An idealised dream for the visiting foreigners, especially the French, Italians, Germans; just what they were looking for. She admitted that sometimes they lavished gifts on her as well as money, but none of them had been her 'romantic', her dream man. When she meets him then she could have as she put it, "a normal life." Tom wondered if she would ever find that particular dream. Would she ever give up the well paid work of the hotel and the nightclub? Or would it eventually give her up as she got older?

Well she could always go into the catering trade, he concluded later. It turned out to be a very good and somewhat large lunch. The trout was done with almonds and a butter sauce, and served with some spiced potatoes and a passably decent salad by Czech standards. It was preceded by the obligatory glass of Czech Becherovka liqueur and followed by apple strudel – which Susanna assured him she had made herself – and cream. All this was washed down with a bottle of Czech Ryzlink white wine. Not the best, but the third glass was always better than the first Tom reckoned.

As soon as each course was finished she not only cleared things away, but also plates, cutlery, glasses were all washed, dried and meticulously put back in their place. Of course, it could have been the anal retention he thought of earlier, but more kindly he surmised it could just be that this was a woman who was very proud of her things – the things she had got from her hard work - and was determined to preserve them. She was indeed a determined woman. A woman who could completely detach what she did with men in hotels and nightclubs from systematically and vigorously wiping down her stainless steel sink drainer. She lived a fragmented life with different identities in two completely separate worlds. Much like her country Czechoslovakia under the communist regime prior to 1989, one was an unreal world of 'working for a better tomorrow' and the other a mundane, grey world.

Tom thought she had a very, very tough mental approach to her life. Maybe for a thirty-two year old Czech woman a tough mental approach was needed. This was not just about survival. This was about doing what she thought necessary, what she would do to make life better. Better than the panelaks' dull, grey apartment block daily grind; better than scratching a living for survival and not knowing just how long your job would be there for in the future. Above all, as Susanna told him, better than being sucked into a marriage with a Czech man who would most likely end up loving his beer more than her. The men drank more beer per head of population than any other country, while the women constantly made themselves beautiful, looked after the home, children, and their biggest 'child', their man. These Czech men had it all Tom thought, but for some crazy reason most of them just pissed it away and never realised just how good what they had was. Why, why? This was another of the great mysteries of life in the Czech Republic that taxed Tom's brain. Something he spent a good deal of his time trying to figure out during his stays in the Czech Republic, without much success.

What he was certain about, sat there in Susanna's flat feeling totally stuffed after the lunch she had cooked him, was that she was very beautiful, in a sort of striking Czech way. Her whole manner and style produced a calm feeling of beauty. She had just cooked him a lovely meal and yet she still looked immaculate. Not a hair out of place and through it all she looked extremely cool. But in his current contented, stuffed state, he realised with a start that he needed a reality check. He needed a tough mental approach, just like Susanna's in a way and shouldn't get sucked into the imaginary romance of his present situation. After all only a few days earlier he'd convinced himself he was in love with Jana, and always had been for four-and-a-half years. So, he was determined he was not going there with Susanna. He was in love with Jana and was not going to fall in love with Susanna. Not like the Italian she told him about, who told her he had left his wife and four children for her. Who sent her flowers every day and who desperately, so, so desperately wanted to marry her, wanted her to be his alone. To have and to hold from this day forth, or whatever the Roman Catholic equivalent was Tom thought. Any 'day forth' would apparently do for the Italian, although the sooner the better seemingly. To the Italian, she told Tom, she was a, "bellissimo dream, a fairy-tale in the mystical magical city of Prague," where she had first met him in the club in which she'd worked.

Tom understood what she was telling him only too well. He'd been there, done that, and got the T-shirt, although not with a prostitute of course. This is precisely what had happened to him with Dita, the spell of the magical city of Prague woven with the charm, and in Dita's case great charm, of the Czech woman. Dita was definitely a different sort of Czech woman to Susanna though. She was a very correct and proper sort of woman in every part of her life. For Dita, there were no two separate disconnected lives like Susanna's. Yet, in her way, Dita was very similar in outlook to Susanna. For both of them everything had to be in its place, just so. Order and responsibility were key parts of Dita's world, especially with timekeeping and getting to appointments on time. Being constantly late was one of Tom's worst traits. Something she hated in him, and was never slow to tell him, even though in fact Dita herself was never the most punctual person, although she hated that and always got angry with herself over it. For different reasons to Dita's, order and responsibility were central to Susanna's world.

Similarly, Dita would treat Tom at times almost in the way an Italian mother fussed about her son. She would ruffle his hair like he was a little boy and it seemed that nothing was too much trouble for her as far as Tom's needs were concerned. It appeared as if it was her duty to ensure not only that Tom had enough to eat, but that he had more than enough. He was always complaining to her, "You will make me fat."

"No, no, it's normal, you need to eat, Tom, otherwise you will lose your health," was always her reply.

A strange sort of medicinal logic he thought. One he couldn't quite fathom. Now here was Susanna doing and saying much the same thing. Eating and providing a, "good kitchen," as Susanna put it, was an essential part of keeping healthy in the Czech Republic and for Czech women very much part of looking after their men. For Tom this summed up the whole problem. The Czech women had to be beauty queens, housewives and mothers, all rolled into one for their men, not to mention being good in bed. Yet they spoilt the men constantly with their fussy attentions. Ironically, it was the women who overfed them with masses of meat, starch-ridden dumplings, apple strudel and cream, and who kept them constantly supplied with beer. Every time he had ever visited a Czech woman's flat, or a Czech couple's flat, he had immediately been offered a beer by the woman, quickly followed by the offer of something to eat. Any response of, "no, no, thank you," was greeted with a strong reply of, "yes, yes, it's for men, good Czech beer." Very strange, it was almost as though the Czech women bred and fed the fat, boozy Czech beast that they most disliked. Or maybe it was just their way to keep them docile, again very much in the way that the Czechoslovak communist leadership attempted to do with Czech and Slovak people over many years.

No wonder then that Susanna wanted something different; that she was determined and very single minded. That she could detach herself from her 'normal life' in Ostrava in her flat from her 'other life, her work' in the hotel bar and in the Prague club. Yet, in many ways she was doing the same thing in both lives, servicing men. How many other late twenties and older Czech prostitutes had similar schizophrenic lives he wondered?

Anyway, for Susanna it seemed to work and suit her. The flat was nice. The furnishings, although by no means grand or even expensive by western standards, were certainly newer and more modern than in the few other average dowdy Czech flats Tom had visited. Also, as he had realised, Susanna appeared single-minded enough to mentally get by with coping with her two very different lives. So, he ate his good meal in the manner of a good Czech man. Drank his wine and chatted with her. She offered him coffee, with a proud accompaniment of, "it's Italian," and when he accepted she told him to go and relax on the sofa in the living room while she cleared up and made coffee. He sat stuffed and contented on the sofa, still mystified as to just what could be wrong with such a life for the Czech men and why they had such a love affair with beer. While she washed dishes in the kitchen and prepared his coffee his mind managed to move away from his bulging stomach to wonder about what she was expecting? Was she now 'working'? Should he offer to pay? Or was this really to do with the fact that she actually did like him?

Maybe it was just the same in the relationship between Czech women and their men in the realm of sex as it was in every other aspect between them inside the home. The women took the lead. Well, that was just how it seemed to Tom. He didn't have to ponder for very long over just what Susanna was expecting in that respect. She appeared with his coffee on a tray, accompanied by another Becherovka liqueur and a few small cakes, which again she proudly announced she had made for him earlier. Setting the tray down on the coffee table in front of him as she bent over facing him she gave him one of her long lingering fixed eye stares he had experienced so well the night before. She then sat herself down so close to him he thought she was going to be wearing his shirt and trousers. Crossing her wonderful long legs, she wrapped herself around and into him, uttering a soft question, "you like me Tom?"

"Err … err … yes, very much," was all he could stammer, getting warmer by the second.

"You want to take a shower before we go to bed," she whispered. Not waiting for his reply, she continued, "I will go first while you have your coffee. I will call you when I'm finished. Don't let the coffee get cold."

While she took her shower the question of whether this was a business transaction as far as she was concerned went completely out of his mind. After about ten minutes she shouted to him to come to the bathroom, which was just off the main hallway. As he reached it the door was wide open and there she sat. In the bath, totally naked and spraying herself with the shower head to remove the soap from her superb curves. If this was a dream this was where he would normally wake up and find himself sweating in his own bed. But this was no dream, far from it. A vision maybe, Christmas even, and here was his very, very early present. She almost nonchalantly told him, "your turn, Tom. I will see you in the bedroom. There are clean towels there. You know how to operate shower?"

"Yes, yes, it will be okay, thanks," he said in a somewhat strained almost high-pitched tone.

With that Susanna stepped out of the bath, offering him a full view once again of her magnificent arse, dried herself off a bit more and told him with another wink, "don't be long Tom, I will be waiting. You wouldn't want me to fall asleep would you?"

He remembered that when he was a kid at secondary school there was an extremely sadistic bastard of a gym teacher who delighted in giving you one minute to get showered and dressed after gym sessions or after swimming lessons. Tom, along with most of the other kids, hated the bastard. He was thinking now maybe he should be thanking the bastard! It was the quickest shower Tom had taken since those frightening school gym days. Inside five minutes he was curling into the lovely welcoming warmth of Susanna's body in her king size bed. He'd never been in her bedroom of course, let alone her bed, but he simply went through the only door in the flat he hadn't yet been through hoping it wasn't a broom cupboard or something, and there she was, laying under the flimsiest of dark blue silk sheets with her blonde hair tumbling down over her shoulders and the covering sheet.

Around two hours later he was back in the shower feeling a little exhausted. She was in the kitchen, somehow still looking immaculate in a blue silk dressing gown and again making him coffee. There had been no mention of money. No mention of payment, but strangely now her detached mood had returned.

"You must be tired. You have to leave early tomorrow don't you? I will call you a taxi for after you have had your coffee, Tom, for fifteen minutes time?"

Again, strange, he thought. It was as though she was determined not to let anyone get to her. Not let anyone get inside her head. He wanted to say no, it's okay there's plenty of time. After all it was still only just gone seven-thirty in the evening and still light outside in grimy Ostrava He wanted to tell her that he would like to talk with her some more, spend a little more time communicating out of bed so to speak. But he didn't tell her that. Maybe she really just wanted him to go anyway. Maybe that was her way of dealing with it. He just agreed with her. "Okay, thanks. Yes I am a little tired and you must be too," was all he could make himself say.

Just before eight she grasped his hand as they walked down the flights of stairs of her block of flats and out into the polluted Ostrava air to his waiting taxi. He wished her good luck, told her to take care and said goodbye with a small kiss on her left cheek. She told him, "Make sure you come and see me next time you come back to Ostrava, Tom. You have my phone number so don't forget your Susanna." With that she wished him a safe journey to Prague the next day and sent him on his way.

As he sat in the back of the rickety old Skoda taxi speeding back to his hotel, again past the numerous greying and blackening tower blocks, Tom wondered just how many others she had wished the same farewell to. Just how many others she had told, "Don't forget your Susanna?" Although he tried to reconcile that with the fact that as she had not asked him for any money that afternoon it was surely a sign that she liked him. She had obviously not been 'working'. If he came back in ten years' time though would she still be doing the same thing? Frequenting the same hotel bar in Ostrava and the same club in Prague, 'working' and convincing herself it was all for a better tomorrow?

Would Susanna, and probably thousands of women like her in the new liberal democratic utopia of the Czech Republic, still be living the same dream in ten years' time? Would she still be, "going to give up this type of work at the end of that particular year," as she told Tom she was going to at the end of this year? Would Susanna ever give up now? Could she, he wondered? At least not until her clients and her body gave up on her. That was the saddest thing of all, and maybe that was the thing that for him most epitomised the new post-

1989 Czech Republic. Susanna was a woman whose life seemed ordinary to her tower block neighbours in Ostrava no doubt, but who had another completely different life on some evenings in a hotel in the city and in another city, Prague. But she was a woman who, like the Czech Republic itself in many ways and maybe even himself, was living for a dream; the dream and hope of eventually having, "a normal life," as she put it, whatever that was, and a better tomorrow? Wonder what that is, that 'better tomorrow', Tom thought as his taxi whisked him through the now murky Ostravian streets and back to the comfort and safety of his nice westernised hotel room.

Life in his visits to the Czech Republic was very safe for Tom, relatively speaking. He could visit, perceive, observe, maybe even judge, but some women in the Czech Republic like Susanna had to live the reality, even if it seemed to Tom that their reality was in fact a belief in a dream. Back in his hotel room sat on his bed relaxing from his afternoon exertions Tom wondered if in some respects he was being just as determined, just as self-interested and single-minded as the 'Czech Susannas'. He had looked at Susanna and at Czech women in their thirties he had met, and had developed, nurtured even, an image of them and their life, a dream. An image that he wanted to believe in, wanted to see. He had tried to look beneath the surface of the 'Czech Susannas' and see just what was hidden there, but in doing so had he really just liberated something from them? Drawn off something from them for his own selfish means and use. To make himself feel good he had stolen something from them ultimately. Stolen a perception, a judgement, which was not really his to make but he had made it, formed a view and made it for his own benefit, for his own feeling of well-being not for theirs.

It was then that his own feeling of well-being overwhelmed him and he dozed off into a real dream world, contented and certain that his afternoon had not, indeed, all been a dream.

16
Stalin's granny

Sitting in his taxi as it laboured through the grimy streets to Ostrava station at ten o'clock on Wednesday morning to catch his 10.45 train to Prague guilt began flooding over Tom. It was his emotional payment for his night and afternoon with Susanna. What was that all about? Some sort of necessary emotional moral cleansing process that would clean out his soul and enable him to get on with his life? Yes Susanna was beautiful, but yes she was 'damaged'. Her profession saw to that. The pollution of the beauty of her image in Tom's mind was through instant guilt. It was not a guilt born of unfaithfulness to anyone else. It was guilt of unfaithfulness to himself. He knew that as soon as he did what he'd done with Susanna he would feel degraded and still unfulfilled. "Hmm ... obviously a man thing," he softly murmured in the back of the rattling taxi. "What was it that made me do it?"

He couldn't dismiss it easily, no matter how much he tried. Just what had he done? How the bloody hell could he have been convinced only a couple of days before that he was still in love with Jana and then go and sleep with a prostitute? Not once, but twice. What the hell was he thinking, or rather he wasn't thinking at all really. Guilt, angst, confusion were just a few of the many thoughts and emotions that now muddled his brain, along with the most worrying thought of all, resignation. What if this was now his life, full of complete unreliability and lack of will power to resist, even when the opportunity he'd been waiting for over almost five years was now only a few days away. Maybe this is all there is for him now, a life of hope destroyed by his own weak will? Why, why had he done it? He just couldn't get past questioning his own stupidity. Okay, so only Susanna would know about it, but he would know about it and that was what was tearing him up inside his head. For a few fleeting moments he tried to rationalise it because he wasn't yet with Jana, hadn't even kissed her properly and certainly hadn't slept with her. So, it would be only as something that happened before her, before they were together, if his hope with her ever materialised. This attempt at guilt removal was washed away though by the words 'a prostitute, a bloody prostitute' refusing to be erased from the forefront of his brain. There is no way he could ever rationalise that in his own head, and definitely not in Jana's. What's more, over the last two days he had not even given one passing thought to Jana and how he would deal with telling her how he felt about her over dinner in Prague that night. What was that telling him? What if, just like Tomas, the main character in Kundera's 'The Unbearable Lightness of Being', he was torn between the responsibility, the burden that would give weight and purpose to his life, and the lightness and freedom of constant womanising? What if his one chance with Jana had gone almost five years previously?

His worrying thoughts were brought to an abrupt end on his arrival at the station when he found his train was delayed until 12 noon. Only one thing to do he thought, get some energy inside him to replace what he had expended over the last two days with Susanna. Some coffee, hot and strong, and he set off in search of the station buffet.

"Revolution, what bloody revolution?" Tom recalled a Czech asking him rhetorically two years after 1989. Standing in the queue at a somewhat smelly and run down Ostrava station restaurant, as it was mislabelled, he was experiencing that questioning phrase in practice. There were four people ahead of him in the queue, but no one was actually being served. Not that there was much to serve to them anyway. Some very sad looking curled edge sweaty meat sat uneasily on some dark, tough looking bread. The meat was doing a not very passable impersonation of salami, but there were only about six of those delicacies anyway. They were complimented, if that's the right word, by half-a-dozen distinctly dodgy looking meat pasties of sort, or at least that's what they looked like. Of course, there was the obligatory káva – coffee - most definitely Czech style, black and thick, with plenty of sludge in the bottom of the cup no doubt. Every time he drank it anywhere in the Czech Republic he always vowed never to look into the bottom of the cup when he finished, but could never resist doing so.

Behind the grubby, cheap, Formica laden counter was undoubtedly Stalin's granny; a fierce looking, very large woman, in the sense that she was most likely taller lying on her side than she was standing up. Probably younger, but looking at least in her mid-sixties and dressed in a decidedly grubby multi-stained, what had very limited pretensions to pass itself off as a white overall. Her grey hair was partially stuffed beneath one of those pork pie type hats, although Tom noticed that the moustache she sported had retained its natural dark colour. It seemed that she was determined not to serve anyone at all. Maybe she had already fulfilled her quota of people served in the 'five year plan' and was definitely not going to serve anyone else. Tom stood transfixed. This time not by the beauty or sheer youth of some Czech girl, but by the ironical, almost 'back to the future' humour of it all. Mrs. Stalin was not serving anyone, but then equally no one in the queue ahead of Tom was pushing her or cajoling her to do so. In any case, he reckoned they had probably all decided that when it came to it they couldn't see anything they really fancied anyway. Meanwhile, they all stood stock-still and gazed into the far distance that projected itself – obviously falsely - as the serving area behind the counter. It was like some still life painting. Or like those paintings of Jesus and his disciples at the Last Supper, which art gallery tour guides throughout the world seemed to go into raptures over, but Tom couldn't quite see why. To him it seemed like thirteen blokes on a boys' night out, like an Old Testament version of a boys bash and bloat out down the local curry house, with the required Balti curry washed down with a few pints of amber nectar. Only in JC's case, them being Mediterranean types, his lads went for the red vino, which was even more ideal of course for the one that Leonardo da Vinci definitely painted as a woman.

Anyway, there was definitely no Balti on offer in Ostrava station restaurant. Even if there had been, Mrs. Stalin was certainly not going to serve it up to anybody. She had better things to do than wait on customers. She was treating Tom and his fellow queuers to an Olympic level exhibition of cleaning, using of course the much prized East European bright yellow heavy duty rubber gloves. They looked as if they were equipped to put out fires, and were accompanied by very gritty looking wire wool – no doubt plucked from Mrs. Stalin's own fine bristly head of hair – and a distinctly murky bowl of soapy water. Or at least water attempting an imitation of being soapy, but doing a better job of looking extremely greasy, such that it wouldn't have looked out of place in a distinctly down market kebab cafe. Everything, from the glass case containing the salami type meat and bread to the counter and the empty shelves behind her, was being scrupulously and systematically cleaned. No doubt in accordance with the pre-1989 instruction manual and directive number 86934 within it, on cleaning empty restaurants. Tom wondered if eventually she would get round to him and his - what by now he felt as he had seemed to have been with them an interminable length of time – life-long associates in the queue. But would they each have to first be inspected and scrubbed up with the rubber gloves and wire wool, so as to be deemed fit in the great Stalinist scheme of things to be served in such an auspicious establishment?

In fact, it was nearly fifteen minutes that he had stood there observing the daily grind of life in post-revolution Ostrava, although it didn't really matter as he had another hour to kill before his train. What was amazing though was that no one gave it the usual, "prossim," or the Czech equivalent of, "when you're ready, luv," or, "don't mind us, we'll just wait," or even, "oi, any chance of some service?"

"Service, what's that?" Tom found himself muttering, much to the curiosity of his fellow queuers. Perhaps in Ostrava Hlavní Nádraží restaurant there just simply isn't a Czech word for it. Or maybe his fellow queuers knew better than to try and hurry or harass Mrs. Stalin. Tom gave up and decided to go back outside to the platform to ponder the finer points of the station's architecture of steel and corrugated iron. In any case, he couldn't possibly have brought himself to try the local delicacy of the curled edged meat, now so nicely imbued with the smell of the soap imposter greasy water, let alone following it with the thick muddy coffee. "Revolution, what revolution?" Well, for sure it wasn't a catering one in Ostrava station.

Part Four:
1989 and 1994; decision time for Czechs, Slovaks and an Englishman

17
"One of you is going to die."

"One of you is going to die." It was a matter of fact chilling statement, which instantly struck fear and bemusement through Jiří Kaluza's whole body in early November 1989. Not waiting for any response or interruption the StB officer, Tomas Musil, ploughed on dispassionately.

"The Russians have a plan to discredit the hard-line fools and dinosaurs that supposedly currently lead our party. They want them removed and replaced with a Czech 'Gorbachev', who will stop the infection threat to the socialist commonwealth from spreading from Poland and Hungary by putting in place some small reforms to placate the people and isolate the dissidents."

Jiří sat there in stunned silence with Martin Šmid in the StB officer's grey, spartan office in the Dejvická Prague 6 district listening to what seemed to be his or his companion's impending martyrdom. As the tall erect Musil, pacing up and down his office paused for breath and turned away from the far wall to face both men once again, Jiří could maintain his disciplined silence no longer.

"What? What is this about, and just what have we done that warrants our death? We have both served the party and socialism in Czechoslovakia well. I don't think we can be faulted in our efforts for the party and the cause. We have done just as we were instructed, and infiltrated the dissident and student movement so well that we are completely respected and trusted by them. In fact, we are both trusted members of its leadership. It is clear that no one suspects us of being StB spies. I don't understand? One of us is to be sacrificed, killed, for a new Czech 'Gorbachev'?"

"That's precisely why you two, and ultimately one of you, has been chosen," the officer interjected, "because of the very fact that you are totally trusted and respected inside the student movement. Your death, one of you, at the hands of the Czech Security Police acting on behalf of the Czechoslovak hard-line party leadership on the 17th November demonstration commemorating the death of a student killed by the Nazis fifty years ago will be an outrage. So much so that the Russian KGB is sure that the existing old party leadership will be forced to resign in shame and a new reforming leadership can then be put in its place. It will completely undermine the tide of reforming dissent in this country and the socialist commonwealth will be secure. That is what the Russians are certain about."

Musil paused, and waited, enjoying his deception and to a degree even the two men's anguish and discomfort. Then he put them out of their misery.

"Of course, you will not actually die. Your death will be faked on the demonstration. One section of six special Security Police officers will pick you out and confront you under the arches on Národní after the march has been halted there by the Security Police. The demonstrators in general will be attacked by them at that point, but one of you two, whoever is chosen, will ensure you are at the front of the march on the right of the front row near the arches. The six special officers will grab you and you will unfortunately have to take some beating to make it look real, but they will be careful and you, of course, will react immediately by falling to the ground. The one of you who is not chosen for the beating will make sure he is also near the front of the demonstration so that he can spread the story of what happened amongst the dissident and student movement with real authority and detail over the next few hours and the next day.

Then, once the area has been cleared of demonstrators and the general Czech Security Police, a show will be made of your body being collected from under the arches by an ambulance and you will be taken away on a stretcher covered completely with a blanket, as if you are dead. We are sure some of the more curious people who live in the apartments above the shops in Národni opposite the arches will witness all of this and spread the word of your death. Our operatives will do their best to ensure that their actions in collecting your body do not go unnoticed. Anyway, we have ways, and the Russians certainly do, of ensuring the western media learn of your death very quickly."

Jiří at least felt reassured that should he be the one chosen he wasn't actually going to die. He couldn't resist asking though, "how will it be decided which of us it is to be?"

"The Russians will choose," Musil told him. "They have your files."

That wasn't exactly something that filled Jiří Kaluza with comfort or joy, and his concerns about the whole business rapidly returned. Being on a file held by the Czechoslovak Stb is one thing, but being on a file held by the Soviet KGB was an entirely more worrying predicament. After all, he'd obviously been on the Stb files since he was recruited by them in his first year as a student at Charles University, being very sympathetic to the cause of 'the party'. It was also where he'd first met Jana Sukova and immediately became attracted to her, although he had never ever tried to recruit her or tell her about his connections and work for the Stb.

While he was trying to digest the much more worrying fact that he was now on the KGB files his concern was at least slightly alleviated by Musil continuing with, "the KGB are inclined to choose you at the moment, Šmid. From your file they believe that far less is known about you and your background amongst the student and dissident movement,"

Jiří Kaluza could certainly relate to that assessment. He had only met Šmid at student dissident movement events and meetings so certainly had no idea about his personal background. He didn't even have any idea whatsoever just what he was supposedly studying at Charles University, or indeed even in what faculty he was studying. Šmid was a tall, thick set, quite distinctive dark black haired man, with thick bushy black eyebrows to match. His voice was deep and exuded an air of authority on whatever subject he was pronouncing on at the student dissident meetings, and yet he had the ability simultaneously to manage to almost melt into the background at meetings once he had made his pointed contribution. To Jiří he came across as a shrewd manipulator. Despite his short contributions and input, and his shadowy presence, on many occasions in meetings he seemed to be able to somehow manage to guide decisions quite effortlessly in the direction he tentatively suggested and ultimately wanted.

Jiří's temporary relief at not being the one chosen for the fake death was instantly removed, however, when Musil added, "the Russians believe you are more of a risk Kaluza. They say you are far too involved, I think that's the polite way they put it, with this woman in the student movement, Jana Sukova. You're much too close to her they say."

Again this stunned and concerned him, raising all manner of questions in his mind. "Too close? Too involved?" How the hell did the KGB know that, or believe they knew that? It didn't take more than a mini-second for him to answer his own thoughts. Obviously, he had been under surveillance by them, and even more of a concern, so had Jana. While he was thinking that through in his head and frantically trying to recollect whether he had any suspicions at any time of being followed or under surveillance, Musil threw another 'curve ball' and almost casually spat out a further name at him.

"The Russians also say she, this Sukova woman, is much too friendly with westerners and foreigners. She spends far too much time in their company for her own good, particularly an English university lecturer, a Tom Carpenter. It seems she has been spending a lot of time with this Carpenter man, far too much time for the Russians' liking." Musil's tone changed from an almost 'matter of fact' reporting voice to a much firmer, aggressive and directed one as he added, "you should be much more careful, Kaluza, just who you become friends with. Anyway, the Russians reckon that because of this you would be too much of a risk. You're much too well known by Sukova and her friend Carpenter to be able to 'play dead' on the demonstration."

Forgetting for a moment his somewhat precarious subordinate position to the Stb officer, Jiří Kaluza couldn't help himself in responding quite firmly, "so, while I have been infiltrating the student leadership, and getting 'too close' as they put it to Jana Sukova, the KGB have been watching me, as well as her," adding as some form of self-defence statement, "and this Tom Carpenter, I've never even met him."

"Everyone watches everyone in this country in this time, Kaluza, surely you realised that? Suspicion and fear is everywhere. We live in dangerous times. Western agents are everywhere throughout East and Central Europe at the moment trying to destabilise our great socialist system because their governments see it as a real threat to their unfair, greedy, privileged for the few, capitalist system. If we are to preserve our superior societies and way of life throughout the socialist commonwealth we must be on our guard and be suspicious at all times. Above all we must be aware of those we associate with, and be very careful just who we call 'friends'." Musil was hovering directly above Jiří's face and staring intently at him as he ended his 'lecture' with, "why should you, or this woman Sukova, be any different or above suspicion? And if you or her have nothing to hide there is no problem is there?"

He was probing hard, obviously trying to see if there was anything Jiří would reveal from his reactions that he didn't already know. Seeing nothing he decided to be more direct. "Foreigners, westerners, and those who associate with them, are under the most suspicion. You've never met him, this Carpenter man, you say?"

Feeling on solid ground as at that time he hadn't met him, Jiří reiterated, even more firmly than previously, "no, never. I don't even know what he looks like. He could walk in here now and I wouldn't know who he was," although he couldn't resist an, "I assume the KGB could tell you that though?"

"Well, what do you know about him? Has Sukova spoken about him to you? What is he doing here?" Musil reeled off a machine-gun barrage of quick fire questions, obviously again trying to unsettle his agent and observe his demeanour and reaction. But there was nothing Jiri could be caught out on as he just relayed what little he knew from Jana about Tom Carpenter.

"She's mentioned him a few times, that he's a lecturer at a university in England and that she met him at an academic conference in Belgium, Spa I think, last year in the autumn. So, she hasn't known him very long, although I think she likes him and they seem to get on quite well. She says he is here researching Czech history, from the sixteenth century I think she said. She did say he was interested in what was going on at the moment across East and Central Europe. What is happening, and has happened, in Hungary and Poland and to some extent here, seems to interest him, although she reckons it's just a curiosity about the news and from an academic perspective."

Musil once again stopped prowling back and forth across his office, peered down at Jiří across his desk and murmured a barely stifled, "hmm," followed slowly and deliberately by, "anything else?"

"No, no, I don't think so, sir," Jiří replied, this time remembering his precarious position and giving the officer more respect.

"What about where Carpenter is staying? What about his friendship with Sukova's friend, Dita Králová?" Musil asked firmly once again, obviously highly suspicious still that Jiří was holding back something.

While one more disconcerting thought flashed through his mind that Dita had obviously also been watched because of her association with Tom Carpenter, Jiří just offered a 'matter of fact' response of, "Jana Sukova told me they are lovers, Carpenter and Králová, and he stays at her flat in Dejvická. That's really all I know though. I've met Králová a couple of times with Jana Sukova. I don't think she likes me, at least that's the impression I got. She seems a very serious type of person, and very serious about her academic work according to Jana Sukova. But, as I said before, I've never met this man Carpenter, and so I really know very little about him except what Jana Sukova has told me, and now I've told you."

Musil was a well-trained Stb officer. He knew perfectly well how to remain cool and calm while inwardly instantly analysing what he had heard and thinking how best to probe a little deeper for more information. To Jiří though he appeared satisfied with what he'd told him, and anyway there really wasn't any more he could tell Musil. Nevertheless, the Stb officer gave it one more try just to be sure, followed by what Jiří interpreted as an order.

"Anything else you might have forgotten to tell me?" he asked firmly, again hovering over him and menacingly peering straight into his face.

"No, nothing, nothing else," Jiří immediately replied.

"Good, well Kaluza you had better probe your friend Sukova a little more about this man Carpenter. The KGB would like to know a lot more about him. I'm sure she can tell you more if you ask her diplomatically. You can do that can't you?"

"Yes sir, of course," was all Jiří could say while now hundreds of questions were running through his brain. Who was it that was watching him, and who was watching Jana and the pair of them when they were together? Who was watching Dita? From what little Jana had told him about Dita and from the very few times he had met her, he reckoned Dita would be apoplectic if she even had the slightest inkling that her and Jana were being watched by the KGB, especially if she thought it was because of Jana's friendship with Jiri.

Through all this Šmid had just sat silent, knowing better than to get involved, not that there was anything he could have contributed anyway. He had never been introduced to Jana and had only seen her a few times at student dissident meetings. His interest and attention was only re-aroused when Musil turned to him after his exchanges with Jiří and informed him, "anyway, the KGB has decided upon you, Šmid. You will be the one supposedly killed in Národni on 17th November. You will be fully briefed by us and by the KGB a day before, as will the selected Security Police officers who will administer the beating. You will carry on as normal up until that night. Do not speak to anyone about this obviously, and the same goes for you Kaluza. Do you both understand?"

Both men simultaneously uttered the same short sharp, "yes sir."

"You, Kaluza, have a different task. I want daily reports through the usual channels on what you have found out about Sukova, her friend Králová, and this Englishman Carpenter. Anything and everything, I want to know it all, and so will the Russians. What they do, where they go every day. Who they know and who they talk to, even where they shit, especially if they are shitting on our socialist country!"

Musil was much more agitated and forceful now than he had been throughout the whole meeting and he ended with, "is that clear?"

Once again Jiří just replied with, "Yes sir."

"Good, you can both go now." The Stb officer almost barked at them with a parting, "we will be in touch, and remember, you are being watched at all times by the KGB wherever you go, even more so now. If this goes wrong, especially before the event on the 17th, we will know where to look and who to blame."

As he entered the lift with Šmid and descended the four floors from Musil's office, and began to analyse and go over what had just happened, it dawned on Jiří that the Stb officer knew all along who the KGB had chosen for the fake death. So, the rest of the meeting was really about testing Jiří and seeing just what he knew. Seeing if he was going to admit to knowing what Musil and the KGB already knew about Jana, Dita, and Tom Carpenter, and his association with them. He was being checked up on and tested. And now he was being tested on whether he could keep to himself what the KGB had planned for the 17th November demonstration and Šmid's faked death.

"Dangerous times indeed," he murmured after he'd parted from Šmid and emerged onto the street into the pale late autumn Prague sunlight.

18
17th November 1989

Sitting on his Prague bound train from Ostrava towards the end of May 1994 Tom knew he really now had to use the journey to do some serious thinking about how to approach his impending dinner with Jana that night. "Maybe what happened on 17th November 1989 was the best place to start," he muttered to himself. "After all, that's when most people think the 'Velvet Revolution' began, so maybe it's as good a place as any." So, he would try and go over it again in his mind and recall the signs that gave him hope with Jana.

He had gone to the demonstration with her on the evening of 17th November, and for each of them there was a different reason to be there. For Tom, it was to observe, and to try and get some idea just what was going on in Prague at that time in terms of the strength of dissent and opposition to the communist government. For Jana, it was simply just to be there, another body protesting in the multitude, sending a peaceful message of dissent to the ageing dinosaurs that ran her country supposedly in the name of socialism and the people. "We have to be there," she had argued with the immovable and reluctant Dita earlier in the day. "It is our duty to stand with others in protest."

"What others are these that you are so friendly with, so eager to stand in solidarity with?" Dita mocked her. "Your comrades? You know as well as I do, Jana, that most Czechs don't give a shit. There will be a few hundred, maybe a thousand of your new friends and comrades there fighting the good fight to free our country at this oh so critical point in its history." Dita's voice got more and more mockingly sarcastic. It wasn't one of her personality traits that Tom found most endearing. Her smile, her beautiful brown eyes, her flowing shoulder length hair and her brilliant bright intellect, yes they were overwhelming. But her anger and her sarcasm, her pessimism over some things and her almost personal possession of feelings and views on her country, were the worst traits of her character. He found those parts of her not only unappealing, but also found it very, very sad that someone so clever, so beautiful, should have had such cynicism ground into them by years and years of the communist system.

"Come on, please. It'll be exciting and I want to be there, and with you, my best friend." Jana was now pleading. "It's important!" Her voice was getting louder as if the more she raised it the more important it would seem to her friend. "It's the seventeenth of November, the fiftieth anniversary of the student demonstration against the Nazis. Now we have a chance to show these Stalinist thugs that run our country that they can't push us around anymore. To show them that things have to change and that they are history."

"Listen to you. You sound like some political agitator," Dita interrupted, never having seen her closest friend like this before. "Anyway, you're getting carried away by the ramblings of a few students who have nothing better to do when they should be studying, and by the abstract dreams of a few so-called intellectuals and middle-class play writers." Dita was never one to do anything without complete calculation and caution. She was reminding Jana in her own way that she was also never someone who just went along with the herd.

"What do you think? That because Gorbachev says everything must change, can change, will change, that some scared stiff frightened Czech police guy with a huge thick stick will not be scared enough to lash out at you with it? Oh yes sure, like in Národni or Wenceslas some helmeted young police guy in the front line and frightened out of his life is not going to lash out at you with his bloody big heavy stick, but instead is going to engage you and the other students and the intellectuals in a deep philosophical discussion about the merits and problems of bloody glasnost! And yeah, the intellectuals, they'll be at the bloody front of the march getting hit, of course they will!" Now Dita was almost screaming and Jana knew that she'd won the argument. If Dita was raising her voice it was because she knew that really she should go to the demonstration. She felt guilty, but also very, very scared. Not so much scared of the police guys with the sticks, but scared of letting herself become too optimistic, and scared of being let down yet again by a false optimism that the system really would change; scared of being let down by a false hope.

Tom watched and listened to the debate between the two women - a polite way of putting it - while all the time he sat in an armchair in Dita's flat. At one point he tried to contribute with, "well, in East Germany," but he got no further than that and it only caused Dita's voice to raise to a new, even higher pitch as she screamed back at him, "oh yeah, East fucking Germany! That'll make the police guys with the sticks think won't it! Anyway, what's it got to do with you?" Now her fire and screams were turned directly on Tom. "It's not your bloody country! And it won't be your fucking head! Anyway you, or at least your bloody country, let us down lots of times before remember. First you gave us to the Nazis in 1938, then to Stalin in 1948, and then you did nothing to help us in 1968. Why the fuck should we be optimistic and believe anything you say!"

"Okay, okay," Tom decided retreat was the best form of defence, not to say self-preservation. He had seen Dita like this before, although never swearing so much. She very seldom swore. She would get more and more angry then she would burst into tears, upset with herself for getting so angry and so upset. Mmm ... I suppose there must be some logic in there somewhere, whatever it is, Tom thought as he watched the discussion develop. The logic must be universal and female. He wasn't about to voice this little philosophical gem of his aloud to the two women at that point though. He was intelligent enough to fully realise that to do that would have resulted not only in Dita turning on him but both of them, and he would have been better off then facing the scared police guy with the, "big bloody stick." He certainly would have had more chance of surviving with less of a sore head and ears. Although he did briefly ponder the merit of pointing out to Dita that he wasn't actually personally responsible for the failure of his country, as she put, and the west in general, to help the Czechs in 1938, 1948 or 1968, but very quickly thought better of it.

Despite all of Dita's protests Jana was still adamant that she was going, and Tom was keen to go with her. "I want to see for myself, Dita. I need to experience it. To be able to try to explain to my friends and colleagues in England the feelings of people living here about the system they hate. I have to go. I'm going to the demonstration with Jana."

He was determined about it and eventually Dita reluctantly, grudgingly gave way. "Go, see for yourself. See the pity and the pointlessness of it all. Then you will know, but don't expect me to come. I've had my expectations raised too many times in the past and this will not be any different."

People gathered for the demonstration at Vyšehrad, a large park area in the south of the city incorporating the ruins of Vyšehrad Castle. In answer to Tom's question on the metro on the way as to why the march was starting there Jana told him that the legend was that the castle had been the home of Princess Libuše, the youngest daughter of Krok, Prince of the Czechs. Krok had three daughters, all of whom were magicians and prophetesses. Libuše was the wisest and most enlightened, and after her father's death she was elected to succeed him in 710. It was then that she founded Psáry Castle, as Vyšehrad was first known. According to the legend Libuše also prophesised the founding of the city of Prague, and founded Prague Castle - Hradčany - in 717. The relevance of Vyšehrad, Jana informed him, to finally answer his question, was that it was the political and religious centre of the country until that role was assigned to Prague Castle in the twelfth century. Vyšehrad had continued though to be a kind of hill top fortress guarding the southern approach to the city alongside the river. So, Tom could understand why it was rather appropriate that the march should start from this ancient political centre of the country, although now there was a cultural and exhibition centre at Vyšehrad that was very much in the monolithic 1950s style of so many he had seen across Eastern Europe and in the Soviet Union, where obviously the original concept and architectural monstrosity had been conceived. Impregnated and brought to maturity no doubt by the Great Cultural Leader and intellect Comrade Stalin, Tom chuckled to himself.

It was a cold, but dry early evening. There was a real end of autumn, start of winter chill in the air. As people spoke to each other clouds of their warm breathe puffed out into the evening air. Tom was glad that Dita's last instructions to him were to take his scarf and gloves, and his warm coat. At least if he was to end up shivering it would be from fear and not the cold. Most of the demonstrators wore anoraks. Not the thin, plastic looking sort that were so evident and denigrated in Britain, but mainly the thicker, padded ski type that were made for warmth. Tom new that most Czechs were great ski enthusiasts, so although they weren't exactly of the expensive sort the anoraks were very functional and warm against the descending cold night air. Some were quite bright – reds, sky and royal blue, and the occasional yellow and pink – and still looked obviously quite new. With their wearer's equally brightly coloured scarves, bobble-hats and gloves, they made a stark patchwork of vivid colour through the gathering throng of marchers. Most though were of the much drabber and faded dark green, black, grey or very dark blue variety and had clearly seen better days. Tom guessed that predominantly the wearers of those were the students.

"It's going to be big, very big, Tom!" Jana exclaimed. Her excitement was growing. Her movements were becoming more and more animated and her smile broader by the minute as she saw and greeted friends waiting to start to march. They excitedly hugged each other and exchanged the usual kisses on the cheek greeting. She introduced Tom to them as a, "curious, sympathetic English Professor friend." Many of the demonstrators carried lighted candles. As Prague took on its early evening mysterious dark side so the light from the candles stood out more and more as a symbol of a sea of dissent. A light of hope in the darkness Tom thought as he began to feel the growing atmosphere sweeping over him, and over most of the people waiting to march. The symbolism of it all was growing stronger and stronger. It was a strange mixture of a whole raft of feelings that was going through his body. It was as though he wanted to burst into tears at the sheer despair, unfairness and inhumanity of it all, but at the same time his spirit was uplifted by the overpowering mood of the mass of collective optimism and resistance that was unfolding before his eyes, and of which he was now very much a part.

"Thank you for bringing me," he blurted out to Jana as he surveyed the swelling crowd of demonstrators. It was all he could think to say to her then. He was trying to tell her how much he appreciated the moment, the opportunity to just be there and experience it all, but all he could express in such a developing emotional situation were the five words he uttered.

She looked surprised at his remark. "Well, thank you for coming," was all she could think of replying as the expectant excited smile across her lips got even broader. "But nothing has happened yet, Tom. First you have some walking to do."

"But do you really fully understand what is happening here, Tom?" Jana asked a few minutes later. "I think you have some idea of course. Some idea that it's about demonstrating to these corrupt so-called communist bastards who have destroyed our country for forty years that enough is enough. That they are finished – history - and that we are not going to just go on putting up with it anymore. It is more than that though. It is also about the way in which we will show them that we have had enough and that their time is up. I'm not sure you fully realise and understand that part, that the way in which we do it is important. How would you put it in English? The methods we use, the mechanisms, I think is the best way I can put it.

This demonstration is important firstly because of what it has been called for, the symbolism of commemorating the killing of a student by the Nazis fifty years ago. October 28th 1939 was the twenty-first anniversary of the independence of the Czechoslovak Republic, and there was a major student demonstration against the Nazis and their occupation of our country. Jan Opletal, a 19 year old medical student at Charles University at the time, was seriously wounded in clashes with the Nazis on the demonstration and he died a few days later. His funeral was attended by thousands of students and it turned into another anti-Nazi demonstration. The Nazis retaliated on November 17th 1939 when they ordered universities and colleges to be closed down. More than twelve hundred students were sent to concentration camps, where nine were executed.

Ever since then Czechs and Slovaks have recognized November 17th as International Students Day. Today, this evening, this demonstration is important because it also signals now to the Stalinist regime in our country that people are beginning to take control over their own lives again. We are starting to take back our public spaces for all our people – the squares, the streets, the traditional gathering places like Wenceslas, like Národni, like Vyšehrad. That's one of the reasons why the demonstration and march is starting from here tonight. We are reclaiming for ourselves the traditional places of protest and demonstration. Of course, they were also traditional places of celebration, but celebration for all the people not just the chosen people in the communist bureaucracy and the party faithful. That's what really frightens those bastards. That's what really makes them shit themselves. That they can't control the public spaces they've stolen from us, because they can't control us anymore. They can't frighten us into submission. That's why it is such a pity that Dita can't be here to see this and to be a part of it. She really is very, very strong you know, Tom, and as you saw she can get very angry. She really is with us in spirit you know. She hates these corrupt communist bastards just as much as the rest of us do really. It's just that she has been ground down by years of unfulfilled hope and optimism. You are very, very lucky to have her. For her, you are her hope and her optimism now. I think you know that she likes you, loves you, very much."

With that defence and praise of her closest friend, and her explanation of the finer points of the demonstration, Jana now had Tom's full attention. Here he was about to march off in a historic demonstration of thousands of bodies, but he could have been anywhere at that particular moment as far as he was concerned, but anywhere with Jana, not with Dita. His vision was focused on one person, Jana, and not the thousands now gathered around him in Vyšehrad waiting for the march to start. This woman, who was increasingly making an impression upon him – one he hadn't expected or anticipated, let alone accounted for – was coming across to him as someone not only full of life, full of optimism, full of hope, but also bloody clever, bloody intelligent. The more she spoke the more he became transfixed. The, "communist bastards," as she put it, may not have been able to control the Czech and Slovak people any more, but within himself Tom was beginning to experience a mixed up feeling about Jana that he didn't understand and increasingly couldn't control, and of course her last comment about Dita loving him very much only added to his confusion.

"Since these bastards corrupted our ideals, well our parent's ideals anyway, they've taken away our public spaces, our places of spontaneous celebrations and demonstrations. They standardised everything, every part of life. In doing that they tried to drain life out of us. They even turned our public spaces, our squares, into 'state spaces', as though they belonged to some faceless entity, the faceless bureaucracy maybe. Do you know, Tom, my mother told me that since 1953 even the arrangement of processions for things like May Day celebrations were formalised and absolutely controlled. Even the order in the procession and celebration for things like flags and the portraits of those corrupt communist shits was standardised and controlled for the whole country. Those so-called spontaneous demonstrations would have their order of marching and every detail decreed by the faceless bureaucrats in Prague, and probably, who knows, really in Moscow. All the banners and slogans were written and arranged by the communist party bureaucracy. We'll show those bastards. Show them what a real spontaneous demonstration, a spontaneous march, is all about. They're our squares, our streets. They always have been. Now we're going to take them back, and most of all it's our country and we're going to take that back too."

"Not that our parents ever really gave up, Tom. They just got worn down by it all; by the struggle just to make ends meet every day. They got tired from just trying to get things each day for everyday life, the necessities of life – work, food and somewhere to live. Even throughout that time though the protests still went on in the nineteen-seventies and eighties, they were just more underground I think you call it. They were simmering under the surface of life in what was called the 'second culture'. Everyone knows about samizdat, even in the West. It was happening in Russia, but it was also happening here. Writers would meet in someone's flat and would bring copies – probably a dozen or so – of their latest work criticising the regime through literature. They would usually be carbon copies because, believe it or not, the police kept a close watch on photocopiers. These copies would be distributed among those people who it was thought could be trusted. At one point there was even a so-called 'underground university' where people would meet, study, and discuss works and texts smuggled in from the West. The dissidents who ran it would travel around to different parts of the country to meet different groups of students."

"Also of course there was the music, Tom. Rock groups like Plastic People of the Universe and DG.307 formed a musical underground movement. They used to play in secret in pubs, in barns on farms, and even at weddings. Young people used to travel halfway across the country to hear them play. The communist regime described them as drug addicts and alcoholic layabouts so as to frighten the parents of the teenagers and young people who went to hear them. They were supposedly corrupting the morals of the country's young people. Then in September 1976 the 'Plastics' were arrested, brought to trial and sent to prison. At least their music had spirit. It was strong rock with moody atmospherics, and a lot different from the boring shit on May Day parades and what was generally on the radio and TV. My mother said it gave people happiness for a short time and some glimpse of what could be. That's really why the regime didn't like the 'Plastics', because they gave people hope, Tom."

He hadn't heard such talk since the anti-Vietnam war demonstrations he'd been on in London in the late nineteen-sixties. There was optimism and hope then, the 'sixties' optimism and hope of the young. He told Jana this as they stood there waiting to march, but was surprised and knocked back by her response.

"Oh yeah, Tom, Vietnam but what did you in the West do about Czechoslovakia in 1968 and the crushing of the 'Prague Spring' by the bloody Russians? Dita was right about that, Tom. The West did nothing to help us then. That was the real time of hope for my parents and their generation. They were brave then, but great changes that they made towards a better way to live for everybody in this country were swept away in a few hours, almost overnight by bloody Russian tanks! And what did the West do? I'll tell you, Tom, nothing! They did nothing. Vietnam yeah, but Prague, oh no fuck them!"

Now he was getting a politics and international relations lesson like he'd never had before, and all in the middle of the reality of an actual huge political event, not in some abstract, safe, hermetically sealed lecture theatre from a dusty old, unemotional, anally retentive professor. Somehow though what was happening then in the autumn and early winter of 1989 felt more certain, more substantial than the events of the Prague Spring of 1968 or of the anti-Vietnam war demos he'd been on. Maybe he felt that because of what he knew was happening across the rest of East and Central Europe in the second half of '89. Maybe it was because of Jana's infectious enthusiasm and her optimism. Maybe he was just getting caught up in the whole tide of the mood of whatever was happening. For whatever reason though he was sure that this time it all felt much different, and he was definitely beginning to feel differently about Jana.

As Jana had reminded Dita earlier when pleading with her to go with them, and as she had just explained to Tom, the demonstration had been called for 17th November in order to commemorate the fiftieth anniversary of a demonstration by Prague students in 1939 against the Nazi occupation, and against the Nazis closing the universities. What was strange about the 1989 demonstration though was that the communist authorities had given permission for it to take place at all, at the time of a somewhat unstable political climate in Prague, not to say across the whole of East and Central Europe.

Dita had expressed just such suspicions to Jana during their heated discussion about whether she and Tom should go and whether she would join them. "Something just doesn't make sense. It just doesn't add up," she pointed out. "Why should our own thugs in the government allow such a demonstration? You should be very suspicious, Jana."

"Oh no, you are always suspicious, Dita. It is because everyone says it's simply a demonstration about an anniversary relating to the Nazis and nothing more, even if it is really about demonstrating against the present corrupt bunch running the country. Even they would not dare to ban such a demonstration in case they are labelled fascists themselves," was Jana's rationalization.

While they waited for the march to start Jana told Tom that from Vyšehrad the demonstration was going to march alongside the River Vltava towards the centre of the city. Then it would turn right from the side of the river by the National Theatre into Národni. Eventually at the top of that wide boulevard the demonstrators would turn right again into Václavské Náměstí, Wenceslas Square. In true Czech tradition this was not in fact a square at all, but was another wide boulevard, similar to many Tom had seen in Paris. The march would go to the top of the square by the statue of Saint Wenceslas and there speeches would be made.

By the time the march actually moved off it was indeed huge, just as Jana had suggested earlier. "There must be hundreds of thousands of people here now," she shouted to Tom as she took his hand and pulling him behind her managed to weave her way towards her friends fifteen or so rows from the front of the about thirty abreast march. There was singing, some chanting, and thousands of candles and flowers. Tom took a deep breath; something was welling up in his throat and deep down in his stomach. He was desperately trying not to let it reach his eyes, which were definitely misting over. Even the rare short silences on the march affected him deeply. At times he found it difficult to get his breath as the emotion of the occasion swept over him. Such a vast crowd, a sea of pleading humanity, he thought. Why, oh why, would things not change? How could they not change? How could they fail to change under such pressure? He could now see just why Jana was so insistent that things would change. Like Jana, he now felt a hope and optimism that this time it would be different.

She glanced sideways at him as they linked arms like most other people on the march. She stopped singing for a brief moment, saw his eyes and said, "Here, Tom," while handing him a tissue from her pocket. "Well, well, so even you Englishmen have a soul," she added as she burst into an excited laugh. She hugged his arm, giving it a squeeze as she did so, and broke into another broad smile that quickly changed into a more rueful one when she said, "I just wish Dita was here. This would surely convince her." For almost an hour they marched, arm in arm, singing and chanting with Jana's friends, as well as with complete strangers; Tom only pretending to mouth the Czech words to the songs and the chants as Jana shouted to him, "my, my, I never knew your Czech was so 'dobry', so good, Tom."

It was a completely peaceful march, a pleasant stroll in a beautiful but growing cold after dark city. What was there to worry about Tom kept thinking. There was absolutely no sign of police harassment, just a very few police flanking the long wide column of marchers on either side. Even they were joking with the demonstrators it seemed from the sounds of their occasional conversations and laughs.

After just over an hour of marching they turned into Národni and passed the lit-up glimmering roof of the imposing and impressive National Theatre, past Café Slavia on their left where so many of the dissidents including Havel met regularly to smoke, drink and discuss politics, usually under the watchful gaze of two or three secret police in plain clothes. Then suddenly halfway up Národni, alongside a passageway of covered arches, the march came to a halt. After they'd been standing there for a few minutes Jana asked, "What's happening? You're taller than me, Tom, can you see?"

"It looks like masses of riot police in white helmets with batons and guns ..." Tom's voice tailed off as it grew audibly quieter and a lot more concerned. Now the fun of it all had instantly disappeared. These were real police, this was real social and political struggle, and even in the cold night air he started to sweat a little as Jana gripped his arm a little tighter.

"Really, why, why are they stopping us here now?" she asked, even though deep inside she knew and felt the fear of the answer. The almost permanent smile she had worn on her face throughout most of the march had gone from her lips. They were tighter, tenser, more serious, as was the previously more relaxed playful grip she had on Tom's arm. On hearing her questions a woman immediately in front of Jana turned around and spoke to her in Czech, quickly, very quietly and with a deadly serious look on her face.

"It's the State police, hundreds of them. A thousand maybe this woman thinks and they're not letting us go any further," Jana translated what the woman had told, adding with a heightened concern in her voice, "and look, they are at the sides too."

Tom looked quickly to both sides. Not only were there some twenty or thirty deep police with batons, guns and riot shields stretched right across the front of the march, but there were also groups of them at least ten deep blocking each of the side roads off Národni. Now Tom was really worried. There was absolutely nowhere for the marchers to go, no escape. It flashed through his brain that were she there with them Dita would no doubt have been saying, "I told you so," although not in a very calm manner.

He'd seen these police tactics before, but that was the British police during the 1984-85 miners' strike and on numerous antinuclear demonstrations he'd been on throughout the 1980s. This though was the Czech State police with far bigger batons, as well as guns, and not just handguns, but what looked like short repeating rifles and even some machine guns. This was serious stuff.

The atmosphere was growing tenser by the minute. They stood there blocked in for what seemed an age with the thirty or so marchers in the front row of the demonstration eyeball to eyeball with the armed police. Some of the marchers sat down. An hour passed by. Tom could see that some of the marchers at the front had put flowers in a few of the police gun barrels. Then the singing started again. "Maybe the atmosphere is getting better. Maybe nothing will happen. Maybe they will eventually let us go on," he tried to reassure Jana.

"Yes, maybe they just wanted to frighten us and make sure there was no damage to the shops or buildings, keep us under control. Just to show us that they could, that they could stop us at any time they wanted. Maybe that's what they think, or rather what their officers think," she agreed. As she did so she relaxed her anxious tight grip on his arm, squeezed it much more gently and began to smile again.

Then it happened. Suddenly and for no apparent reason, without any warning, the police began to lash out with their batons into the crowd. People screamed loudly in fear, pain and despair. Panic instantly spread throughout the march. Some at the front of the demonstration tried to fight back, but more and more of the batons were whirling and thrashing through the air. It was like the police were cutting corn in a field with scythes. The crunching of hard thick sticks on bone though was much more audible and frightening than corn being cut. There was chaos everywhere. People tried to move back away from the batons and the police in their white helmets, but the police just kept driving into the crowd and pushing them further and further back into the packed dense body of the march. Demonstrators stumbled over one another in their effort to retreat from the crunching pain of the batons and groups of three and four marchers fell on top of one another. It seemed to Tom that the police were deliberately trying to force people back under the arches of the passageway at the right-hand side of the street. It was total mayhem in there. The police violence and attack on the marchers was at its worst under those arches as people seemingly had nowhere to go to escape. The screaming panic of the marchers fused together with the screaming rage and shouts of the police attackers to form a blurred explosive cacophony; a noisy cocktail of fear, panic and pain that echoed and rebounded off the walls of the arches in the narrow passageway.

Tom grabbed Jana's hand and tried desperately to drag her back and away from the police and their batons. She was crying and screaming at the top of her voice. "Why, why, why won't they ever learn, the bastards?" With her fear and anger she was gulping for air. Tom virtually lifted her off the ground as he clutched her around the waist and shouted at her, "this way, quick, quick, now!"

They had been pushed under the arches and he was frantically trying to get both of them out of that hell hole. The white whirling batons were moving at such a speed that the whole scene was a blurred mess of vision and sound in their heads. The screams and the crack of baton on bone were piercing. Tom had managed to get them both furthest away from the front line of the baton wielding police so he turned to push Jana out from the passageway first and into the side street of Mikulandská, through the advancing police ranks. Then he briefly heard a loud deep male Czech voice shout something, followed by a barely audible low hiss as a baton sped through air and the crunch hit him. A thud landed across his shoulder blades, and a hot searing pain raced down his arms and across his back. He lurched and stumbled forward, fortunately out from under the arches and straight through the police racing past him, but not before another one of them caught him a sharp blow across the back of his legs just below the knees as he charged past the stunned falling Englishman.

The 'face' wielding that baton landing the second blow on Tom's body was a face full of anger, but also full of fear. It was a very young face, maybe nineteen years old at the most, with eyes open wide and very large pupils betraying the fear. The young voice, shouting and ranting in Czech, displayed the anger. There was a fine line between the two blurred instantaneous emotions of anger and fear, and they produced an extremely volatile mixture when added to the wielding and thrashing through the air of a long thick stick making contact with Tom's body. Later, when reason had replaced pain in his senses, Tom realised that the young face was angry at having to be there at all and be in such a dangerous situation. Despite possessing and wielding the long thick stick he nevertheless obviously felt no longer in control of the situation, or indeed of himself and had no idea just what might happen next. What did happen next was that the stick made rapid and extremely painful contact with Tom's legs, immediately followed by his yelping cry as the pain again seared through that part of his body. His cry of pain was accompanied by yet more and rapid screaming Czech verbal abuse from the young police guy as he raced on and into the main body of the brutal violent madness under the arches in the passageway. As Tom hit the cobbled road from the second blow he felt physically sick, from the pain and from the fear of what might still be coming his way in terms of a beating. All the police though were too busy charging past him to get at the main body of marchers still trapped under the arches. In the hazy corner of his brain he heard Jana screaming at him, "Tom, Tom! Get up, get up! Quickly, get up now!"

He tried to shake his stunned head and get his brain to tell his body to move, muttered, "I'm okay," although he clearly wasn't and Jana put her hand under his arm and hauled him up.

"Come on, quick," she implored him.

"I'm bloody trying," was all he could reply as he gasped for air. They could still hear the screams and shouting from the continuing mayhem and chaos behind them as they stumbled off down the side street of Mikulandská and into the relative safety of the dark and cold Prague night.

Jana pushed him into a doorway in a street about half-a-mile from Národni and propped him up for a minute to get his breath and try to recover a little. In a very low and serious tone she whispered in his still ringing ears, "Well, Tom, now you know. Now you have seen what it's like. What the problem is. Why we want to change it all and how much they are determined not to let us. Now you have seen the reality of it. It's a good, but painful lesson don't you think? I'm sorry that you had to experience that very practical lesson. I'm sorry I asked you to come. I didn't want you to get hurt. I really didn't think that would happen."

"Yes, well I've certainly seen and experienced the painful reality, but you don't have to apologise for bringing me. It was my choice, I wanted to come," was all he could think to say through deep breaths as he dealt with the pain across the top of his back and his lower legs. "No doubt tomorrow I'll have the bruises as evidence of the reality of my practical lesson, but what did that bastard say just before he hit me? I'm sure it wasn't excuse me could you move aside please, sir". At least he still had his sense of humour, even if the rest of his senses were completely intact at that point.

"Err ... no, I think it was more like 'you fucking pig, do you think we want to be here because of you'. He was as scared as you and me, Tom, and that's just what it's all about. Fear is everywhere in this country and has been for forty years. It almost killed the hope, but not now. You saw for yourself how many people came tonight to demonstrate their opposition. Those Stalinist bastards can't kill the hope now. More and more people are starting to believe things can and will change. And the chanting, Tom, you heard the chanting on the march. In English it meant 'this is it, now is the time'. They can't control that. They can't stop it forever. They can't stop us and our voices anymore." She was rambling, but he realised from the conviction in her voice and the look in her eyes that Jana really did believe something big was happening and that her life was about to change dramatically.

By the time they got to Dita's apartment Tom was in a state of some shock and was still breathing heavily. The adrenaline of the exciting events of the evening had died away somewhat, and the real deep soreness of where he had been hit by the police batons was beginning to kick in. The pain and shock of it all was increasingly dulling his senses, making him a little dizzy. He leaned heavily on Jana as he groped in his pocket for the key to the door to the apartment and his weight against her caused them to make a stumbling entrance once they got the door open. They were met with the greeting that he had been expecting and fearing ever since the heavy thud of the police baton had landed across the back of his shoulders. A greeting he feared almost as much as the baton, though not physically of course.

"What, what's happened? I knew it! You are crazy to go there, Tom! And you, Jana, you are even crazier to take him!"

Dita was only just beginning to work up her, "I told you so," anger. She reached her right hand up towards the top of the back of Tom's coat where it was split right across his shoulder blades from the first baton blow and with her other hand she pointed to his jeans that were torn to shreds across the knees from where he'd hit the Prague cobbled street in his fall. As she grabbed the split opening at the back of the top of his coat she exclaimed, in a voice that was growing louder by the second, "look at this. Look! This could have been your head, Tom!"

"It's okay," he wheezed. "I'm okay it just got a little hectic." He tried to brush away Dita's concerns and sound as calm as possible in an as understated English way as he could manage.

Jana found that amusing. "Yes, a little hectic," she laughed as she repeated Tom's phrase. "But he's alright really, Dita. He'll have some bruises, but he'll be fine."

For her friend it wasn't funny though. Dita wasn't going to let it go that easily. "Look at you. You are really lucky it wasn't your head that the bastards cracked. Then we would be rushing you straight to the hospital." Tom though was getting off comparatively lightly. Most of Dita's anger was directed at Jana. Even though she was her best friend she was not letting her off the hook.

"You are a bloody fool, Jana. He was a bloody fool to go, but you are a bigger bloody fool to take him!" Now she was shouting at Jana and her friend had stopped laughing.

"But people said there were at least a hundred thousand of us there tonight, Dita. A hundred thousand! You really should have been there. You really should." She was shouting back and pleading with Dita to see the positive side of what had happened.

Dita's dismissive response was simply, "oh yeah, of course I should have been there, Jana, and then I would have a sore head and bruises just like him, and like all the other bloody fools that were there will have in the morning."

For another five minutes the two women stood and screamed at each other. They traded the kind of insults related to stupidity and lost opportunities that only real friends can exchange, some in Czech but mostly in English, no doubt for Tom's benefit. Then suddenly they stopped, stared at one another face to face for a few seconds and then hugged each other so tightly that Tom thought they would never part as tears streamed down both their faces. Meanwhile, he just sat there on Dita's settee holding and rubbing his shoulder and his legs, but being completely ignored, just like the foreigner and outsider that he was, intruding on a very private and personal argument and a bonding that he could in no way explain. Then he heard Jana speak softly into her friend's ear while they were still embracing, "it is happening, Dita. It is changing, it really is."

On his Prague bound train four-and-a-half years later he recalled that it was then, as the two Czech women hugged one another late on that 17th November evening in 1989, that he knew why and how he could be in love with them both, as well as in love with their country.

19
18th November 1989 and the beginning of Tom's 'revolution'

"It is not bravery. It cannot really be described, cannot be put into words easily. Sitting there waiting, knowing that eventually you will be hit. Hit very hard, very, very hard by a long white, thick, heavy stick. Hit by someone in a police uniform who is really just as scared as you; someone who may be so scared that he is completely out of control, lashing out into the crowd with his long white stick. Not even because he hates you as an individual and certainly not because he hates what you stand for, what you are demonstrating for. No, he is lashing out at you because he is petrified. So you just sit there also in fear, trying not to let it show on your face but knowing that after all the face to face rituals have been played out and observed then the violence will begin. Once all the talking and taunting between the front line of demonstrators and the front line of 'white batons' are gone through, then it will start. It will not last long. Time flashes by once it starts and you are really frightened, really scared of course. It speeds past when the red hot searing pain of the thud of that long white stick hits your head or your leg, or the arm you quickly thrust up to try and fend off the assault. So, it is fear. You sit there, stand there, march, chant, sing, and demonstrate, only because the life you suffer, the life you hate is more meaningless, more repellent, more awful, than the fear in your stomach while you sit there waiting to be hit. That fear is fleeting. It's over in a few hours and alongside you there are others who for those fearful few hours you feel are 'with you' as a collective body in a common friendship of demonstration, a common bond of wanting something to change. The alternative though, the everyday pointless mind-numbing life that we live here, is with you all the time and for all parts of your life. Every single minute of every single day, week, and year of the rest of your life, that depressing, life dulling pain is always there. That is why we protest against it and demonstrate."

Jana had introduced Jiří Kaluza as a close friend and a leading activist in the student dissident movement As he answered Tom's question about what it was like to be at the front of a demonstration he was staring into the Englishman's eyes but his mind was elsewhere outside of the cafe in which they were sitting and talking. It was focused on his instructions and orders to spread rumours from his StB superior Tomas Musil, It was mid-afternoon on the day after the 17th November demonstration and Tom had phoned Jana at lunchtime in order to try to find out the latest news.

"What's happening now?" he'd asked her. An excited Jana's voice rattled down the crackly phone line.

"Everything, everything is happening! Now it is really starting to happen!" she told him at the top of her voice.

"What, what's happening precisely, Jana?" Tom repeated, none the wiser through her excitement.

"People say Havel has returned to Prague. He was out of the city yesterday and so couldn't make the demonstration. Seems he is trying to get all the different opposition groups – the students, actors, artists, intellectuals and the dissident church leaders – to combine and form some sort of broad based organisation to focus the opposition and continue the demonstrations."

Although her English was excellent Jana was talking so fast that Tom was having trouble understanding her. He managed to repeat a few of her key words aloud though, "What, Havel is combining the opposition groups, forming a broad organisation to continue the demonstrations? So you think things are really starting to happen then?" In addition the phone line wasn't good and throughout the conversation he had a strongly vociferous critical running commentary resounding all the while in his other ear from Dita whose phone he was calling from, as she picked up his repeated phrases.

"Yes, yes, it's all starting again. How many times have I heard that over the past ten years or so? Nothing will happen, except that a few people will get very sore heads just like you did last night, Tom, and some broken bones from the police and their batons." Dita's cynicism seemed unshakeable.

Nevertheless Tom ploughed on with his search for information from Jana. "So, will there be more demonstrations soon? When and where?"

"There are strikes right now throughout the city and they will be throughout the country soon!" she shouted down the phone at him. "The actors are on strike and some of the TV people. The theatres are closed and the students are on strike of course. The talk is that they are trying to get the factory workers to strike. There is to be another demonstration in Wenceslas tonight. Everyone says there will be a quarter of a million people there." Jana's voice was squealing with excitement as the words tumbled out of her mouth at a rapid rate and down the phone line. This was a completely different sounding Jana phone voice from what Tom always thought was such a soft, cultured, and quite sexy telephone voice.

"So, what are you doing now, today?" Tom asked her.

"I'm going to meet my friend Jiří at two-thirty at the cafe in the Arts Faculty of Charles University. He is an, how do you put it in England, Tom, older student? She didn't wait to let him answer, "Anyway, he is twenty-eight and is very involved in the student organisation of the strikes and demonstrations. He was on the demonstration last night of course, but being one of the student organisers he would have been at the very front of the march so we never saw him."

Finally getting a word in as she caught her breath, Tom rattled off," can I come?"

"Sure, it could be a little dangerous though, the city is buzzing with excitement and it's not easy to know who to trust or who is or isn't watching us. You had better bring your security, that nice safe British passport of yours," and she followed that with a little excited laugh.

"The Arts Faculty, opposite the Rudolfinum Theatre, behind the Jewish cemetery?" Tom checked.

"Yes that's right. See you there at two-thirty," Jana confirmed. "Oh," she remembered, "sorry, I almost forgot. How are your shoulder and legs?"

"They are black and blue, with a few nice big bruises, Prague mementos. Sore, but I'll be okay, and not as sore as my ears are from Dita's scolding and from trying to talk some sense into me, as she puts it."

"That's good then. Hope the bruises disappear quickly. You'll have to get Dita to massage your shoulder for you. Not sure your ears will mend so quickly though from what I know of my good friend," Jana added with another small chuckle. "See you at two-thirty. Take care." With that there was the clunk of her receiver going down and she'd gone.

The telephone had barely left Tom's hand when he heard, "are you mad again?" ringing in his ears. "You, not even a Czech, are going to meet one of the leaders of the student demonstrations, and on a day like today after all that happened last night in the city and all that happened to you as well! Didn't the beating knock any sense into you? Or maybe it just knocked all the sense out of you. And what about your shoulder, you said this morning it's very sore. If you get picked up by the secret police for even sitting at the same table as one of the leaders of the demonstrations they will take you straight to the airport and throw you out of the country. They will never let you into Czechoslovakia again! Where will that leave us then, Tom?"

Dita was now not only cynical and unsympathetic, but also angry again. Tom had seen her like this before and nothing, no logic however logical, no appeals to morality however seemingly the right thing to do would remove her anger. Usually, because she got so angry about something over which she had so little control, her anger ended up in her own tears of frustration and unhappiness. He hated seeing her like this, so unhappy. It was almost as if she knew Jana was right – Jana with her optimism and enthusiasm for the cause and the fight – but she just couldn't bring herself to be so unconventional as to join the demonstrations. It wasn't that Dita was scared, or even frightened. Tom knew it wasn't that. To have an Englishman staying in her apartment, virtually living with her, was a pretty brave thing to do at that time. No, it was just something else. Something inside her that constantly restrained her, so unlike her free spirited friend Jana.

"Well I know all that you say could happen," he tried to reason with her, "but I'm sure it will be alright and I'm going anyway. It will be exciting finding out what is really going on after last night. Why don't you come? You should be there. After all, you're right, I'm an Englishman not a Czech, a foreigner in this country, but you are a Czech. This is your country. You should be there," he tried to convince her. It was a funny kind of attempt at rationalisation, designed to appeal to Dita's logic on her terms, but she wasn't having any of it or more precisely anything to do with it.

"You go if you must. You took absolutely no notice of me trying to persuade you not to go on the demonstration last night, so why should I expect you to take any notice now? Try to remember though, Tom, it will not only be you that will have to bear the consequences if you get arrested, it will be both of us. If they catch you they will want to know just where you are staying and that will mean trouble for me," she pointed out to him in a now very serious mood.

"I know, I understand, Dita. I really do, but I will be careful, very careful," he responded. The next hour passed almost in silence between the two of them. Then, just before two o'clock Tom grabbed his coat and scarf, made one last plea to Dita to go with him, and rushed off to get the metro to meet Jana at the Arts Faculty café.

Jana and Jiří Kaluza were already sipping their coffee by the time he arrived, a few minutes late. The Arts Faculty café was a long, quite narrow, arched ceiling room, almost like the restaurant carriage of a train, with the counter running virtually the length of one wall. Around each of the dark wood tables were groups of four 'seen better days' faded green velvet padded chairs. The place was humming with chatter. It was packed with what were obviously students and two older looking quite soberly dressed men, who looked somewhat out of place in their suits and ties. The noise of the talking, the arguments in some cases, about the events and the demonstration of the previous evening was intense. As he descended the three steps at the entrance to the café it hit Tom like a wall of sound from some Pink Floyd track of his own younger student days. As with all Czech cafes the air was thick with cigarette smoke, combining somewhat uncomfortably with the general musty stale atmosphere of the place, the sort that left a pungent taste in the mouth for seemingly hours afterwards. It seemed that everyone in the room except him and Jana was puffing away. No wonder the walls and ceiling were a grubby darkish brown, no doubt from years of nicotine abuse.

He'd joined Jana and Jiri on a circular, also faded green velvet padded, bench seat at the far end of the café. Jana was buzzing as she introduced Tom to Jiří. The excitement of the demonstration of the night before and the unfolding events in Prague shone through her eyes and across the rest of her face. She had greeted him with a huge hug and a kiss on the cheek, as well as her broad smile. Her long dark ruddy-brown hair had obviously received very little attention when she got up that morning, but somehow to Tom it looked wonderful as it tumbled down over her shoulders and the white roll neck jumper she wore. As she stood up to greet him and introduce him to Jiří the impact upon him of her tumbling hair was matched by how trim and slim she looked in her tight fitting pale blue jeans. Maybe it was not only the effect on her of all the excitement, he told himself. Maybe it was all getting to him too and sharpening his perceptions.

Jiří was the archetypical dissident student. He had the 'uniform' down to perfection. Tall and very slim – almost unhealthily, bordering on anaemic, so Tom thought – he too had the roll neck jumper on, but in his case like his jeans it was black as were his boots. He had the regulation student agitator thin very black lined beard running all around his chin, only interrupted by the briefest of goatee beards at the base of his narrow, elongated face. His hair, of course, was a shiny dark black. Maybe he had gone for the metallic black finish on his revolutionary model, Tom pondered. For sure he wouldn't have looked out of place in any of those old black and white newsreels of the student demonstrations in Paris and London in the late 1960s. The obligatory chain of cigarettes were constantly lit, puffed at, left in the ashtray to smoulder while he talked, and then puffed away at again whilst dangling precariously from the corner of his mouth. The existence of a cigarette, in or out of his mouth, and the plumes of smoke he blew out into the heavily polluted atmosphere of the café, had no effect whatsoever though on his excellent English.

Halfway through his answer to Tom's, "don't you get scared," question he noticed Tom looking around at the two older soberly dressed men. "Don't worry about them, they are just StB, Secret Police," Jiří told him. "They are always in here. It's a sort of game we play. We watch them watching us, watching them. The game is just a mirror of our Czech way of life really."

Jesus Christ! The thought briefly went through his mind that if Dita was here she would be dragging him out of there by the scruff of his collar. Good job he never managed to persuade her to come.

"So," Jiří continued, "people who don't understand, mainly westerners actually, Tom – what is it you call them, liberal do-gooders? – they think, say, that people demonstrate here because as our lives are so mind-numbingly boring we have nothing to lose by demonstrating, that we feel nothing. They couldn't be more wrong. We feel everything, and not least fear, and then pain when the baton strikes. We live monotonous lives in a soul-less system, but we are not soul-less downtrodden demonstrators with no feelings. We demonstrate and want to change the system precisely because we have a soul. Of course, for some it's a Czech or a Slovak soul, and we know that can be an unusual soul, Tom, but nevertheless it's a soul anyway. And feelings, we have feelings about what we don't like. What we've got, that's what we don't like. The system we live under every day, and we have feelings about what we want, something different from this, to be freer. We demonstrate because we have optimism. Optimism that the system is as Havel said, 'built on sand'. Optimism that we can have something better, a better life. With our optimism we also have our humour and our irony. Not all the demonstrations have been quite so serious and have ended in such violence. In August this year there were some demonstrations and quite weird protests organised near the Charles Bridge, but on the other side of the river to the National Theatre, near Kampa Island. For instance, there was a protest by 'The Society for a Merrier Present'. They dressed themselves up as a 'Merry Security Patrol' and charged down the street known as Political Prisoners' Street wearing water-melons as helmets and leading plastic dogs on wheels. They pretended to beat people up on the street with batons made of salami, cucumbers and French bread. Their idea was to parody the way that the police were beating up demonstrators. To show their protest against the Soviet invasion of 1968 they made a whale out of chicken wire, paper and tree branches and sent it down the Vltava River from Kampa Island on an inflatable mattress. Also, one day in August a big model of a duck suddenly appeared floating down the river. In English the name of our communist President, Husák, means duck. The model was wearing a placard which read 'I don't want to be President'. So, Tom, fear is easier to deal with if you think like all that, with optimism but also with humour and irony, contempt almost for the stupidity of the present system and regime. Fear is easier to deal with if you think like that when you are sitting there waiting to be hit again and again with the long thick white baton."

Tom was speechless, flabbergasted. At first he thought the guy's optimism was contagious. He felt he had just been exposed to a very persuasive philosophy lesson far more potent and relevant than any he had ever experienced in his undergraduate days from some boring, almost dead, English political philosophy professor. Or, for that matter, far more pertinent than any he had endured from some of his pontificating colleagues in the university bar. Now he was also excited. He glanced sideways at Jana. She was positively glowing, and it was nothing to do with the warm smoky atmosphere inside the café. Her smile was now even broader than the one that greeted him as he had walked into the café and she was touching his arm, patting it, and prodding him in the ribs. "See, see, it's really happening, Tom" she told him eagerly. "This time the people and the demonstrations are not going to be frightened away, not even by the police batons. Now even Dita will have to accept it that it's happening and it will all change."

Dita sure will have to accept it he thought as he nodded agreement to the beaming Jana. As for accepting things were happening, something was definitely happening to him, but it had nothing to do with demonstrations and revolutions, at least not the possible social and political revolution that might occur in Czechoslovakia. No, it had much more to do with his personal 'revolution' in relation to Jana. That was when he began to realise that he'd got it wrong the night before when he believed he was in love with both women. That was the moment he knew he was falling in love with Jana and out of love with Dita. At that point he wasn't in love with the both of them but just with Jana he was convinced as his train clattered its way to Prague four and a half years later. Around the time of the 18th November was when his feelings about the two women changed, and throughout all the things that happened so quickly after that in the rest of that year as he spent more and more time with Jana.

His thoughts went off on a tangent as he continued to gaze into the distance out of the train window. "What about that guy Jiří though?" Something was nagging away in Tom's brain about him and he couldn't quite figure out what it was. What was it that Petr had said to him during their Friday afternoon stroll in Brno a few days ago about some people at the time of the 'November days' of 1989? "You never really knew who to trust. There were Secret Police informers and infiltrators into the dissident movement everywhere, people who were not what they seemed or pretended to be."

"People were not what they seemed, or pretended to be," Tom repeated on his Prague bound train, adding, "so, was Jiří Kaluza really what he seemed, a dissident student?"

One rumour that was buzzing around the Arts Faculty café when Tom arrived there on that afternoon of 18th November 1989 was that a student had been killed by the State police on the demonstration the previous evening. "It's a guy called Šmid, Jiří says," Jana told him that afternoon soon after he arrived, explaining "this could be a huge thing for the communist government bastards to try to deal with, Tom, especially with the demonstration having been called to commemorate the killing of a student by the Nazis fifty years ago. It could really mobilise most of the people against the government not just the students, and be the start of the end for them." Jiří quickly interjected and recounted in quite some detail for nearly fifteen minutes just what had happened. How the student Šmid had been brutally beaten and attacked by the State police under the same arches in the passageway that Tom and Jana had scrambled out of as Tom was hit by the police batons. He then went on to give information on Šmid's personal background in quite some detail.

Maybe it was because this guy Jiří seemed so close to Jana, and that she seemed really drawn to him, that made Tom not really take to him. Maybe it was just jealousy over Jana's obvious admiration for him, bordering on hero worship, but Tom remembered starting to question in his own mind that afternoon in November 1989 just how could this guy know so much detail about what had happened to Šmid, as well as his personal background, so soon after the events of the night before? Where the police had taken the body, what the guy was studying, what the police were saying about it, he seemed to know an awful lot of detail so quickly. After all this was still only eighteen hours or so after it had happened and the State police were not exactly renowned for their communications skills and openness. Yes, of course Prague was full of rumours and stories at that time, but Jiří seemed to not only know so much detail but also be completely sure about it. Looking back on it now Tom felt it was almost like he was broadcasting an authorised version of what had happened, or more accurately what the State police wished people to believe had happened. "Yes, and what bruises did Jiří have from the demonstration the night before?" Tom muttered in his empty train compartment. He was supposedly at the very front of the demonstration according to what he told Tom in the Arts Faculty café that day, but he didn't seem to have any of the soreness or bruises that Tom exhibited.

When Tom had tried to interrupt Jiří's detailed explanation of what happened to Šmid, and raise some questions about how he knew so much about the details and be so sure of them, he was brushed aside as the Czech continued with his 'State bulletin', almost like he was trying to keep up with his autocue. Tom's attempted question and scepticism also drew some stern looks from Jana, something he certainly didn't want to provoke further thinking it might damage their growing friendship. So he withdrew from the conversation and just sat there listening more and more incredulously and all the while with growing doubts about Jiří's student revolutionary credentials. Tom's academic analytical mind picked up a number of bits of fine detail about Šmid and what had happened that Jiří relayed in his 'bulletin', and each time he mentally wondered hang on mate, how could you know that and how do you know that so quickly? In the turmoil that was Prague at that time information was definitely power and Jiří seemed to possess an awful lot of detailed information about what had happened the night before, not least about someone, Šmid, who very few people seemed to have known or heard of, as Jana confirmed when Tom asked her about him later.

As Tom and all the Czechoslovak people were to find out later in the years that followed, in fact Šmid wasn't exactly who or what he seemed. An investigation by a commission set up by the new post-communist government found that Šmid certainly wasn't dead, but was an agent for the StB Secret police who had infiltrated the student dissident movement. The StB plan, supervised by Soviet KGB agents in Prague at the time of the November 17th demonstration, was to fake the killing of a student, Šmid, thereby echoing what had happened under the Nazis on the student demonstration fifty years earlier. They believed this would totally discredit the old hard-line Czechoslovak communist leadership in the eyes of the Czech and Slovak people and they could be replaced by a more reform minded communist leadership under a 'Czech Gorbachev' type leader. It didn't quite work out like that of course.

On 18th November in the Arts Faculty café Tom put his suspicions about Jiri down to jealousy and ultimately he was more concerned about his bruises and aches and pains from the blows he'd suffered the night before, plus he didn't really want to get on the wrong side of Jana of course. But Petr's comment in Brno, "people were not what they seemed, or pretended to be in the communist period," kept leaping into his brain now. If Šmid wasn't who he pretended to be, maybe Jiří wasn't either. Maybe he was a Secret police infiltrator too? After all that day in the Arts Faculty cafe he'd also made quite a point to Jana and Tom about the dangers of Dita having Tom, a foreigner, staying with her at that time, following his seemingly innocent enquiry about just where Tom was staying. Then during the ensuing crazy days of the rest of November and early December Dita received quite a few very strange phone calls to her flat, in one of which the caller specifically asked to speak to Tom Carpenter. She simply told them there was no Tom Carpenter there. Because she was by then very much caught up much more positively in the fervour of the on-rushing events Dita put most of the calls down to some fool getting the wrong number, although her concern and suspicions were heightened by the one when the person specifically asked for Tom, as she wasn't slow in telling him.

Anyway now his train was pulling into Prague main station, Hlavní Nádraží, and there was nothing really that he could definitely recall linking Jiří Kaluza to the strange phone calls, and maybe he was indeed just a very well informed dissident student. His suspicions of four and a half years ago had to be left for more pressing matters and his impending dinner with Jana that evening.

20
The 'Revolutionary Days' and change – for everyone

Prague Hlavní Nádraží railway station is not the most salubrious or worthy of entrances to the beautiful city of Prague, and it can hardly be described as a terminus. The train from Vienna that Tom had used a few times in recent years on his journeys to Prague arrived at the city's other railway station, Holešovice. Hlavní Nádraží, the main station, was better than Holešovice, although only marginally.

A couple of years previously on a journey from Vienna Tom noticed and recognised the American film star Gene Hackman sat a couple of rows in front of him in the first class carriage. From what Tom gathered from overhearing his conversation with his traveling companion Hackman was heading for a meeting with the Czech President, Vaclav Havel, at Prague Castle. As Holešovice station definitely doesn't give the appearance of a major terminus in a capital city, Hackman rose from his seat as the inter-city express entered the station, questioned his woman travelling companion as to whether this was, "the end of the line," and then spotting Tom rising from his seat ventured the same question to him, preceded by, "hey, buddy, do you speak English?" Tom's first words of reply were, "we invented it Mr. Hackman," drawing what he preferred to determine was a slight smile from the star's lips. It was his next response which always made Tom chuckle whenever he thought about it. Never in a million years did he ever think he would find himself saying to Gene Hackman, "Yep, Mr. Hackman, this sure is the end of the line for you." That definitely drew a wry grin from the movie star.

He remembered that incident once more on that late Wednesday morning as this time his train pulled into Hlavní Nádraží and he wondered if it would prove to be his, "end of the line." That evening over dinner he would get his answer from Jana. At least he hoped he would once he had told her how he felt about her and then summoned up the courage to actually pose the question. He still wasn't exactly quite sure just what form that question should. Although he was certain that he wanted to get across just how he felt about her.

Hlavní Nádraží railway station was an armpit of a place, as Tom preferred to refer to it. Old 1950s or 1960s style soulless, characterless, communist concrete. After you descended the stairs from the platform - which was usually full of people struggling with suitcases and bags as there was no sign of anything as functional as an elevator - you emerged into a smelly, grubby passageway and then the booking hall. This felt equally grubby and included the added attraction of the seemingly obligatory, for eastern and central European railway stations, grimy looking kiosks. These sold very unappetizing, usually soft and soggy rolls containing the merest sliver of tasteless cheese and ham or meats of extremely dubious health, dusty faded label bottles of coke, water, and the odd can of drink. Of course the kiosks also stocked the multitude of cheap cigarettes, the smoke from which filled the booking hall from the mouths of their users. This also nicely contributed to the general stale smell of the place.

Although it certainly didn't feel as threatening as Ostrava station, and he had never actually encountered any problems there, Hlavní Nádraží station booking hall was a place Tom always felt it was best not to linger in, not that he had ever felt the need to. There were always a few drunks, down-and-outs, and generally unsavory looking people mingling about the place. So he strode briskly through it out to the taxi rank, jumped in a cab and uttered the name of his city centre hotel. Twenty minutes later he had checked in, dumped his bag in the corner of the room and was slumping on his hotel bed. It was eleven-thirty. Eight and a half hours to kill, well seven and a half if he allowed himself plenty of time for a shower and to get changed before his meeting with Jana at eight.

This was it then. This was the day he had waited for and thought about throughout his visit, or at least tried to think about throughout his travels around the Czech Republic. Wednesday had finally arrived and the stark reality was now rushing towards him, the stark reality of the fact that on that evening in Prague he would find out precisely how Jana felt about him. Assuming, of course, that he could summon up the courage to ask her, and assuming that he could actually decide on some sort of strategy about how to raise the subject. Decide how to play it? How to bring the conversation around to it? It began to dawn on him that even when he had thought about it during his travels over the past ten days he hadn't actually come up with any definite plan about how to play the evening with Jana. Every time he started to think about it he'd done what he was very good at, let his mind wander off at a tangent thinking about some related but not directly useful past incidents. Maybe that was it. Maybe there was a message in that for him. Perhaps his mind was trying to tell him something he didn't want to recognise. He'd been very good at thinking about the past, but not the future. He'd managed to completely ignore and avoid the future in terms of how to deal with what he wanted to tell Jana.

As he pondered these options he began to wonder again if there was nevertheless something, just something, that the past between them, and between him and Dita, could point him to. Give him some clue about just how to approach the evening. Something he could use that evening to try and convince Jana of the way he felt. Uncomfortable as it was to think about it, he wondered if maybe there was something in the way he and Dita had finished their relationship that might help him. Something he could learn from that. In any case Jana was bound to bring it up that evening once he started telling her how he felt about her. Dita was her best friend so the whole business of how to handle that situation was a minefield. It was no good avoiding it. He'd have to face that whole situation and think it through if he really wanted a positive response from Jana. So, he settled himself down on the somewhat too soft from over use hotel bed and tried to concentrate on that, going over just how it all went wrong with Dita.

He knew that after the 17th November 1989 nothing had been the same. Not just for Czechoslovakia, for it was after that day that people really began to believe that nothing could remain the same in that country any longer and things would change. Something would happen, even if most people didn't seem sure just what that something would be. Now though, four-and-a-half years later, Tom realised it was also a day that something changed between him and Dita, as well as between him and Jana as far as he was concerned. Quite what it was he was unsure. Dita herself changed, or at least the staunch pessimism she had always exhibited about nothing really changing in her country seemed to just quickly melt away, in the same way eventually as the communist regime that she had lived under all her life. It seemed as if Tom's beating on the demonstration at the hands of the State police had opened a valve. Let out all her steam. The day immediately after the demonstration she still kept up her pessimism, but within a couple of days she began to be more and more positive. Then she very quickly began to channel all the energy and passion she had put into her negativity and frustration into instead positively supporting Jana, even joining her on the growing – in number and size - demonstrations.

Tom watched as Jana and Dita's bond of friendship became even stronger during those 'November days', while his own feelings and admiration for Jana grew infinitely greater. He realised now that it was clearly more than admiration. He couldn't really describe it, couldn't easily put it into words, but being on the 17th November demonstration with her, seeing her wide-eyed optimism and her determination just made her even more attractive for him. "Was that when it started then?" he mumbled in his Prague hotel room, "the hope?" Was that when this strange triangle of two Czech women friends, very good friends, and the intruding outsider Englishman all changed? For sure something changed between him and Dita. It never really felt the same again. He believed now that it was probably really all down to him that things changed. It was all down to his growing feelings for Jana, but maybe just a part of him thought something also changed in Dita. She became more and more attached to everything Jana did in relation to the demonstrations, the strikes, and what came to be known as the 'Velvet Revolution'. Although Tom was always there it just seemed that as far as Dita was concerned he became more and more of an 'outsider' looking in; an Englishman, a foreign outsider looking in on the Czechoslovak revolution, and an outsider looking in on Dita and Jana's friendship. Theirs had always been a very, very strong Czech female friendship and now they were fighting and struggling for their freedom alongside thousands of other Czechs and Slovaks. No matter how much he tried, there was no way he could relate to that or really be part of it. He would always be an onlooker, an observer. He'd soon learned over the few months that he'd known her that Dita's personality was such that when she was convinced of something, when she took up a project or cause, she put everything into it, every part of her. She took it over as much as she could and almost took charge. For Dita, the struggle, the revolution, became hers and Jana's, and of course the Czechs' and Slovaks'. It was not Tom's, as she was quick to tell him in the heat of the moment quite a few times after 17th November. "It's not your country. It's not your life. It's not your struggle," was the way she was always very fond of putting it.

As Jana told Tom in their phone conversation on 18th November, Václav Havel, who had been out of Prague on the previous day, returned to the city and quickly set about trying to formalise the opposition movement. The two 'umbrella' opposition movements that were to form the focus of the revolution, 'Civic Forum' in the Czech part of the country and 'Public Against Violence' in the Slovak part, were formed within forty-eight hours of the 17th November demonstration, before Tom's bruises had disappeared or his sore back and legs for that matter.

For Tom the next few 'November days', in truth the next few weeks, was a whirling, rushing blur of activity. Telephone calls from Jana to Dita's flat would provoke a furious scrambling for coats, scarves, gloves and hats as Dita and Tom both dashed out together into the cold Prague winter air to meet her on a demonstration, or a strike, or for a student meeting in one of the many Prague theatres. Tom remembered vividly it was both of them, as Dita was now well and truly caught up in the fervency of the revolution. There were no more arguments between Dita and her best friend, or between Dita and Tom, about, "nothing changing." Soon it was always Dita who took control. From then on Dita's suggestions to him that, "maybe you shouldn't come, after all if they catch you they'll know you're a foreigner, and then God knows what might happen," were much calmer, more gentle and considerate than before in attempting to deter him from going on a demonstration. A couple of times Tom's reaction was to smile at these comments and then allow himself a small chuckle at the way she had changed. Dita, however, immediately firmly responded, "It's not funny, Tom. This is a serious business, not some game."

Blimey, how she's changed, Tom thought, although he definitely kept that well and truly to himself. Then again, maybe looking back on it now in some respects she hadn't really changed. Even when she did eventually get swept up in the excitement of the revolution she still wanted to be in charge, in control. When Dita did something it had to be done properly. Once she was convinced something was the right thing to do she threw herself into it a hundred per cent, determined to get it right. On a few occasions Tom even saw her trying to tell Jana where they should go and what needed to be done by the strikers, the students and the demonstrators. Jana though knew her friend very well. She would just smile and agree. Tom pleasantly recalled that once while doing just that Jana gave him a quick knowing wink over her friend's shoulder. It was as if she was saying to him, "it's okay, I've known her a long time and I know it's best just to agree with her, even if she knows, like me, that nothing will happen that way." From his experiences in their country he'd learned that this was very much a Czech way of dealing with things and issues.

One of the most poignant memories in Tom's mind was that on the 20th November they were all there together in Wenceslas Square, jammed into the wide boulevard with a quarter of a million others; all three of them chanting in Czech the equivalent of, "this is it," and, "now is the time," although in Tom's case he just tried to follow rabbit fashion what the two women chanted. Jana and Dita were singing in Czech at the top of their voices with the huge crowd. All three of them laughing, smiling, and hugging one another in the cold Prague night air as their hot breath floated off joining thousands of others. Trying to keep warm, trying to hear the speeches from Havel and the other dissidents, and then roaring their approval and clapping furiously at what was said. It was an incredible feeling, a truly wonderful shining moment. Something he'd never experienced before and guessed he'd never experience again. Not only to be in such an exciting situation, in such an exciting place at such a moment in history, but also to be there with two incredible women. As he sat there on the bed in his Prague hotel room looking back on it in that way he almost wondered why he believed four-and-a-half years on he now needed hope about meeting Jana that evening and explaining just how he felt about her. How could anything replace those feelings of that night in Wenceslas Square with the two of them? Why would he want anything more? Why put himself through the minefield of feelings about one of the two women and thereby endanger all the good thoughts and memories he had about the good times the three of them had shared in the past, and not least endanger the two women's friendship?

During the rest of those happy days of November 1989 and on into December the demonstrations, meetings and strikes came thick and fast. At first it was the university and high school students demonstrating, along with the dissident intellectuals and some church leaders, after November 17th though they were soon joined by the country's industrial workers. Tom smiled again now as he recalled Jana telling him and Dita at the time in Dita's flat how the support for the demonstrations and strikes had spread to the industrial workers. "How do you English put it, Tom?" she asked him, adding before he could answer, "I think you say that for the communist regime it's the hay that breaks the donkey's back now that the workers have joined us."

"Err ... something like that," he told her, "but actually, it's straw and camel's back."

She laughed out loud, replying in her mischievous way, "camels? But there are no camels in England, Tom, only donkeys I'm sure. Everyone knows that."

That night towards the end of November in Dita's flat Jana told Tom and Dita that her father had said that the march through Prague on the twentieth, and the demonstration in Wenceslas Square which the three of them had been at, had reminded him of the mass protest in 1967 that had swept away the hard-line communist leader Antonín Novotný and saw him replaced by the reformer Alexander Dubček, ushering in the Prague Spring reforms. "Tears filled up my father's eyes when he told me this. Even he, who had given up hope of ever seeing this, now believes something is going to change, and this time for real, permanently, forever," she told them. Tom remembered thinking at the time that this was a serious, caring Jana, one that was just as charming as the smiling, happy, laughing one.

Dita, now well and truly caught up in the mood of the time and definitely one of the dissident demonstrators, added, "Yes, and even the official radio and national TV are reporting the demonstrations." Positively possessed by the excitement she went on, "and not just in Prague, but also the demonstrations in Ostrava, Bratislava and Brno are all being reported on radio and TV. The daily mass rallies are being reported live and uncensored, including calls for an end to the Communist Party monopoly on political power. Of course that crazy old communist leader Jakeš and the hard-liners are saying that the protesters are just trying to create chaos and anarchy. Apparently we are wreckers, he says. Can you believe that ignorant old man's arrogance? Well, he is completely out of touch with reality. He'll see. He's history, bad rotten history, along with the rest of his crooks and cronies."

It was indeed an amazing period. An amazing time, and one Tom would always remember for all sorts of reasons, not least the change in Dita and the change in his feelings towards Jana. Within a week or so of the November 17th demonstration Prague was awash with crudely printed leaflets. Walls, metro stations, and even the metro trains themselves were covered with previously suppressed dissident posters. Suddenly people were getting as much, if not more, information from these sources as they got from TV and radio. What came to be known as the 'subway samizdat' became the most effective means of finding out about daily events and demonstrations opposing the regime. One of the leaders of the dissident opposition group Civic Forum had apparently called it, "a war on walls." One afternoon Tom was standing with Dita and Jana waiting for a metro train and after an announcement on the station tannoy they excitedly translated it for him, explaining that the announcer had just given out the time and place of a rally later that day where people were going to hold hands and form a chain of human solidarity. The announcement had apparently ended with the information that the workers on the metro would be honouring and supporting the

General Strike called for the following Monday from noon till two o'clock in the afternoon.

At that time it seemed as if the whole of the country had found the confidence and strength to speak out, to make their voices heard and to demonstrate. It reminded him of the saying that you can hold down the lid of a boiling kettle for only so long before eventually the steam will blow the lid right off. By the end of November 1989 the people of Czechoslovakia were at full steam and the lid was about to be blown off the communist system, blowing the communist crooks, as Dita was fond of referring to them, clean away. Day after day the demonstrations went on, and grew larger and larger as each day passed. The biggest one took place on November 25th, the ninth consecutive day of marches and protests. On a very cold winter's night, lit up by thousands of candles held by the protesters and by the millions of puffs of hot breath streaming from their singing and chanting mouths like a vast smouldering bonfire about to ignite and burn away forty years of oppression, around a million people converged on the Letná field in the north of the city, near the Sparta Prague football stadium and not far from Prague Castle. Just like in Národní on 17th November there was tension in the freezing Prague air. This time though it was not a tension of fear and uncertainty. This time it was a tension of confidence, excitement, expectancy and hope. It was an excitement born from the belief that something was changing, and it was a confidence amongst millions of Czechs and Slovaks gathered at Letná on that momentous evening that they could make it change. Once more Dita, Jana and Tom were there, linking arms with each other and with people they had never met before in their life. Swaying and singing while people jangled their keys in unison and Jana explained to Tom that it was the people's way of signalling to the communists that, "it was time for them to give up the keys to Prague Castle and go." There the three of them were, together, listening to speeches in the very cold Prague early evening as a light snow fell. Speeches this time not only from Havel, but also from Alexander Dubček, who was greeted with a thunderous roar and prolonged applause from the demonstrators. The previous day the ageing hard-line communist leadership group had resigned, only to be replaced by a younger neo-Stalinist leadership. Havel told the Letná crowd, "The new leadership is a trick that was meant to confuse." Havel and the millions of Czech and Slovak demonstrators were not now about to fall for such a cosmetic change. They felt and believed in their new found confidence and hope, and they wanted the whole corrupt and rotten system swept away.

As he stood there in the cold listening to Havel, with Jana and Dita on either side of him their arms linked in his, Tom wondered just how much longer the communists would be able to withstand all this growing public pressure? At that point one of the newly appointed Prague city communist leaders attempted to address the crowd but he was whistled and booed off the stage before he could say a word. Tom just stood there smiling in total admiration at the two women as they, along with a million other steamy voices, screamed resign in Czech at the tops of their voices. Now he was beginning to wonder just how much longer personally he could cope with all this and his inner struggle about his feelings for the two women.

The night before the Letná demonstration the national TV station had reported that power struggles were taking place in the communist party organisation in towns and cities across the country. At the time he thought that they mirrored the much more minor personal struggle and indecision going on in his own heart and mind. In both cases, Czechoslovakia's and his, total increasing turmoil was occurring. Translating some of the speeches for him Dita told Tom that Dubček symbolically told the demonstrators at Letná that they should, "act in such a way as to bring the light back again." For Tom though, every time he saw her, went on a demonstration with her, the light was now increasingly shining like the flames from the million candles that night at Letná, but it was shining in Jana's eyes not Dita's.

Quite early on the morning of the twenty-fifth, the day of the Letná demonstration, Jana arrived at Dita's flat, once more bubbling with enthusiasm and news. "It looks like the two hour General Strike we – she had long given up referring to 'them', or 'the students', now everyone against the communists was 'we'; all part of it – have called today is going to be a complete success, total stoppage. This will show the bastards!" The words came tumbling rapidly out of her mouth as soon as Dita opened the door to her flat.

"The college classes and the schools are all shut down, just like the theatres. Posters about the strike and the demand for the communists to resign are all over the city, stuck up everywhere - in shop windows, in the metro, on the trams and the buses, on street lamps, and even on the metro elevators. Everywhere! The students have set up work groups in classrooms, lecture theatres and gymnasiums, and they're spending days and nights typing up appeals and declarations, and posters."

She was in full flight verbally and was barely stopping to take a breath. Tom just stood there listening intently to every word that rushed out of her mouth, while Dita helped her friend off with her coat and scarf, pausing only briefly to tell him, "to pour Jana some coffee." As the two women followed Tom into the kitchen so that he wouldn't miss any of Jana's news, she carried on.

"Teams of the students have gone out to the factories and the large work places throughout Prague as well as all over the country. They are going to try to persuade the workers to join the strike and the demonstrations tonight. The students even have videos, lots of copies of videos, of the police beating demonstrators on the march on 17th November. One of them is being shown constantly on a TV set in the window of the Magic Lantern Theatre, which Civic Forum has taken over as its headquarters."

Jana paused for breath, and for a sip of her coffee, and even Dita beamed one of her smiles that had so mesmerised Tom in the past as she quickly interjected, "well, my dear, Tom, maybe you will be a film star, or is it a video star? Maybe we can get a copy. It might be worth it, just to see you getting some sense beaten into you by the nice Czech policeman with the big baton you met on that night of the seventeenth!"

With that the two women burst out laughing, going on for another five minutes with various jibes about Tom's new found stardom, and pretending to ask for his autograph. The two of them only stopped when Jana exclaimed, "we must go to the demonstration at Letná tonight. It will be huge! The students have called the strike today a 'Strike for Democracy'. There is even a rumour that the demonstration at Letná will be live on TV tonight right across the country. Who knows, Tom," she winked, "maybe you will also be a TV star now."

At noon that day the lights went off and cafes and bookshops across the city closed. In the Old Town Square they were joined by souvenir shops and high up in the tower of the beautiful Gothic style Týn Church on the square a solitary bell tolled. The whole period was a very strange surreal one for the Englishman as he stood with Jana and Dita in Old Town Square at noon watching events. Throughout all those November days, day in and day out, night after night, the three of them went on demonstration after demonstration. The whole of their intertwined lives was taken over with the events of the time. The whole of the country seemed to stop, as though it was trapped in some sort of time warp. In fact, Czechoslovakia was freeing itself from a time warp that had engulfed it for forty years and so the struggle went on, day after day.

On the twenty-seventh of November another two hour General Strike again brought the whole country to a standstill. Over 900 factories and other businesses closed. All public transport stopped. Only hospitals, nursing homes and some food shops stayed open. A strikingly poignant sign of the determination and new mood amongst the people was given through the way that many of the public clocks in the city were deliberately stopped at five minutes before twelve. Some of the posters across the city showed a clock with its hands in the same position. It symbolised the fact that the time was up for the communists. It was time for them to go, time for a new shift to come on. The call for free elections was everywhere now. People who remembered, who were there, said it was the biggest show of dissent since February 1948 when ironically demonstrations orchestrated by the communists toppled the multi-party democratic Czechoslovak government. Now it was the Communist Party of 1989 in Czechoslovakia that was falling apart under the pressure of genuine popular protest, protest organised and led by the dissident umbrella groups Civic Forum and Public Against Violence.

On the twenty-seventh Tom and Dita met Jana in late morning in Národní, at the end of the street by the river and the National Theatre. By noon the street was full of thousands of people who, like the three of them, gathered for the march to mark the General Strike. Leading actors and actresses came out into the street from the many theatres around Národní to wave to the strikers and demonstrators and shout encouragement. On every window, even those of the Beryiozka, a restaurant run by the Soviet government, and those of Čedok, the Czechoslovak state travel agency, there were signs stating 'Generální Stávka', General Strike. On balconies, on poles and lampposts, and in windows everywhere the Czechoslovak flag fluttered, with its blue triangle to the left and a band of red and one of white running across it. Ribbons in the colour of the flag were pinned to every lapel and even to the collars of dogs. Television cameras were everywhere, but not this time to take pictures of the marchers for the communist Secret police. Now they were taking pictures for all of Czechoslovakia and beyond to see. One of the cameramen told Dita that pictures of the strike demonstrations all over the country were being shown live on national television. "They are showing demonstrations in České Budéjovice, where even the workers at the Budvar brewery are on strike," he happily told her, "and of the miners on strike in Banská Bystrica in Slovakia, and even from the demonstrations in Kavčí Hory. Amazing!" Dita explained to Tom that Kavčí Hory was the mountain outside Prague where the television transmitters were situated.

"Now it's clear, the whole of the country supports the students. Supports us," Jana emphasised to her two friends. "My friend Jiří Kaluza told me last night that there were rumours everywhere that things are getting so bad for the Czechoslovak communist bastards, so out of control, that the Russians have taken over running the show. There is a rumour again that they are trying to put a kind of 'Czech Gorbachev' in power to replace the old leaders, someone who is more of a reformer, to try and keep people happy and take the sting out of the situation. We've heard that rumour before of course, but Jiří says it's much stronger now and could well be true. He said he's heard that Zdeněk Mlynář has been flown to Moscow to meet with Gorbachev and that he will be asked to take over."

"Zdeněk Mlynář," Tom asked? "Didn't your friend Monika tell us some rumour before about him and Gorbachev being long-time friends?"

"Yes, that's right, she did," Jana confirmed. "He was one of the leading reformers in the Communist Party in the period of the Prague Spring in 1968. After the Russians crushed the reform movement in August 1968, and put in their own Czechoslovak 'puppet' hard-line leaders, Mlynář was eventually expelled from the party in March 1970 at the start of the so-called 'normalisation' period. Jiří said that Mlynář was at Moscow University with Gorbachev when they were students in the 1950s, and that they have been friends ever since. Don't ask me how he knows that, I have no idea. There are so many stories and rumours all over Prague at the moment, but Jiří is usually right."

"Fascinating and very interesting," was all Tom could get out of his wide-open mouth at the time. Although sat there on his Prague hotel bed four and a half years later this struck him again as something else that Jiří seemed remarkably well informed about, especially for a so-called dissident student. It only fuelled further his retrospective suspicions that perhaps Jiří Kaluza wasn't exactly what he seemed? How had he known all this? Where did he get his instant information? Was he really what he seemed? Maybe he really had been one of the people Petr in Brno had talked about – a Secret Police agent who had infiltrated the student movement?

There were lots of rumours buzzing around Prague at that time of course. Who knows how many of them were true, and whether anyone ever did find out, ever could find out through that hazy time of intrigue and chaos whether stories such as the one about the 'Czech Gorbachev', and Gorbachev and Mlynář meeting during the 'November days', were true? Tom couldn't even be sure now that his recollections of all the details of the rumours and stories of the time were accurate.

There was one recollection that was always quite vivid though. A recollection he was always sure he had the details right about, not least because of the impact it had on him and his feelings at the time. At one of the dissident meetings Tom went to during those crazy days he heard a dissident actress who was a long-time resident of Prague explain to the crowd assembled in the theatre that she believed that over the forty years in which the communists had been in power people had become soured. She told the crowded theatre that it was similar to a woman being made to marry the wrong man. "It is like a young woman who is very much in love with one man, but she is forced to marry another man. But she lives on, she has children and she carries on in a kind of muted way, as if it were a normal life, even though in her heart she knows it isn't normal. Then one day she sees the lover of her youth on a bridge, the man she was in love with before she was forced to marry someone else, and suddenly she comes alive. We, Czechs and Slovaks, are like that woman. Our lover may still be on the other side of the bridge, but at least he is now visible."

Sitting in his Prague hotel room Tom recalled just how poignant that comparison and imagery had been for him then as he sat and listened to the woman in the theatre in the 'November days' of '89. That simple analogy had made him fully realise now in 1994 just what he had to do, what he was determined to do as he did not want to miss his chance to come alive and cross to the other side of the bridge to be with his 'right woman', Jana. He may not have worked out a clear strategy yet but at least he had strengthened his conviction that he had to take his second chance with Jana and tell her just how he felt.

21
Tom Carpenter – 'voice' of the reform communists

After the 17th November demonstration and in the days that followed Prague was alive with rumour and counter rumour about the various groups struggling for political control. About who was talking to who, and who was making deals. Once again thanks to his connection with Jana and his growing feelings for her, a few days after the demonstration Tom found himself in the middle of it all.

"Monika says Tomas Plašil wants to meet you. He wants to give you an interview."

Telling Tom this Jana seemed excited, like it was something really important. Tom was just confused though.

"Plašil? Why does he want to give me an interview? I'm an academic not a journalist. Doesn't he know that?"

"That's just the point, Tom. There is no way he'll talk to a journalist, especially a western one. It would be far too dangerous. No one trusts him and his reform communist friends. The hard-line communists around Husák hate the reformers like Plašil and his boss Adamec, and the dissidents just don't trust the reformers. A communist is a communist to them, reformer or hard-line. They all say one thing and then do something else as far as the dissidents are concerned."

Taking a sip of his coffee in the small old Czech style café in the Zizkov, Prague 3 district, near the University of Economics where Monika worked, Tom listened intently to Jana's explanation but was still none the wiser.

"What does he expect me to do with this interview with him, assuming that I do it of course?"

"Monika said Plašil and the reformers think that getting their reform views and ideas heard in the west will get them support from important people and governments there, and the reaction and influence of those people will prevent the Russians coming into our country with their tanks like they did in 1968. She said he knows you're not a journalist, but talking to you will not arouse the suspicion of the hardliners. You will be seen as just another interested academic probing around trying to find out what's going on, but not supporting or promoting any side or views in particular. After all, it's not like you're being watched or followed or anything. So, you're safe. It will be safe for you, and safe for Plašil and Adamec, not that he will be there or meet you. You know that I am not sympathetic towards any of the communists, the hard-liners or the reformers, and Dita certainly isn't, but just think, Tom, what a chance this is to really get some insight into what is going on inside the communist party and the government. Also, Monika says Plašil reckons you will easily be able to pass on what he tells you to some journalist contacts back in England. With everything that is going on here and in Eastern Europe at the moment they will be desperate to get hold of what you can tell them. So, what do you think? Monika says she can arrange it for tomorrow afternoon if you can make it? Please, Tom, please do it for me, and it could be so important for the future of my country."

Her eyes were open wide, staring into his face and pleading with him. How could he refuse? Nevertheless, he managed, just, to hesitate. "I don't know, I need to think about it Jana. Plašil is a political advisor to Adamec after all, one of the leaders in the communist party. So he will be a shrewd political operator. What if it's all bullshit? What if it's all a trap? And what the hell do we tell Dita? She'll go crazy. You said she's hardly sympathetic towards any of them and in fact she hates all those communist bastards as she calls them. Reformers or hardliners, they are all the same to her. What will she say and do if it is all a trap and I end up getting kicked out of the country, with her in deep shit because I'm staying at her place? It's bloody risky."

"Look, Tom," Jana pleaded, "it can be tomorrow afternoon, you don't even have to tell her unless something goes wrong, which I am sure will not happen. It'll be our secret, Tom. Something just you and I can share."

"Yep, Jana, you and me and half the Czechoslovak communist party, plus a whole load of western journalists and the western world in general if I succeed in getting journalists to publish it. And Dita will go ballistic if it is published and she finds out afterwards, not only because it is dangerous but because I didn't tell her about it beforehand. It is a lose, lose situation with Dita whichever way."

As he said that to her though he couldn't help briefly thinking just what did that mean, "our secret, just something you and I can share." Was she starting to feel about him the same way as he was beginning to feel about her? Anyway, now wasn't really the time to think about that. Jana was being insistent on him meeting Plašil and she wasn't going to let him off the hook easily by giving him time to think about it.

"Come on, Tom. It's a great opportunity. The reform communists are reaching out. It would be stupid to not at least hear what they have to say. Please, please, Tom," and she once again added, "do it for me."

Once again she was staring intently straight into his face with those lovely brown eyes of hers open wide again and just a faint hint of a mischievous smile spreading across her full lips. How could he refuse?

"Okay, okay, but if it all goes wrong you can be the one doing the explaining to Dita."

"Great! I'll go to Monika's office in the university right now and arrange it for tomorrow. Shall I suggest you meet her at two o'clock at the university to meet Plašil at three, if that's okay with him, and wherever he thinks it's best to meet?"

"Okay, whatever. I must be mad, but I'll wait here and have another coffee, or maybe I need something stronger, while you go and arrange it."

Half-an-hour later she was back at the café, cheeks slightly flushed, partly from excitement and partly from rushing the quarter of a mile to Monika's office at the university and back.

"Well?" Tom asked while she dragged back the rickety wooden chair and slumped on to it to catch her breath while at the same time struggling to remove her coat.

"Yes, yes, it's fine. It's all arranged, but can you get me some water please and another coffee?"

Beckoning over the already approaching waitress Tom ordered the water and coffee plus another beer for himself, having decided while Jana was away at the university that what he had just agreed to did, indeed, require something stronger, like alcohol.

"Monika called Plašil while I was in her office and he's happy to see you tomorrow at three. She says you should meet her in the university lobby at two-fifteen."

"Is that it?" Tom responded, a little agitated, "nothing else?"

"No nothing else, Tom. What else were you expecting?"

"Well, for a start what am I supposed to ask him about?"

"Oh, don't worry about that, I expect he'll do most of the talking, and anyway Monika said she'll help you and give you an idea of what he's expecting on your way to meet him. She said he speaks good English, so no translation will be needed. Oh, and she did say he'd insisted on no tape recorders, paranoia is everywhere in this city at the moment and everyone is listening to, and watching, everyone."

"Oh thanks, that last bit is very reassuring I'm sure. Basically, I'm going to interview and be the 'voice' of someone who is under surveillance; and under surveillance by whom, the Czech StB, the Russian KGB, the dissidents, or even all of them?"

"Don't worry, Tom, Monika will look after you. I think she is quite sympathetic to the reform communists actually, but I am sure she wouldn't have suggested this and you to Plašil if it wasn't completely safe."

Jana had composed herself and was now sipping her coffee when she lifted her eyes to fix another gaze on the concerned Englishman and simply said a very warm and soft, "thank you, Tom, thank you very much. If you can get what Plašil tells you out in the western media it will mean a lot, not just for all the people in this country who are struggling for some sort of change here, but for me especially in our friendship. You are showing you trust us and I think that is important. I will always remember this and these times between us, Tom."

More good signs, but again this wasn't the time or place for personal feelings or relationships, so all he could offer her in reply was, "yes, yes I appreciate how important it is to you, Jana, and I am pleased that I can help." His reward for that was a gentle squeeze of his hand as she reached across the bare wooden café table and smiled broadly at him.

At ten past two the next day he arrived at the busy University of Economics lobby in Zizkov. The place was bustling with students, some carrying a book and all seemingly rushing up or down the stairs at the far side of the wide lobby, no doubt to a lecture or for an appointment with their lecturer for which they were already ten minutes late. The lobby was a drab place with plenty of concrete decorated in pale green and grubby looking pale beige that in a few places was flaking off the walls. It had definitely seen better days and had a real bare and spartan communist feel to it. The obligatory black and white photos of the Czechoslovak communist leaders Gottwald, Husák and Jakeš hung over the small sliding glass fronted reception booth to the left of the entrance to the lobby. Apart from that, a small clock, and a small wooden most uncomfortable looking bench that Tom headed towards to sit on while he waited for Monika, there was nothing to occupy his vision except the passing students. He placed himself at one end of the bench so that he had a good view of the staircase down which he assumed Monika would appear from her second floor office. His black laptop shoulder bag contained only a foolscap pad and a couple of pens, and not the 'banned' tape recorder that he had left at Dita's, telling her as he left her flat only that he was going to spend the morning in the National Library and then meet Monika in the afternoon to discuss a possible future academic article. Not exactly the whole truth, but he persuaded himself it was not a complete lie, and if everything went okay he'd tell her the whole truth later, but only with Jana present for safety. Should he succeed in what he was being asked to do and get his interview with Plasil into the western press he would have to tell Dita anyway before she heard about it on the Prague rumour mill.

As the clock in the lobby showed precisely two-fifteen Monika came down the stairs, spotted Tom immediately, and kissing him on both cheeks greeted him with an almost cheery, "hello," followed quickly by, "thanks for doing this, Tom."

"No problem, my pleasure," was his instant reply, although clearly neither of those statements was entirely correct as far as he was concerned.

Monika was a short, quite stocky woman, about five foot two or three inches tall. He had met her a few times before of course and she came across as a quite fussy, almost pedantic woman, for which every detail was important and everything had to be done totally correctly, no doubt a result of her communist academic training. She was an economist, and political economy was the subject she taught at the university. Her regular work attire each time he had met her previously was a sober dark blue or grey jacket and skirt with a white or pale blue blouse and sensible flat soled black shoes. The dark blue with the white was her choice today. Her dark short cut hair was showing some early strands of grey, betraying her fifty years. As they set off out of the faculty lobby she told Tom, "We have to get a number nine tram first, and then the metro from Hlavní Nádraží."

Tom, who had no idea quite where they were headed other than that Jana had told him the day before it would be somewhere on the outskirts of the city, just said a brief, "okay."

As they walked the two hundred yards to the number nine tram stop Monika started to tell him something about Plašil, his background and what Tom could expect from their meeting. Although he couldn't help noticing she seemed somewhat agitated and anxious, and was continuously looking behind them.

"Plašil and the reform communists, Tom, want to try and, I think you say, get their voice heard? Get their ideas and views across and heard in the west. They are very strong supporters of Gorbachev and what he is doing in Russia and they think that if they can do something similar here in Czechoslovakia they will be accepted in the west like Gorbachev and not feel threatened. Their problem is that they are hated on both sides, by the hard-line communists on one side and by the dissidents on the other, who are very suspicious of them and don't trust them. So, they are caught between the two groups."

"I see, but just what does he expect me to do?" he asked as they boarded the number nine tram towards the Hlavní Nádraží metro station.

"Basically you just need to listen to him, Tom, and make some notes, but no tape recorder. Jana told you that?"

"Yes she did," he confirmed.

"Good. He will do most of the talking and you can just ask him a few questions at the end if you have any. From what he said to me when he asked if I knew anyone in Prague from the west he could talk to I think he will just tell you what the reformers want to do and what they see as the way forward out of the current political crisis for Czechoslovakia. He wants to somehow get that published in the western media, so I guess he will ask you about that and if you can do it? I think that obviously Adamec, his boss, is behind it, but it would be far too dangerous inside the communist leadership for him come out publicly with it, so he is using Plašil."

"Well, I do know a couple of journalists in England who work for The Guardian and the BBC, so I guess they will be interested, although I don't really know any western journalists in Prague at the moment," Tom told her. "And unless I go back to England soon, which I don't think Dita would be pleased about, it could be difficult to get what Plašil says back to London."

"The Guardian and the BBC would be perfect and I'm sure we can work out a way for you to get it back to London without you having to go yourself. We have our means and channels. So, you can tell him about the possibilities with the Guardian and the BBC, but I'm not sure you should mention the problem about getting it back to London. I don't think he would want to be involved in that. If it got out that he'd also helped to get the story to the western media it would means big problems for him, and ultimately for Adamec, inside the communist party. The hardliners would make great political capital about what they would call political collaboration with the west to undermine the communist system here in Czechoslovakia."

She seemed very pleased with what he had told her about his media contacts in England, although he was somewhat taken aback by her comment that, "we have our means and channels." Just what did she mean by that? As far as Tom was concerned Monika was just an academic economist. He had no idea or information about her political background, if she had one, although he was now sensing that she was somewhat more than a little sympathetic to the reform communist's cause.

As they got off the tram at the Hlavní Nádraží stop he couldn't help noticing once again that two or three times she glanced anxiously behind them. He was about to ask her about it when she told him, "we have to get on the 'B' line metro and change at Muzeum." It was at that point that she told him that Plašil didn't want to meet them at his office and so they would be meeting him at the flat of a friend of his. With all this secrecy he decided it was best not to push it and ask then just exactly where that was.

From the Hlavní Nádraží metro they took the 'B' line train one stop to the Muzeum station and transferred there onto the 'A' line to the Hradčanská metro station near Prague Castle. As they emerged up the stairs from the metro station Monika told an increasingly bemused Tom, "we have to get the number twenty-two tram now." Tom assumed it would be from the tram stop for trams heading further out of the city, towards the north-west and the airport. So he was somewhat surprised when she guided him towards one heading in the other direction, back towards the city centre. He still didn't question her about it. After all it was her city and being not entirely familiar with all the tram routes in that part of Prague he thought it best to remain silent and trust her. Also he had concluded from their previous meetings that she was a stickler for detail and so surely knew the best way to get to wherever it was they were going.

After four stops, during which time she again seemed to be checking out all their fellow passengers, she indicated they should get off. A totally confused Tom couldn't remain silent any longer. "But this is Vltavská metro station, Monika. I know this is your city and not mine, but why didn't we just come straight here on the metro from Hlavní Nádraží? It's only two stops on the same line. And forgive me for mentioning it but you seem really rather agitated and I'm wondering why you've been looking around behind us all the time?"

"Yes, I'm sorry, Tom, you're right of course, we could have come straight here on the metro, but I was afraid we might be being followed. I should have told you earlier. It is a very dangerous time here at the moment. Nobody trusts anyone, and everyone is watching everyone else. I am sure Jana has made you aware of that. If you are feeling really uneasy about this now you can still decide not to do it."

"No I'm okay, I think, but I wish you had explained this back in the faculty when we met. I might have been more nervous of course, but at least I would have known what was going on."

"Good, and again I'm sorry I didn't explain earlier. Plašil's friend's flat is only a short five minute walk from here and I promise not to act so nervously from now on. If it's any reassurance I am pretty sure we are not being followed."

Not exactly completely reassuring Tom thought, but at least he knew now just what had got her so nervous and agitated, and she obviously hadn't mentioned this to Jana. A few minutes later Monika was pressing an intercom entry button marked with the name Winkler for the flat in which they were going to meet Plašil. It was on the second floor of a grey, functional looking building, obviously built during the communist period. After a voice welcomed them the entry door clicked open so they could ascend the four flights of stairs to the flat. Plašil, at least that is who Tom assumed it was before they were formally introduced, was standing in the open flat doorway to meet them. He was a tall, gangly, slim man with a small dark moustache beneath his quite large protruding nose. Monika had told Tom that he was forty-one years old, although his well-worn face suggested he was older. He was wearing a pale green, quite cheap looking open necked shirt and light grey well-worn trousers. As Tom and Monika removed their shoes in the hallway, as was the custom in Czech homes, he asked them if they'd like coffee or water or both. "Coffee would be good thanks," Tom replied, followed by Monika's, "yes, for me too please."

The apartment living room was very basically furnished with an old battered brown leather settee and a couple of light green cloth equally old and worn armchairs. A dark brown wood coffee table sat between all these in the middle of a faded large square beige rug on the wooden parquet floor. Along the whole of one side of the room was a large floor to ceiling bookcase overflowing with various texts, some in English, but overwhelmingly in Czech. From this Tom guessed Plašil's friend was an academic. Maybe they were also a friend of Monika's. A few faded framed photographs of what looked like nineteenth century Prague were hanging on the wall opposite the bookcase. Tom planted himself in one of the armchairs and Monika in the other.

While he was wondering how to begin Plašil brought the coffee. He needn't have worried. The Czech started talking straightaway as he settled onto the settee.

"Monika tells me you have some useful contacts in the English press and with the BBC."

"Well, it all depends on what you call useful," Tom told him. "I know some people, but it depends really on what you are going to tell me and how interesting they find it."

Tom was stunned by the immediacy of Plašil's next sentence and revelation. He'd assumed there would be some verbal foreplay while the Czech tested out whether he could really be trusted, but that never happened. Either Monika had done a good job convincing Plašil that Tom could be trusted or else he, and the reform communists that he claimed to represent, were desperate.

"Adamec sent me to Moscow a month ago to see Gorbachev. I was to ask him to send some Soviet political advisors, as we call them, to persuade the hard-liners in the Czechoslovak communist party leadership here to begin some reforms similar to those Gorbachev has introduced in Russia," Plašil instantly revealed.

"Err ...," Tom stammered, clearly visibly shocked at such an incredible revelation about the involvement of Plasil's political boss, one of the leaders of the Czechoslovak communist party. Yes, that definitely would be of interest to the English media and press for sure he thought, but before he could relay that to Plašil the Czech added, "But of course you can't use that. That would be political dynamite, I think that is the way you put it in English. Gorbachev and the KGB would most certainly not be happy if that came out in the western press, and nor would the communist party hard-liners here."

Monika had stressed to Tom very forcibly on their journey to meet Plašil that he had insisted that he would designate very clearly and directly what couldn't be used from what he would tell Tom, and he immediately reminded him of that with, "Monika told you that I would say if any parts of what I tell you couldn't be used?"

"Yes, yes, of course," Tom instantly confirmed.

"So, you cannot use that, or this; Gorbachev sent three Soviet political advisors to Prague for two weeks, but they did nothing except drink and party with prostitutes. Adamec then sent me back to see Gorbachev and I told him that, and do you know what he said to me? He said you asked me to send them, but you didn't ask me to tell them to do anything. Fucking Russians, they play fucking games with us. Gorbachev wants 'clean hands' in the west, with no sign of any public involvement by him and the Soviets with what is going on here, or in Poland, or the rest of Eastern Europe. He wants to be liked by bloody Thatcher, Reagan and the rest of them, but all the time the Russians are deeply involved behind the scenes and the KGB is fucking with our country. And you know what? It's all going bloody wrong. It's a complete mess now and I can tell you that unless something drastic is done quickly it will all end badly, for Czechoslovakia, for all the Czech communists – hard-liners and reformers - and for the Soviets."

His tone had increased as he became more and more agitated, and he was now leaning forward on the edge of the settee and jabbing his finger into mid-air.

Blimey, Tom thought, this is a bombshell but I can't bloody use it. Shit! So, just what does he want me to use and get out in the western media? With that in mind Tom tried to move things on.

"Yes, I can see that's incredible. Thanks for telling me that, but what is it that you want to tell me that I can use and try and get published in England?"

"Gorbachev wants a reform communist leadership here, a Czech 'Gorbachev'. He wanted Zdeněk Mlynář, but he refused. Everyone knows that this time the Russians are not going to come riding into Prague on their tanks like they did in 1968, but they still want to control and change things to what is best for them. There are splits politically inside the Soviet communist party leadership though about just what that is. On one side there is Gorbachev and the reformers and on the other side there are the old style hard-line communists who want things to go back to the way they were before Gorbachev took over. On top of that we are caught in the middle of all this here in Czechoslovakia as reformers. The dissidents don't trust us, even though there have been some contacts between us and some of those groups. The hard-line Czechoslovak communists hate us, and the KGB certainly doesn't trust us. So, we need a 'voice', some way to get our views heard here and in the west. Do you think you can help us, Tom? The State media is changing, becoming more open, and we are getting more and more of our people into positions in the State television and radio. Adamec is open to a whole range of reform ideas and I can tell you more about some of them if you want, and you certainly can use what I tell you about them."

"Okay, that sounds good, and maybe I can try and put some kind of article together from that and try to get it to my media contacts in England," Tom confirmed.

Plašil was more relaxed now, not so agitated, and was once more sitting back in the settee. He spent another hour going through various things that Adamec and the reform communists wanted to introduce, and after shaking Tom's hand firmly and thanking him profusely he showed him and Monika to the door of the flat. Monika told him that she would obviously be in touch soon to let him know what had happened to the interview and Tom's success or otherwise in getting it published in the west. As they descended the grey concrete stairwell she asked Tom what he thought about what Plašil had told him.

"Well, the mere fact that they want to get their arguments and views over and publicised in the west is certainly some revelation. I can say that straightaway and I'm sure the western media will be very interested, but the whole thing is a minefield. The Russians are split god knows how many ways, the KGB are clearly all over Prague doing their worst, the Czechoslovak Communist Party leadership is split and in a mess, and according to Plašil the dissidents don't seem to be much of a force politically. Although, if what he said about some contacts having taken place between the dissident groups and the reform communists is true, I'm sure that will be of interest to the western media. The key thing is time, things are moving so fast, changing every day. The whole country is in turmoil, not to mention the rest of Eastern Europe, and the reform communists around Adamec may just simply run out of time if the whole thing explodes politically and the Czechoslovak people start to take matters into their own hands. Gorbachev, and the Soviet reformers around him, just don't seem to understand that. Rumour has it that he is a very indecisive man and takes an eternity to make decisions. If that's true events may just overtake anything he and the Russians try to do, by the time they decide just what to do of course. I'll try and get what Plašil told me, what he said I could use, out in the western media as soon as possible, but it could take a little time and events here are moving so fast that I think it may well turn out to be old news by the time I manage to get it published. I'll try as quickly as I can of course, and if I need some help from you and the channels and means that you have that you mentioned earlier I'll get in touch. I'll also keep you updated on how successful or not I've been."

"I think you might be right, Tom," she told him as they exited the building, "but thank you again for coming and for trying anyway." At that point though she began to look anxious again, adding, "I don't want to alarm you, Tom, but I'm pretty sure that the man in the doorway across the street has been following us. I'm sure I saw him on the tram and the metro."

22
December 1989 and the cold reality

Tom remembered thinking at the time would it ever end? Not just the communist regime, with every day that went by in that November and December of '89 it became clearer and clearer that they could not, would not survive, but would his own experience in that period ever end? A period of perfect happiness, total excitement, constant activity and friendship between the three of them, Tom and the two women now totally in his life. He knew that at some point it would all fade away, this fantasy time. It would all come to a halt and then the day-to-day reality would mean him having to face his dilemma and deal with his feelings about the two women. Then one of them, Dita, who in the 'November days' had eventually begun to enjoy true happiness in her country after waiting for it all her life, would be hurt and suddenly be very, very unhappy.

Then it did end. At the end of December after six weeks of frantic activity for the three of them and the rest of Czechoslovakia the communist regime was swept away. On December 10th the Communist President, Gustav Husák, resigned, and on December 29th Václav Havel was elected as the new President by the country's representatives in Parliament, many of whom had previously preferred to lock him up in prison. Havel became Czechoslovakia's first non-communist President since 1948. Alexander Dubček was appointed the Chairman of the Parliament and it was agreed that free parliamentary elections would be held in the following year. For Tom this represented another peculiar Czechoslovak irony. Havel, who had not been allowed by the communists to go to university because of his perceived well-off background, had been catapulted to power most of all by students and the student dissident movement from the country's very universities that he had been prevented from attending.

Much of Havel's literary work contained the thread of what the writer called 'the absolute horizon' – the moral and philosophical judgements that give human life its meaning. Even now, four and a half years later, Tom's stomach still churned over as he recalled the moral and philosophical judgement he'd already made by the time Havel became Czechoslovakia's new President. A judgement he'd hoped would give his life real meaning, but one he couldn't bring himself to face. Tom's visa had long expired by the end of December 1989 of course, but that wasn't the major moral and philosophical issue that taxed him at the time. Anyway, no one in the wildly celebrating new Czechoslovakia seemed to be really bothered about such bureaucracy at that particular moment in time.

So, it wasn't the question of his expired visa that occupied his mind daily. Instead, the increasing cold of the Prague winter was matched for him by the growing cold reality of just how to deal with his personal moral situation with Dita, and thereby Jana. That was what concerned him most. As was his way, he had resolved at the time that he would not tell Dita the whole truth. He would not, indeed felt he could not, tell her that he was really utterly and totally in love with her best friend, and anyway could he really tell Jana that before he told Dita? No, he was convinced at the time that the situation would have been impossible. While he grappled with just how to raise it at the end of December 1989, what to say, in effect the issue was forced and resolved for him. Not one to stand on ceremony while others organised things, Dita had decided just what her life, and by association Tom's, should look like post-1989 after the fall of the communist regime. Just what their life together should be in the new democratic Czechoslovakia. Over a dinner she had specially prepared for the two of them in the evening on New Year's Day she told him she wanted to discuss something very serious with him. "Now all the old barriers have been swept away we can all have a new start," she explained.

"What are you saying?" Tom tentatively interrupted, fearing only too well that the moment he had dreaded and studiously avoided was about to descend upon him. Dita had dressed up especially in a simple, but elegant and effective little black dress. Even at that most difficult of times Tom still found himself thinking how lovely, charming, and most of all very happy she looked. Her wide brown eyes were sparkling. She obviously believed that as her life had changed because of the changes in her country she could now complete the picture and make things perfect in her personal life.

"Tom, do you realise how happy I am?" she pointedly asked him.

Not really what he wanted to hear right then as he sat there desperately hoping not to have to face what he feared was coming his way, but Dita went on, as determined as ever.

"No one knows for sure what will happen now in this country of mine, but for certain the old soul-destroying ways are gone. Life will change for everybody and everybody will hope for, dream of, a better life. On top of all that I also have you and now we can be together all the time."

He was beginning to sweat a little as he thought this is terrible, awful. How can I be so cruel as to kill her optimism? She will be so hurt.

"Over the past few days I have thought a lot about it, the changes and us, Tom," she continued. "For a start we in this country will be able to travel abroad much more easily. I will be able to come to England with you now, very soon."

"Yes, yes, of course you will," Tom agreed, not knowing quite what else to say, and thinking that's okay. If that's all she means I can deal with that now and face the real issue at a better time. As usual he was once again putting off the difficult moment, but Dita didn't stop there and had no intention of doing so. She had something much more in mind, something much more concrete and committed.

"But it's much more than just that, Tom. I do mean that now I will be able to come to England in the next few weeks, but I am also talking about the longer period, Tom, and us being together."

He slowly half-nodded a sort of tentative jerk forward of his head. It was all he could think to do. He couldn't utter a word. Nothing would come out of his mouth. His throat felt dry and he could feel it closing up. It was probably just as well that he couldn't speak as Dita seemed to take this as a positive sign. For her he was obviously listening intently. She was just pushing on, organising the rest of their life. So much so that she didn't even notice he was now quite visibly sweating. Tom felt as though liquid was gushing out of his forehead. Christ, my head's leaking, he thought.

Then it came. The moment he couldn't avoid, the question that really cornered him. Well, it was more a statement of intent really that floored him with the unexpected killer punch, the unforeseen knock-out blow. When it happened he never even saw it coming. Never even ducked or weaved. He couldn't. He had no time to and was like a 'sitting duck'. All that stuff about travel just lulled him into a false sense of avoidance security, but Dita meanwhile was just totally full of optimism and excitement about the prospects of their new life together.

"You can come and work here now, Tom. Get a job in one of the universities. They will be looking for western lecturers, and be desperate for western ideas and western views. Everything will open up. The courses in the universities will change completely now. You will be perfect for the new Czechoslovakia."

Bang, right on his jaw! His head was reeling, just as it had been on that night of 17th November in Národní when he had been so rudely introduced to the large thick Czech riot police baton. He muttered, "Err ... um ...," but Dita was ploughing on, impervious to his hesitancy.

"Then we can live together here in Prague. You love it here and I don't really want to leave my home city, especially not now when it will be an exciting time with so many changes happening. After all, Tom, it will be much easier for you to get a good academic job here than it would be for me to get one in England."

She was right about that of course, but now she really had him on the ropes and was moving in for the knock-out blow.

"We can live here at first. It will not really be big enough, but it will be okay while we look for somewhere bigger quite quickly." She had clearly thought it all through.

"A bigger apartment, but still near the centre will be nice. Although when we have children I would like to have a house with a garden in a nice area just on the edge of the city. I think you call it 'in the suburbs', Tom, but not in that part of the city with all those concrete blocks of paneláks. You know, not in an area with all those masses and masses of big tower blocks of flats."

Wham!! That floored him completely and knocked all sense out of him. He was well and truly counted out. If it wasn't for the fact that so much sweat was now pouring out of his head to let him know it was still there he would have thought it had completely fallen off his shoulders. There was no feeling in it whatsoever and his eyes were open so wide it felt like they were going to pop right out of their sockets. He couldn't even feel to blink, but he must have been on autopilot because his automatic reaction couldn't stop one key and vital, although ultimately dangerous, word repeatedly spluttering out of his mouth.

"Children, children?" he had to say it twice, as though he was convincing himself he'd heard her correctly.

"Yes, Tom, of course I want children, and you do too, I know you do really." The old pre-'November days' Dita had returned, the one in control and planning everything.

"We've talked about it before. You always talk so fondly about your son and daughter from your previous marriage. You've always gone on about when they were little and growing up. So I know you like children."

He tried to lighten the moment by interjecting, "yes, I love children; I went to school with them." But that didn't work, didn't deflect her. Dita didn't get his joke at all and just looked at him briefly a little quizzically before charging on and putting her case for their future.

"It will be lovely to have our own and watch them grow up in a new free Czechoslovakia."

Tom's anaesthetic was wearing off. The feeling was slowly coming back into his face and head. It was just like the feeling as an injection at the dentist starts to wears off and you begin to feel the muscles in your face again. He stuttered, "But my kids are grown up. Well, they aren't even kids any more, Jim's nineteen and Karen's twenty-three. Yeah, they're great now, but hold on a bit, Dita. First you're talking about us living together. Then, it has to be here in Prague you've decided and with a job at a university for me, which you reckon will be easy for me to get. Then it's a larger apartment we need, then a house, a garden, and then kids. Phew!" With that he blew a large puff of air out of his mouth in a sigh, followed by, "that's a huge leap from where we are now."

In truth it was a far greater leap than he was letting on, far bigger than he was telling Dita. He hadn't added his feelings for Jana into the equation, but he wasn't about to introduce that factor, that issue, at this particular delicate moment. Instead he focused, somewhat unfairly he later recalled, on the issue he knew that he could argue best over and on which he could put up the best argument.

"I'm not sure I want to have any more kids," was his counter-attack. "Not at my age. I mean I will be in my sixties before they are grown up and leaving us."

This was getting trickier he thought, as even he was now talking about an, "us." He stumbled on though, beginning to sound more and more incoherent. "I just don't know. It's all a bit too much, kids and all that. Not now. Why now? Why do we have to talk about this now?" Now he was rambling completely, struggling against the tide that was Dita and her 'five year plan' that sounded to Tom like something the former communist regime would have adopted. He'd got up from the table and was pacing up and down the room flailing his arms about like a drowning man. All he could think to say as the final part of his argument now was, "why can't we just enjoy for a few more weeks all that has happened since mid-November?"

Dita's facial expression had changed completely. It was now a mixture of surprise, bewilderment, and impending tears. Then she threw him another curve ball.

"But I've talked to Jana about all this and she said it was so obviously meant to be. She said she could see, everybody could see, just how happy we are. How perfect we are together."

Tom felt his face flush. This was terrible. At just the mention of Jana's name he was starting to blush. Fortunately for him Dita was too caught up in her own emotions to notice.

"I ... I can't believe this. I can't believe you are not as happy about this as I am. "Why are you so reluctant, so negative, and so cautious? Isn't this what you want? I am sure it's what I want, Tom. So, so sure, it is what I want more than anything, Tom."

Small trails of tears were starting to fall from her eyes. She was shaking her head and insisting in an increasingly loud voice, "Tell me, tell me it's what you want. I know it is! I know it is!"

Now she was working herself up into the sort of despairing temper and fervour he had seen her in a few times in the past. He just sat there motionless on the settee he'd slumped into after his agitated march up and down the room. He really didn't know quite how to respond. When things didn't go or work out quite as she'd planned Tom had seen Dita work herself up before into what was almost like the temper tantrum of a young child. Except in her case the anger was often directed at herself, or at least the impossibility of the situation and her inability to change or affect it.

"I'm just stupid," she was now shouting. "Stupid for convincing myself that something could be perfect. Why, why do I do it? I should know that nothing can work out perfectly, should know that something always goes wrong."

Tom still hadn't a clue just how to respond, although fortunately for him he had no chance to as Dita was now in full flow. Her self-flagellation went on, over and over, round and round, stronger and stronger, for another fifteen minutes. When she had finally exhausted herself Tom calmly said, "It's not you." God he thought, how often has he said or heard that, adding quickly, "I just don't want to rush."

Delay, delay, avoid the issue, avoidance and delaying tactics, that's the best way to play it at the moment, he decided. "We don't need to rush, we really don't, Dita." He couldn't resist or leave the issue of kids though, "but I'm really, really not sure about kids. We need to talk more about it, rather than you just presenting me with this is how it's going to be."

He nearly made it, nearly got away with calming the situation, but that last bit blew it. It was definitely the wrong thing to say.

"What do you mean by I'm presenting you with this is how it's going to be!" Her voice was raised again. "Oh I'm not trying to force you, Tom. I thought, I believed from all you've said, all you've done, that was what you wanted. I don't want to make you do something you don't want to, Tom!" Now she was angry and sarcastic.

"That's not what I meant," was all he could find to say, but he was simply digging himself a bigger hole. For fuck's sake put down the shovel was what was going through his mind. "I just need some time, some time to think about all this."

"To think, think about what? What can there be to think about?" Dita was not going to let go. She was like a Jack Russell terrier. She had her teeth well and truly into Tom's leg, or seemingly Tom's future life, and was not about remove them.

"If you feel the way I thought you did, the way you've said you do, what can there possibly be to think about, Tom?"

Now he was well and truly cornered. There was no way out. No avenues open to him. It was checkmate. In that situation Tom resorted to what he always did, what men in general always do, shout, wave his arms about and try to retreat by leaving the flat.

"I need some air! I need to go out for a while! I can't talk about this now." With a grab for his coat in the hallway and a slam of the door behind him he was out of the apartment hurrying down the flights of stairs and on to the street.

The freezing cold Prague January evening air was a welcome relief after the oven-like heat of the confrontation he had just experienced. The streets around Dita's apartment were quiet and deserted. The night air was still and silent, unlike the whirlwind and turmoil he had just left. Through all that turmoil though even he now realised what had changed, but as he wandered around the streets the more he tried to think about just what he should do the more nothing would come. His foggy brain was empty. All that was in there was a growing, dull, thudding headache engulfing the space between his ears. Gradually his mind meandered to where he was, strolling on the streets of Prague in the cold night air. In contrast to his and Dita's situation this was a Prague air that was full of happiness and expectancy now after the 'November days'. It somehow had a smell and an atmosphere that was newer and different from the oppressive air of the past forty years. What a contrast between his own hopeless situation and the optimism of the newly free Czechoslovak people – or at least most of them, with the exception now of Dita he guessed.

And that's the way it was. Their relationship drifted on for a few more brief, yet long and painful weeks. Nearly a month went by. There were long silent periods of hours and almost days. There were extended periods of avoidance, when they both talked about everything but the major issue that would shape and affect the rest of both of their lives one way or another. Overall though there were no more major arguments such as the one they'd had on that sad Prague evening at the start of the new year of 1990. At times they did briefly speak of the future and discussed it fleetingly, but it was never taken on into a full-blown discussion. They never got down to details and the nitty-gritty. It seemed like neither of them wanted to push it. Tom certainly didn't, and it increasingly seemed to him that Dita was too afraid of what she might hear if she did push to discuss it. Tom felt that Dita, maybe sub-consciously maybe consciously, didn't want to push it to the limit for fear of getting the answer she most wanted to avoid - that they had no future together. That Tom could not bring himself to commit to her and to living with her in Prague, let alone have children in the future. Eventually she seemed resigned to the situation.

So, it died. It just plain and simple died Tom decided, as he sat in his Prague hotel room four and a half years later. It just wasn't physically practically possible for it to live. That was how he rationalised it anyway. Cleared his conscience maybe, as in reality he knew full well that his feelings for Jana were somewhere there in the equation? Just how Dita rationalised it he never knew. He never found out. What he did know was that she took it very, very badly. She was deeply hurt, distraught for weeks after he finally left Prague. Ironically, it was Jana that he heard all this from in a couple of telephone conversations they had during the two months after it ended. Dita wouldn't talk to him. Maybe she couldn't talk to him. She just ignored his calls and letters. Although just why he wrote and what precisely he expected to achieve other than to ease his conscience he couldn't figure out. According to Jana, Dita just simply couldn't bring herself to talk to him. That is how she dealt with it he supposed.

So, it just eventually wilted and died. The initial hope and optimism of their relationship, so bright at first in those Prague revolutionary days early in the year of 1989 and even into the summer of that year, had died by that autumn and the craziness of the 'November days'. Seemingly at first it had been so strong, and for Tom so perfect. It had appeared to be what he wanted so much, what he sought after. Yet it collapsed as swiftly and as simply as the communist regime in Czechoslovakia. Maybe, as Havel had said of the communist regime, it was really merely, "built on sand", built on a dream and with no real foundation within Tom himself. His dream of love with a charming, lovely, clever Czech woman may indeed have given him hope, but events, circumstances and changes within him had convinced him that Dita was not that woman but that her best friend was.

23
The end of the line?

As he thought about the events in his life and in this country five years previously, his relationship with Dita and his attraction to Jana, he once again tried to reconcile his dilemma through Kundera's novel 'The Unbearable Lightness of Being'. For Tom, Kundera got it dead right when his main character, Tomas, tormented himself with the dilemma of whether he wanted the responsibility of someone close to him in his life, the responsibility of a relationship and of his feelings for them, or alternatively the 'lightness' through the lack of responsibility in his own freedom and in concern only about himself and his feelings. Was Tom really a man who was simply just like Tomas, aware deep down of his own inaptitude for love, an inability to love, and consequently he merely felt the self-deluding need to simulate it? Was it better to be with Jana and take the chance, or remain alone? Why should it turn out to be any different to what happened with Dita and his time with her? Hadn't he felt the same way initially about Dita five years previously as he now did about Jana - excited, expectant, and hopeful?

Recalling Kundera brought the author's idea of 'eternal return' into Tom's thoughts, implying a perspective from which things appear other than as we know them. Things were as they were then and not necessarily as we imagine them to have been or interpret them retrospectively. Maybe his 'eternal return' - to hope and the new chance and opportunity to actually finally meet the 'one' - gave Tom a perspective from which things appeared other than what they actually were. He had always managed to convince himself in his search for his 'ideal woman' that this one and this time would be different. He was good, very good, at interpreting and re-interpreting the past differently from what it actually had been, and usually getting it very wrong.

Okay he decided, stop all this introspection and moping around in the hotel room on a bright, sunny Prague May afternoon, the best plan of action was to get out and get some daylight on the subject. Go out for a pleasant afternoon wandering the cobbled streets and cafes of Prague, searching for inspiration and thinking through in his mind just how to approach the evening. Should he come straight out with how he felt about her as soon as they sat down for dinner in the restaurant, or should he wait and build up slowly? Let her see just how well they got on and recall how well they had got on in the past. Show her just how much he liked her. Then he could tell her his feelings towards the end of the meal. While he pondered this laying on the bed though all that kept leaping into his mind was a line from a Tom Waits song, "If you live in hope you're dancing to a terrible tune." Just hope that's not an omen he thought.

Tom had always thought Prague meant different things for different people. For some the magical city meant constantly gazing upwards at wonderful architectural feasts, superb buildings, and looking downwards to the cobbled streets and alleyways, what had been called the 'music of the stones of Prague'. For others Prague simply meant music, great tunes and immense musical themes humming inside their head. The tunes of Mozart or Dvorak, Beethoven, Smetana, Suk or Chopin, all of whose music invaded and echoed through the cobbled streets like some perfect match to the architecture, especially in the late afternoon of dusky autumn or of the dark cold winter days. It was Prague's very own original supermarket 'musac' he decided.

For others, especially the young British tourist groups of single men, the post-1989 Prague meant beer, cheap gallons and gallons of it, as well as the nightlife of course of clubs, bars and sex clubs. That was just another side of Prague, which in its own way matched the grubby cobbles of the city on rainy dark winter nights. Rain always had the effect of making Prague seem dirtier. It should have cleansed it, but strangely it brought instead a wet, grimy film over the cobbles and pavements. It was the first initial falling of crisp white snow which always appeared to cleanse the city. Covering up its grimy imperfections and for a few fleeting hours making it look like a pristine fairytale, especially when the snowfall came in the night. Of course the snow soon turned to an even dirtier, messier kind of slush. Initially though, it definitely gave the city a glistening new white coat, adding even more to its mystery and stillness when it came at night.

This wasn't winter in Prague though this was late May, early summer. So, by the time he had roused himself from lazing on the bed and stepped out of his hotel at just after noon the sunlight was streaming down and shimmering off the golden domes of some of Prague's churches. He'd decided on a light lunch at Cafe Slavia down by the National Theatre and the river, followed by the obligatory stroll across the Charles Bridge with its artists and stalls. He remembered again that Dita had told him when she first kissed him there that if you kiss someone on the Charles Bridge you will always return to Prague. Here he was in the magical city yet again so it must be true then; after all he'd been back many times. The question uppermost in his mind now though was would he ever get to kiss Jana there?

Prague has been a city of Bohemian rulers, a city of artists and of musicians. Its past is reflected in its many different styles of architecture, side by side. It's a city of happiness and suffering, and of so many legends and stories. One of the legends tells how the city was formed where four elements could be found in good harmony - fertile life giving soil, pure water, healthy air, and sufficient fuel for fire. As Tom began to stroll the streets of Prague on that afternoon he reflected that despite the warm early summer sunshine of that day the pure water and healthy air of Prague was long gone, lost at times unfortunately in the air polluted smog of the city traffic.

For some people Prague was the city of Franz Kafka and literature. It was words and literature that filled those people's heads. Kafka's Prague, with a soul of its own, appeared timeless to Tom. It remained untouched. In much the same way as his selective memories of Jana, his preferred optimistic signs, had remained untouched, fuelled and tinted by his hope. Indeed most of Tom's meetings with Dita and Jana had started in the very heart of Kafka's Prague, in and around Staromětske náměstí, the Old Town Square. Many of his rendezvous with the two most important Czech women in his life were framed by the buildings around the square - the Astronomical Clock at the Old Town Hall, the Disneyesque Tyn Church that of course far pre-dated the era of the Disney Fantasia, the Kinsky Palace, and the Church of St. Nicholas. All of these framed Kafka's daily life, and provided Tom with pleasant memories of waiting for and meeting Dita and Jana.

In the 1890's Kafka's Prague was a city flourishing due to the great technological progress of the age. It was also a place of deep social conflict. Workers demanding a political voice and power took part in mass demonstrations. Tom contemplated how the past was destined to recur in the city. The demonstrations he had witnessed in 1989 in Prague were the descendants of many more before them.

Cafe's played a major role as cultural centres and meeting places in the literary and intellectual life of Prague, in a similar way to those in Berlin, Paris or Vienna. Newspapers could be read in them, gossip listened to or overheard, and discussions held with like-minded people. It had been like that during the dissident period pre-1989, as well as during Kafka's time and no doubt at all other times in the city's past two hundred years or so. The Prague cafes were Tom's spiritual home, or so he liked to believe. Cafe Slavia was one such place. It was once renowned as a meeting place for Prague's intellectuals and dissidents, although now it was usually full of tourists. In a way Slavia most resembled Tom's Prague. Not as a place full of tourists, but in its pre-tourist days as a representation of Prague as a city of literature. Most of all it was always a place that provoked him into thought. Prague, and especially Slavia, always had the effect of raising in him thoughts about his life and the grand sounding 'meaning of life'. This time was no different as he sat in a window seat in Slavia with his beer and lunch of bread, cheese, salad and the usual Czech pickles on the side.

As he noticed that the Cafe had more than a sprinkling of middle-aged men in it his mind began to wander. Who were they? Were they all staring emptily into space ahead of them, daydreaming perhaps of the younger woman who had simultaneously enriched and destroyed their existence? Anyway, that's what he romanticised. His mind was wandering, observing, but avoiding it seemed any thought of his strategy for the evening. Avoiding the hope, and instead enjoying the moment.

However, staring out of Slavia's large windows at the passing trams and the mass of humanity getting on and off them as he sipped at his beer Tom eventually decided that he really had better start concentrating on just what he was intending to do that evening. How was he going to play it? For a start did he really know just what he wanted? He knew, or thought he knew, that he wanted Jana, but in what way? Was it the romance and excitement of initially being with someone, and in Prague, or was it more? Did he want to be with her forever? Was he carried away with her charm, her personality, her striking looks, or was it more? Was that enough though to want the responsibility to be with someone and share your life with someone day in, day out? Tom always believed he did, and was always convinced that when he found someone he would know what he wanted and would know that she was 'the one'. Know that was it, the 'real thing', and yes he was certain that Jana was 'the one', the 'real thing'. She was all he wanted. But again, was he really sure he wanted to be with someone now though, rather than have the space of being alone, being on his own, enjoying Kundera's 'lightness'? His thought process was going round in circles, indecisively, as always. He'd been on his own for some time now. He knew what that was like, but for a long time he hadn't experienced being with someone and sharing his life with someone. Even when he'd been with Dita it was only for relatively short periods, and that was nearly five years ago. So how could he know what sharing his life completely with someone would be like now? He recalled that Kundera had written, "We can never know what to want because, living only one life, we can neither compare it with our previous life nor perfect it in our lives to come." So how could Tom compare what had gone before in his relationships with what he believed he wanted now with Jana?

What if it really was just the surroundings that he was in love with, the intoxicating romantic atmosphere of Prague? Its winding streets and narrow cobblestone paths that reveal café after café. Maybe Prague, or even the whole Czech Republic, was Tom's 'ideal woman', his real love affair. The country certainly gave him a warm comfortable feeling inside. It made him happy most of the time. Made him feel free and yet feel that he belonged. A feeling especially of belonging to the city of Prague was how he felt every time he was in the city. The feeling he got each time he arrived there. What's more he could leave and return when and as he wanted. The city would still be there for him and welcome him. Still make him feel good and feel happy, feel safe, and yes, comfortable. Prague was always forgiving, no matter how long he had left it. No matter how long he had been away. The city always accepted his 'lightness of being' completely, without any hint of complaint.

Yep, his was a true romance with the Czech Republic, and in particular with Prague. Maybe he should just settle for that rather than trying to find an ideal woman who would be a soul mate. The trouble was he just couldn't convince himself to do that. He'd persuaded himself that what he really wanted – what was his ideal, what he was really searching for – was a Czech woman. To find and fall in love with a Czech woman, and eventually to be with her for the rest of his life, that would combine the romance of the country he was in love with and his ideal woman. Now of course he was totally convinced that all that, everything that he wanted, all that he sought, was in Jana and was represented by her.

He was certain now then, what he wanted was clear in his mind. It was Jana and to be with her. All he had to think about now though was how to tell her that evening over dinner. Of course there was the minor matter of hoping that she felt the same. He'd sat there in Cafe Slavia pondering over all this long enough though. It was time to get out of the smoky atmosphere of that place and back into the Prague sunshine. As he summoned the waiter and paid the bill he changed his mind and instead of the Charles Bridge he decided that he'd stroll across the Most Legií – the bridge at the bottom of Národni - and go into the little park there by the river at the other side of the bridge.

The slap of the heat of the early summer's day warmed his face as he sat on a bench in the middle of the park after his short walk across the bridge. He knew the park quite well having been there quite a few times, sometimes with Dita in 1989, sometimes on his own. Strangely it was never crowded, even though it was by the river and right in the centre of the city. Maybe it just wasn't big enough for the Praguers. Certainly there was nothing in it to interest the tourists, who'd come to look at the buildings and the architecture of the city not its solitude. So, the park was full of the faint murmuring of a warm day. A few people lay or sat on the grass in the sun and some sat on the benches. There were isolated individuals enjoying a few warm moments, as well as couples and small groups of people. The low murmur of conversations between couples as they strolled past

Tom's bench was accompanied by the pleasant background singing of the birds. It was a restful, peaceful environment. Its calmness, right in the middle of a big capital city that was full of frantic almost manic tourists, reflected his own state of mind. The calm before the storm, or more accurately the calm before the trials and uncertainty of what he intended to undertake later in the evening. The calm before the realisation of his hope maybe?

As he sat there he felt he had space and time to think. All around him there was the very faint low noise from people talking as they strolled through the park or sat there in that small Prague green space. He just sat and watched, listening to and overhearing Czech conversations even though he couldn't really understand them. Imagining just what it was they were talking about, or in some cases laughing about on that warm sunny afternoon. In Tom's mind though there was a complete silence, the silence of expectancy and hope as well as the space in his mind to shape that hope over and over again in his head while the Praguers passed him by talking and laughing. Sunshine, silence, and space to think were always an extremely compatible mixture of ingredients for producing optimism within him.

What was right in front of Tom now was a picture of human serenity. For him this was the soothing virtuous face of Prague. All so different from the Prague in turmoil that he'd witnessed four and a half years earlier in the 'November days' of the revolution. Now the conjuncture, the moment, was a more personal one. In 1989 it was all about the condition, the 'human condition', of the seething mass of Czech and Slovak humanity in Prague and in other parts of Czechoslovakia and Eastern Europe. It was all about their collective determination and actions in demanding change. Actions that were designed to change the world they inhabited. It was about their awareness of their collective power and ability to do just that because of the circumstances that had arisen.

On this sunny warm day it was Tom's individual 'human condition' that was being given the opportunity to take actions that could change his life perhaps. He was certainly aware that the conjuncture of his visit to Prague earlier that year, and the message about Jana that he got from Monika just before she delivered her lecture to his students, had provided him with circumstances to pursue what he was convinced was his long term interest in Jana. He was determined not to miss his opportunity to act. An opportunity that he thought had passed him by.

As he sat there on the park bench his mind began to wander between his work and his own present situation, hoping that somehow his work methods would offer him some clarity in approaching his upcoming personal situation. The academic in him prompted him to equate the historical context and circumstances of the events of November 1989 with his own 'human condition' and historical context now. His brain meandered onto the role of Gorbachev and the change he brought about to the Soviet Union's policy in the East and Central European states during the second half of the nineteen-eighties – the so-called 'Sinatra doctrine', the phrase given in 1986 to that change of policy by Gorbachev's press secretary, Genadii Gerasimov. In response to questions from western journalists about just what the Soviets intended to do in respect of their role in their 'satellite' Central and East European states in the light of Gorbachev's policies of *glasnost* and *perestroika* inside the Soviet Union the press secretary said the Soviets were going to apply 'the Sinatra doctrine'. They would let the individual states do things their way, and he related this new policy to the Frank Sinatra song 'My Way'.

However, Tom always reckoned that the policy had much more in common with Mozart's opera 'Don Giovanni'. Consequently, he argued it should really have been labelled 'the Mozart doctrine'. In the opera, based on the life of Don Juan, the central character, the 'well respected in society' Don Giovanni, disguises and masks himself while carrying out his womanising pursuits. From various bits and pieces of details of events that came out publicly in the years after 1989, and after the collapse of the Soviet Union at the end of 1991, and from his own research and what he had been told by Monika and Jana, Tom always believed that the Soviets had been saying one thing publicly about their policy in East and Central Europe in the late nineteen-eighties while in fact 'wearing a mask' and acting in a completely different way politically behind the scenes in those countries. Publicly they espoused 'the Sinatra doctrine' of political and military withdrawal, and non-involvement. Meanwhile, throughout that period they were hiding behind a 'Don Giovanni type mask' and operating the 'Mozart doctrine', largely through the activities of the KGB, by attempting to replace old hard-line leaders with communist leaders that resembled 'East and Central European Gorbachevs' in their reforming policies and approach.

The rumour of Zdeněk Mlynář's long-term friendship with Gorbachev that Dita's friend Monika had told her, Jana and Tom about in August 1989, as well as the one later that year of Mlynář being flown to Moscow in November 1989 by the Soviets to meet Gorbachev and asked to take over the leadership of Czechoslovakia as a kind of 'Czech Gorbachev', were prime examples of his 'Mozart doctrine' theory for Tom.

Also, there were other 'Mozart doctrine' examples across the Central and East European Soviet 'satellite states'. According to several members of the then German Democratic Republic (East German) Communist Party Central Committee, during the build-up of demonstrations in the days preceding the fall of the Berlin Wall the new East German communist leader, Egon Krenz, telephoned Gorbachev for advice on how to deal with the crisis. Gorbachev is reported to have advised that the border between East and West Germany should be opened to provide an escape valve, and thereby stop any unrest that threatened to see the communists removed from power; a plan that obviously went disastrously wrong. In Bulgaria, an emergency plenum of the Communist Party Central Committee took place on November 10th 1989, the day after the fall of the Berlin Wall. At it Bulgaria's President, Todor Zhivkov, was forced to resign and was replaced by the reform communist Petar Mladenov. A few days before the emergency plenum Mladenov made an unscheduled stop-over visit to Moscow on his return journey to Bulgaria after a trip to China in his capacity as Foreign Minister, and was rumoured to have met with Gorbachev. Suspicions also lingered over Moscow's role in the events in Bucharest in December 1989. Ion Iliescu, who became Romania's first President after the 1989 revolution, was also a close friend of Gorbachev having, like Mlynář, attended university with him in Moscow in the 1950s while studying law. Also, Silviu Brucan, a central figure in the initial post-1989 National Salvation

Front government in Romania, visited Moscow in November 1988. Brucan claimed to have had contacts, "in the Kremlin," during his visit, where the talks had been of, "a political nature," with an emphasis on, "the resistance movement in Romania," and a conspiracy to remove Ceaușescu. He claimed to have met Gorbachev and secured reluctant Soviet agreement to the overthrow of Ceaușescu, but also to have been told not to expect any Soviet intervention in assistance.

The irony of all this Tom thought as he sat there on that Prague park bench was that Mozart's 'Don Giovanni' had its premiere in the city's Estates Theatre in 1787, and as he contemplated all these things he began to wonder whether maybe, just maybe, there was some parallel lesson to be learned for his own life and his 'human condition' from 'the Mozart doctrine'. He'd certainly masked his growing feelings for Jana during those final days of his time with Dita at the end of 1989. What though if he was always permanently exhibiting a masked face and in reality just enjoyed the 'chase' and the womanising. He stopped himself immediately. Halted his thought processes then and there. He didn't want to go there in his head. Somewhere in the back of his mind though there was still this nagging thought of maybe his actual recurring 'human condition' was to always be a Don Giovanni, although certainly without the success rate of the opera's main character.

Anyway, he tried to convince himself, all that was history – the events of 1989, Mozart, Sinatra, and his own, what seemed lovely at first, Prague 'opera' with Dita. Again the academic in him reminded him that all historical facts come to us as a result of choices of interpretation by historians influenced by the standards of their age. Now he really was slipping into academic mode, and academic speak, and on such a lovely, tranquil, warm relaxing day. Nevertheless, he always felt that he did believe that the way we see things in our personal lives, interpret things, read into things – the smallest things like someone saying, "I'm looking forward to it" – is influenced by what we want to see. What we want to remember and how we want to interpret and remember it. What we want to believe or hope. The events of November 1989, his relationship with Dita and how it ended, the encouraging signs that he now believed he saw from Jana, were all seen through his eyes and interpreted through his mind, clouded maybe by his hope. So, what if he was simply using the past and that crazy and exciting time in 1989, or his recollections of it, to validate his hope for the present?

No doubt the events of November 1989 were interpreted hundreds of different ways. Each one of the multitude of the people on the march of November 17th or in Wenceslas Square on the subsequent nights undoubtedly had their own small space of recollection and memory of their experience of the time and events. In relation to Jana though Tom only had his own space of recollection and memory of those days in the months towards the end of 1989. His optimistic interpretation of her little sayings, her touches, laughs and smiles, and their conversations was what he clung to. There was only one other interpretation in existence. Only one other recollection, or non-recollection, and that was Jana's, and for all he knew that could be completely different to his. His hope was that it matched his of course. As his doubting side kicked in again he cautioned himself that maybe Jana had just been on some sort of adrenaline rush from the time, on a high because of the events and situation of the period. What if she was like that with everyone at the time just because of the excitement of those November days in 1989? One thing was for sure, pretty soon he'd find out whether Jana's actions and feelings of those days really did match his historical recollections and interpretation of them. Soon he'd be put out of his misery of expectation. One way or another in a few hours he would be released from his agony of hope.

As he adjusted his seated position slightly on the hard wooden bench he started to worry that he'd be going in to unknown territory with what he was about to tell Jana that evening, be going in blind so to speak. Had she even given it a second thought? Had she wondered why he was so keen to meet up with her again? What was she looking for? Hoping for? What did she really think of him? Was he just a good friend, or was he more to her? He went over and over as many memories as he could. Went over and over every little word he could recall she had ever said to him, or at least he imagined she'd said to him. He analysed and re-analysed it in his mind as he sat there staring into the sunlit open grassy space in front of him. Went over and over every faint touch of his arm she'd made, every faint smile she'd given him, every wink of her eye to him. It was then that it dawned on him that he actually knew very little about her. In fact, he really didn't know her that well at all. The nearest he'd come to knowing anything about her as a person was only during those crazy 'November days' of 1989, and after all that was an exceptional time. He knew nothing about her past, her family, or her future ambitions then other than to live in a free Czechoslovakia.

Now the fear and doubt was starting to creep over him again. The self-doubt and the fear of having got it all completely wrong, read all the messages and signals wrongly. After all what was it that made her the person she was? He thought he knew what it was that made her attractive for him, but he now realised that actually he'd never even had a conversation with her at all about, for want of a better term, just what it was to be her. No one ever asks anyone that specifically of course. A string of different conversations at different times can usually tell you a lot about what a person thinks about themselves though. God knows he was always having them, with others and with himself, and usually with himself in empty hotel rooms.

He decided he needed to think this through a lot more. Spend the time left to him on that sunny, now late afternoon, trying to work this through in his mind. He started with the obvious. She was Czech of course, but just what did that mean? Tom always found that to ask a Czech just what it is to be a Czech generally drew a response that referred to certain national qualities or dispositions, and to what Czechs considered to be their national traditions. In that respect, Czechs were just like other nationalities in identifying what traits and symbols determined their identity. It was all about the self-images they attributed to themselves. For many academics at the heart of the Czech self-image was the belief in the equality of individuals in nature; in 'academic speak' an egalitarian ethos in the natural state. The failure of a Czech individual was put down to a lack of effort or hard work. It was generally not the Czech belief to put it down to a lack of intelligence, as that would admit an inherent inequality.

In that respect Dita was not your average Czech. The 'clever versus thick' dichotomy, or the idea of the 'egalitarian ethos in the natural state', was never one that caused a great problem for her. It was simple for Dita. Some people were, indeed, naturally stupid or thick. Not that thick was a word Tom had ever heard her use, whereas stupid was one of her favourites. Tom even suspected that there were times when she believed him to be stupid, usually over some of his actions that she thought he made without thinking, like stooping down to help to his feet the blood-stained student running from the police that night in March 1989 in Celetná in Prague. For Dita sometimes Tom just naturally did stupid things, and some of her countrymen and women were naturally stupid, as were some men and women of other nationalities. Tom recalled she seemed to reserve her greatest 'stupid' condemnation for politicians. They, and pre-1989 Czech state policemen and women and the Secret Police agents, were idiots, though for Dita the latter were dangerous idiots.

It had been suggested to Tom though by his Czech academic colleagues that the typical representation of their nation was through the expression of ordinariness, together with a healthy common sense approach. If Tom was sure that some of his British academic colleagues were definitely educated beyond their intelligence, from his experience he believed that many Czechs, if not most, possessed intelligence beyond their education, beyond the level of their education. Or in the communist period it seemed, intelligence despite the ideological form of their education. The Czech intelligence was based on an ability to see the simplest answers and the simplest way forward. To do the simplest things, usually in order to approach the problem from a different angle and thereby get around the issue without actually confronting it. The embodiment of this approach and element of Czechness is the central character in Jaroslav Hašek's novel *The Good Soldier Schweik*, written in the early nineteen-twenties. Schweik was very adept at finding very simplistic ways around things, and thus avoiding confrontation. In that respect maybe Tom had some claims to 'Czechness' in the way he tried to avoid confrontation with Dita over their future on that evening at the beginning of January in 1990.

One thing most Czechs were proud of was what they describe as 'golden Czech hands'; hands that could cope with everything they touch because of the Czechs' talent, skill and ingenuity. In the years between the two world wars Czechoslovakia was the tenth strongest industrial power in the world. The country was famous for its engineering plants and its successful light industry, as well as the production of glass, shoes and textiles, not to mention its breweries and beer production of course. Czechs and Slovaks produced a wide range of quality goods, from pins to locomotives. The first president of Czechoslovakia during this period, Thomas Garrigue Masaryk, encouraged what he called 'Czechism'. For him this uniqueness was based on a humane, democratic politics and a cultured lifestyle, alongside Czech ingenuity, invention, talent and skill.

Before the events of 1989 however, and the change under the communist regime, any characteristics that might have been perceived as typically Czech were not portrayed as being important. The official communist ideology emphasised the socialist character of Czechoslovak society. What were important were the characteristics of the new socialist man and woman. Characteristics that Czechs were encouraged to embrace, and which Dita hated intensely. For her these ideals killed everything she loved about life – individualism, creativity, diversity, difference - the ability, talent and opportunity to be different. So, for Dita most of the changes after 1989 were a welcome relief, even though initially she believed they would never happen and only became a 'convert' to the 'Velvet Revolution' late in those 'November days'. For her the post-1989 changes in her country were a reawakening and release of Czech talent and creativity that for forty years had been suppressed. One of the few things she didn't like about her surroundings in the post-1989 period though, and was not slow in saying so, was what she perceived as the incessant, seemingly increasing rudeness of many of her countrymen and women. Waiters, shop assistants, bureaucrats and officials especially, seemed to have been subjected to some kind of 'rudeness course' as part of their job training as far as Dita was concerned. In many cases it seemed to be a requirement of the post. "Must have great ability to be rude and to ignore the public! Under no circumstances embrace anything that can be described as service!" seemed to have been part of the job description for most of them she suggested to Tom on more than one occasion. This attitude most definitely existed before 1989 of course, but the new liberal democratic values of post-1989 had in no way eradicated it. Next to

Tom's occasional stupidity or stupid actions, and the stupidity of politicians, this was the thing that annoyed Dita most.

Yet despite her cynicism, and at times disdain for her fellow citizens, Dita was very proud to call herself Czech. She would criticise her country and its people to Tom, but at the same time she'd leap to its defence and defend Czechs vigorously if an Englishman, like Tom, or any foreigner dared to criticise her fellow citizens or her country. In this she was the embodiment of what it was to be Czech, self-critical, but just that, 'self'. It was not for other non-Czechs to criticise. Dita saw the Czech national tradition and character very much in the same way as Thomas Masaryk, rooted in a democratic, well-educated and highly cultured nation. That's where she got her pride in her country from, from that image and ideal, and she had her own high ideals, her well merited self-belief, a belief in her own abilities and talent. She also had her parochial beliefs and values about such things as family and home life, and both these aspects of her own Czech character were wrapped up in a resilience and determination.

As he now strolled on through the park and along the river embankment Tom remembered that two years before he'd seen in an academic journal the results of a survey of the Czech character that had been carried out in January 1992. Seventy-six per cent of the traits most often mentioned by Czechs as characteristics of themselves were distinctly negative ones. The most prominent were envy, excessive conformism, and cunning. Did Dita fit this picture of an average Czech, he wondered? Probably not, she certainly never looked upon herself as average anyway, and as far as Tom was concerned he would never describe her as average. She was very intelligent, even if at times he felt it was what he described as an immature intelligence.

"Hang on," he mumbled as he momentarily stopped his casual strolling with a jolt, "what's all this about Dita? I'm supposed to be thinking about Jana and what I know about her so as to sort out how to deal with this evening. Enough of Dita, start trying to figure out the best way to approach dinner with Jana this evening. Start thinking about what he actually knew about Jana, about her 'Czechness'?" What all this was telling him, however, was that he knew far more about Dita than he did about Jana, not least because he'd spent much more time with her. One thing he was now sure of was that as far as his feelings were concerned Jana would never be an average Czech. He could never foresee describing her as that. Yes, for him she embraced the Czech cultured lifestyle and ingenuity and had the national characteristics of Czech talent and skills. He had to admit though that in terms of Jana's personal qualities, and whether for instance they might have anything in common with the other characteristics identified in the academic survey, he really didn't know that much about her. He'd obviously spent some time with her during those exciting days over the two months at the end of 1989, but that was in extremely exceptional and different circumstances, and for a lot of the time he was only in her company with Dita. Most of the time it was always the three of them rushing off to demonstrations. It was the three of them racing through the Prague wind as it screamed over the cobbled streets and swirled the falling snow into their panting faces that frantically puffed visible warm air into the cold night. Nevertheless, in the warm late afternoon Prague sunshine now he wasn't going to entertain any doubts at this stage. He was convinced of what he wanted to do and was determined not to let this opportunity, this second chance with her, slip by. No negative thoughts. Anyway, he'd find out a lot more about her and her character later that evening for sure, and hopefully for a long time in the future. Maybe it would just be 'chemistry' between them, like he had sensed in the 'November days' of 1989 that would do it, that would produce what he hoped for. Just what was this 'chemistry' though, an attraction between people, something that so many of his friends who were in relationships were so fond of telling him was the key? He guessed he'd experienced it with Dita, and yes it was instantaneous, an instant attraction. It was her captivating charm perhaps? With Jana he reckoned it just grew and grew during the autumn of 1989, slowly building to a crescendo, just like the events of the year of 1989 and the 'Velvet Revolution' itself.

In terms of Jana's character he knew some things about her as that was what had attracted him so much in the first place. Her enthusiasm, her optimism, her energy, determination and sense of humour, and her all round charm of course, were all part of her personality that he couldn't resist. Then there was her very proud 'Czechness'; all those historical stories she had told him about her country on demonstrations and during the 'November days'.

This always happened to him. Walking, strolling almost aimlessly in Prague was guaranteed to start him thinking. It never failed. Another part of Prague's magic perhaps, another influence and characteristic of the city? Strangely, it was usually mostly his work that it got him thinking about. He never normally found academic work concerns filling his mind outside office hours, but in Prague it was always different. An idea for some new academic journal article perhaps or some future research project often leaped into his brain while wandering in Prague? It was nothing that ever changed the world, or would ever change the world of course. He was far too cynical about academia to ever think that. An idea or two though that easily transformed and extended into a five or six thousand word article that placated his university department and its 'research, research, research', 'publications, publications, publications', hunger and demands. The initial thoughts for those often came to him while his mind floated through the Prague cobbled alleyways. Some would call it inspiration he supposed. He preferred to call it his form of mental bonding. Somehow or other his clearest thoughts - the time when his mind was at its clearest and sharpest – always came when he was mentally attached to the streets and alleyways of the city he loved most of all, Praha. The Prague surroundings, the city around him, always fused together perfectly with his inner thoughts, complimenting them and in some way sparking his brain into life like jump leads on a slumbering car battery, even a battered old Skoda one.

This time though it was him that Prague was prompting review of, prompting him to take a good hard look at himself. The city had seen many momentous events throughout its history and maybe it was that historic atmosphere that provoked his 'grand' thoughts. Somehow or other Prague always managed, 'Kafkaesque', to link the personal, the fortunes of the individual, in this case Tom, and the more macro grand level world issues and debates. He'd concluded quite some time ago that this was a very complex and contradictory city and country, full of contradictory and complex inhabitants. Czechs could perceive themselves as petty minded on the one hand, but on the other hand highly cultured and well educated. At one and the same time they could consider themselves both parochial and internationalist, while embracing high moral internationalist ideals. Sometimes this produced a self-deprecating charm in his Czech friends that he found most endearing. Nowhere were these contradictions played out more than in Czech cultural interests and concerns. Tom had once been told by Dita, for example, that Smetana's music was considered by some Czechs to be inferior to Dvořák's because it was too parochially Czech. Yet for other Czechs Dvořák's music was considered inferior to Smetana's precisely because it was too cosmopolitan and not Czech enough. "Hmm, sometimes there is just no winning with the Czechs," he muttered.

While Tom believed Dita was fiercely defensive of the Czech nation to foreigners, he also knew she could easily participate in this national self-contradiction and self-deprecation. Whereas it seemed to him that Jana was altogether much easier on her country, on her fellow citizens, and most of all on herself. Dita was always preparing for life, always planning, usually meticulously. At times it looked like it was the planning that she enjoyed most of all, even more than the event being planned, whereas Jana just enjoyed the moment, enjoyed the day. For her everything would always work out okay anyway. Jana lived for the day. That was one of the main things that really attracted him to her. Yep, it was Jana's laid-back spontaneity that he was attracted to. So, he should just take it easy tonight, not rush it, just let the evening develop, so she, the both of them, were completely relaxed before he tried to tell her how he felt about her.

For Dita nowhere were the Czechs such a proud, cultured nation as they were in her home city of Prague. She would justify her belief about this by constantly pointing out to Tom the number of theatres and bookshops in, "her city". She was never slow to compare that to the numbers in London, arguing that in proportion to the population the Praguers, "had many, many more. Even in the flats and houses of ordinary workers and farmers a great number of books can be found," she would tell him proudly. Although quite how she knew that to be the case he could never fathom, but he was for sure never going to challenge her. He did though remember a story in the British press that when Czechs began traveling to Vienna after the opening of the borders with the fall of the communist system at the end of 1989 they had flocked to the museums and galleries rather than to the consumer stores and supermarkets as the newly free East Germans did in Berlin.

Even geographically, Dita on behalf of her fellow countrymen and women was never slow to claim unique distinctiveness, and for her, like many people, Prague was the 'middle of Europe' – 'Mitteleuropa'. Tom often felt that it was really that magical atmospheric feeling, one of being in 'Mitteleuropa', which swept over him whenever he arrived in the region. 'Mitteleuropa' stretched from Prague to Vienna and to Budapest. Between all of these three capital cities was Brno. Now, even after his short visit and even though it wasn't a capital city, it felt like that city was the 'middle of Europe' rather than Prague, Vienna or Budapest, as his friend Petr in Brno had never been slow to tell him; if not strictly geographically the 'middle of Europe', then certainly in its feel and its atmosphere.

He recalled a conversation with Dita in which he referred to his academic work in Prague being about Eastern Europe. "Oh, really, Tom, just where does this Eastern Europe that you are so fond of talking about begin," she taunted him? "Not in Prague or Budapest I hope. Bucharest, Sofia, Moscow even, yes that's Eastern Europe. We Central Europeans can agree that those cities are in Eastern Europe, but be careful when you put us all together for your convenience or you will definitely upset us Czechs and Slovaks." It was one of Dita's more light-hearted, sarcastic moments. Equally though it was one of the fond ways she would gently correct and make a point to him.

Now Prague, the city he loved, was doing it to him again. Making him think, and think deeply about things that were very important to him. It was also making him calmer. As he continued his stroll out of the park and into the quieter back streets of the city that tourists never found or bothered with he realized he was once again experiencing the contradictions and disjuncture that are the magical city of Prague. For Tom it was a city of atmospheric tranquility, at least it was away from the tourists. A city that somehow managed to control you, influence you, own you even, but at the same time set you free, make you feel free and as though you hadn't a care in the world. Through its atmosphere, its way of life, its mystery, its shadows and light, and that in-between dusky twilight, the very charm of the city seeps slowly into your consciousness at every street corner, through every cobblestone. It made him feel great just to be alive and in Prague. He remembered standing in the Old Town Square very late one crystal clear night with very few other souls in sight and just gazing at the magnificent buildings that surrounded him, that had captured him as they crowded their way into his inadequate vision. That feeling, of just how great it felt to be alive and in such a lovely wonderful place, came flooding over him. It gathered him up and then and there cemented him into the cobblestones of Prague forever he reckoned. It was truly a precious and unique moment. One he was sure would never come again, just like Dita's dazzling smile directed at him at the conference in Spa in 1988, or Jana's overwhelming excitement at times during the 'November days' of 1989.

In all this grand scale philosophising he'd still not thought about the micro detail of the coming, now fast approaching, so important evening with Jana. He hadn't even decided where to take her for dinner. Right, he told himself, get focused Tom. First question, where to go for dinner? Anywhere too grand might scare her straight away. After all she just wasn't a grand restaurant type of woman. Taking her somewhere too special might start her thinking what's all this about? Why is he taking me to such a posh and quite expensive place? He didn't want that sparking off awkward questions before they'd even sat down. Timing was going to be everything. Didn't want her getting curious about the evening until she was relaxed and he was good and ready to raise his important subject about her and him. He was certain though that one question that was going to come his way would be about him and Dita, and that was going to be a key moment. Once again he pondered his acute dilemma; how could he and Jana have any kind of relationship when he'd supposedly once been deeply in love with her best friend?

Taking Jana somewhere too down-market for dinner though might suggest to her he was not really very serious about what he was going to tell her. Anyway it should be an appropriate setting. "Can hardly take her to MacDonalds," he murmured as he was returning across the Most Legií. He dwelt on it for a few minutes as he leaned on the wall of the bridge and looked up the river at Prague castle dominating the skyline. That view jogged his memory about an Italian restaurant he'd been to before down by the Charles Bridge, just a hundred yards or so along from the National Library, but with good views of the river and the castle. Good setting, good food, possibly a bit more expensive than Jana would expect, but not that much more. It should be alright. It wouldn't seem too special, and you're always safe with an 'Italian'.

As he strode purposefully along the Smetanovo nábřeží towards the restaurant he tried to work out the rest of his tactics for the evening. He'd wait until they'd ordered their food before raising what he wanted to tell her; how he felt about her. "No, no," he muttered, he'd decided earlier that he should wait until much later in the meal when she was completely relaxed, especially after a couple of glasses of wine. Wait until they'd finished eating, that would be best, and then begin to raise it over coffee. Maybe hint at it through the meal, with a compliment here and there. Tell her how well she looked, but definitely wait till coffee before getting to the crunch, the defining moment. Yep, that's the best approach. Any other way and timing might mean a very awkward situation throughout the meal. Not that for one minute he believed there was any possibility she'd turn him down of course. No, no, he was now more confident than ever that it would all turn out well. He was sure she'd respond positively and be very happy about what he told her, about how he felt about her. He'd seen and heard all the good signs over that dinner with her ten days before. He'd gone over and over things from the 'November days' of four and a half years ago, and of course as far as he was concerned, from his perspective, there were nothing but positive signs, real hope. Be positive, it's all about positive thinking he told himself. There was just the awkwardness over Dita of course, but that was in the past now, nearly five years ago. Maybe Dita had moved on, found someone else perhaps. Yep, over coffee it would be then and that would at least give him a chance to find out if Dita had met someone, which would definitely make things a lot easier and much less awkward.

By the time he'd booked a table at the restaurant and spent twenty minutes trying to explain over and over to the completely disinterested waiter that he really wanted a table with a nice view of the river and the castle – without any sign that he'd managed to get through to him or any expectancy that was what they would get – it was just past five o'clock. Now it was time to head back to his hotel and maybe grab a nap for an hour before getting ready for his big night of fate and hope.

24
The hope

There are some very few and far between times when everything seems right with the world, with your world. When everything seems in its place, everything is wonderful. At the end of a warm late spring or hot summer's day, that time when there is a glow about your body from the day's sun and everything seems at ease with life. For Tom it was laying on a hot white sandy southern Italian beach in the late afternoon hearing the sounds of only Italian voices and the gentle waves of the clear blue sea. Everything then was warm and restful with not a care in the world. A first date was like that for him, or to be more exact, that time just before the first date with a new woman. Just before she turns up wherever or whenever you have arranged it. Now was one of those times. It wasn't a first date of course, but he still felt a calm expectancy about meeting Jana again. He had a nice warm feeling that everything was okay and would be alright. Yep, he felt confident. Confident because he believed he knew his feelings and confident that they would be returned by Jana. At that time everything was fine on that warm early summer evening in the magical city of Prague. Everything felt good and everything was right, fine, and calm. Now finally he had arrived at the point in his life that he'd been searching for and it would all be okay.

He could even rationalise what had occurred over the past ten days of his journey around the Czech Republic now. Susanna in Ostrava, his various encounters with different women in Brno and Liberec, they were just him getting it all out of his system before he told Jana how he felt about her. That was how he justified it, a sort of ten day 'stag party', last rites and all that. Once he was with Jana none of that would ever happen again. After all it had never happened while he was with Dita, so it was just a temporary aberration, a temporary release valve.

As he was indulging in this self-justification he drifted into his hour's nap and woke on his hotel bed to the irritating beeping of his bedside travelling alarm clock. A careful shave – didn't want to nick himself and have to turn up with talcum powder and toilet paper dabbed all over his face – followed by a shower and a calm putting on of the trousers and button-down collar blue shirt he'd selected to wear and he was almost ready. "That's good," he reassured himself as he sprayed on his deodorant and not too much after-shave, "keep calm and don't get too hot. Don't want to turn up sweating like a pig."

He'd resolved to leave his hotel in plenty of time to make the ten minute leisurely walk to meet Jana under the astronomical clock in Old Town Square. It was still quite warm outside so he didn't want to get all hot and bothered rushing through the aimless herds of tourist at the last minute to get there by eight. That was likely to happen later anyway when he started talking to her about his feelings towards her. The open necked shirt was a good move too. He wouldn't get hot through being strangled by a tie, and anyway that just wasn't Jana's style. She would immediately be spooked by him turning up in a tie. She was much more laid-back and knew that ties were not usually Tom's style. Of course she was always very smartly dressed in her own way, and very elegant, but not formal. He couldn't ever remember seeing her formally dressed, even in the conference at which he met Dita and her in Spa. One Czech female national characteristic he was certainly sure she possessed was the ability to take the simplest basic clothes and make them look fabulously elegant and beautiful when she wore them. He never ceased to be amazed at how she and most other Czech women did it. Perhaps it was indeed their 'Czech golden hands'.

Walking in the evening sunshine towards the Old Town Square his confidence began to waiver. The doubts started to creep up on him again. Was he really reading the signs correctly? Once again his academic side surfaced and reminded him that history is always written from the viewpoint of the victors. The history of 1989 and the events in Prague and across eastern and central Europe that brought about the fall of the communist regimes would doubtless be written from the perspective of those that overthrew and removed those regimes, from the perspective of the dissidents in Prague in the 'November days' of 1989. Even if the previous communist rulers really understood or were capable of conceiving just what brought about their downfall, it wasn't likely to be a version widely in demand or circulated. They were the losers. Not many people were likely to want to hear their views or believe their version of events. As he turned into Bétlemské náměstí he recalled that the famous historian, E. H. Carr, had written, "When we attempt to answer the question 'What is history?' our answer, consciously or unconsciously, reflects our own position in time ..."

Tom's personal history of his journey of the past ten days and of the past four and a half years, his personal destiny with Jana, must have two versions then, a successful one and an unsuccessful one. Having been so certain of the outcome less than an hour before, now just ten minutes or so before he was due to meet her he realised he really wasn't so sure which version would prevail. Which version would stand the test of history? He hoped of course that it would be the successful one. He thought he'd convinced himself of that, but now he was quickly re-running the arguments over and over in his brain. He tried to seek some comfort in his academic approach and applying that to the question he came up with the same successful answer over and over again. First ascertain the facts Positivist historians had always contended then draw your conclusions from them. It has been argued of course that facts speak for themselves, but the 'academic Tom' knew that wasn't so. Facts are selectively chosen, as is the context in which they are chosen, so the question revolved around his selective memory or otherwise, and his selective interpretation of his past meetings with Jana. As the academic part of his brain clunked into gear it began to haunt him once again that the picture of optimism he had formed in his mind about pursuing Jana now, and telling her in no uncertain terms in a few hours just how he felt, might only be based on what he knew or thought he knew. After all it was only based on his side of things, his interpretation of what he took to be facts and signs. What about the missing bits of the puzzle of his personal history of the situation; Jana's perspective? What about her interpretation of events, her interpretation of their meetings and time together back in 1989?

Now he really was much less certain, much less calm and much less optimistic. Doubts came flooding into his mind. How could he know for certain? How could he tell? He wanted to believe the positive optimistic side of course, but what if he really was merely deliberately ignoring the negative signs? Worse, what if he had simply obliterated them from his memory deliberately over the past four and a half years? Maybe he'd just over estimated some of the things she had said to him, some of the things they had done together, and chosen selectively to remember what he'd interpreted as the good signs. As he proceeded to make his way through the alleys and passageways towards the square he remembered another academic lesson from his undergraduate days – that the history we read is not really factual at all, but merely a series of accepted judgements. From his academic work he, more than most people, knew that judgements are always biased, even if often only subconsciously so. Were all the good signs that he recalled what really had happened between them, or were they simply what he thought had happened? Was his interpretation of them what Jana intended or just something he hoped and wished for? He wanted to believe that what he saw as her growing closeness to him during the 'November days' of 1989 was the truth, wanted to believe it had actually happened, but now could he be so sure? Or was it that he had drawn this conclusion simply because he had based his analysis and his interpretation of the situation on his own selective facts? Facts that he'd chosen to remember, chosen to select, rather than others that might draw him to a very different conclusion. He knew very well too that the very selection and ordering of the facts of the various situations they had been in four and a half years ago would have undergone subtle changes in his mind as he constantly went over and over them during the intervening years, and even would have changed slightly as he went over them during the past ten days on his travels around the Czech Republic.

"Okay enough, stop being a bloody cynical academic and start being an optimistic human being. This is just last minute nerves. Of course it will all be okay," he muttered as he now emerged out of the shadows of the passageway and began to stride more purposefully in the fading sunlight towards the square and the astronomical clock to meet her. He was determined that his was not a case of selective memory, or selective facts. His interpretation was the truth. The absolute optimistic truth of how Jana felt. The real signs of how she felt. There was the, "you were my Englishman," comment about when he first came to Prague in December 1988, and her, "it was me who liked you, really, really, liked you," comment of only ten days before over dinner. Then there were all the smiles, hugs, winks, touches, the squeezing of his hand occasionally, and even tears of joy that they'd shared in the crazy days of November and December 1989. Plus she was perfectly happy, seemed quite pleased in fact, to meet him again for dinner tonight after their evening together ten days ago. And what about Monika's contact and what Jana had told her to tell him about getting in touch? Why would she do that if she wasn't still interested in him? Then there were Jana's emails to him after that. All the, "It is good to hear from you again, really!!!. I am looking forward to seeing you in Praha …it's great to hear from you again!!!. Love Jana," comments. Not forgetting the, "really," and three exclamation marks. How could anyone interpret those emails and the language in them as anything but positive? "Yep," he muttered again reassuringly, "there are lots of reasons and causes to be optimistic, couldn't possibly be otherwise when you look at the facts."

Most of all he returned again to the 'cause of all causes', the key factor in his analysis as he was approaching the Astronomical clock. Jana's, "my Englishman, my Englishman," comment, that he began muttering to himself like some chant of a secret society or sect, no doubt one of the 'sacred order of Czech women'. Seeking yet more reassurance he tried to recall her exact words and felt the need to not only recount them in his head, but quietly aloud. "You were my Englishman, Tom … because it was me who liked you, really, really, liked you." To any passing tourist who overheard he must have seemed like some poor mentally disturbed soul who at any moment might start chanting this over and over louder and louder while rocking back and forth in a crouched position. At one point he even found himself questioning aloud, "was there one 'really' or two before she said 'liked you'," as if that was the key to his whole future life in respect of Jana. Eventually he came back from his trance to some sort of normality and reassured himself again with, "but that's what she said, that's definitely what she said ten days ago." Some passing tourists were now indeed turning to look in bewilderment at this muttering seemingly deranged man. Realising this he silently continued his circumspection with, why would she tell him all this at this point in time? She didn't need to. It was getting on for five years ago now. She didn't need to tell him and could have kept it to herself. There could only be one reason. She wanted him to know, and know now. She wanted to take the chance that he felt the same way. It was obvious, anyone could see it. This wasn't subjective analysis of selective facts. It could only be looked at one way. There was no other conclusion that could be drawn. It was simply the case that Jana felt the same way and was now taking her chance, her opportunity. A chance she thought had gone and would never come again. A chance she realised she had to take now as it might not come again if she let it pass her by once more.

Now he was totally convinced and in a very positive frame of mind once again as he slowly weaved his way through the tide of tourists, being almost dragged along in their babble towards the square. It was a very pleasant warm evening and he was on his way to meet the woman he was convinced was the one of his dreams, the one he'd spent his life searching for. What could possibly go wrong? His mate Steve was wrong this time. This time Tom's hope and optimism would at last be fully justified. This time he had read the signs correctly and got it right, and his hope would be fulfilled.

By the time he reached the clock tower it was ten to eight. He was ten minutes early and time enough to calmly prepare himself. As he stood there watching the tourists gathering to see the clock put on its show on the hour at eight he wondered which way she'd come into the square? Which way he'd first catch a glimpse of her? Then there she was, five minutes early, weaving her way serenely through the tourists from out of Železná, the street leading into the square from the Estates Theatre. She looked gorgeous and even more beautiful than the week before. She was wearing a simple olive green and white patterned sleeveless cotton summer dress. It was set off with a silver necklace that shimmered and sparkled as the fading sunlight hit it, in just the same way that her eyes did when she took off her sunglasses to say, "Hi," and kiss him once on the cheek. Her mass of dark ruddy-brown hair lay on her exposed shoulders, perfectly complementing the green and white dress.

Once he'd got past his breathe being taken away by the way she looked his first impression was that she appeared to be very happy to see him. Her smile told him that. She did, indeed, look very, very happy. Happy to be there he hoped. Happy maybe that she was getting a second chance to tell him just how she felt.

"I've booked a table for eight-thirty at an Italian restaurant by the Charles Bridge. I hope that's okay," he tentatively asked? But without letting her respond he added the justification, "I just thought that with the tourists we might not be able to just turn up and get in somewhere."

"That's fine," she told him. Tucking her arm into his she joked, "come on let's go. Do you remember the way, Tom? And this time in our new free city we don't have to keep ducking out of the way of secret policemen in every street and alleyway, or even policemen with big sticks that you were so attracted to on that night in 1989. I've got lots to tell you that I didn't get round to telling you about last time, but I'll save it for later in the restaurant."

That intrigued him a little. Although not in such a way as to prompt any trace of doubt in his mind as she was definitely in a very, very good mood. Arm in arm they weaved their way through the legions of tourists following their tour guides' coloured umbrellas or long sticks with coloured ribbons tied to them held aloft so their flocks with cameras dangling around their necks could keep track of them. German, Italian and British voices were babbling all around as they made their way out of the square and down Karlova towards the Charles Bridge. Of course the most multitudinous of cameras decorated the necks of the Japanese tour groups. Jana again referred to dodging the secret police in the past only this time joking that the tourist groups were far harder to avoid, and in many cases were much more lethal. She was certainly very excited about something. He just hoped that it was the excitement of meeting him again and spending the evening together.

Eventually they reached the restaurant and she told him, "Oh, I know this restaurant. It's very good, with real Italian food cooked by Italians. It's owned by an Italian family. I like it, though I've only been here once before."

A good choice, a lucky choice, Tom congratulated himself. A

good start, and so far, so good, was what was going through his by now racing brain. He was desperately trying to stay calm, even though his mind was speeding on uncontrollably thinking about what lay ahead later in the evening. Thinking about what he intended to say.

Jana picked up on his nervousness as much to his surprise they sat down at the perfect corner table that the waiter led them to. "You okay, Tom? You're very quiet. Perhaps our hot early summer weather and all the travelling has tired you out? We don't have to have a long dinner if you are really tired, especially with you having to travel home to England tomorrow."

"No, no, really I'm fine," he responded quickly, trying to sound much more relaxed and upbeat. "How could I not be, being here in this wonderful city of yours and having dinner with such a lovely beautiful woman." It was all his brain would let him conjure up and as soon as it came out he could feel that strange embarrassing ache of the sickliness of a remark like that deep in his stomach.

"I bet you say that to all your women," she mocked him.

"What women? I don't have 'all my women'," he desperately tried to reassure her, and simultaneously hoped she was really just floating a statement out there to obtain the answer she wanted – that he was not 'with someone' and wasn't in a relationship. Then just as he was extracting the positive from what she said the first grenade landed slap in his lap. His first tricky moment came much, much earlier than he'd anticipated.

"I bet that's what you used to say to Dita all the time, Tom. Telling her she was a lovely beautiful woman I mean. After all she is beautiful."

"Err ... I ... well," he was drowning, struggling for air and the right words. Not only stunned by the mention of Dita so early in the evening – that wasn't in his plan, wasn't in the script, it wasn't supposed to happen like that – but also he was totally unsure of just how was the best way to respond to that? "Yes, she is beautiful, but not as beautiful as you," might really pull the pin out of the grenade far too early and blow the whole evening to smithereens. But, "no, Dita wasn't really that beautiful," would hardly impress her best friend, and she would know it wasn't true anyway and that he didn't really think that. She'd see straight through that, and him. After all he had spent six months with Dita, pursuing, wining and dining, and being with her. An answer like that would hardly help the evening along and what he intended to say to Jana later. So, he decided on diversion tactics. Avoid answering the question. That was the best way to deal with it.

"How is Dita? Well, I hope? I think I asked you the last time we met and you said she was fine but still heavily engrossed in her academic work?"

Unfortunately for Tom, Jana's response had as an equally unsettling effect on him as her previous question.

"She's more than well, Tom. She's very, very well, and I'm sure you'll be glad to know, very, very happy. She's married now. Didn't I tell you last week? Sorry, I was sure I did. Can't think how I didn't. How I let something so important slip my mind and not tell you. Anyway, she's been an 'old married woman' for just over six months now. He's a lovely man, Martyn, a classical musician. He plays the flute in the Prague Philharmonic orchestra. Well, he'd have to be some sort of clever and talented man for Dita wouldn't he? They have a house in Prague 6, Dejvice, with a nice garden. Dita loves it. Everyone can see that she's very much in love with Martyn. They seem perfectly matched."

Tom sat there desperately trying not to let his jaw drop too far. Trying to not look too flabbergasted, while Jana just ploughed on with telling him just how happy her friend was now. It wasn't that he was hurt, upset, disappointed or anything like that. It wasn't like he had any feelings for Dita now. It was just so unexpected. Not at all in the equation he'd worked out for his fateful evening with Jana. For a very fleeting moment he thought that maybe she was telling him so enthusiastically all about how happy Dita was just to 'rub his nose in it'. Show him Dita was getting on very well without him, but then the reality of the positive side of what he was being told dawned on him. If Dita was happily married, had found her 'Mr. Right', then surely that would mean less of a problem for him in revealing to Jana just how he felt about her.

"Oh, that's lovely, I'm really, really pleased for her. Do give her my congratulations," gushed out of his mouth as he tried desperately to sound enthusiastic and not merely relieved.

"Yes, I think she now realises that what happened before between you and her wasn't quite right, Tom. It wasn't meant to be. Not that she regrets it of course. I know that she was happy then too, very, very happy. But some things just don't work out do they, and then the real right situation, the right time, the right person comes along and everything is for the best."

He nearly jumped straight in there and then with what he'd now gone over and over in his mind for what seemed a thousand times and told Jana just how he felt about her. Her comments about the, "right person," and the, "right time," offered him the perfect opportunity, but that definitely wouldn't have looked good he quickly decided. Then the realisation dawned on him that given the news he'd just heard about Dita's marriage it might be very difficult to tell Jana at all that evening just how he felt about her. What if she thought he was only doing it to prove a point to Dita. To show he could 'pull' her friend to piss off Dita. That would be disastrous, but when was he going to get another chance if he didn't take the plunge that evening? He was leaving for London tomorrow and it would be three months before he came back for his work. He could come over specially to see her of course, but she would wonder why he was coming to see her even before he got there. At that point therefore he thought his best bet was to 'play it by ear' through the rest of the evening. See how the evening developed. Hope it would feel right later on at some point in the evening. Hopefully the right time would arise, maybe towards the end of the meal just as he'd originally planned. Yep, stick to the original plan and don't be blown off course by the news about Dita.

At that point their conversation, or rather him listening to Jana's philosophy about the way things had worked out for the best for Dita, was interrupted by the waiter hovering and asking what they'd like to drink.

"Wine, I think," Tom responded immediately, without revealing that what he actually thought was more on the lines of, "a bloody great big bottle of wine quickly please!"

"White wine okay for you, Sauvignon?" he checked with Jana.

"Yes and some water without gas please," she added, telling the waiter in Czech, "voda neperlivá prossim."

At least that gave him the chance to change the subject. "Right, food, now what shall I have," he said a little nervously. He was never very good at menus and choosing at the best of times, and this wasn't exactly the most settling of them. He'd always change his mind about three or four times before the waiter took the order. This time it was even more difficult as he was getting more and more nervous as the evening was progressing and he knew that at some stage he'd have to take his 'leap in the dark', take his opportunity. To calm himself down a bit he decided that general everyday 'chit-chat' was the way forward. There was no doubt that the news about Dita's marriage had completely thrown him off track and destabilised him somewhat, especially as he had planned a nice calm start to the evening with a few nicely placed compliments about Jana's dress for instance. That's just what he'd reckoned would build up perfectly to what he wanted to tell her over coffee at the end of the meal. At least everything had started off extremely well in the square and on their walk down to the restaurant, which also turned out to be a good choice and one she liked. That had certainly initially relaxed him.

So, to get back on track he asked her more about her work. He'd asked her a bit about it when they'd met ten days ago of course, but now he wanted to get her talking a lot more about herself and her life. She was working in the office of an environmental non-governmental organisation - an NGO, as she put it – in Prague city centre in a street just off the top of Národní. She was the Personal Assistant to the director and Tom listened intently as she told him it sounded much grander than it really was, and that she was really just a person who dealt with all and everything for the director. As she went on to say how much she enjoyed it though, and how well she thought the job was going, he managed to glance carefully into her eyes a couple of times. He was sure that she'd definitely tried to hold eye contact, sure once again that was a positive sign. Then she asked him about his work and how his week had gone travelling around, "her country." He made her smile with his very selective stories of 'pivo' nights in Brno, and even got her laughing aloud when he told her how he'd met, "Stalin's granny," in the Ostrava station buffet. He talked about how, "interesting, educational and useful workwise," his time with

Petr had been in Brno. Although, of course, he never told her how interesting, educational and introspective his time with Susanna had been in Ostrava.

Now he was beginning to feel more comfortable and more relaxed. She seemed very interested in his work and that gave him yet more positive vibes. She was asking him all about his research and how often that would bring him back to the Czech Republic in future? How long was he likely to have to stay each time he came? When was the next time he was likely to come to Prague? Yep, he was determined and definitely going to do it this evening he decided. Definitely take his opportunity, especially after the news about Dita and the positive signs he was now getting. His hope was in full flight. How could he possibly have got it wrong after all this? This is just what he'd been waiting for through all those years. This was the right thing at the right time, and Jana was definitely the right one for him.

They were finishing their main courses. Tom was clearing his plate of the last small pieces of potato, mopping up the quite delicious tomato and olive sauce that had engulfed his chicken, while simultaneously internally taking the equivalent of a very deep breath and thinking, okay just the pudding then. Then along came another positive sign. Jana reached across the table as he topped up her wine glass and placing her hand on his arm said, "Well Tom, I've told you all about Dita, but what about you? Is there a special woman in your life now?"

Once again though he was thrown off balance and for the very briefest of moments he thought about taking his opportunity there and then. Leap in and say the equivalent of, "no, but what's my chances with you?" Or even, "yes I'm looking at her now I hope." But he didn't. He just offered her a weak smile and stuttered a little, telling her, "err ... no ... no. No one at the moment," tantalisingly adding while he had the chance, "there was someone, but I'm not sure if she realised she was or even still is special to me. Who knows? She may do. She may still be that special one. I live in hope. You just never know when the opportunity just might come along."

He was talking about her of course, but she just sat there smiling sympathetically at him without giving any sign that she was aware of that. He interpreted her question as yet another good sign though, reckoning she might be asking it just because she wanted to check if he was still available. As a result he decided to push things on a little and see if he could confirm his assessment. Test her out a little.

"Opportunity is a funny thing," he said. "It comes along and sort of smacks you in the face when you least expect it. Look how I met Dita." He paused very, very briefly, although it seemed like an eternity to him, then added carefully and deliberately, "and met you?" But she didn't bite, didn't take the bait or react at all. Maybe she just missed the point. Maybe she thought he was just joking, but the only response she made was to his comment about Dita. Even that was a fairly non-committal, "yes, I suppose that was a surprising opportunity for you, and Dita as well of course."

"I'm still looking for the one, the right person at the right time I suppose," he went on. "But I do think I may have found her. I've just not really had the chance to tell her how I feel."

Now he was teetering on the edge of the cliff. Should he take his leap now? The time did seem right and he calculated he wasn't likely to get a better chance. She seemed totally relaxed and happy. Maybe the wine had something to do with it, but she was certainly smiling a lot and seemed totally at ease with him, and in turn he was feeling more and more comfortable.

"Really, Tom, that's good. Who is-" she began to ask him. Before she could get any further though he interrupted her and threw in one more check, one more attempt to gather further information before going for his big revelation.

"What about you though?" he asked her. "Anyone special for you at the moment, maybe someone you also haven't told yet just how you feel?"

That would do it he thought. He'd just given her the perfect opportunity to give him the clearest indication if she really, really did like her Englishman. That would end all this verbal shadow-boxing and maybe her answer would save him from having to make his leap in the dark. Hopefully she'd just come straight out and reply simply, "Yes, it's you, Tom. You're the 'special one' for me." Maybe she would, anyway that was what he hoped.

It wasn't like that though. Wasn't even remotely within a million miles of the answer he wanted to hear. Initially the first part of her answer was fine, just perfect enough in fact to build up his hope and expectations even more.

"Yes, Tom, there is someone, someone very, very special to me. Someone I've known since those crazy 'November days' of 1989. We had such exciting times on demonstrations and rushing to meetings. Mad, mad times, it was sheer madness. I think now that's when I first really fell in love with him. I liked him a lot before that time, but somehow those exciting, frantic 'November days' just drew us closer and closer together. It was like we had so much in common and were fighting for it together."

He moved forward expectantly onto the very edge of his seat and placed his elbows on the table with his chin cupped in his hands, staring at her full in the face and listening intently. Wonderful! Bloody magic he thought. It just had to be him she was talking about. Who else could it possibly be? At last, at fucking last! This was 'it', his moment had come. No more pissing around with various women. No more tacky squalid episodes with prostitutes. His 'bubbles of hope' were flying beautifully, soaring higher and higher. But then ... then ... just in the very deepest corner of his hearing senses he heard the faintest of pin-pricks. Not a big bang, no big pop followed. Just an excruciatingly, painfully slow, low hiss of deflating dreams and hope.

"I'm sure you remember him, Tom, Jiří, Jiří Kaluza. You met him in the Arts Faculty cafe the day after the demonstration on the 17th of November in 1989. We've been together, really together, living together for nearly a year now. We're getting married in the autumn, in October. It would be great if you'd come. Dita and Martyn will be there of course, but I'm sure that will not be a problem now, Tom, will it? Tom?" She was confused because in all the pleasure she was experiencing in telling him her news and about her happiness she'd only just begun to realise he was showing no sign of any reaction at all. His facial expression was completely lifeless and he was looking quite numb as the blood seemed to be rapidly draining from his face.

He was paralysed, sitting there just staring into space. Jana's happy and even more radiant face was in that space, directly in front of him. His mind and his senses though were experiencing just one massive power cut. There was absolutely no way that he could see her, no way that he could focus. His world went black, like a total eclipse of the sun. All he could hear in the deep recesses of his mind was his mate Steve's voice in his ear uttering smugly, "see, see, told you, it's the fucking hope that kills you, mate."

Slowly his senses returned as his ears picked up Jana's, "Tom, Tom are you okay? You look a little pale."

"Yes, yes, I'm fine," he told her, although he clearly wasn't as he tried to get the blood flowing through his brain and his veins again. "I was just a little surprised. The two of you, you and Dita, will both be married." Realising that she looked even more confused at that statement, and despite his speech faltering as the words stumbled out of his mouth, he somehow tried as quickly as possible to cover his excruciating embarrassing disappointment by adding, "Or at least one of you is already married and the other one is getting married. Who'd have thought it?" It was all he could think to say, and now he felt the blood was definitely returning to his cheeks as his embarrassment at the thought of what he'd almost told her flooded into his face. Hoping desperately that she hadn't noticed the growing scarlet hue of his face he finally got to the, "I'm so happy for you," bit, telling her, "That's great news, great news, congratulations." With that he struggled to his feet and leaned across the table to give her a kiss on the cheek, praying that he wouldn't inflict a third degree burn on her face with his embarrassed heated cheeks. Just a few minutes earlier of course, he'd hoped that he'd soon be giving her a different sort of kiss, one full on the lips having told her how he felt about her and having received a positive response.

"Thank you, Tom. I'm very, very happy. Well, you probably noticed that."

"Yes, you certainly do look radiant with happiness," he told her. By that time what was actually screaming through his brain like the sound of some air raid warning siren was, "thank God I didn't tell her how I felt. How awkward would that have been?" In fact, he was desperate now to get out into the soothing and calming night air of Prague, but that wasn't going to happen quickly. He reckoned he would have to sit there for another half-an-hour or so at least being happy for her while they had coffee. That meant more conversation, which would be difficult now with some of the shock and numbness that lingered in his brain. So, in an effort to overcome that and kick-start his thought processes he asked, "What is Jiří doing now then?" and tried as much as possible to look interested. What he was really bitterly thinking was is he still a student drop-out revolutionary? Maybe he's got his own entrepreneurial 'how to organise a revolution' business, 'Revolutions-r-us' maybe? And hang on, just a minute, bloody Jiří, what about all that stuff about him and the Czech Secret Police, about how he seemed to know so much about them and what was going on with the Russians in November 1989. Tom thought he never really liked him then and had lots of suspicions about him. Now Jiří had just become much less likeable.

"He works for Price Waterhouse now in Prague as an accountant." Jana's reply was another surprise. "He finally finished his qualifications two years ago and now he has a really good job with them, earning plenty of Czech Krowns eh, Tom."

"That's great," he replied, thinking that he'd have to start sounding a bit more original with his enthusiasm soon and stop replying to everything with, "that's great". In his mind though, he was thinking, so the great revolutionary is now an accountant. Hmm ... no doubt the student uniform black roll neck jumper and jeans has been dumped and replaced with a very respectable sharp suit and tie, and I bet the revolutionary regulation thin black lined beard all round his chin has gone too. This guy is definitely a survivor, and obviously knows all the right people when it suits him.

"An accountant with Price Waterhouse, yes that will certainly be well paid I guess." He was desperately trying to sound as enthusiastic as possible, but couldn't resist one probing enquiry. "I remember thinking when I met Jiří back in 1989, Jana, that he seemed to know an awful lot about what was going on in Prague, seemed to know a lot of detail about what was going on with the Russians and that guy Šmid who was supposedly killed on the demonstration. I always wondered how he knew so much of that stuff, so much information that he seemed quite fond of telling to everyone. Did you ever ask him about that? Has he ever said anything to you about it?"

She looked bemused and confused as she responded, "That's a strange thing to ask now, Tom. Jiří was very involved in the student dissident movement as you know. He was on the organising committee so he had access to all sorts of information that they picked up from a lot of their contacts during that time in the autumn of 1989. I can't say I've really gone into any great detail with him, but we did have some brief conversations about it and those times obviously, and he always says that there were hundreds of rumours going around Prague then so like many of the other students he heard a lot of things."

"Did he know Šmid very well?" he pressed her.

"Šmid? No, I don't think so. In fact I'm sure he didn't, Tom. Why would he? Anyway, the investigation by the new government after 1989 found out that Šmid wasn't who he pretended to be, and as you know now he wasn't really killed on that demonstration on 17th November. He was a StB Secret Police agent, Tom, as I'm sure you know. What would make you think that my Jiří would know him or have anything to do with him?" Now she was getting a little agitated and added, "I'm really not sure why you're so interested now in all that, Tom, or what you are implying? Lots of people in this country now don't want to talk about what it was like here before 1989 and what happened here. Many people think that the past is the past and it should be left behind."

That last point made him think that maybe she did have some suspicions after all about Jiří Kaluza's past and his role in what happened in 1989, especially on the 17th November demonstration, but was determined not to think about it and certainly not discuss it. Also, she was now being very protective of her future husband as her, "my Jiří ," reference indicated strongly. So, back off, back off, a voice was telling him in his head. He wanted to tell her that he definitely thought that Jiří might have been a StB agent as well as Šmid and in fact he was pretty well convinced that was the case. Now he was rapidly thinking better of it though. To tell her that now would just seem like 'sour grapes', which of course it was, but he decided it would be pointless given her present happiness and the way she obviously felt about her intended. So he settled for trying to extricate himself from the awkward moment by replying, "nothing, please don't misunderstand me I'm not implying anything. I am just curious because I've got an idea for another academic article about that time and what happened here in Prague. I guess the academic in me never really switches off." That was definitely not true, but it was all he could think of in order to try and lighten what was now turning out to be a difficult moment in an increasingly difficult evening.

Having thought that he got out of that predicament okay she gave him yet another obstacle to manoeuvre around as she asked him, "Well, Tom, who is she, this 'special one' of yours. This woman you've found who you think might be the right one for you? I've been so carried away monopolising the conversation with my news about Jiří I didn't let you finish telling me all about this woman you know who you think could finally make you happy. Dita and I are very happy now, so it would be great if all three of us friends were. Come on then tell me all about her. Is she Czech?"

If only he thought, if only you knew Jana. The moment had definitely passed and there certainly didn't seem any point in telling her now how he felt. That would be disastrous. The hope had gone. So, he settled for making something up.

"She's someone I met a few weeks ago on holiday at Easter," he began to tell her. "No she's not Czech, she's English. Her name's Sara and she's a solicitor. She's lovely. Tall and slim with short blonde hair and is the same age as you. She's got a great personality and a really good sense of humour. She's always laughing and really good fun to be with. We seem to be getting on very well. I think she likes me and I reckon she knows I like her, but I've not really had a chance to tell her. The trouble is Jana that ... that ... " He stuttered a little and paused, trying not to let his voice break up as the words came out of his mouth, as he was now really talking about Jana again. Desperately trying to hold it all together he went on, "the trouble is that I'm not very good at judging these things, not very good at judging whether a woman really likes me or at acting on it. I'm always just that little bit too late in telling women how I feel. At least, I am with the women I feel about in a special way."

Now it was her turn to reach across the table. Squeezing his hand affectionately she told him, "Just tell her, Tom. Tell this Sara as soon as you can. You are a lovely, lovely man. She would be very lucky to be with you. If she doesn't feel the same what have you got to lose by telling her? If you don't, Tom, you might regret not taking the chance, not taking your opportunity, for the rest of your life."

Bloody precisely! If only you knew he was thinking as she said it. His feelings about Sara were, of course, just something he made up on the spur of the moment in order to avoid any possibility whatsoever that Jana might think that he had been talking about her. He had met a woman called Sara on holiday at Easter, but he could hardly claim to know her very much or be involved with her, let alone claim that she was the 'love of his life' or the 'special one' he'd been searching for. So, in answer to Jana's encouragement about his feelings and the fictional 'love of his life', Sara, he settled for a, "yes, you are right," response and tried to make it sound as upbeat and positive as he could in the circumstances.

Meanwhile, in his head he was thinking that at least he'd tried and given it a good go with Jana. He recalled some of the times that he hadn't tried, been afraid to, hadn't given it even a small 'go', been too scared to really. Scared of just what he didn't know of course. Scared of failing perhaps, afraid of the embarrassment of being refused? Maybe that was it. Now of course he wished he'd been braver in the past and less afraid of rejection and failure. In particular, he wished he'd been braver with Jana in those 'November days' of 1989, and yes, okay, braver with some of the other women since then as well, but most of all with Jana.

The determination, will and the certainty of just a few hours before had almost drained out of him now. A small seed of hope must have lodged itself deep inside him though and the root of it was refusing to be weeded out. For some unknown reason at that moment his mood improved a little and a small part of his determination returned. Maybe it was reflecting on his previous lost opportunities that did it, or maybe it was Jana telling him that he was, "a lovely, lovely man." Anyway, somehow he drew on something inside him and decided there was still a chance and that he hadn't completely given up hope. The Czech and Slovak people hadn't given up hope over the forty or so years before 1989, and compared to that this was a minor challenge. Perhaps, just perhaps, if she knew, really knew just how he felt that would change things. Maybe she had just always been waiting for him to show his feelings towards her and that would do it. Maybe that was it, she had waited for so long for him to actually tell her how he felt that she had given up hope and moved on with Jiří. He took another deep breath and decided to try just once more.

"Perhaps me and you should have got together as a couple earlier," he suddenly blurted out clumsily. "Maybe we both would have been, could have been happy a lot earlier in our lives, maybe during the 'November days'?" His voice just tailed off, expressing perfectly the way he was fishing for something, anything, from her. Also, although he was hardly focusing on that at the time, expressing perfectly the way the hope was drifting away and draining out of him.

It was a very awkward pathetic sounding effort. It just wasn't meant to sound like that at all of course. It wasn't meant to sound the way it came out of his mouth at all. At first Jana laughed, thinking he was joking. Slowly though it dawned on her that he might be serious, and she became much more sensitive and quieter as she looked him in the eyes and smiled warmly, asking him, "Tom, are you serious? That's very flattering really. I had no idea. I mean I know we were good friends in the 'November days' and I grew very, very fond of you, but you were with Dita, my best friend, so there was no way there could have been anything that serious between us. I certainly wouldn't have done anything like that to my best friend, Tom. Of course I am still very fond of you, but now I am very much in love with Jiří, who I always liked very much, and you've moved on too from what you have just told me about Sara."

Bugger! That fabrication didn't help at all, he realised.

"And I am marrying Jiří, marrying him because I love him, Tom."

"Yes, yes of course you are, Jana. I understand totally. It's just me reminiscing and wallowing in nostalgia that's all. I must be getting old," he told her with a slight chuckle, frantically trying to lighten what he felt was even more growing awkwardness and embarrassment.

She reached across and squeezed his hand once again, telling him, "It's okay, Tom. We will not ever speak of this again. It will only ever be the two of us who will know what you said."

"Of course, of course," he agreed, seeming to need to repeat it twice in order to convince not only her but also himself. He still couldn't let his suspicions about Jiří Kaluza go though. "So, tell me a bit more about Jiří," he asked. "What exactly was his position in the student dissident movement? It might help me with my article and give me some idea of the structure of the movement."

Once more looking a little puzzled at his enquiry, but seemingly accepting his reason, she explained that, "he was on the student organising committee at Charles University for the November 17th demonstration. He was always very active in the student dissident groups when I first met him a year before in 1988. After he met you that day in the Arts Faculty café he said he liked you, and that he was very impressed that as a westerner, as he put it, you were not only very interested in what was going on with the demonstrations but also took part in them with Dita and I. In fact, he asked me quite a lot about you over the next few days and also even before he met you on 18th November as I had been talking to him about you quite a lot before then, especially about your relationship with Dita."

That simply confirmed Tom's suspicions about the great 'student revolutionary leader' even more, and he couldn't resist a further question. "Did he know that I was staying at Dita's place then?"

"Yes of course, Tom. He asked me a couple of times about it, saying that Dita should be very careful as it was especially dangerous at that time to have a westerner staying with you, but of course I never mentioned it to Dita. As you know she would have freaked out, Tom, and she didn't like Jiří very much then anyway. She has, I think you say, warmed to him now though and is very happy for me.

"I don't remember us meeting or seeing Jiří on the demonstration on November 17th. Obviously he was there? Where was he, near the front?" he asked her.

"No we didn't see him then, Tom. He was busy organising the march before we set off, but yes he was right in the front row. He was lucky though, he didn't get hit by the police so he didn't have your scars of the 'Velvet Revolution', Tom, your bruises from the police baton."

"That was lucky for him then. I thought from what he told us in the Arts Faculty café the next day that he must have been hit, lucky … yes, he was lucky." Tom couldn't resist one final heavily doubt laden comment though of, "he seemed to know an awful lot about what happened that night so I assumed he must have been right in the thick of it at the front of the march. Strange how some people are luckier than others in those situations." He did manage to resist going the whole way though and suggesting that she was about to marry a former StB informer, or even an officer, who knows? It was completely clear to him now that trying to convince her of that fact would hardly drive her straight into his arms.

The atmosphere of the dinner had changed, certainly as far as Tom was concerned. He was glad that within what fortuitously seemed a very short time – no more than ten more minutes – he had paid the bill and they were standing outside the restaurant awkwardly saying their goodbyes in the still warm Prague air.

"Have a good flight home," she told him, and as if to emphasise that he should forget any embarrassment from what he'd said earlier she added, "Please keep in touch. I want to see you at the wedding in October, and with Sara I hope. I won't take no for an answer, Tom, and Dita will be pleased to see you, really she will. I'll email you the details so you can make your plans and get some flights."

He just stood there with a somewhat silly feeling half grin on his face, nodding in agreement at her requests. He felt like a damp rag. Like every sense of feeling that had built up over the past ten days had been rung out of him. When she asked if he was going to share her taxi, saying she would drop him off at his hotel, he declined, telling her it was okay he was going to walk and take in the last bit of Prague night air before leaving for London tomorrow. So, after she gave him a small gentle kiss on the cheek and waved him goodbye through the taxi window, she was gone. Just like his long held hope she instantly disappeared into the Prague night.

He wandered, stumbled almost, off to the left of the restaurant after he'd stood watching until her taxi had completely disappeared from his view. In his numbed despairing state, not thinking or realising where he was going and with no sense of the direction in which he was headed he suddenly lifted his head to see that he was on the Charles Bridge and almost exactly at the place on the old bridge where he had first kissed Dita back in the spring of 1989. He'd been really happy then. Really enraptured by Dita, totally obsessed and captured by her charm, her smile, her intelligence, and by what he described as her Czechness. Where did all that go wrong?

How did he fall out of love with her? When she whispered, "kiss me," on that spring early evening in 1989 at the very spot on the Charles Bridge where he was now standing five years later he felt completely happy and at ease with his world. Maybe that is just the problem. He is never satisfied with being completely happy it seems. After all in the autumn of 1989 he'd then gone and fallen in love with Jana. Why, he now wondered as he stood there on the bridge late into the night and a few couples wandered past him arm in arm, why was he not satisfied with Dita? Why could he not have just been happy with her? What was it about her best friend Jana that made him think that being in love with her, and being with her, would be even better? Better than being completely happy with being in love with Dita? How could he have really thought that?

He could have been with Dita. Could have still been with Dita and could still have been happy with her. If only it hadn't been for the 'November days' of 1989 and Jana, and the time he spent and enjoyed with her during that crazy exciting time he might still have been with Dita. Counterfactuals – 'the what could have been' – are always simple and straightforward though, because the premise is always false. The academic in him reminded him of that, and the false premise in his case was that he wouldn't have got frightened and panicked by the immediacy of Dita's fast-track planning of the rest of his life over dinner that evening in her flat at the beginning of 1990. He did though, and he knew really now that he always would have done, whether he had fallen in love with Jana or not. He had to admit, however, that the frightening panic wasn't the main reason for him falling out of love with Dita. That was just an excuse. The real reason was his growing love for Jana and the feelings that he obviously imagined she held for him in the 'November days of 1989'. His misguided interpretations had concocted a huge counterfactual in his mind about what could have been between him and Jana five years before and in their future.

Now he wasn't with either of them. Now there was no Jana and no Dita. No more counterfactual, and unlike the people of Czechoslovakia who had struggled and fought so hard to change their lives in 1989, for him there was no more hope of a 'Czech dream'. He'd managed to blow it with both of them. He wasn't to be given his second chance with Jana. "We don't really get bloody second chances," he muttered. "We make our choices and our decisions, and for the big ones, the really important life-changing ones, we get one chance and no second go."

Standing there and staring out at the great River Vltava flowing underneath the centuries old bridge he wondered if now it really was all too late for him. Was it time to give up the 'hope' and to become as cynical as his mate Steve? Now he was resigned to believing that he would never find the 'love of his life'. Or maybe he had found it, but threw it away. Blew it and missed his chance. Maybe that was it. He'd had his chance and he'd missed out on his unconditional perfect love. Anyway, as he recalled Susanna's 'favourite', Charlie Chaplin, had once written, "perfect love is the most beautiful of all frustrations because it is more than one can express."

"So what's the point," he asked himself? "In terms of perfect love, true love, the love of one's life, just what is the bloody point of all the hope? It just kills you in the end. Maybe hope is just for countries like Czechoslovakia and for people like the Czechs and Slovaks in 1989, and through all those frustrating grinding years before."

We all remember the good times, he thought. The times of sun, sand and sea, or of parties with friends and relatives that go on long into the night, but it's the bad times, the hard times that shape us and make us what we are. The times of divorce or of separation, the times of illness, of broken limbs, or even of a broken heart, the times of disappointment, and of course the times of the death of a loved one or family member, or of a good friend. To retain hope through any or all of these makes us what we are as individuals. All of these are in their own way temporary bad times though. Generally these moments will all eventually pass. Although they are seemingly and realistically disastrous periods for the individuals affected, they are relatively minor periods when compared to over forty years of repression for a whole country, over forty years of bad times that invaded every aspect of life for most Czechs and Slovaks after 1948. That was indeed a trial and test of hope, one that the Czechs and Slovaks eventually came through. From that perspective, and in that context, he again realised that his hope and optimism of the past ten days, and his eventual utter disappointment and despair over Jana didn't bear comparison.

Unable to get his personal disappointment out of his head his rational introspection led him to one hopeless conclusion about himself. Finally it all became clear to him through the Prague darkness - his eternal dilemma and infinite contradiction. The constant never being satisfied and always looking for someone and something better was merely a symptom. The cause of his problem was that he wanted to be with someone, but he didn't want the responsibility of being with someone. The premise of Kundera's 'Unbearable Lightness of Being' was dead right in Tom's case. He wanted to be with a woman, but didn't want the responsibility of being with just one woman. Yes he wanted to have someone special, to be with someone special, and to be someone special for a woman, but he couldn't face or accept the responsibility of being and having that special one. That was what led to his constant searching and his constant hope. "Totally and utterly hopeless," he mumbled, standing in the near darkness on the beauty that was the Charles Bridge.

For Czechs and Slovaks their hope had materialised at the end of 1989. For some of them for the better over the four-and-a-half years since then, for some of them not so, and for some like Susanna in Ostrava it had materialised into some kind of surreal 'double life world'. For Tom his hope over those four-and-a-half years just hadn't materialised at all. Prague had captured his soul, full of hope, in its dusky magical twilight just a few hours earlier and now it plunged it despairingly into the city's dark shadows.

Gazing out into that darkness from the six hundred year old bridge in utter bewilderment he recalled that as he was about to marry Byron had said, "I am in all the misery of a man in pursuit of happiness." Tom was far from being about to get married, that was Dita and Jana's fate, but at this time he could certainly relate to the sentiments of that comment by another favourite Englishman of Jana's – her favourite poet.

They Say that Hope is Happiness

1
They say that Hope is happiness –
But genuine Love must prize the past;
And Mem'ry wakes the thoughts that bless:
They rose the first – they set the last

2
And all that mem'ry loves the most
Was once our only hope to be:
And all that hope adored and lost
Hath melted into memory

3
Alas! it is delusion all–
The future cheats us from afar:
Nor can we be what we recall,
Nor dare we think on what we are.

(Byron, 1814)

Printed in Great Britain
by Amazon.co.uk, Ltd.,
Marston Gate.